1216 EATON   12/31/00

MW01284572

"A wonderful book that truly touches the Mexican soul!"

—VICTOR VILLASENOR, BESTSELLING AUTHOR OF
RAIN OF GOLD AND *WILD STEPS OF HEAVEN*

King of the Moon will enthrall all who love Baja... a novel of depth and delight... a story you will want to read again and again."

—GRAHAM MACKINTOSH, BAJA LECTURER, AUTHOR OF *INTO A DESERT PLACE*

"Kira's love for Baja, and its people, shines through in this novel. *King of the Moon* is a story of the human struggle, but more than that, it's a story of humanity. This is a 'fish story,' and Kira has landed his readers a big fish."

—ALAN RUSSELL, AUTHOR OF *THE FAT INNKEEPER* AND *MULTIPLE WOUNDS*

"Make space on your bookshelf between Hemingway and Steinbeck! Gene Kira's *King of the Moon* is one of those rare and exciting works that manages to bare the soul of a Baja few people will ever experience. A tiny fishing village will touch your heart and stir your emotions in ways that will recast your perceptions of Baja forever. A book to read again and again."

—HUGH F. KRAMER, PRESIDENT, DISCOVER BAJA TRAVEL CLUB

"If you have an ounce of love for Baja and its people, you will get a ton of pleasure reading Gene Kira's *King of the Moon*."

—ROBERT LAWRENCE HOLT, AUTHOR OF *N.Y. TIMES* BESTSELLER *GOOD FRIDAY*

"If you've ever fished, camped or visited the beaches in Baja California, you will treasure *King of the Moon,* a meaningful insight into the people who are the real heart of the peninsula. You've been there, you've met the people, and now they come alive in the pages of this novel. Kira brings the Baja soul alive. A must read for the Baja buff!"

—SHIRLEY MILLER, CO-FOUNDER, MEXICO WEST TRAVEL CLUB

Additional comments on following page...

"(A novel of)… breadth and depth. I enjoyed it so much that it was hard to put down."

—FRED JONES, EDITOR, *CHUBASCO*, VAGABUNDOS DEL MAR

"There are stacks of travel books on the market that paint dazzling pictures of Baja's many allurements. But it has awaited the brush of the novelist to capture the souls of her people. Kira's action-packed saga of the panga fishermen inhabiting the cliff-lined southern shore of the Sea of Cortez is a must for anyone who has, or still longs to travel in Baja. I have visited all the places portrayed in Kira's novel but missed seeing into the hearts of their people. *King of the Moon* completes the picture."

—JACK WILLIAMS, AUTHOR OF
THE MAGNIFICENT PENINSULA AND *BAJA BOATER'S GUIDES*

" …Very funny, yet tragic, as the joys and sorrows of human nature are played out in a small tropical fishing village."

—NEIL KELLY, CO-AUTHOR OF *THE BAJA CATCH*

"A good yarn! Captures the magic spirit of Baja—the unique culture, the remarkable people, the governing sea. Authentic, adrenaline-pumping fishing scenes, romance, and unforgettable characters. The author knows and cares about the people of Baja and provides an insight into their lives and their trials and triumphs. Beautiful descriptions of life in a fishing village on the Sea of Cortez, the enduring love of the women, and the indomitable spirit of the fishermen."

—GINGER MCMAHAN POTTER, AUTHOR OF *THE BAJA BOOK IV*

" …Captures the essence of life and the indomitable perseverance of the human spirit in a time and place that is both magic and believable. Gene Kira writes one hell of a fish story."

—MATTHEW J. PALLAMARY, AUTHOR OF *THE SMALL DARK ROOM OF THE SOUL*

KING OF THE MOON

A NOVEL OF BAJA CALIFORNIA

BY

GENE KIRA

APPLES & ORANGES PUBLISHERS
VALLEY CENTER, CALIFORNIA

King of the Moon
A Novel of Baja California

ISBN 0-929637-03-8
Copyright © 1997 by Gene Kira
Map, jacket, and book design Copyright © 1997 by Mary E. Gifford

Printed in the United States of America

Published by Apples & Oranges, Inc., P.O. Box 2296, Valley Center, CA 92082

First Edition
2 4 6 8 9 7 5 3 1

Library of Congress Cataloging in Publication Data

Kira, Gene
King of the moon : a novel of Baja California / Gene Kira. -- 1st ed.
p. cm.
ISBN 0-929637-03-8 (hardcover : alk. paper)
1. Fishing villages--Mexico--Baja California--Fiction.
2. Fishers--Mexico--Baja California--Fiction.
3. Family--Mexico--Baja California--Fiction. I. Title.
PS3561.I647K56 1996
813'.54--dc20   96-6249
                                      CIP

BOOKS BY GENE KIRA

with Neil Kelly

THE BAJA CATCH
A Fishing, Travel & Remote Camping Manual for Baja California

*   *   *

UNDERSTANDING SOCCER
Rules and Procedures for Players, Parents & Coaches

*   *   *

KING OF THE MOON
A Novel of Baja California

ACKNOWLEDGEMENTS

Special thanks to my wife, Mary, for her very fine and sensitive editorial comments throughout the writing of this book.

Also, to Bob Holt, a wise, always cheerful, encouraging voice on the phone that brightened many days and nights at the word processor.

And to Neil Kelly—the greatest Baja angler of them all.

And to the following generous people, each of whom commented on the text or helped in some other invaluable way: Mike Bales, Linda Bonin, Andy Bullard, Bruce Burns, Coco Corral, Robert Cullen, Joe and Lynne Cummings, Dempsey Doyle III, Rona Freedman, John Haddon, Brooks Harper, Laurie Hope, Fred Jones, Josie Kelly, David Kira, Hugh F. Kramer, Roger Lawrence, Graham Macintosh, Russ Merritt, Shirley Miller, Sra. Doris Ortega, Matthew Pallamary, Ginger McMahan Potter, Fernando Ramírez, Lori Roach, Alan Russell, Ignacio Santos, Fred Schreier, María Serrano de Alba, Honey C. Shellman, Martín Verdugo, Ronny Verdugo, Victor Villaseñor, Al Walters, Kwan Wang, Barbara Weston, and Patricia and Jack Williams.

— *gsk*

AUTHOR'S NOTE

In the words of the immortal Huck Finn, this is "mostly a true book; with some stretchers" in it.

The villages of Caleta Agua Amargosa and Las Ramalitas and the characters and events in this novel are fiction. Nevertheless, they are composites of things that occurred in Baja California during the 1960s. If you were lucky enough to find yourself in that magical world, you may recognize your experience somewhere in these pages.

It has now been a third of a century—thirty-three years—since my first trip to Baja California, and more than three years since I began writing every day on *King of the Moon*. The table beneath this keyboard is stained with the tears of that marvelous journey.

So, if this story touches your heart, as it does mine, you may know that, for better or worse, the author wrote it with sincerity, passion, love, true feeling, and most of all, *con corazón*.

For Mary, Abigail, and Gifford... and for all pangueros and their families everywhere. May the winds be gentle and the seas kind to you always.

— Gene Kira, November 1996

… And smale foweles maken melodye,
That slepen al the nyght with open eye
(So priketh hem Nature in hir corages);
Than longen folk to goon on pilgrimages …

GEOFFREY CHAUCER

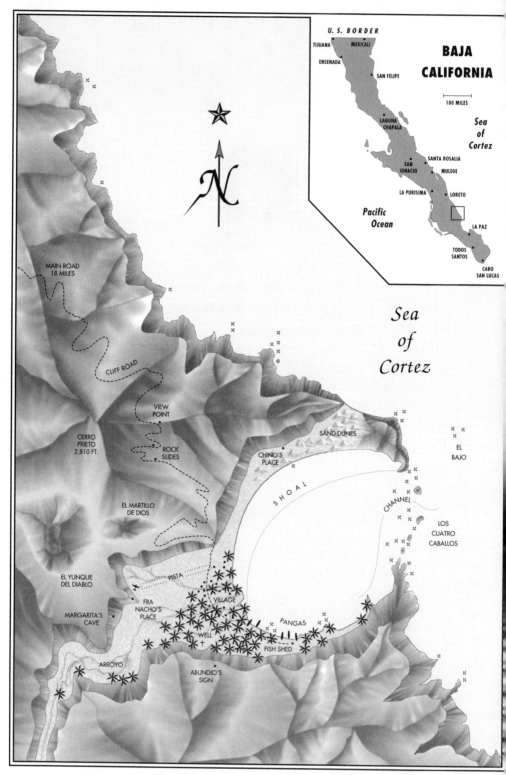

Caleta Agua Amargosa, B.C.S., México, c. 1967

1/4 MILE

Somewhere in the arroyo, the lonely old rooster was calling again in the middle of the night.

"*Cock-a-doodle-doo!*"

"*Cock-a-doodle-doo!*"

Over and over, the bird sent its solitary cry through the palm trees and up to the desert stars; and in the village below, Abundio Rodríguez stirred, dreaming on his cot.

Old, ugly, half-dead thing...

Do you wake me just to entertain yourself?

Quiet!

Let me sleep a little longer...

In the comforting dark, Abundio sighed drowsily and pulled a blanket up. Perhaps he would sleep just a little more.

But too soon, it seemed, a woman's voice called out.

"Bundo! Get yourself up! Chino has already gone down to the boat."

Abundio opened one eye.

It was morning now, and Socorro's calloused feet stood beside his cot. Beside them, the bristles of her broom swept the hard dirt floor. Her voice came again as he rolled over and turned his back to the sunlight streaming through the open doorway.

"Get up, Bundo! You go to Las Ramalitas today."

"Acch... "

"You drink too much, husband."

"Ah, well... better a famous drunk than an anonymous alcoholic."

"You? *Famoso?* Right now, your own mother wouldn't recognize you."

Abundio rolled back to face the room.

"Crazy, ragged old bird."

Socorro stopped sweeping. She stared at him, gripping her broom with both hands.

"What do you say?"

"His singing wakes me up every night. Don't you hear him?"

She resumed sweeping.

"Bundo, *who* are you talking about?"

"Never mind... did you say Chino was here?"

"Two hours ago. He said he would wait at the boat."

Abundio raised himself on one elbow and squinted at the beach. Two men were in the water, casting nets for bait fish. Beyond them, the awakening sea stretched flat and calm, and just above the horizon, the early June sun hovered—fat and yellow and blinding hot.

There was a skiff running fast in the distance, cutting across the islands, a rolling line of diamonds in its double wake. Two small boys stood up in the bow as the skiff disappeared beyond the edge of view.

Pablo and his sons.

Socorro leaned her broom against the table and she went to the corner of the room, where she carefully counted a mixed collection of bottles containing clear drinking water.

"We still have enough water for two more days."

He sat up, with his hands on the edge of the cot, and he raised his voice a little louder than necessary.

"It has *already* been decided. I will go to Las Ramalitas... *today.*"

"We still have flour and oil."

"We are almost out."

"The motor is broken."

"Today, the motor will work."

Socorro took up her broom again and began sweeping in silent, dusty circles around the cot.

She was exceptionally short—well under five feet—and her body was round and thick like a little beer barrel. Her handsome face was sun-darkened to the color of roasted chestnuts and her hair was streaked with wide rivers of gray. She had tied it, as she did each morning, into a thick braid hanging down the middle of her back.

And she wore, as she did each day, a simple blouse and skirt of white cotton, held at the waist by a sash woven in patterns of red and blue.

She wiped her hands and went outside to the fire barrel, smoking under the palm-thatched porch roof. There, she checked a thin, round sheet of dough that had been cooking on a piece of cast iron. When the tortilla was blistered and slightly browned, she lifted it with her fingertips and added it to a stack on a board beside the barrel.

She threw a handful of dry twigs into the fire, watched them crackle up, and then went back inside to sit on the cot with her husband.

"The wind will probably come again this afternoon. If it does, stay with Ramón tonight."

Abundio looked out at the water, noting the sparkles raised by the first morning breezes on the horizon.

"There will be no wind today. But if there is… we will stay with Ramón. We will come home tomorrow."

He struggled up from the cot.

He was a very large and powerfully conceived man, a massive giant nearly two feet taller than his wife and a full head taller than any other man in the village.

But he was gone badly by.

His legs, once hard with sinew, were heavy and shapeless, and they wobbled beneath him like drunken tree trunks. They were covered by a pair of baggy black pants, held up with a piece of yellow plastic rope whose ends he had burned to stop them from unraveling. Over this belt, his bare belly pushed out, round and smooth, as though he were perpetually carrying a sea turtle made of tanned human flesh.

His dark brown face was still dreamy and half-full of the night. It was split horizontally by the outstretched wings of a mustache that blended gradually into a gritty, three-day beard and a mass of stiff, black hair.

And his hands were enormous, tormented, work-twisted, fisherman's hands, inlaid with overlapping cuts and punctures and the memories of missing pieces. The bones popped and snapped as he flexed them.

He walked unsteadily to the doorway and he leaned his forehead against his crossed wrists on the wall above the frame, looking out at the silent, slowly moving sea, the rising tide, filling yesterday's muddy footprints one-by-one.

For another minute, he stood there, watching the water, summing up the tasks of the long day ahead.

Then he ducked out to the porch. He lifted a bucket of cloudy yellow water over his head and he rubbed his face as the musty-smelling liquid ran off his elbows and soaked into the sand. He took a mouthful, but resisted the urge to swallow, and spit it out again.

Socorro's voice came from inside the house.

"Bundo, remember to take your boots. The motor... "

He cut her off as he used the knuckle of his right thumb to squeegee water from his eyes.

"*Socorro!* Stop worrying! The motor will work today! But... I will take the boots just in case."

The boots hung from one of the crooked mesquite poles supporting the porch roof. They were round-toed military boots, dull black and heavy. Abundio turned them upside down, knocked them together a few times, and slung them on his shoulder.

Socorro came out with the tortillas wrapped in a large red handkerchief. She brushed a strand of hair from her face with the back of her wrist, and she stretched herself on the tips of her bare toes as he bent over to let her kiss him on the cheek.

"Bundo, drink something before you go."

"I am all right."

"Then take the good gallon with you."

"Chino has some... from yesterday."

She held on to his arms, looking up at him.

"Husband, we could easily wait another day."

"I promise, if the wind comes again, we will stay tonight with your brother."

He searched through the thin cotton material of her blouse, tickling her. She kissed his cheek again, more softly, then dented his belly with a stiff finger.

"Truly, you are an old goat."

"I am a man of infinite passion and romance."

" ...and a very bad hangover, *borrachón.*"

His hand opened inside her blouse.

"Perhaps... I will not go to Las Ramalitas today after all."

"Perhaps Chino has already left without you."

That was a definite possibility, given the hour and the fact that the winds had made the sea dangerous by mid-morning each day for the past week.

THE VILLAGE OF Caleta Agua Amargosa was as quiet and dry as a deep hole dug in the sand.

Abundio Rodríguez strolled toward the beach—with his boots around his neck and his warm package of tortillas swinging from one hand—and the only sound he heard was the distant tink-tink of goat bells coming from somewhere in the arroyo.

The tropical morning air was already very hot, and it was heavy and humid with the salt smell of the edge of the sea. Abundio stayed beneath the tall palm trees that formed a shady canopy over the village. He hopped across a gully cut by the spring rains, and he followed along it, passing by most of the two dozen dwellings between his house and the boat launching beach.

About halfway to the water he came to a bright pink house made of concrete block. This fine house had a smooth, poured concrete floor and a milled wooden door with metal hinges. It was the only house in the village with a tar paper roof, rather than palm thatch or sheet metal, and on part of the roof the tar paper had been covered with red clay tiles. The front door stood open. Abundio stopped when he saw the dusky silhouette of a woman inside.

She did not come out, but remained hidden in the shadows. Her low, cool voice came through the screen door.

"*Hola,* Abundio."

"*Buenos días,* Margarita."

"Pablo has left for Las Ramalitas. He took his boys with him."

"Yes, I saw them go."

She came to the door and peered out. She had been watching him, from a window on the front wall of the room. Her head was covered by a long, heavy black *rebozo*, a woven shawl reaching almost to her feet.

"You look tired, Abundio."

"It was the rooster."

"The rooster?"

"The old featherless one that lives by itself in the arroyo. It calls every night. Don't you hear it?"

"I have not heard it, Abundio."

She opened the screen door.

"Are you and Chino going for water today?"

"Yes."

"Is the road open today, Abundio?"

"No. I don't think so."

"You haven't eaten... "

"I must go now, Margarita."

"Would you like some eggs... or fish?"

"Margarita, I am sorry. I really must go. Chino is waiting for me."

CHINO WAS NOT at the boat, but a good pair of oars had been left in it. There were also some empty water bottles and gasoline cans, and a crate of empty garbage bags.

The skiff's outboard motor hung on the transom with its cover off, and a collection of screws and springs and other small metal parts from the carburetor lay spread on the stern seat.

Abundio tossed his boots and tortillas into the boat and set out down the beach in search of his partner. Keeping to the band of coarse sand and flotsam at the high tide line, he headed toward a grove of very tall palm trees standing at the water's edge on the south side of the bay. He came to a group of several other brightly painted wooden skiffs, pulled up on the beach with their bows almost touching the tree trunks. In the shade between two of these *pangas*, a cluster of men sat on the sand talking, sharing a case of warm beer, and smoking cigarettes.

One of them called out to Abundio.

"Hola, *chingón*."

"*Buenos, cabrones*. Have you seen Chino?"

"He went back to his house."

"How long ago?"

"A long time. Are you going to Las Ramalitas today?"

"Yes. We're out of drinking water. And Socorro needs flour."

"Us, too, amigo. But it's going to be rough this afternoon. Better wait a little longer. Who knows? Maybe they'll fix the road today!"

"Hah! And maybe pigs can fly!"

"Sit with us here… in the shade! Do you want a beer?"

Abundio didn't stay, but he accepted four open bottles of beer anyway.

Now, he doubled back up the beach, heading north, with the morning sun striking the right side of his face.

He dangled three of the beer bottles by their necks between the fingers of his left hand, like baseball bats in a rack, and he drank hungrily from the fourth. The warm beer fizzed as it ran down his throat, and it seemed to evaporate to dust before it hit his stomach, not even touching the thirst that had been growing there since the night before.

Abundio walked up the beach, switching bottles as he drained them. The heat rose quickly, and beads of sweat formed on his rounded shoulders and ran down his back in rivulets. Soon, his pants were soaked, but he walked steadily to an area of low sand dunes on the north side of the bay.

Far back in these dunes, Chino Zúñiga lived alone in a lean-to shack he had built with mesquite poles and palm leaves. Chino's sand-bound house was the only dwelling on the north side of the bay and it was impossible to find unless you knew exactly where to look. Even Chino's footprints were erased each day by the afternoon wind blowing in from the sea.

Abundio followed the beach to a formation of three knee-high rocks protruding from the sand at the high tide line. There, he turned to his left and entered the dunes. He climbed through the multitude of sand hummocks marching slowly landward here, each as high as a man, each topped by a ragged crown of dry grass, or the thorny, long-dead branches of some unlucky bush buried by the wind.

Abundio soon lost sight of the water but he kept his direction by taking bearings on the high cliffs rising up behind the dunes. As he got farther from the beach the noises of the sea became muffled and then died away and the air grew very hot and still.

There was little life or movement in these silent mounds of sand, not even lizards, just a few flies here and there.

Chino, why do you live so far away, all by yourself?

There is plenty of space under the palm trees with the other men.

Why do you parch yourself like a piece of beef jerky in these godforsaken sand dunes?

As Abundio struggled toward the cliffs, he tossed his empty beer bottles aside, flipping them end-over-end to see if he could make them stand in the soft sand. Shining with sweat, he emerged onto a wide, flat area at the base of the cliffs. Chino's house wobbled in the heat waves rising slowly through the brilliant white.

Abundio cupped his hands and shouted.

"Hey! Where are you!?"

No answer came back through the folds of heated air.

Abundio began to think he had wasted the sweaty trip. But then, he heard a rough hissing sound coming from behind the shack and he found his friend and fishing partner there, squatting beside the flame of a blow torch sitting on the ground.

Chino had piled sand around the base of the torch to keep it from falling over and he was holding a large kitchen spoon in the sputtering flame. An outboard motor lay on the dirt beside him.

Chino was fifteen years younger than Abundio and—at five feet, nine inches tall—nearly a foot shorter. As always, he was dressed in a ragged set of military fatigues, missing its pockets and sleeves, and faded to a powdery light shade of greenish gray.

Chino's body was built light and springy, and very tough. It was so lean, every cord and muscle showed clearly beneath a thin layer of tightly-stretched skin the color of smoked fish. Even his face seemed taut to the breaking point. It was narrow and long, and when he smiled, it pleated itself into deep furrows that made him look like a Gothic altar saint, carved in dark rosewood and come to life.

Despite his thin, almost scrawny appearance, Chino was quietly acknowledged to be the strongest man in the village, even stronger than Abundio. And, to Abundio's constant amazement, his friend never sweated. Even here in these sweltering dunes, and even during their hottest days in the boat, when the air was perfectly still and they sat in the sun hour after hour tending their lines, Chino's faded fatigues remained as dusty dry as the sand in which he lived.

Abundio looked down at the back of his partner's head, hidden beneath a bush of tightly-curled black hair. Chino's deeply-lined face studied the bowl of the spoon as it began to smoke and glow a dull orange.

"Quick, Bundo. Find me a sinker."

Abundio didn't see any of the egg-shaped bits of lead they used to weight their fishing lines. Besides, what could Chino possibly want a sinker for?

Chino shifted the spoon quickly back and forth from one hand to the other. He wrapped the front of his shirt around the handle.

"Hurry! It's getting hot!"

"I don't see any, *mijo*."

"Over there. In the bucket. Get a small one. Four ounces or less."

Abundio found the sinker.

Chino dropped it into the red-hot bowl of the spoon. The gray lead sagged and its surface wrinkled and broke apart as it melted and became a liquid mirror.

Still squatting, Chino shuffled to the outboard motor. He held the spoon carefully with both hands to avoid spilling the quivering lead.

"Help me with the motor. Hold it level where the crack is. Right. Just like that. Don't let it move."

Chino laid the bowl of the spoon against the motor casing and carefully poured the lead into a jagged crack near the propeller.

The liquid metal solidified instantly as it filled the crack. Chino moved the spoon along, pouring as he went. A curl of acrid, gray smoke rose up and there was a sizzling sound as the oil on the motor casing was vaporized by the heat.

Abundio felt his fingers begin to slip on the oily motor. As he shifted around to save his grip, the top of his head bumped Chino's shoulder.

A silvery stream ran down the side of the motor casing and a glob of molten lead landed on Abundio's big toe, making a tiny puff of smoke as it splashed itself into a thin, lacy shield covering his toenail and cuticle. Abundio gasped.

"*Carajo!* Goddammit!"

Chino's concentration remained unbroken as he hurried to finish before the shiny hot liquid coagulated in the spoon.

"Bundo! Stop moving around! I'm almost done."

"*Pinche cabrón!* It's on my foot!"

Chino continued to pour, keeping his eyes fixed on the remaining half-inch of the crack to be sure he filled it completely.

"What's on your foot, amigo?"

"The lead! The goddamned lead!"

Chino finished pouring and threw the hot spoon away into the sand. He took his time, carefully inspecting his work, and then he looked, expressionless, into his partner's wide-open eyes.

"It can't be the lead, amigo."

Abundio stammered in disbelief.

"Why... why not?"

"It would be burning the hell out of you."

Chino had just enough time for half a grin to form on his narrow face before it was time to jump up and run. He easily outdistanced the larger man, hooting and scuttling like a monkey, and he had to circle the shack only twice before Abundio gave up.

They stood in the shade, panting and laughing, while Abundio caught his breath, his bare belly heaving in and out like a big brown jelly fish swimming for its life. He was peppered with sand from head to toe.

Abundio let out a series of loud coughs and bellows and a final belch. He was thirstier than before, from his long, hot walk up the beach, and he searched in the rags and boat parts scattered around the shack.

"Where's the water?"

"In the boat. But we have two beers left."

"Only two?"

"We'll get some cold ones at Las Ramalitas, eh?"

The bottles had been in the sun and half the beer boiled out through the necks as soon as the caps came off.

Abundio drained his bottle in one swallow and hurled it against the cliff behind the shack. Still thirsty, he tilted his head toward the newly repaired outboard motor.

"So, our other motor will not start?"

"The carburetor is totally *jodido*. We need to have Ramón buy a new one in Loreto."

Chino threw his bottle against the cliff. The dark brown glass exploded like fireworks and tinkled down on a cone of shards almost as high as the shack.

Abundio looked around one last time—to be sure there was really nothing more to drink—then turned to his partner.

"Where did you get the oars?"

"From Pablo."

"Didn't he go to Las Ramalitas?"

"Yes, but Margarita made him leave his oars for us."

Abundio ran his fingers over the outboard motor and its shiny new ornament of lead.

"Will it hold, mijo?"

Chino shrugged and spread his hands, face up, with his elbows held against his ribs.

"It will have to. At the moment, amigo, it's all we've got."

Using a dry twig as a guide, Chino poured oil through a screw hole in the side of the motor. Then they tied it to a wide plywood board and lifted it between them like a body on a stretcher. Chino shifted his end of the board around behind his back.

"*Ooopla!* I wish we had a pickup."

Chino had used the English pronunciation "pickup," rather than the Mexican "pee-cup," and for a moment Abundio did not understand him.

"A what, mijo?"

"A pickup. A truck."

"Ah, *sí!*. A nice new one, preferably a red one with four-wheel-drive and air conditioning."

They started down through the dunes with Chino in the lead carrying the much lighter propeller end of the motor behind his back. Abundio followed with the heavy end, its weight pressing his bare feet into the sand.

Chino looked back at his partner, who was leaving a chaotic trail of holes and ridges as he staggered with his load.

"Pretty heavy, eh?"

"Not bad. How many horses does it have? Fifty, no?"

"Thirty-five."

"Ah... well. Do you think it will start, mijo?"

"It was running fine the night we hit the rock. Remember?"

The rock? Yes... he did remember it. Where had that been, exactly? In many seasons, they had not gone back to the southern islands. But the fishing was poor that year, and the price was high, and it had been worth the risk, almost fifty miles to a place Chino knew of, between the biggest island and the coast. There, the hidden pinnacle lay beneath the water's surface at only eleven *brazas*, sixty-six feet deep, its highest point measured carefully with eleven outstretched double arms' lengths of the weighted line. They had lowered the heavy sinker again and again into the fathomless depths of the channel, almost the entire day, until they had found it. And then, in the darkening twilight, they had filled the panga with an incredible number of the tasty *huachinango*, the true red snapper.

"That was the best day we ever had on huachinango. Do you remember, mijo?"

Chino's grin deepened the lines in his face.

"And they were so big, too. Those fish would have paid us plenty."

Abundio smiled to himself and nodded silently as they rounded a low sand hill. With the price so high, they could have lived for a month on that one day's catch, even after being cheated by the buyer who came to Agua Amargosa twice a week.

"We had at least a hundred huachinango, eh, mijo? Plus all the *cabrilla*."

"It was sixty-six huachinango. And one cabrilla."

"Is that *all*, mijo? I'm sure I remember it was much more than that."

"I counted as we threw them overboard."

"Ah… "

What a sad sight! All those beautiful fish thrown back into the uncaring sea! All that food and beer and gas turned into nothing but scraps for the nameless worms creeping over the bottom! But there had been no other choice. The unlucky rock, *"Chino's Rock,"* they named it later, had lain just a few inches under the surface, and they had struck it at full throttle in the dark while running their precious load toward the lighted beacon at the little bay of San Evaristo. By the afternoon of their second day adrift in the sun, the fish were not salable at any price, even to the bastard buyer from La Paz. Chino had long since given up trying to free the drive shaft of their motor. The huachinangos' once translucent flesh had turned to grayish putty and bubbles of gas had begun to make a honeycomb pattern beneath the skin. So they had thrown their wealth back into the sea and they had drifted in their open skiff for another five days and a half before they were found. By then they had passed beyond suffering and they had simply lain on their backs in the bottom of the panga with the sky becoming smaller and smaller above them and even the cruel sun itself a shriveled, darkened pinpoint, fixed above the endlessly curving sea.

The plywood board blocked Abundio's view of the ground. He placed his bare feet carefully in the sand to avoid stepping on a stick or sharp stone, and he shifted the rough wood to a new place on his hands.

"It was lucky Pablo found us way down there, no?"

Chino turned halfway around and smiled.

"It was lucky his sister made him go look for us. If it weren't for your Margarita, I think Pablo would have let us drift all the way to Mazatlán."

Abundio studied the mane of tight black curls on the back of Chino's head. A sprinkling of sand stuck to his shirt.

Your Margarita? Abundio wondered what his partner knew of that. He and Chino had come to trust and depend on one another during the past seven years. But Abundio knew very little of Chino's life before he appeared in Agua Amargosa one day as a hitchhiker on the fish truck. He had always assumed that his friendship with Chino existed exclusively in the present. Perhaps he was wrong.

They could see the beach now. As they squeezed through the narrow, overgrown opening between the last two sand hills, Chino used one hand to grasp a thorny, overhanging branch and hold it aside while they passed through.

"You know, amigo, if Pablo ever finds out that his own sister has given us all his secret spots… *Oops! Dammit!"*

Six inches of brittle twig broke off in Chino's hand. The thorny branch whipped across Abundio's face, catching him square on the forehead just above the eyes.

"Puta madre!"

The big man went down on his knees, taking his end of the motor with him, and the rough plywood tore the skin on his palms and pinned his hands in the sand. Chino quickly lowered his end of the board and helped Abundio stand up.

"Bundo, are you all right? The branch, it broke itself."

"Sí. Sí. I am fine. It is lucky I was looking down."

Thorns had punctured Abundio's forehead in several places. A thin line of blood ran down the side of his face.

Chino gripped the larger man's shoulder.

"Your hands are cut. Let me take the heavy end."

Abundio brushed his partner's arm away.

"Sorry, mijo. But this is a job for a big strong man. Like me. Not a skinny little chicken like you."

Abundio bent to take his end of the motor again, but Chino waved a finger back and forth a few inches in front of his nose.

"We shall see how strong this little chicken is."

Chino removed his shirt and folded it into a pad, leaving a flap of cloth that he tucked into his belt behind his back. With Abundio's help, he lifted the heavy end of the board, placed the plywood against the pad, and resumed the lead.

Abundio was still unable to see his feet, but he walked easier now because of his lightened load. When they reached the beach, they turned to their right and headed south along the firm sand next to the water.

Lıke a pair of ants, then, wrestling a bit of forage to their nest in the morning sun, the two men crept down the shore of the bay, the smaller man in front with his shoulder muscles pulled tight by the heavy motor, and the larger man following behind, shining with sweat in the quickly rising heat.

Both the bay and the village on its shore were known by the curious Spanish name of *Caleta Agua Amargosa,* or "Cove of Bitter Water," and both had been cut off from the outside world for the past three months, ever since an early March rainstorm had buried the only road with rocks and mud.

The bay was three-quarters of a mile across and C-shaped. Its only outlet was a wide, rocky channel opening eastward to the Sea of Cortez.

The entire shore of the bay, and indeed the entire stretch of coast that it stood upon, for twenty miles in either direction, was backed by high cliffs built of layered pink, green and gray rock so brilliant and pure in hue that when the sun shone down in the hot afternoons it hardly seemed possible the colors could be real.

From a distance, all these cliffs, and also the high mountains rising endlessly to the sky behind them, appeared to be composed of naked rock, free of plant life, for rain came infrequently to the sere desert around the caleta.

But when the rains did come, especially in late summer when the hurricanes hurled themselves over the mountains to the west, the desert was awakened by lightning and torrents of water, and the brittle sticks hidden between the rocks burst forth overnight and the cliffs and mountains became festooned with a mantle of green. In the course of a few weeks, the mantle grew so thick and high in places that a man could not see over it or force his way through it, even with a machete, for the tendrils and leaves became entangled in an intertwining, solid mass. Buds appeared, then flowers of every color and description, huge, succulent blooms half a foot across, long strings of waxy, orchid-like flowers, humble clusters of flowers no bigger than a pinhead, and the whole of it became alive with a teeming multitude of ants and beetles and flies and other insects, suddenly jarred to existence and frantic to gather strength and mate and die before the land returned to its barren state.

Along much of this rugged coast, the multicolored cliffs plunged straight down into the sea, leaving not so much as a foot of beach to stand upon, and the dark waters that churned against the rocks held the bones of many fishermen's skiffs that had been shattered for lack of a place to land.

But at Caleta Agua Amargosa a providential thing occurred. At this point on the coast, the cliffs suddenly turned inland, forming a blind *arroyo*, or canyon, several miles long, that ran back into the mountains.

At its eastern mouth, the canyon's walls opened out to face the sea. In eons past, huge slabs of rock, as tall as skyscrapers, had sheared away from the eroding cliffs and had fallen across this opening. These rocks now lay just beneath the waves, poking up here and there to form a chain of four rugged islets protecting the bay within.

Inland, the canyon floor was covered deep with alluvial sand and rocks that washed down from the mountains when the storms were strong. This sloping *bajada* was piled hundreds of feet high at the canyon's upper end. Gradually, the slope descended to the water's edge to form a perfect, curving beach of pure white sand. Along the south wall of the canyon, and around the south shore of the bay, a grove of very tall palm trees grew lush and green all the way down to the beach.

It was in the shade of these palms that the fish camp had come into existence, gradually, over the seasons.

The first fishermen to visit the caleta were on their way to somewhere else, or else on their way back, and they had merely rested overnight in the open lee of their canoes and pangas while a storm blew over or a reluctant outboard motor was persuaded to function well enough for the long ride home.

Later, as the fishing grew less profitable in the waters to the north and south, a cluster of seasonal shanties, made of mesquite, driftwood, cactus ribs, and palm leaves, was thrown together on the beach, and the fishermen would camp for a few weeks while they salted their catch and then hurried home to their families.

Still nameless, the caleta might have remained indefinitely an almost unknown, miraculously sheltered pocket on a forbidding coast, an unlikely haven where a panga could hide from the wind or load up with fish whenever the price justified the trip.

But one day there came to the canyon the sound of pounding hammers and splitting rock. Somewhere far away, a great amount of wealth had been dedicated to the ending of the caleta's anonymity. Over the course of a single summer, men fought their way from the main road in the west, over the high mountains, and down the very cliffs themselves, to the floor of the canyon. It was not a legitimate road they cut, but more of a plunging, twisting trail clinging to the sides of the cliffs. It was so narrow in places one could not get out of a pickup, for on one side the door would be stopped by the face of the cliff, while on the other, it would open over nothing but air.

Soon after the road was built, though, the caleta's only source of fresh water, a shallow, hand-dug well located part way up the canyon, ran low and then turned salty, unfit for drinking, and as suddenly as its fascination had grown, the wealth that had built the road found other interests and the caleta was abandoned.

Within three seasons of its birth, the road was washed away by storms and soon after that it was forgotten, and in the humidity and heat of summer, only the nomadic panga fishermen, the lizards, and the crabs took refuge in the shade beneath the caleta's towering palms.

And so it remained, while year-by-year most of the worthwhile shark and huachinango and cabrilla in the great God-given waters of Loreto to the north and La Paz to the south were brought into the pangas and taken to the markets to be eaten by the hungry people of those cities. Gradually, as the seasons became more difficult and the fish grew fewer and smaller, the fishermen began to think of the old road again, and of the caleta's almost untouched richness.

One year, they came not in their pangas, but in rusty, swaybacked pickups. They brought picks and shovels and iron bars and long levers cut from the resilient trees of the desert, and they rebuilt the abandoned road with their backs and their calloused, gloveless hands. They cleared the landslides rock-by-rock, and they bridged across the washed-out hairpin turns with mortarless stonework, built with a skill learned as they toiled. The work went slowly, but at last the road was reopened all the way to the caleta, and with it came women and children, and most importantly, the twice-a-week fish buyer from La Paz with drinking water, supplies, cash, and ice for the fish shed.

The fish shed was built before the first house went up. It was eight feet wide and twelve feet long, and its walls and roof were covered with corrugated sheet metal. On its concrete floor, a heavy wooden box held layers of freshly caught fish and ice, covered thickly with tarps. Each day's catch was added to the box, together with another layer of ice, and each Tuesday and Friday the fish were weighed by the buyer and thrown into the back of his insulated five-ton truck, in exchange for food and drinking water, a handful of money, and a fresh supply of ice.

With this routine established, several dozen families came eventually to live under the shady palms along the caleta's southern shore. Each morning the pangas were launched to pull and reset the baited lines and on the beach each afternoon a long row of boats sat blistering in the tropic sun. And after work, in the cool evenings, the lantern light from the houses and the voices of laughing children would mingle and dance beneath the desert stars.

It was to this remote, almost unknown village on the east coast of Mexico's rugged Baja California peninsula that the fisherman Abundio Rodríguez had brought his wife Socorro and their small daughter María in the sixth winter following the reopening of the road.

And now—three months after the road, the village's livelihood, and its only source of drinking water had yet again been cut off by rain—it was this same Abundio Rodríguez, fourteen seasons older and quite a few pounds heavier, who struggled down the beach, carrying an outboard motor of doubtful reliability, with his best friend and fishing partner, Chino Zúñiga.

ABUNDIO CLENCHED HIS teeth. His hands were shaking from the strain of carrying his end of the board. To keep the motor from slipping, he was forced to let the edges of the plywood ride in the cuts on his palms. His eyes burned from sweat running down off his wounded forehead. He was thirstier than ever.

"Hey, Chino, are your arms getting tired?"

"*No hay problema*. How about you, amigo?"

In front, Chino was whistling *"La Cucaracha"* softly as he strode along at the edge of the water. Chino carried the much heavier crankcase end of the motor and his burden was made all the greater because he was the shorter man and the board was lower at his end. Every now and then, he let go with one hand and whipped it through the air to restore the circulation in his forearms. Each time he did this, the board tipped precariously to one side and its edges dug into Abundio's hands.

"Does that bother you, Bundo?"

"It is nothing."

"*Muy bien!* Looks like we'll make it to the boat without stopping."

Abundio was not confident he could go the remaining two-hundred yards without a rest. He extended his lower lip and snorted a blast of air upwards, trying to blow away the sweat and gnats that plagued his eyes.

Fifty yards from the panga, they came to a group of boys fishing a reef of submerged rocks extending out from the beach. Each boy had an old beer can with thirty yards of fishing line wound around it. Tied to the end of each line was a large fishhook and an old spark plug, or a rusty bolt, or some other bit of metal for weight.

On the sand, a kitchen knife rested across the carcass of a dead mullet. The fish's long body had been cut into slices about an inch apart and the boys were using the half-moon shaped pieces as bait.

With the hook pushed through a piece of mullet, a few feet of line was unwound from the beer can and whirled around and around until it had enough speed to be thrown out over the reef. The can was held by one end and pointed in the direction of the cast as the line spun off and the bait landed in the water.

Abundio called to one of the boys.

"Hola! Any luck?"

"*Nada.*"

The boy indicated a pile of twenty or thirty striped grunts lying at his feet, several of them still alive. The small, perch-shaped fish had snagged themselves as they tried to steal bits of bait with their tiny mouths. In disgust the boy had thrown them on the beach to die. Similar piles of puffers and grunts and lizardfish and other incidental catches lay at the feet of the other boys.

Abundio seized the opportunity for a rest, halting so abruptly he nearly pulled the plywood from Chino's hands.

"One moment, mijo! Let me help these boys."

Chino lowered his end of the motor. He opened and closed his hands and rubbed his arms.

"*Bueno*. I'll go take our other motor off the panga."

"I'll be right there! This won't take a minute."

"No hay problema, amigo. I need to find us a wrench anyway."

Abundio turned to the smallest fisherman of the group, a deeply tanned boy of perhaps three years, with big, dark eyes and a white streak of dried mucous on his upper lip.

"Here. Give me your line."

Shyly, the boy handed his beer can to Abundio, who wound in the line and was about to put on a piece of bait when he discovered the rusty hook was broken off at the shank. He called out to the oldest of the group, a very thin boy of about twelve with a shock of straight, black hair hanging down over his face.

"Joselito! You rat! You gave your little brother a line with no hook!"

Joselito continued to watch his bait.

"He doesn't know the difference. Besides, I don't have any more hooks."

Annoyed, Abundio went to Joselito and stood over him with a baleful scowl. He shook a big, fat finger at the side of the boy's head.

"You shouldn't play tricks on your brother. If you come to my boat, I'll give you a hook."

Joselito tossed his hair aside as he pulled his line in hand-over-hand.

"A new hook?"

"No. But it will be better than what you have. Meanwhile, give me your line."

Abundio put on a fresh bait and walked up the beach with his darkly tanned retinue following closely behind. At the edge of the reef he stopped and waded out to thigh deep water. He whirled the line over his head, shouting.

"Joselito! Look here! The big yellow rock. See it?"

The boys could see the large round boulder clearly, just under the surface. It was actually dark brown, but it looked distinctly yellow because of the way the light refracted through the water.

The tide was coming over the reef in a ruffled flow that turned glassy smooth where the rocks dropped away to a deeper, sandy bottom. Abundio's yellow boulder sat right on the edge, where the smooth and ruffled waters met.

"Joselito! When the tide is coming in, throw your bait to the rock. Just like this!"

Abundio's chunk of mullet landed on the yellow spot. As it sank, the current sucked it down over the edge of the reef and it disappeared into deeper water.

A second later, Abundio felt a quick double tap on the line. He jerked it back violently with both hands to set the hook. He backed up to the beach, letting the line slip through his fingers a little when the fish pulled strongly.

It broke the surface with a splash and the boys cheered as Abundio played it out and let it swim back and forth in knee-deep water. Its swirling purple and bright green colors told them it was a good-sized hogfish, a large member of the wrasse family and an excellent dinner.

Abundio turned to his court of wide-eyed believers.

"All right! Who wants to catch this fish for *mamá*?"

They crowded around, squealing and jumping and grabbing for the line, but Abundio held it high above their heads and sought out the small one with the broken hook.

"Here… see if *you* can catch it!"

The boy was so astonished to be chosen that he dropped the line as it was thrust into his hands. Abundio gave him the beer can. He knew what to do. He took the can and ran straight into the palm trees, not stopping until the hogfish had been slid out of the water.

Joselito, the oldest, stunned the fish by striking its head with the back edge of the kitchen knife. With three swift strokes of the razor sharp blade, he cut out the fish's gills and guts, and he grabbed it by its lower lip and rinsed it clean. It took all his strength to hold it out to Abundio.

"Here."

"No, Joselito. It was your line. Have little brother take it home."

"Thank you, Bundo."

Abundio knelt down and placed his stiff, work-thickened hands lightly on Joselito's shoulders. He looked straight into the boy's eyes.

"Listen, Joselito, the yellow rock will always feed your family. By tomorrow, there will be another fish there. The little crabs float off the reef. Always on the rising tide, night or day, it doesn't matter. The big fish are lazy and fearful, like us, and they hide under the yellow rock, waiting for the crabs to come."

Joselito's eyes swept slowly across the sparkling clear water.

"Bundo… are there any more yellow rocks?"

Abundio threw back his head and laughed.

"Yes, you little coyote! Of many colors! But this is the only one in the caleta. Now, Joselito, you must promise never to tell anyone!"

Joselito pointed his chin toward the other boys, who had put a long stick through the hogfish's mouth and were noisily carrying it back to the houses.

"What about them?"

"Do not worry. They are too young to remember."

At the end of the beach, Chino was working on the panga. Abundio went to the outboard motor, tested its weight, and called the boy.

"Joselito! Give me a hand here!"

Working as a team, the man and boy grabbed the lighter end of the plywood board and dragged it to the boat. They untied the motor and held it on the transom while Chino used the borrowed wrench to tighten the mounting bolts.

As Chino attached the fuel line, Abundio searched in the crevices and debris in the bottom of the panga. He found half a dozen fishhooks in various stages of rusty decomposition and he gave them to the patiently waiting Joselito.

"Listen, Joselito. We will see your *papá* today in Las Ramalitas. Do you want us to tell him anything?"

Joselito looked back toward the houses.

"Please tell him... tell him... we are fine... but my mother has no oil or salt."

"Or water?"

"Yes... we need water too."

"And flour?"

"Yes... we are out of flour."

Abundio waited a long moment.

"Anything else?"

Joselito's fingers tightened around his new fishhooks. He stood up straight with his mop of hair covering his eyes and his knees sticking out like door knobs on his long, thin legs. He had not seen his father for nearly three months, ever since the week following the terrible storm.

"Please tell my papá... tell him... my mother misses him. She wishes to join him in Las Ramalitas."

Abundio waited another moment.

"And you too?"

Joselito looked down at his feet.

"Yes."

Abundio knelt again and faced the boy, but did not touch him.

"Joselito, I promise to speak to your father. Perhaps he is ready for you now. Meanwhile, it is your job to take care of your family here until things get better."

"I am!"

"I know you are, Joselito. And I am proud of the job you are doing. Ask me if you need more hooks or line."

"Thank you, Bundo. And thank you for the yellow rock."

Joselito turned and ran off toward the houses, and Abundio shouted after him.

"Hey, beach rat! Remember, the rock is a secret! And tell Socorro I said to give you some water and flour. We have more than we need."

Joselito's thin brown arm waved as he disappeared into the palms.

CHINO HOPPED INTO the boat to test start the motor. He squeezed the rubber gas bulb several times and pulled out the choke button. A dozen powerful yanks on the starter rope produced no result.

"Pinche motor. *God,* I hate these things."

"Chino, it's been so long. Perhaps the spark plugs?"

"Right."

The electrodes were covered with carbon and rust. Chino scraped them with a knife and rubbed them in the sand until they were clean. But another twenty pulls on the rope did no good.

"Ayy… amigo. It isn't going to start."

"Let me try, mijo."

Abundio took his place at the motor. On his very first pull, it surprised them by coughing and stuttering, and Chino leapt to take over.

"Look out, amigo!"

Chino braced his feet against the transom and pulled a dozen times in quick succession, getting more and more coughs with each pull.

"Bundo! Keep pumping!"

Abundio worked the gas bulb and choke while Chino pulled with all his might.

"Oooof…! Oooof…! *Oooof…!*"

The motor woke with an unmuffled roar audible two-hundred yards away, and Chino killed it instantly to keep the water pump from burning itself out. He slumped over, panting deeply as Abundio laughed and clapped him on the back.

"Hah! Chino! Nice work! For a minute, I thought you were actually going to make yourself sweaty!"

Chino shook his head, laughing too.

"Bundo, you lucky cabrón! I don't know why, but these things always seem to come to life when you touch them."

They hopped out of the panga and stood near the bow. Chino tilted his head back toward the village.

"So, amigo. Did you show them Pablo's yellow rock?"

Abundio nodded.

"And?"

"A big hogfish."

Chino drew some squiggles in the sand with his toe.

"Another of Pablo's secret spots given away."

Abundio shrugged his big, round shoulders.

"Pablo has more than he needs."

"Pablo, yes. Us, no."

WITH THAT SUCCINCT assessment of their professional qualifications Abundio had no argument, for even though they had benefited for years from a covert knowledge of Pablo Santos' fabulous collection of secret fishing spots, Abundio Rodríguez and Chino Zúñiga were still the two worst fishermen in Agua Amargosa.

Not that they suffered from insult or lack of comradeship because of their bad luck. Far from it. The partners, due to Abundio's size and Chino's strength and well-known temper, were given a generous berth by the other men of the village. The worse their day's catch, the wider the berth became, and the buyer from La Paz had learned early in his career never, ever, to make jokes about the size or number of fish they brought to his scales, except on those very rare occasions when they had bested one of the other boats.

In some ways, the star-crossed pair had actually benefited from their uncanny bad luck, for by dint of their unflagging persistence through many an embarrassing and unprofitable season, they had earned the genuine respect and affection of the other fishermen, and they never lacked for a beer to drink in the afternoon shade, or the gift of a few dead mackerel or mullet to be used for bait the following morning.

And by any accounting, their lack of skill had not really cost them that much, for, with the sole exception of Pablo Santos himself, the fishermen of Agua Amargosa were so poor it was difficult to tell them apart anyway.

HALF A DOZEN men emerged from the palm trees. As they approached the panga, one of them shouted ahead to Abundio and Chino.

"Hola, chingones! Ready to go?"

Abundio waved for them to keep coming.

The first man to arrive went to the stern of the panga and inspected the patch on the motor casing. He scraped at the lead with a fingernail, and a large flake of it came off and fell to the sand.

"Chino, is this your old motor from San Felipe? The one that almost killed you?"

Chino grunted as he and two others grabbed the bow of the panga and swung it around to face the water.

"Sí."

"We couldn't believe it when we heard it start up."

The panga weighed very little and the men slid it easily into the water and floated it ankle deep. Abundio and Chino hopped in. With a light shove, the boat glided out a few yards from shore and curled sideways, away from the breeze. Chino went to work on the motor as Abundio waved to the men.

"Hey, cabrones. What do you want from Las Ramalitas?"

"Beer and women."

"Too expensive. How about some dirty pictures?"

"Tu madre."

The men disappeared into the palm trees, leaving the two partners adrift in the morning sun. Chino tilted the prop into the water and began huffing and puffing on the rope.

Abundio bent down in the bow and popped out a fist-sized roll of cloth that had been stuffed into a jagged hole in the hull, just below the water line. Quickly, he placed a foot on the hole to slow the inrushing sea water. He wrapped the plug in black plastic from one of the garbage bags and stomped it back into the hole with his bare heel. The leak slowed to a steady drip that ran down the inside of the hull and collected in a small pool just in front of the panga's forward seat.

The motor gave no sign of starting. The boat drifted in the breeze and the prop skeg dragged slowly across the sandy white bottom and caught on an embedded stone. Chino sat on the stern seat and looked out toward the four rocky islets guarding the entrance to the bay.

"The wind is coming. We need to get started right now."

Abundio waved for Chino to get out of his way.

"Mijo, we need a more experienced man for this."

"It is my motor."

"Yes. But it is *my* boat, and *Capitán Rodríguez* orders you to move your skinny ass over."

Chino chuckled as the big man took over on the starter rope.

"Hey, capitán! Ensign Chino requests permission to pee."

After three big pulls, Abundio was ready for a rest. He plopped down on the rear seat, with his hands draped over his knees.

"Permission to pee is granted, ensign. But please, use the proper equipment. Don't dribble all over my ship as you usually do."

"*Sí capitán!* And where is the proper equipment?"

"Behind you. And after you pee, please bail the water from the swimming pool."

The water leaking through the hole in the bow was a couple of inches deep. Floating on it was a plastic bleach bottle with its bottom cut out, turning it into a bailing scoop. Chino relieved himself, emptied the scoop over the side, and used it to bail the bow out. He gave the cloth plug a couple of kicks.

"Ensign Chino reports the swimming pool is now empty."

Abundio, breathing hard, was ready for another rest.

"You show excellent promise, Ensign Chino. Perhaps someday I may recommend you for a promotion."

"Actually, capitán, I just wish you would start this worthless piece of shit so we can get to Las Ramalitas before it sinks."

Abundio turned and stretched himself to attention, looking as big as an outhouse as he stood in the middle of the panga with his belly sucked in as far as possible and his finger stabbing through the air.

"*Ensign Chino!* You better show some respect for this fine ship! After all, it was you who put the hole in her beautiful loins."

"Hah!"

The partners shared another laugh as they floated only ten feet from shore after two-and-a-half hours' work.

It was true, Chino knew. He had been at the tiller the night they hit the rock. Margarita had said to look for exactly eleven brazas and she had been dead right. They had never found another red snapper spot to compare with that one. How did Pablo do it? It was almost as though his eyes saw through the water. Well, no matter. They had hit the rock and cracked the bow of the panga and wrecked his Evinrude motor. It had been his most valuable asset the night he fled San Felipe and came down the long lonely road to Caleta Agua Amargosa.

Over the seasons, they had placed many layers of fiberglass over the hole in the bow, but the boat's spirit seemed to be broken, and the constant flexing of the weakened strakes always caused the patches to come loose. At some point, they had given up trying to fix the underlying fault and they had begun plugging the hole with rolls of cloth, resigning themselves to a routine of bailing the bow out every so often.

Chino used a fingernail to pick at the layered patina of fish scales and dried blood covering the inside of the panga. He thought of the rock and the terrible days that followed it.

"You know, amigo, I really thought we were going to die that time."

Abundio sat down and snorted.

"After the third day I really didn't give a damn."

"Neither did I. It's amazing how simple it seemed."

SEVERAL FISHERMEN REAPPEARED on the beach. They began whistling and laughing and one of them called out.

"Hey, are you guys back from Las Ramalitas *already?*"

Another man waded out and grabbed the bow of the panga.

"*Ayy!* You better believe it! This is the fastest boat in all of México!"

Chino gave the man a look that made his mouth drop open and his hand jump off the gunnel as though it had been red hot.

They fell silent. Chino waved for Abundio to get out of his way. Grabbing the starter rope, he spoke without looking at the men on the beach.

"Push us."

As a group, they waded into the water and guided the panga away from shore. The water rose to their knees, then their thighs, and then almost to their waists, before Chino released them.

"Enough."

They waved cheerfully as the boat glided into deeper water.

"Chino! We'll wait here in case you need us!"

Chino did not answer. But Abundio waved back and smiled.

"Thanks, cabrones! We'll see you tonight."

Chino braced his feet on the transom and pulled the rope so hard the motor tilted into the half-up position. The group on the beach twittered and whistled. Cursing to himself, Chino locked the motor down. On the next pull it almost caught. Then it roared with a cloud of bluish smoke that bubbled up in the water behind the panga.

CHINO LET THE motor idle as the boat slid out over the white sand bottom. Fifty yards from the beach, the water turned to light turquoise, mottled with rocky patches, and then it deepened to the aquamarine of the inner channel. When the engine was warm and running smoothly, Chino opened the throttle wide and the skiff rose up and skimmed across the dead flat caleta.

As they passed inside the first of the four channel islets, Abundio stood up to watch for rocks. He braced his calves against the middle seat and scanned the water ahead, looking for dark patches. When he spotted one, he raised a finger and looked back to be sure Chino saw it too, and Chino would apply a little pressure to the tiller to miss the rock as they shot by it.

Using this sign language, the partners passed just inside the second island, then the third, and they headed for the fourth and final island, where they would turn sharply out to the open sea.

The four channel islands of Agua Amargosa were connected by almost continuous reefs that made it difficult for the fishermen to take shortcuts between them. The islands were similar in size, averaging about twenty-five feet high and a hundred yards long. Although each had its own character, the islands had never been given individual names as far as anyone knew. They were referred to collectively by the fishermen as *Los Cuatro Caballos*, "The Four Horses," although in appearance they bore no resemblance to those animals at all.

The innermost island was so low it disappeared beneath a few inches of water twice during each monthly cycle when the moon was new or full and the tides rose to their highest level. Its yellowish substance had a spongy, rotten feel under the foot and it was positioned in the near shore current so that it caught the village's floating refuse, the orange peels and the decomposing carcasses left when the people cleaned their fish on the beach. It was a pestilential place, avoided by the inhabitants of Agua Amargosa.

Although the second island was also low, it never sank completely beneath the waves, even during the highest tides. It was composed of a single, flat slab of gray rock, chopped off vertically all around the edges. Its featureless surface was barren except for a pile of fist-sized cobbles at one end. In the middle of the pile, the central shaft of a cactus clung to life in the salty air, its famished limbs withered away or perhaps never grown. For some reason, the water around this island was as infertile and unproductive as the island itself and even in the early days the men of the caleta had rarely bothered to fish near it.

Abundio looked over his shoulder at the dull black boulders that formed the third island. The largest boulder was shaped like the top half of a skull. It wore a white-bleached cap of bird droppings and there were three crevices that formed its eyes and nose. Despite its ghastly aspect, the third island's waters thrived with life and Abundio hoped to see a school of bait fish leap into the sunlight, the silvery explosion announcing the presence of hungry yellowtail or perhaps barracuda attacking from below. But he saw nothing, and he turned forward again to watch for rocks.

Now the panga entered deep, open water and its bow began to undulate up and down as it felt the first swells coming from outside the caleta. Abundio, still awkward in a boat after a lifetime of fishing, bent forward and steadied himself with a hand on the gunnel. It was more difficult to see the rocks out here because the water was a darker, cobalt blue and the sea breeze created shadows and ghosts beneath its surface.

Out here, both Abundio and Chino scanned the horizon for signs of dorado or perhaps tuna. The best fishing near the caleta was in the area just outside the third and fourth islands. Chino yelled forward over the wind and the steady drone of the outboard.

"Anything, amigo?"

Abundio shook his head.

They went straight toward the last island, a dark red spire thrusting a hundred feet above the waves. It was the largest and highest island in the chain and it stood alone, challenging the open sea at the outer end of the channel.

As they approached within fifty yards of the island, Abundio saw the shiny black hulks of a squadron of sea lions basking on a ledge just above the water line. Chino drove the panga straight toward them and some of them began to raise their pointed heads and bark in annoyance.

Abundio held a finger in the air and waited for a light patch of sandy bottom to appear. When they were twenty yards from the now raging and combative sea lions, Abundio jabbed his finger to the right and dropped to his seat as Chino threw the tiller over and the panga cut through a gap between a submerged rock and the island.

They skirted around the end of the island and out onto the open sea. Then Chino turned the panga north to run parallel to the cliffs that would be their companions for the next two hours, nearly all the way to Las Ramalitas.

Abundio settled down on the middle seat. He felt among the garbage bags in the milk crate, finding first his boots, then Socorro's package of tortillas. He rolled two tortillas into a tight tube, took a couple of bites, and then raised the remaining half to Chino.

"Some tortillas, mijo?"

"Don't we have anything else?"

Abundio bent over and made a pretense of searching at length through the milk crate.

"Well, let me see... Ah! What luck! Here is a whole fried chicken! But wait! Here is something even better! Pork tamales! There must be twenty of them here! And a nice fillet of dorado, grilled with butter and garlic! Ayy, mijo, this is truly a lucky day!"

Smiling, Chino waited for his partner to finish.

"Sounds good, amigo. But I think I'll just have a couple of tortillas for now."

"*Ah!* An excellent choice, mijo! The tortillas are very good today. In fact, I happen to know Socorro made them herself."

Abundio rolled three of the flat sheets of plain, unleavened bread into a very fat tube and handed it back.

Chino took a couple of bites and then grew silent as his eyes searched the silky flat water ahead for signs of sea life. Occasionally, he made small corrections with the tiller to keep them headed for a high, rocky point floating above the sea haze a dozen miles to the north.

After a few minutes, Chino slowed the boat a little and spoke in a voice just audible above the sound of the motor.

"Amigo, how is Socorro today?"

"As always. She will never give up the caleta."

"Never?"

"I don't think so."

"And you, amigo? How much longer do *you* think we can stay?"

Abundio dragged a half-empty water bottle from beneath his seat. He unscrewed the lid, gave some to Chino, and then took a long drink himself.

"I really don't know, mijo... "

Abundio took another deep swallow and again passed the bottle to Chino. It came back with less than an inch of water in it. Abundio sat crosswise on the seat, looking down at the bottle between his legs. The vibration of the boat made standing waves inside it, and now and then, a drop jumped out of its neck. He lifted it and drained it.

" ...perhaps only God knows."

Chino certainly needed and deserved a better answer than that, but Abundio had none. Perhaps there *was* no answer for the little village of Agua Amargosa. No future role in God's plan. Why, God, should you destroy the only road to our village, built with so much honest work? Why did you, on a single night, send such a flood, to wipe out our road and cut us off from the fish buyer's truck? From gas for our pangas, and food, and even water to drink? Such a rain! So much effort! Just to cull a meaningless fishing village from your list and scatter its families over the sea? Why, God, did you create the caleta in the first place? And why would you bring us to it, if you only meant to drive us away again?

Abundio chewed his last piece of tortilla. The panga hissed easily northward over the swells. Behind them, one after another, the Four Horses of Agua Amargosa sank slowly from view.

"More tortillas, mijo?"

"Actually, I think I am ready for a nice piece of chicken now."

"Hah!"

Abundio looked past Chino's shoulder as he rolled another fat, triple tortilla tube and handed it to him. Behind them, the panga's foamy wake trailed over the swells to the south, and on the horizon, a range of jagged, lavender mountains rose up to the sky.

From this distance, only the higher mountains far back from the coast were visible and someone unfamiliar with them could not have guessed where the sheltered entrance to the cove of Agua Amargosa lay. On their way home, Abundio and Chino would watch for a singular, flat-topped peak with the name of *El Yunque del Diablo*, "The Devil's Anvil." They would run south until the exact center of the anvil lined up with a lower pinnacle called *El Martillo de Dios*, "The Hammer Of God," and they would keep the two mountains lined up while they closed on the coast and searched for the four islands of the entrance channel.

Abundio sat watching as the panga sped north and El Yunque del Diablo and El Martillo de Dios moved slowly apart.

"Mijo, you are right. We must convince Socorro it is too dangerous to stay any longer."

"She will never give up the caleta, amigo."

Abundio looked up in surprise.

"But that's what I said!"

Chino laughed.

"And you are right, amigo! Your woman, she's a tough one."

"Socorro says she will be buried beneath the palm trees."

"I believe her! And she will see the two of us buried there first!"

Abundio felt relieved that his partner seemed willing to give their situation more time to work itself out. But how? Even Socorro had to admit that once their money jar ran empty they would have to abandon the caleta. No, Socorro would *not* admit it. Of all the people in the village, she and perhaps Fra Nacho seemed most intent on remaining, even if the damned officials in La Paz *never* removed the rockslide that had cut them off from the world.

Chino's voice came out of the dull growl of the Evinrude motor.

"In a few more weeks, amigo, there will be no gas for the panga."

"Perhaps, we will catch enough to pay for that at least."

Chino shook his head.

"Not with those bastards at Las Ramalitas."

"Perhaps they will lower their commission."

Chino shook his head again.

"Impossible, amigo."

Indeed, their situation did seem impossible. By panga, it was almost a forty-mile round trip to buy water and supplies at the fish camp of Las Ramalitas. The cost of gas alone made everything twice as expensive as in those easy days when the fish truck brought everything they needed to the caleta. And to make things worse, the fishermen of the Las Ramalitas *cooperativa* had been charging them a usurious twenty percent for the privilege of selling fish to *their* buyer, who came south from Loreto.

"Shall we fish outside, mijo?"

"Better not risk it. Let's try the point for cabrilla."

"I am sure the patch will hold, mijo. The lead is still stuck to my toe."

"Hah!"

As they approached the high promontory ahead, the mountains behind the coast turned from purple to gray and then brown. Barren areas appeared, dusty tan and rocky, polka dotted with the widely-spaced shrubs of the desert.

Chino set a course directly toward the cliffs and Abundio readied their fishing lines as they neared the sheer rock wall.

There were four lines of heavy, yellowed nylon monofilament as thick as the lead of a pencil, each wound on its own wooden board about a foot long.

Working quickly, Abundio attached ten-foot leaders of lightweight monofilament to the ends of two lines. Each leader held four, small feathered lures, less than an inch long, spaced eighteen inches apart on loops. Hidden inside each lure was a small, lightweight hook with a gap of about a third of an inch.

Next, Abundio tied large single hooks about a yard from the ends of the remaining two lines, using short leaders of heavy monofilament. These big, bare hooks were more than an inch wide and they were forged of heavy steel to resist bending.

Finally, he attached egg-sized sinkers to the ends of all four lines.

"All set, mijo."

Chino took the panga to within twenty feet of the cliff. In here, the swells slapped against the vertical rock face and reflected back on themselves, raising short, foam-topped peaks that jumped and fell and flicked drops of water on the gunnels of the boat. Chino put the motor into neutral, but did not kill it.

"Let's catch some bait, amigo."

The partners stood on opposite sides of the boat, steadying themselves against the gunnels. They each lowered a small-feathered line into the water, playing it out between the fingers as its winding board flopped over and over on the bottom of the panga and its sinker descended the face of the underwater cliff.

The sinkers touched the sea floor about a hundred feet below the surface, and they began to jerk their lines up and down a few inches at a time to make the feathers dance enticingly among the rocks.

Almost immediately Abundio felt a series of weak taps on his line. He let it rest a moment and the tugging subsided. Slowly, he raised and lowered his feathers a few feet, and he felt the taps begin and then stop again.

"Mackerel. Two of them."

Chino quickly wound his feathers in, and he readied the lines with the big hooks.

"Wait for a couple more... just in case."

"I'm sure I have two, mijo."

"Just one more, then."

"All right."

Abundio raised and lowered his line slowly, feeling the very faint struggles of the two mackerel that had taken his feathers. The school had moved away, and he waited for it to turn back and investigate the vibrations his two captive baits were sending through the water.

"Come back. Come back, little sisters. Your friends are getting all the food."

Chino stood with the heavy lines ready.

"No more?"

"Another minute. They will come back."

Now, Abundio felt the taps again. This time they did not fade away, but sent a steady, barely discernible throbbing to his fingertips. He pulled his line up slowly, looking into the dark green water for signs of his fish. They came up—four mackerel—spiraling and darting around as they neared the surface. He held them out of the water while Chino removed the uppermost fish and ran one of the big hooks crosswise through its nose just in front of its eyes.

Chino lowered the impaled mackerel into the water and held it beside the boat by putting his foot on the winding board. He stuck the other heavy hook through the nose of a second bait.

Abundio tied off his feathered line, allowing the last two mackerel to swim beside the boat. He took one of the baited lines and let it trail through the water as Chino slipped the motor into gear and the panga bobbed slowly toward a cluster of white rocks about a hundred yards out from the cliff.

Halfway out, the motor died. Chino cursed it while he tied off his baited line and grabbed the starter rope. After ten pulls he cursed again and prepared himself for harder work.

As a light, southeast summer breeze began to push them slowly back toward the cliffs, Abundio decided to lower his live mackerel bait to the bottom.

"I will try to catch us something."

"Good idea, amigo. And you better check the swimming pool."

"Ayy! I forgot."

The run up from the caleta had loosened the plug, and the water in the bow was several inches deep. It took Abundio a few minutes to bail the boat dry with the bleach bottle scoop. Then he placed the end of a short wooden fish club on the plug and began pounding with their heaviest sinker.

"Careful, amigo. Don't push it through."

"Mijo! Do not worry! I am a man of infinite capability with any type of tool. Also with wine, women... *oops!*"

The plug popped up in the water just outside the boat. It floated there, supported by the air trapped in its plastic wrapping. Still holding his baited line, Abundio knelt down over the forward seat and clapped his free hand on the hole. He hollered back.

"Mijo! Use the gaff. Hurry, before it sinks."

Chino hopped forward holding the long-handled hook they used for pulling large fish into the boat. With the wooden shaft in his hands, he stood just behind Abundio, who was still on his knees in the bow holding back the water.

"Sí, *capitán!* And whom... oh, excuse me... *what* should I gaff?"

"You better stop clowning around! We don't have any more plugs!"

Chino scratched the needle-sharp hook across the seat of the big man's pants, making a small ripping sound.

"But, *capitán!* You are doing such a fine job! Perhaps you only need a little... encouragement."

Abundio was laughing so hard his belly was bouncing on the seat. The water was up to his elbow.

"You treat him like a son! You show him how to live well! "

"Hah!"

Chino lowered the hook beside the boat and snagged the plug just as it sank from view. He swung it over Abundio's back and plopped it into the swimming pool. Abundio quickly jammed the plug into the hole and gave it half a dozen good, splashing kicks.

While Chino worked on the motor, Abundio bailed the bow dry again and then turned his attention to his line. His mackerel bait swam fitfully in the shadow beside the panga, its mottled green back and silvery belly showing bright in the black water. Abundio lowered it to the bottom, raised it a couple of feet, and held it there. The stiff monofilament transmitted the tethered fish's uneasy vibrations as it tried unsuccessfully to hide its loneliness and nakedness in the open water.

Abundio sat with his knees against the gunnel, waiting for something to take his bait. He held the line loosely in his fingers so he could let it slip if necessary to keep a heavy fish from cutting him or pulling him off balance.

As Chino worked on the motor, the panga drifted slowly toward the cliff. When they were only a few inches from the rock face, Abundio grabbed an oar to push them away. But as he did, his mackerel vibrated strongly, stopped, and then vibrated again. Abundio put the oar down and allowed the gunnel to grind against the cliff.

"Something down here, mijo."

Chino looked up from the starter rope. The line running over Abundio's finger trembled slightly as the terrified mackerel strained against the hook in its nose a hundred feet below them.

Abundio backed up to the middle of the boat, letting the heavy monofilament take a turn over the gunnel. He had just raised the bait a couple of feet when the large fish struck, pulling him right back to the gunnel and jamming his knuckles against the wood. Chino leapt to his partner's aid and grabbed the line from behind. With four hands breaking its escape, the fish made half a dozen surging pulls and then rolled over and spiraled toward the surface as they hauled it in.

Abundio peered down into the dark water, waiting for the fish to show. Although he had been doing this for nearly all of his forty-two years, no matter how many fish he caught, he was always thrilled when he saw the first ghostly swirl of deep color, for it was only then that he knew what the gods had sent him. For Abundio, the act of fishing had always seemed submissive rather than active. One launched a boat upon the sea and sacrificed a mackerel to the depths, and then one simply waited. Nothing more. Sometimes many fish would come. Sometimes nothing. It seemed to Abundio that he really had little to do with it, other than to launch the boat and sacrifice the mackerel, and he was always grateful and filled with wonder when he first saw that wild, living thing that had come to him of its own volition.

The fish reached the surface. It was a good-sized grouper, heavy bodied and a little under four feet long, with dark, irregular, hand-sized blotches stamped all over its head and sides. It was stunned from being wrenched so suddenly from deep water and it wallowed beside the boat while they put two gaffs into it and pulled it aboard. It lay bleeding and gasping silently through its fat lips while Abundio removed the hook from its jaw and Chino hurried to lower another bait to the bottom.

"Maybe one more."

"Sí, maybe one more."

Abundio pushed them away from the cliff. He put another live mackerel on his line and dropped it quickly into the water.

But they scraped along the cliff for an hour, feeling nothing but the occasional vibrations of their baits, while the big grouper died on the floor of the panga, and its ring-shaped markings faded to an even gray, and its fins began to dry and curl.

Chino tied off his line and resumed work on the motor. The sun had gone behind the cliff. As they drifted in the narrow band of shade beneath its rocky face, the partners began to reflect silently on the possibility of having to row the remaining ten or twelve miles to Las Ramalitas.

Without warning, both baits were hit with such force that Chino's line immediately snapped off where he had tied it to the boat. Abundio's line burned him as he tried to snub his fish and keep it from diving back into its rocky den. With Chino helping, they stopped the fish at the end of its powerful turn and they held it suspended as it surged and pulled. Abundio felt a worrisome rasping on the line that meant the fish was sawing it against the sharp edges of its cave.

"Mijo, can you feel it rubbing?"

Chino was pulling with every bit of force he could muster.

"Yes! Yes! What a fish! Damn! It's going to cut us off."

"No it won't! Let go! Let go of the line!"

Chino understood. He released the line, and Abundio let the fish take a dozen yards into the water. Abundio kept throwing out more line until it was completely slack and then he threw out another few brazas for good measure.

"Get ready, mijo. We will have only one more chance."

Abundio rowed the panga directly over the place where the fish had struck. Then he rowed slowly to a point about fifty feet away from the cliff while Chino released more line to keep it from tightening on the fish.

After a wait of several minutes, Chino took up a position behind his partner, ready to pull on the instant required, and Abundio brought the line in, an inch at a time, using just his fingertips.

Far below, the great fish had relaxed from its fight and had returned to its feeding station at the mouth of its cave, with Abundio's barbed hook still embedded in its massive jaw and the heavy monofilament dangling from the corner of its mouth.

As Abundio took up the last bit of slack, the fish again felt the strangeness of the sharpened metal, and with a slap of its thick tail, it shot forward and tried to turn back to the safety of its cave. But this time two men were ready with their hands wrapped in cloth, and the fish was stopped in open water before it could reach the entrance.

"Pull, mijo! Pull! Pull!"

"*Ayyy!*"

The fish straightened their arms repeatedly and they were forced to give it several yards of line, but then it tired and came up like a heavy anchor. It was another grouper, solid brown and two feet longer than the first one, and the partners were barely able to slide it into the boat after gaffing it repeatedly through the gills. The bleeding monster crowded the floor of the panga. Its huge, blunt body looked as big as a cow's. Chino sat gaping at its slow, rhythmic death spasms.

"Amigo, I think maybe this is the biggest *garropa* I have ever seen."

Abundio was still breathing hard.

"My father said these big ones are very old... as old as the churches. He said only God and these fish live forever, unless we kill them."

Chino looked toward their motor, sitting quietly on the transom with its cover removed.

"Two big fish. We need to get started or we will miss the buyer at Las Ramalitas."

"What time does he come?"

"About three o'clock. But he only stays for a few minutes."

Chino cleaned the spark plugs again and squirted a little gas into the mouth of the carburetor. He pulled and pulled, and then sat down with his legs straddling the head of the giant grouper.

"Amigo, I think maybe we are going to miss the buyer."

Abundio jumped to his feet.

"Not with *my* fish! Capitán Rodríguez orders you to move your skinny ass over!"

Chino moved to the middle of the boat but he was not optimistic.

"Amigo, I do not think so."

"That is because you have no faith in the mysterious powers of Capitán Rodríguez!"

Abundio sat facing the motor. He raised his knees as far as his stomach allowed and he put his big feet squarely against the transom. After removing all the slack from the starter rope he took a deep breath and gave a single, mighty pull.

The cantankerous old Evinrude startled them both by exploding to miraculous life with a roar and its usual cloud of thick, bluish smoke, curling lazily up the face of the cliff.

"Hah!"

Abundio twisted the hand grip to keep the motor running. He replaced the cover and let the prop pull them away from the cliff. Then he opened the throttle wide for the run north.

A fresh breeze had come up. Abundio stood at the tiller of the rolling, bucking, heavily laden panga with his legs set wide apart. He leaned back against the motor to steady himself and he shouted into the wind.

"Ensign! Please see to the swimming pool! I have an appointment with a fish buyer and a case of cold beer in Las Ra-ma-*li*-tas!"

Chino shook his head and grinned as he reached for the scoop.

"Amigo, you must be the luckiest chingón who ever lived."

Abundio's face opened wide to the brilliant blue streaming above them. He swept an enormous long arm through the air.

"We, mijo! *We* are the luckiest two chingones in the *whole world!"*

THE TIDE WAS at low ebb. From the viewpoint of the speeding panga, the fish truck and the group of quarreling, gesticulating men beside it were almost hidden behind the high gravel berm that formed the beach of Las Ramalitas.

But as Abundio and Chino skimmed across the bay, they caught sight of the truck's white top sticking up above the gravel and they steered directly toward it. They had one very nice grouper to sell and another they hoped would buy gas and food for several more weeks of waiting for the road to be fixed.

On the far side of the berm, the low whine of the approaching panga went unnoticed as the men on the beach argued. The rear doors of the truck hung open, revealing a pile of shaved ice and fish extending to the roof.

One man, bare to the waist and shoeless, bellowed angrily as he pointed to a row of small cabrilla laid out on the gravel. His large black mustache jiggled up and down as he shook his fist and shouted.

"But how can the price here be *so* much lower than in La Paz?"

He was answered by a short, very fat man who stood with his back turned, adjusting the weights of the scales he had set up beside his truck.

"Sorry… that's all I can pay. Take it or leave it."

"But you are *cheating* us!"

The shirtless fisherman stabbed a finger into the back of the man with the scales and he immediately regretted it, for the fish buyer turned around with a threatening glare and an iron weight in his hand and the group of men tightened around them.

The fat buyer wore tight pants and a very tight shirt. The lacy front of his shirt was open to the navel, revealing a gold chain that glinted in the hairs between his breasts. He shifted a toothpick from one side of his mouth to the other.

"Last chance. I have to get back to Loreto."

"All right then! Take them!"

The shirtless fisherman motioned to two boys standing at the edge of the circle. Together, they helped their father throw the cabrilla into the back of the truck. The buyer counted out some bills from his shirt pocket. He divided the money into two rolls. He handed the larger roll to the shirtless fisherman and gave the remainder of the money to the tallest of the men watching.

The tall man moved close to the shirtless one and spoke in an urgent, confidential whisper.

"Pablo, listen... We don't like it either... But we are just fishermen... The same as you... What else can we do?"

Pablo Santos, the best fisherman of Caleta Agua Amargosa, fanned his pesos in the sunlight. He motioned for his sons to stand back, away from the truck.

"And your twenty percent? What about *that?*"

The tall one spread his arms wide.

"That is fair, Pablo! And you know it! Your people are fishing in our territory. And it is *your* fish that have driven the price down."

"You fish in our territory, too!"

"Yes, yes! But we aren't selling fish to your buyer. Loreto is a very small market. This isn't La Paz!"

Behind them, the fish buyer had closed his truck doors and put his scales away in the cab. He rubbed the buckles of his loafers against the backs of his pant legs to clean them of dust. Pablo jerked his thumb toward the buyer and hissed.

"Your buyer is a cheat!"

"So is yours. It is the nature of the business."

Pablo raised his fist and spoke loudly enough to draw the attention of the other men.

"We have no gas! No ice! We work for nothing! Our families are *starving!*"

As he shouted, Pablo Santos pushed the tall man down, but he jumped up and stood ready while the others surrounded them. The fish buyer climbed on the running board of his truck and smiled to himself in anticipation of watching a good beating. Pablo's sons stood at the edge of the bushes, wide-eyed, with four smooth stones in their hands, ready to defend their father.

"HOLA! CHINGONES! GIVE us some help up here!"

They looked toward the voice. On the crest of the berm, Abundio Rodríguez stood smiling and waving as he dragged a large grouper over the gravel.

Though the grouper was partly hidden behind the berm, they could tell that both the fish—and the man dragging it— were bigger than anyone had seen recently. The buyer got down from his truck and shouted.

"Do you have fish to sell?"

With a mighty shrug of his shoulders, Abundio heaved the grouper through the air. The heavy carcass slammed to the gravel at the buyer's feet, and half a quart of blood and slime shot from its stiff, yawning mouth.

"What does *that* look like? My fairy godmother?"

Everyone but the fish buyer whistled and howled with laughter. Pablo's sons threw down their stones and ran to see the grouper. Pablo met Abundio as he came off the berm.

"Bundo, I could have helped you."

Abundio tilted his head back toward the water.

"Go help my assistant, Ensign Chino."

At first, Pablo thought Chino needed help with the panga, but then he realized the partners must have caught more than one fish.

"Does Chino have more fish?"

"Go take a look."

They climbed the berm. The old panga floated with its bow resting on the gravel and Chino was standing beside it with the larger of their two grouper. He had managed to drag the monster fish to the edge of the water, but it had run itself aground there and he had not been able to move it further. He motioned for them to come down.

"What's the matter, amigos? Haven't you ever seen a garropa before?"

The tall man looked accusingly at Pablo.

"I thought you said you aren't taking our fish."

He shouted down to Chino.

"Eh! Chino! Where did you get it?"

Pablo and Chino caught each other's eyes. Then Chino shouted back.

"At the Four Horses. Near the island with the dead cactus. Very lucky, no?"

The tall one looked down at the enormous fish.

"Yes... very lucky."

He waved to the other men.

"Help them."

Then he shouted to the fish buyer.

"Back your truck up to the gravel. We need a long rope."

The buyer had set up his scales again and he was struggling to weigh the smaller grouper.

"What is it?"

"A very big garropa. At least one-hundred-fifty kilos. Maybe a lot more."

They hurled the rope to Chino, who passed it through the gills of the great fish, and they used the buyer's truck to drag it over the berm. As it slid down the round, black stones, the grouper's body left a wet groove twice as wide as a man.

The buyer glanced casually at the fish. Then he shook his head and folded his arms.

"It won't fit on the scales. I'll pay eighty kilos. Take it or leave it."

Abundio Rodríguez spat out most of the bottle of beer he had discovered hidden beneath the ice in the fish buyer's truck.

His eyes opened wide and he pressed his belly against the front of the buyer's shirt.

"What!? What did you say!? *You pinche cabrón!*"

Abundio held the buyer's loafers down with his bare feet and he sprayed the man's face with a mix of beer and air. The buyer leaned back, pinned against his truck. His chain and shirt were pasted to his stomach by Abundio's sweat.

Frightened, the buyer looked to the Las Ramalitas men and they started to come to his aid. But then they remembered Chino, who was standing back on the berm, watching silently, with his hands hanging loosely at his sides. The tall man raised his arms with his palms held outward, shaking his head.

"Chino! We don't want any trouble here, Chino."

They moved aside as Chino descended the berm and crossed through their midst. Abundio's sweaty belly still held the fish buyer tight against his truck. Chino stared hard into the buyer's eyes. He raised his voice loud enough for everyone to hear.

"Señor, we know this *pescado* weighs more than one-hundred-fifty kilos. But unfortunately, there is no way to measure it. Why don't we just call it one-hundred twenty-five kilos?"

Abundio stepped back.

The buyer was about to protest, but his eyes and the eyes of the other men were drawn past Chino and Abundio to a slender young woman who had appeared on the road behind them.

Her voice rang out like a fine, silver bell.

"*Papá?*"

Abundio turned, and he saw the face of someone whose large, black eyes he had known since the morning they first opened—a lifetime ago and in a world far, far away, it seemed to him, as he stood on the hot beach of Las Ramalitas trying to get a fair price for his fish, with steadfast Chino Zúñiga at his side and these incomprehensibly hostile men all around them.

But although he knew this girl's face as well as his own, to Abundio it seemed strangely inappropriate, disconnected from the long woman's legs striding confidently toward him, the slender arms reaching out to him, the woman's hair falling about her shoulders.

Abundio knew the hours and the minutes that had formed her. But, could these be her lips, so strangely smooth and red? Her little bare feet, shod in golden sandals? Her thighs, shaping the unfamiliar, new white cotton pants? And... could these be his little girl's breasts? Filling the inside of her shirt?

She touched his cheek and she smiled inquiringly into the distant, rarely visited shores of his life.

"Papá?"

Abundio's lips hesitated, and opened, and the name he had given her came out in a dry whisper.

"María... "

"I am coming home."

"But... *la profesora?*"

"We have some time free. May I come today? With you and Chino?"

She placed a slender hand on Chino's arm and allowed it to rest there. Chino stood silently, as Abundio considered this request of one María Guadalupe Rodríguez, nineteen years old, daughter of himself and Socorro, formerly a beach child of the tenuously extant Mexican fishing village of Agua Amargosa, and now a student in Loreto, who, in the nine months since he had last seen her, had changed into something quite extraordinary and unexpected.

"But... what about your things, María?"

"Everything is at Uncle Ramón's camp. The food and water. Also the gasoline. Everything is ready."

Abundio searched his mind for a reason why this miracle should not happen, but he found none. And why should there be? If a child may tie her clothes into a bundle and leave home on the fish truck one day, could not that same child just as easily return in a panga? Where was it written that miracles must have a reason? Why could they not just happen of their own accord? Why be suspicious of them?

"It seems there will be no wind today."

"Then... may I come, papá?"

He thought of the evenings and the days ahead, of her laughter calling him to play in the shade of the trees, the sound of her breathing as she slept on her cot, of Socorro humming softly at the cooking barrel.

"Your mother. She has missed you much. She will be... very happy."

"Oh, thank you, papá!"

María laughed to Chino, who grinned and nodded silently.

Then, as she had always done, María wrapped her arms around her papá's sweaty neck and she kissed his unshaven cheeks, unmindful of the spectacle she was creating by the pressing of her new self against the familiar, comforting, half-naked bulk of Abundio Rodríguez.

"Come, papá! I will show you the way to Uncle Ramón's!"

María steadied herself on Chino's arm as she bent over to remove her thin, golden sandals for the walk down the beach. Abundio felt the heat of the men's eyes settle upon her, and he shouted to Chino with an abruptness that broke the spell.

"Chino! I am going to see Ramón! Bring the panga after you have finished here."

María gave Chino's arm a squeeze.

"Don't take too long!"

She took her father's hand and started him on the sandy path leading to the south side of the bay.

When they were gone, one of the other men whistled and called out in an ululating, mocking voice.

"Ayyy, Chino! You'd better not take too l-o-n-g! Ayyy, ayyy, ayyy! She's *waiting* for you."

In a flash of motion, Chino grabbed the fish buyer's short-handled gaff from its hook on the back of the truck and he whirled around with it. Instantly, the circle of men grew wider. As the one who had whistled turned to run, Chino took two fast steps toward him, and then bent over and struck the head of the larger grouper a savage blow that buried the hook to its shank. Standing up, Chino lifted the massive head as high as he could and he turned to the fish buyer with a beaming smile.

"One-hundred twenty-five kilos, amigo?"

The buyer nodded his agreement.

ABUNDIO AND MARÍA walked hand-in-hand along the ridge of smooth, black stones that formed the beach of Las Ramalitas.

Each winter, the gravel berm was rebuilt by storm waves to the height of a man's head. The berm extended nearly all the way around the bay and it made the launching of the Las Ramalitas pangas a difficult job that required the combined efforts of perhaps fifteen men. Because the semi-open bay offered little shelter from wind and swells, there were only a few days per month that the fishermen felt secure in anchoring their boats in the water overnight. So every afternoon they helped each other drag their pangas to safety above the high tide line, and every morning they worked in teams to slide the boats down again.

Because the land behind the beach was flat and subject to flooding, the fishermen had built their shacks in a long, single row upon the gravel berm itself. Dry salt flats came to within thirty feet of their plastic and tar paper dwellings, and in the afternoons, the houses rattled and shook in the constant wind blowing off the sea.

Normally, the mud behind the houses was as hard as concrete, perfectly level and featureless, but when it rained, the flats became an impenetrable morass. Two roads went back to the main highway. Usually, the fish buyer drove straight across the mud flats. But in wet weather, a much longer road winding through the foothills allowed fish to reach market in Loreto.

Abundio and María headed for a place on the beach a quarter mile south of the main cluster of shacks. Here, the winter berm disappeared and gave way to a series of low, brushy sand dunes. Although launching their pangas would have been much easier here, the fishermen of Las Ramalitas never used this part of the beach because it was cut off by a high rock hill that made it impossible to reach with a pickup.

In this unfavorable location, approachable only on foot or by panga, Socorro's brother, Ramón Ochoa, and several dozen other refugees from Agua Amargosa had created a camp of rough shelters made of driftwood and plastic garbage bags.

Some of the lean-tos held single men. Others, such as Ramón Ochoa's, contained families with women and children who hunkered down out of the wind while the men fished, who kept their belongings wrapped in bags against the flying sand, and who slept on the ground at night with the scorpions and fleas.

In fairness to the village of Las Ramalitas, there was no space for these newcomers on the gravel berm anyway. But even if there had been, the strangers would not have been welcome, for they had become a source of suffering and disquietude.

Their efforts to support themselves had, in truth, increased the amount of fish brought to the truck twice a week, and justified or not, the buyer had seized this opportunity to lower his price. In order to make up the shortfall in their own barely adequate incomes, the villagers had been forced to charge the fishermen of Agua Amargosa twenty percent of everything they caught, a levy viewed by both groups as repugnant but inevitable and necessary for the survival of at least one of them.

The tranquility of the people of Las Ramalitas had been shaken by the specter of the starving colony that had appeared so suddenly in their midst and they wished they could wake one morning to find it gone. Each night, the campfires flickering at the far end of the beach reminded them that the fate of those unfortunate families, and of their own as well, depended on the whims of the gods that controlled the rain and wind, and on the unknown forces that created such things as roads, and they had little confidence in either.

As a youth, Abundio had visited Las Ramalitas with his father a few times and once they had even camped there when the swells were especially small, but the steep beach and the insecure shelter of the bay made it a treacherous stop for a single man and a small boy, and they had for the most part avoided it.

Now, Abundio recognized little of the terrain as María led him through the scattered campsites.

As they passed one of the lean-tos, a feeble voice called out to them.

"Bundo... is that you? Has Socorro come also?"

An old man, tempered to brittleness by the seasons and dressed all in white, came out from beneath the lean-to. He was followed by two small children and a puppy. Abundio lifted the puppy by the skin on the back of its neck. He shook the old man's trembling hand.

"Hello, Carlos. No, Socorro is not here. I came with Chino. How are your family?"

The old man wobbled and pulled on Abundio's fingers. His eyes were cloudy and dull.

"Not good, Bundo. My son is in Santa Rosalia... working at *El Boleo*. They send him into the ground... like an Indian. Ah! Forgive me, Abundio! I am a fool who speaks without thinking."

"It is of no importance, old friend."

The old man wrung his hands, rocking back and forth.

"No, no! I offer my apology to Socorro... and to Ramón, of course."

"It is nothing, Carlos."

The old man nodded to himself. His dim eyes turned south across the sand dunes.

" ...the caleta?"

"Your house stands as always, Carlos."

" ...and the road?"

"Nothing yet."

The old man's face brightened as he noticed María for the first time. He bent close and tugged the buttons of her shirt.

"Ah, María Guadalupe! How tall and lovely you have grown! You will soon make a rich man happy. *Ayy!*"

María gave him a hug around his shoulders.

"Thank you, Carlos. You *are* such a charmer! Come, papá. Uncle Ramón's camp is down by the water."

The old man caught Abundio's thick wrist.

"Bundo... Bundo... what is going to happen to us?"

Abundio lowered the puppy to the sand.

"Carlos, we must be patient. I am sure they will come to fix the road soon."

The old man crossed himself. He got down on his hands and knees and crawled back into his lean-to.

WITHOUT ICE OR a place to store their catch, the men from Agua Amargosa were constrained to fishing only on those mornings when the buyer's truck was expected.

Other days, they worked on their lean-tos, or they kicked a soccer ball on the mud flat or simply lolled about the beach, waiting for something to end their time in limbo. The children played with each other and the women cooked and washed. The daily routine of the dunes was not unpleasant and it was not much different from the routine they had known in Agua Amargosa.

But each afternoon, the wind seemed stronger than before, and each evening the shadows seemed darker as the sun descended toward the western hills and the money jars were dug out of the sand so beans and lard, coffee, sugar, flour and salt could be bought in the village. Already, many of the money jars had run out and their families had left the bay of Las Ramalitas as they had come, in precariously loaded pangas, bound for another village, another place where they might find a way to continue somehow.

Friday afternoons brought a welcome break in the routine for it was on this day that the pangas came up the coast with news and visits from home. At first, there had been up to a dozen boats to be loaded with supplies for the caleta, but as the weeks passed and the money jars emptied, fewer and fewer pangas had appeared on the horizon.

This Friday, only two boats had made the trip. One had brought Pablo Santos and his young sons. The other had brought Chino Zúñiga, as usual, and for the first time, Abundio Rodríguez, who had resisted coming until now for two reasons. First, as de facto headman of Agua Amargosa, he considered it his symbolic duty to maintain the flag at home. Secondly, his wife Socorro, despite all entreaties in the name of logic, refused even to consider abandoning the caleta, and she had made it clear to her husband that a visit north would be thought of as an impardonable act of treachery. In the present case, she had relented only because of Chino's problems with their Evinrude motor and her knowledge that a drifting panga, especially Abundio's panga, would be difficult for Chino to manage alone beneath the cliffs if the winds came up.

Sensing Socorro's concern, Abundio had sprung his hole card on her, describing in elaborate detail the blisters on Chino's lips, the size of his tongue, the color of his fingernails, and the way his eyes protruded during the seven days they had drifted near death off the southern islands. Socorro had finally given her blessing for the trip on the condition that Abundio take his boots in case they had to jump for their lives and climb out over the rocks.

As he reached Ramón's large, well-kept lean-to, with María's hand in his, Abundio hoped the surprise of his daughter's homecoming would help Socorro forget any rash promises he might have made as he negotiated for his trip north.

María unhooked a string loop and opened a door made of chicken wire and black plastic.

"Come in, papá!"

Abundio heard the old Evinrude approaching behind him as he ducked to enter the lean-to.

CHINO HAD THEIR money from the fish buyer. He ran the panga up on the beach opposite Ramón's camp and began loading water bottles and supplies from a pile at the edge of the water.

A few minutes later, Pablo Santos arrived with his sons and they began loading from a similar pile. Pablo lifted some boxes into his panga and then stood blocking Chino's way.

"So... where did you really catch the garropas?"

"You don't believe the Four Horses?"

"I know better than that! Where was it, Chino?"

"Why should I tell you?"

Pablo pointed a finger at Chino's chest.

"*You* know why!"

Chino stepped around the finger and picked up a bag of flour.

"What do you mean?"

Pablo hopped back in the way, waving his arms.

"Come off it, Chino! I know what's going on! I find a good spot and right away your panga is sitting on it. You guys are too obvious! You should at least wait a few weeks."

Chino stepped around Pablo again. He loaded the water bottles, saving the beer for last so he could pad it with extra care. That done, he grabbed a heavy crate and helped Pablo load it into his panga. As they set the crate down, Chino spoke in an even, conciliatory tone.

"You know, Pablo, your boat always catches the most fish."

"True."

"What's your secret?"

"Don't try to change the subject! We're talking about two very big garropas and probably a lot more. Somewhere between here and Agua Amargosa."

"All right. You know the big point with the white rocks off it?"

"There is nothing but mackerel there."

"Really? Well, about a mile south, drift a bait close to the cliff."

"How close?"

"You have to be touching it."

"How deep?"

"About fifteen brazas. We found it by accident. There is at least one more big fish there. It broke the heavy line."

"Chino, you better be telling the truth this time."

"And... if I'm not?"

"I could stop telling Margarita where I fish. I thought of doing that seven years ago."

Chino was amazed.

"You have known for *that* long, Pablo?"

"Do you think I'm blind? I said, you guys are too obvious."

Chino, now, was sincerely puzzled.

"But Pablo, if you have known for so long... why didn't you stop?"

Pablo shrugged.

"You guys never catch anything anyway!"

Abundio came down to the beach and glanced at the supplies. He noted a nest-like, empty space that Chino had created in the middle of the panga. It had been carefully lined with plastic bags and pieces of smooth cardboard.

"What is that, mijo?"

"A place for María... her new clothes."

"Ah... yes."

Abundio went over to Pablo's big green panga. Pablo was in it, trimming his load for the ride south.

"Pablo, your wife is up there. At Ramón's. She wants to talk to you."

Pablo grunted and waved for his sons to follow him. Abundio waited until they were out of hearing distance and then spoke to his partner.

"So? Another of Abundio and Chino's secret spots given away, eh?"

"He already knew."

"I didn't think he would swallow that story about the Four Horses."

"Amigo. He also knows all about Margarita."

Abundio felt an electric current of disorientation pass through him. His knees buckled momentarily, but he caught himself so quickly Chino was unaware of the disturbance this revelation had caused in his partner. Abundio's voice was a cautious whisper.

"What about Margarita?"

"Pablo says he has known from the beginning. For seven years!"

"You mean... about his fishing spots?"

"Of course, Bundo. What else?"

"Nothing, mijo. Let's go pay Ramón."

The tide had begun rising to its evening peak and the panga would be sure to drift if left untended. Chino dragged a grapnel anchor of bent iron rods a dozen yards up from the water and sank it into dry sand.

They started up to Ramón's camp with Abundio following behind.

" ...and what did he say, mijo?"

"Who?"

"Pablo. What did he say about us fishing in his spots?"

"He doesn't care."

"Good! Pablo doesn't own the ocean, anyway."

"Well, I just hope he keeps talking to his sister! If it weren't for Margarita we'd be selling Chiclets to the *turistas* in Tijuana."

"Mijo! Please! I am a fisherman! A prince of the sea! Like my father before me!"

Chino turned and grinned at his partner, the optimistic, always cheerful man who had taken him in as a complete stranger, who had defended him against the suspicions of Socorro and the others, and who had over the years shown him how to respect himself and not wish he were something else.

He put a hand on Abundio's thick shoulder and smiled.

"Sorry, amigo. I was just being realistic."

Ramón's camp was built low, out of the wind, behind the first row of sand dunes. Pablo Santos stood just in front of the lean-to, arguing with his wife. The boys were listening closely as they pretended to play at the edge of camp.

Since Abundio had last seen her, Pablo Santos' wife had transformed herself in a manner something like María's, but in reverse. Whereas María seemed to have matured years during her nine-month absence from the caleta, Lupe Santos seemed magically to have become a youthful coquette again in only one-third that time.

Her plump body seemed ready to burst through her thigh-high, red satin dress and it seemed her breasts and buttocks must pop like balloons if pricked with a pin. Her hair was piled high on her head and held in place by long brass combs, and her eyes were surrounded by butterfly-shaped black marks reaching almost back to her ears. The tops of her feet escaped from a pair of high-heeled shoes covered with red sequins the size of thumbnails.

Abundio wouldn't have recognized the once familiar woman were it not for the vulgar, unnerving pitch of her voice. He winced as she held her hands on her hips and screamed at Pablo.

"You should have brought their clothes! Now what am I going to do?"

Pablo stood facing her. Streaks of dry sea salt mottled the dark skin of his chest and stomach.

"I didn't think you were going to take them today."

"You didn't *think!* Do you know what it costs me to come down here?"

"I will bring their clothes next Friday."

"Idiot! Now I have to miss another day at the tienda."

"I am sorry, Lupe."

Pablo knelt down and gathered his sons to his chest and kissed them.

"It will be better for you in Loreto. Mamá has found work and a place for you to live."

The smaller boy went to his mother. But the older refused to let go of Pablo and cried into his neck, holding on tight with his strong brown arms.

"But papá? Who will help you in the boat?"

"I will be all right, Rubén. I fished alone all the years when you were small. Do you think I am too old and fat now?"

"But who will watch Aunt Margarita?"

"Margarita must learn to care for herself. She is alone today. Is she not?"

Pablo pulled the boy's hands away and gave them to his wife.

"Lupe. I will bring everything on Friday."

"Why can't you come Sunday? Then I wouldn't have to miss work."

"There is no fish truck on Sunday."

"Pablo! Pablo! You aren't catching enough anyway! How much longer can you stay down there?"

"It is almost the season of the tuna."

"Tuna!? How can you fish outside without gas!? Oh, Pablo! You are as crazy as your sister mourning her bastard baby in the moonlight!"

Pablo turned away as though she had stung him with a whip.

"Enough! Lupe! Please!"

He knelt to give his sons a final hug and kiss. They waited for their mother to take off her shoes and they followed her through the sandy dunes toward the village of Las Ramalitas.

María came out of the lean-to with her Uncle Ramón.

Ramón Ochoa was four years older than Socorro and perhaps two inches taller. But except for gender, he was nearly his sister's identical twin, possessed of the same dark skin, the very short stature, the round head, and the unusual steel gray eyes.

Socorro and Ramón had been born on a small rented farm outside the great shipping port of Salina Cruz in the southern mainland state of Oaxaca. In Salina Cruz, goods from around the Pacific were loaded on trains to be transported to the other side of the Isthmus of Tehuantepec. There, they were reloaded onto ships bound for Europe and the east coasts of North and South America.

But with the completion of the Panama Canal in 1914 the trains of Salina Cruz had been silenced and the city had undergone a slow, painful decline. The workmen had left first, followed by the small businessmen and ruling families, and by the time of the Great Depression of the 1930s, the crumbling streets and buildings of Salina Cruz were populated mainly by a handful of officials with little to do.

With the departure of their Mexican clients, the Indians around Salina Cruz were forced to give up their farms. The Ochoa family tried moving inland to the town of Tehuantepec, but they could find no suitable land to rent there, nor in the neighboring state of Chiapas, which was even poorer than their own.

So, in the Indian way, they began walking, barefoot, north up the coastal road, a tiny, doll-like mother and father and four even smaller children, living off the land for a thousand miles, until they reached the port of Mazatlán. From there they crossed the Sea of Cortez by begging passage from the captain of a rotting bark that ferried cargo to La Paz.

From La Paz, they walked northward again, in their fringed rebozos, their stiff, hand-woven *serapes,* and their wide-brimmed straw hats, crossing the mountains from one desert rancho to the next until they reached the outskirts of Loreto. Here at last, the family found work, hoeing weeds and serving as human beasts of burden on a small farm, but they had reached the end of their strength and the two younger children had died of influenza the first year, followed shortly by the father and finally the mother in the winter of 1935.

Socorro was ten when she and Ramón buried their mother in the sand beside their father and their brother and sister. They marked the graves with wood crosses like the ones they had seen in the Mexican cemetery north of town and they bundled their clothes and began to wander.

Ramón, though older, spoke only the language of the Indians. Socorro quickly learned enough Spanish from the other children to find work for them as they moved from rancho to rancho in the rocky canyons and valleys surrounding Loreto.

But as he hoed and carried the cruel loads tied upon his back, and as he watched his young sister's body wither and her bones grow old and twisted before their natural time, Ramón knew he was never intended to live on the ranchos. From the moment he had first experienced the sea, on the crossing from Mazatlán, Ramón had longed to live on it and he began to spend time at the beach, waiting for the pangas to return in the afternoons, standing by mutely as the fishermen worked, leaping to fetch or help whenever an opportunity presented itself. It was not long before the fishermen of Loreto learned that the short, homely, silent, black-skinned Indian youth had hands of iron and could carry as much as any man, more in fact than many of them, and soon Ramón was invited on the pangas to help pull the lines.

That year, when Ramón was fourteen, he earned his first few pesos as a working fisherman. In his fifth season, he earned enough to rescue Socorro from the killing work of the ranchos and allow her to join him in a shack he had built on an island just north of town. But even though he worked hard and drank not at all, and even though Socorro kept the cleanest and best managed household of all the women in the encampment, they were never integrated with the handful of Mexicans who lived on the island, and the brother and sister had only each other, and they longed once more to hear someone speak the language of their parents.

For six lonely years they lived on the sand spit at the edge of the sea. There were years when Socorro never left the island or spoke to a person other than her brother. Though only twenty-two years old, she had been broken to the hoe at the age of five and she had long passed the prime of whatever feminine beauty would ever be granted to her. Isolated and lacking prospects, she gratefully accepted her reprieve from the hills, and she settled into caring for Ramón and sharing his earnings from the pangas.

The sudden landing of Abundio Rodríguez on their beach one windy September afternoon changed everything.

Abundio's motorless panga washed up in the surf directly in front of their shack and he leapt out of it as it capsized, brandishing his one good oar and bellowing for help. They ran down to him, but when they reached him, they stopped, dumbfounded, for they had no knowledge that men could grow so large. Neither Socorro nor her brother stood any taller than Abundio's strapping chest, and his voice seemed to boom like thunder as he shouted at them and struggled to pull his panga from the pitching shore break.

Abundio had rowed and sailed his seventeen-foot wooden boat all the way from La Paz, following the coast and relying on luck and the strength of his manhood to make the dangerous passage. But his mast had splintered as he attempted a foolhardy, wind-driven shortcut between the islands of Danzante and Carmen, and then one of his oars had split, leaving him adrift among the whitecaps of the channel. The southeast wind had pushed him right past the town of Loreto to the lonely sand spit on Isla Coronado that was the home of Ramón and Socorro Ochoa.

They helped wire Abundio's broken oar back together and they gave him food and rest for the night. In the morning, Socorro filled his water bottle and made him a package of tortillas for the final run to Loreto.

But when Ramón returned from work that evening he was surprised to find the big Mexican still there. Abundio had gathered lengths of derelict fishing line and had joined them together with his own hooks and sinkers. He had found driftwood on the beach, and when Ramón came in, he was sitting on the floor of their shack carving a pair of winding boards. In reply to Ramón's questioning eyes, Abundio stood up with his head nearly touching the palm-thatched ceiling and he indicated his handiwork. His voice seemed strangely loud and foreign in their tiny shack as he pointed outside to his beached panga.

"I have no home. You have no boat. We fish together?"

"But señor, your boat has no motor."

Abundio held out his enormous hands, so thickly calloused he could hardly close them. Ramón noticed that he had lost the tip of his right thumb in the rough landing. Abundio smiled his big smile and flexed his incredibly thick arms.

"I am a rower of infinite *capacidad*. I will be the motor. You know how to fish. We will make much money."

Ramón realized that this soft-mannered giant, a socially superior *mestizo,* was offering to be the donkey, while he, Ramón Ochoa, the socially invisible Zapotec Indian, would supply the knowledge and direction for their partnership. Still, he was wary of being taken advantage of.

"We split money... fifty-fifty?"

"Of course, señor!"

That did it. Nobody had ever called him "señor" before with such thoughtless sincerity. There was something different about this man. Something that attracted Ramón and drew a sense of hope and trust from him that he had not known before. Ramón surveyed the knotted, different colored lines, carefully coiled on the floor. They would not last long. And meanwhile, they would lose many hooks and sinkers.

"I would have to quit my job."

"I have nothing else. I make you a promise. I will never let you or your sister down."

And he never had.

Abundio Rodríguez had rowed and rowed like a machine, never complaining, never asking to be spelled. Within two months, they had made enough to buy new lines and real oars. Within a year, Abundio and Socorro had become a pair of nervous, self-conscious, not-so-young lovers, and they had built a shack beside Ramón's, and a year after that, María had been born.

Their fortunes had grown steadily over the seasons, and with their new status, Ramón had found a girl from one of the ranchos and had begun a family of his own. The twin shacks on the shore of Isla Coronado came to be surrounded by the footprints of children.

Eventually, they did so well Ramón made a down payment on his own panga, complete with Evinrude, and the brothers-in-law were able to dissolve their partnership and fish separately. Each afternoon, the two boats were pulled up on the beach side-by-side, Abundio's, motorless as always, and Ramón's, bought on payments from his former employer.

But each year the fishing became less reliable in the reefs around Isla Coronado. On Abundio's recommendation the families moved south to the new village of Agua Amargosa. Abundio had known the caleta for most of his life and he had been correct in calculating that the fishing would be better there. In fact, it was much better, and the two families prospered under the caleta's shady palms. Although their barren island had been tranquil, it had also enforced a bleakness to their lives that they began to recognize only after the move. Socorro, especially, blossomed into a sort of happiness that Ramón had never expected for his sister. In contentment, she swept her floor and watered her geraniums as she watched María grow tall and beautiful, and she cleaved to her man with all her love and tried to ease his journey through the seasons, as each year he grew a little quieter, a little stiffer in his joints, and a little thicker about the middle.

But regardless of whatever else Abundio Rodríguez might have done for him, as Ramón Ochoa emerged from his rough lean-to on the beach of Las Ramalitas, he knew in his heart there was one simple thing that was the most important of all. Twenty years before, Abundio had stood with his head bumping the ceiling of their eight-foot by eight-foot tar paper shack on the island of Coronado, and he had addressed him with the word "señor," and he had meant it. At that moment, Ramón Ochoa had left the hills of Oaxaca for the last time, and he had never looked back.

But now the spring storm had cut the road to the caleta and ended everything, and now, with the new cooperativas and the many new fishermen and their families, there was no longer space or fish for them in Loreto, nor in La Paz, nor even in Las Ramalitas.

Now, nearly all of them had been forced to abandon the caleta, and only a dwindling few clung to the hope that someone, somewhere, would notice their plight and cause the road to be repaired.

Ramón and Abundio wrapped their arms tightly about each other's shoulders and Abundio bent down as they kissed each other on both cheeks. They held that *abrazo* a long time with their eyes closed and their arms locked together. Finally, Abundio spoke to his brother-in-law.

"Adiós, Ramón. We must go now."

"Yes. Yes. The wind. You mustn't get caught under the cliffs."

Pablo Santos pulled out a wad of bills. He paid Ramón for his food and gas, and shook hands.

"Thank you, Ramón. And how much for filling the water bottles?"

"It is nothing."

"*Gracias.* And for hiring the pickup?"

"Don't worry about it."

Pablo left for the beach. In a few moments, they heard the sound of his outboard motor, and then it was quiet. Abundio pointed toward the village.

"Pablo's wife is… very different."

"She had to buy those clothes. She is at the hotel, serving drinks to the gringos."

"She said it was a store."

"I saw her."

Chino and María came out of the lean-to with a garbage bag containing María's things. María also had a plastic shopping bag which she opened and showed to her father.

"Papá, I bought some things in Loreto. Look! Some *chorizo* and isn't this a beautiful ribbon for mamá? Do you think she will like it?"

The ribbon was scarlet red, Socorro's favorite color. Abundio was about to comment on the pleasure it would bring her when he saw the menacing orange and green shapes filling the bottom of the bag.

"*Muertos?*"

"You know how she loves them."

"But, María. So many?"

"The price was very good!"

Abundio and Chino shot glances at each other and resigned themselves to another onslaught of the hell fire these small, misshapen chili peppers would soon bring to their table. Socorro's passion for hot food was rarely satiated, and the peppers she liked to call *levanta muertos*, or "raise-the-dead," were the only luxury she allowed herself with complete disregard for the well-being of others. Unfortunately, María, while bearing no other physical resemblance to her mother, had inherited from her an apparent immunity from the peppers' ravaging chemistry, and the Rodríguez women had conspired for nearly two decades to have them as often as possible.

Chino handed a roll of bills to Ramón, who put it into his pocket without counting it.

"Ramón, that should be enough. If there is any left over, keep it for yourself. We caught two very big garropas today."

"Yes. Abundio said one of them was the biggest he has ever seen."

"How has it gone this week, Ramón?"

"Badly. They all use the nets and spearguns here. They are killing everything. Even fish too small to sell."

"And after they kill them all?"

"They will be gone too. Like the fish."

Now Ramón turned to Abundio.

"How is Fra Nacho? Still breathing?"

"Yes. He is happy. He sits with his flashlight and his music."

María gasped.

"Oh, Uncle Ramón! I forgot batteries for him! It has been so long!"

"No matter. No matter."

Ramón went into the lean-to. He returned with a paper bag which he gave to María.

"Here, sweet baby, give these to him with my best wishes. They are almost new."

María added the batteries to her bag of levanta muertos.

"Thank you, uncle!"

Chino gave Ramón the abrazo.

"Listen, Ramón. We need a new carburetor for the Evinrude."

"I will find a good one in Loreto."

"Thanks."

"Adiós, Chino. And take good care of this beautiful one."

Ramón pinched María's cheek and she gave him a kiss. She and Chino left for the beach.

When they had gone, Abundio spoke.

"Ramón, I need to talk to Luis Medina. His family can't wait any longer."

"Out of food?"

"Yes, and everything else. Joselito fishes from the beach, but that's all they have."

Ramón raised an open hand toward a ragged piece of black plastic tied between some bushes in the distance.

"Luis is over there. By himself. But it won't do any good."

"Is he sick?"

"He is drunk. He stopped fishing three weeks ago."

Abundio watched the Las Ramalitas wind whip and tear at the plastic. One corner had come loose and had caught itself on the spiny branches of a bush. As the plastic rose and fell, it revealed the clasped feet of a man sleeping on his side, half-buried in the sand.

"Ramón, do you have some extra flour? And some oil and salt? Chino will pay you next week."

"Sure, Bundo."

Ramón went inside. As Abundio stood waiting, he heard a man's voice call out behind him.

"Hey, you!"

"Eh... ?"

"Where's Chino? We came to see if he is going to play today."

Several of the Las Ramalitas men stood at the edge of camp. Abundio recognized the man who had spoken as their leader, the tall one who collected the commission money. The man was now wearing a new tee-shirt with a diagonal stripe across the front. Under one arm, he held a soccer ball cradled against his ribs.

"You mean a ball game?"

The men circled Abundio while the leader slowly looked him over, up and down, side to side.

"If... you are up to it."

Abundio pointed to himself.

"You mean... *me?*"

The tall man's eyes roamed all over Abundio's overhanging belly.

"Why not, amigo? You look like you could use the exercise."

Abundio folded his arms and ignored the laughs as two of the men pushed out their stomachs and danced about him, puffing out their cheeks and making rude noises.

"Just a minute."

Abundio went down to the beach, where María and Chino were sitting on the sand tossing pebbles into the water.

"Mijo. Some guys from Las Ramalitas want you to play ball with them."

"We've been playing on Fridays. But nobody came up today."

"You mean... it is us against Las Ramalitas? Every week?"

"Well, yes, usually. But we never win."

"Never?"

"They have shoes. And more players. Besides, they practice. They are better than us."

Abundio spread his arms wide and threw back his head.

"Those *cabrones?* Better than *us!?* We'll see about *that!"*

María had lived with her father's moods long enough to know the danger signs.

"Papá! No! The games are very rough. And some of them have shoes with cleats!"

Abundio had not even heard her.

"Mijo! How many men do we have?"

"Five, maybe six. Seven, if you were to play."

María glared at Chino. She faced her father with her fists held tightly at her sides.

"Papá, you are too old for this. They are very dirty. Even Chino has a rough time."

"Ah, María, do not worry! I am a man of infinite… "

She leaned forward with her fists pressed into her slender waist.

"No! Papá! I am serious! Chino! *Stop* him!"

Chino was startled by the tone of her voice.

"Listen, amigo, there isn't enough time today. Anyway, the wind is coming… "

"The wind is *not* coming!!"

IN FACT, MARÍA was only partially correct about her father's ignorance of the game of soccer, for although it was true that he had not kicked a ball seriously for over twenty years, and although he was much too far out of condition to protect himself in serious competition, Abundio Rodríguez actually had something more than a passing acquaintance with the game the Mexicans called *fútbol*.

Unknown even to Socorro, there had been a period on the beaches and playing fields of La Paz when a certain, oversized youth had won comradeship, many wagers for cash, and uncounted beers and tacos by terrorizing any side that dared enter the pitch against him.

Abundio's height and weight had allowed him to play on even terms with adults by the time he was twelve, but they had also handicapped him with an innate slowness and awkwardness that would be with him for life. He learned early that his value to his team lay not at midfield or in attacks on goal, but at the defensive position that would someday be known as "sweeper." Here, Abundio would conserve his energy by stationing himself motionless near his goal keeper through most of the game. But whenever an attacker threatened to score against them, he launched himself from the goal area like an evil missile from hell, bent on destruction, ruthlessly and shamelessly fouling with his knees and elbows in an effort to take the player out of the game. If he also happened to stop the shot, that was good too.

Usually, Abundio played for an amateur team called *Los Tecolotes*, or "The Eagle Owls," after a beach of the same name a few miles north of La Paz, and typically, visiting sides required only a few minutes to decide that direct attacks against the big, dirty fullback were simply not worth the medical bills. After that, Los Tecolotes only needed to score one or perhaps two goals to win the majority of their matches.

Left more or less to his own devices from an early age, Abundio lived with friends and teammates around the city of La Paz and his routine was made up mostly of hanging around, playing games on weekends, and waiting for those happy occasions when his father would come to take him on fishing trips.

But one day, shortly after the end of the war, word came that Abundio's father had died in the fishing village of El Sargento and the son had hitch-hiked over the mountains south of La Paz to take possession of his inheritance, a square-transomed, seventeen-foot wooden panga that his father had bought the previous year with profits from the wartime shark liver oil market. When Abundio arrived in El Sargento, he found that the panga's motor, oars, and mast had been stolen, along with all of their lines and other things, so he carved himself a new pair of oars and rowed the bare boat back to La Paz.

Abundio played for the Tecolotes another season, and he enjoyed the life of a popular young man, free to roam and explore the city. But he was short on cash. The shark liver market had collapsed with the end of the war, and Abundio found that the death of his father had somehow dissipated his energy, his *joie de vivre*. He drifted away from his team, never to return, and soon his exploits with the Tecolotes became a rarely conjured memory, as though that part of his life were a story someone had once told him long ago.

In later years, Abundio would play fútbol with the children, and on occasion he would join in when the other fishermen invited him to fill a side after work, but in these friendly situations he felt constrained from using his capacity for mayhem, and his weight and natural awkwardness gave others the impression that he was a mere dabbler in the sport. Some time when María was still a child, he stopped playing altogether, and he was not sure if he had ever even mentioned his days with the Tecolotes to either her or Socorro.

A few months after quitting the Tecolotes, Abundio became restless and he left La Paz. He took the old panga and rowed north alone, stopping in the fish camps, seeking out the old places from the golden days with his father.

He wandered up the coast for two months, feeding himself by fishing, or helping on the boats, or picking up odd jobs in the camps, and by and large, he was happy and satisfied, except for a deepening awareness of how much he missed his father and a fear that perhaps one day his own journey would come to an end, somewhere, and that his father's panga would pass into the hands of someone who had never known his name.

Then his mast and oar broke and the southern whitecaps sent him flying straight as an arrow to a pair of lonely Indians keeping to themselves. The tiny, dark-skinned little man and woman spoke hardly any Spanish, and they were more hindrance than help in getting his panga out of the surf, but they fed him and gave him a place to lie down and the woman wrapped his thumb with cloth that she tore from her only dress.

For the remainder of the day, and through the following morning after the man had left for work, she spoke not a word to him. But as he prepared to leave, she appeared on the beach with tortillas and water, and she put her shoulder to the transom and made little grunting noises as she helped him push his panga into the sea.

She stood and watched silently as Abundio hopped in and rowed and rowed against the southern breeze that was trying to drive him back to the beach. He gained a quarter mile toward the town of Loreto, watching her grow small and child-like as she stood with her hand raised and her round brown face shining in the sun. Then he thought of the freshly turned patch of sand they had said was his father, and his arms grew suddenly weary. He stopped fighting the wind and he let it blow him back toward the island.

The woman saw him stop rowing and after a while she ran down the beach and was lost from sight.

As he drifted ashore, almost back to the spot where he had started, she reappeared and came running to meet him. She had gathered up a big armful of old fishing lines from the beach and in rough Spanish she spoke to him for the first time.

"My brother. Very, very good fisherman. But no panga."

Her *brother?* So, they weren't husband and wife after all. Abundio saw that she was much younger than she had first appeared to be, and her eyes were the gray of new steel. The sea wind blew strands of hair across her face as she held the tangled bundle of lines out to him.

That had been the beginning of their gifts to him. Gifts which had never stopped coming and which he had never been asked to repay. Ramón had proven to be not just good but an extraordinary fisherman with an amazing knowledge of the reefs around Loreto, and he was generous in his patience with Abundio's lack of aptitude. Although Abundio rarely did more than row the boat and was hard put to remember the exact locations where they had strung out their baited lines the previous day, Ramón always accepted him as an equal, and he referred to the fish as *their* catch. And Ramón had been genuinely touched and pleased on the evening, so many years before, when he and Socorro had confessed their relationship and had asked for permission to build their own shack beside his.

And certainly, Abundio knew, the greatest gift of all that Ramón and Socorro Ochoa had bestowed upon him was this fine young woman who stood before him now, expressing such concern that her father might be injured, or perhaps disgraced, in a simple, pickup soccer game against the fishermen of Las Ramalitas.

Abundio, not one for false modesty in any forum, nevertheless sensed the need for restraint in reassuring his daughter that he had not entirely lost the powers that had earned him the nickname of *El Tecolote Terrible* on the playing fields of La Paz.

"María, have no fear. Actually, I used to play quite a little bit of fútbol when I was younger."

"When!?"

"Well... in La Paz. In fact... they used to call me El Tecolote Terrible."

Chino swallowed a chuckle, but María's voice shook in exasperation.

"An owl? Papá, what is *that* supposed to mean?"

"It was the name of the team. Anyway... it means I used to be pretty good. And I can handle this bunch of amateurs."

María knew it was useless to argue with her father when he was like this. *El Tecolote Terrible?* Where did that come from? She imagined him in a mask and owl costume, with an embroidered cape and his stomach hanging over a pair of tights. She turned to Chino and jabbed a finger into his chest.

"Chino, if they hurt him, I will never forgive you. Never."

To Chino, it seemed that María's polished fingernail had cut through to his heart. He wished these ball games had never started. They had been friendly enough in the beginning, but lately they had become more than just sport for both sides.

But Chino understood why his partner would seize upon this call to reckless action. For himself, and for the other fishermen of Agua Amargosa as well, the weekly matches had become a way of striking out, of declaring to the unknown that they were still alive, still a force to be reckoned with.

For the men of Las Ramalitas, on the other hand, the matches had become a cathartic tragedy played on a stage of hardened mud, a ritual in which the Agua Amargosa side were stretched out and sacrificed in the sun to ward off the blood lust of that very same unknown.

AND NOW, IT seemed, María had charged Chino with the impossible task of shielding her out-of-shape, overweight father from the slings and arrows that were about to engulf him.

Chino took a deep breath.

"All right, Tecolote Terrible, let's go round up the guys."

"Good."

THEIR FIRST RECRUIT was Ramón Ochoa. At nearly fifty years old, Ramón had never played soccer before the present series of matches. However, he had a pair of high top work boots from his days on the ranchos and the protection they gave his feet and shins had made him Agua Amargosa's top goal maker. In fact, he was their only one. During the preceding eight matches, Ramón had scored Agua Amargosa's only two goals, one by accident and one by design.

Abundio and Chino went from camp to camp, looking for anyone able to play. They came up with seven men, including themselves and Luis Medina, dredged out of the sand beneath his plastic shelter. They gathered on the dry mud flat behind the dunes. Two goals had been set up a hundred yards apart, and big white rocks marked the corners of the field.

El Tecolote Terrible surveyed the opposing side with a professional eye. Las Ramalitas would field a full roster of eleven players. The tall one with the diagonal stripe and three of his teammates wore cleats and looked like trouble. Three more wore tennis shoes and would have to be taken into consideration. The remaining four were barefoot and looked to be of little consequence. El Tecolote spoke to Chino, the nominal captain of the Agua Amargosa side.

"Is it always like this?"

"Usually we have nine or ten."

"And... they *always* win?"

"So far, amigo."

Abundio scratched his unshaven chin. He aimed his thumb at the Las Ramalitas fishermen.

"Listen, we are not going to get many goals against that... "

The troops shuffled their feet in agreement. Only three of them wore tennis shoes.

"But amigos, we need only one goal to win."

There was a crossing of toes and El Tecolote sensed some doubt in the ranks.

"I promise they will not score on us today. Get one goal and we win."

El Tecolote placed his hands on Ramón's wide shoulders.

"Brother, you have the big shoes. Stay up front and shoot immediately every time you get the ball."

He turned to Luis Medina, still dizzy from being in a vertical position.

"Luis, you play *portero*. Do not come out of the goal. After the first attack they will stay back and take long shots only. Just catch the ball and kick it out as far as you can."

Finally, El Tecolote turned to his strongest player.

"Chino, stay in the middle. Don't come back to help me. Keep the ball bouncing high and get it to Ramón."

Chino whispered as he pointed down to Abundio's bare feet and then back toward their panga.

"Amigo, what about your boots?"

Abundio sniffed.

"That will not be necessary, mijo."

They took their places on the field.

From the shade of a dry bush at the edge of the mud flat a young woman's voice called out.

"Chino! You better remember what I said."

Abundio waved and smiled to her as Agua Amargosa took the kickoff.

The Diagonal Stripe won the ball. He easily beat Chino and the others in midfield and he came in on the attack. Abundio rushed to meet him far out from the goal. The Diagonal Stripe took his shot and Abundio feigned an attempt to block the ball, but instead he let it pass beneath his foot and, with perfect timing, he jammed his huge knee hard into the man's exposed leg. The Diagonal Stripe, outweighed by well over one-hundred pounds, turned a perfect somersault in the air and landed on his back as Luis Medina caught the ball and kicked it out to midfield. The Diagonal Stripe did not rise.

The next attacker came down the sideline but Abundio did not run out to defend. Instead, he hung back with Luis. The attacker dribbled past the body of the Diagonal Stripe and chipped a pass to a teammate directly in front of the goal. The teammate jumped up to knock the ball in with his head, but Abundio had jumped just a moment earlier and was already on his way down with his arms spread wide to make it seem like he, too, was trying to head the ball. A sledgehammer elbow caught the attacker on the top of his shoulder just as he jumped, and he was whacked to the ground like a wet rag. He did not get up either. Luis Medina caught the ball again and kicked it back out to midfield.

There were two Las Ramalitas players left with cleated shoes, and they crossed the middle of the field, passing the ball back and forth while Chino and the others gingerly tried to win it with their bare feet. Abundio had made two sprints in as many minutes and he did not have any more left at the moment. But the players didn't press their attack. Instead, one of them lobbed a hopelessly long shot that missed the goal and went out of bounds. Luis kicked it back out to midfield again.

By halftime, Abundio had leveled the pitch by chasing down and taking out the other two Las Ramalitas players who wore the cleated shoes, and the sides stood even with seven men each. The Diagonal Stripe and Abundio's three other victims watched sullenly from the sidelines as their teammates kicked off to begin the second period. But the Las Ramalitas fishermen had suffered enough for one day and they contented themselves with taking long shots from midfield and passing the ball back and forth until time ran out.

The whistle blew at last and María came running onto the field. *Zeros!* A tie! They surrounded the Tecolote Terrible of old and they pounded his wide, sweaty back, and they hugged and swayed and fell together in a howling pile on the powdery dry mud.

CHINO RAN THE panga out of Las Ramalitas Bay at full throttle. He hugged the southern shore, skimming over choppy, waist-deep water on the rising tide, and he turned south as soon as they rounded the point and reached the open sea.

The sun hung two hands above the western mountains. It would be almost dark by the time they reached the caleta.

The wind had come up after all, but not as strong as it had for the past week. As the boat turned sideways to it, the streaming air began to shred the edge of their bow wake and drops of seawater came curling in over the windward gunnel.

Abundio sat facing backwards in the bow, with his head and chest sticking up over a pile of supplies. María was on the nearest seat with her long hair whipping in the wind. She shifted to the right side of the boat in an effort to keep herself dry. Chino tapped her on the shoulder and gave her an empty plastic bag. She leaned backwards and smiled to him as she wrapped it around her legs and hips.

Chino watched the wind tug on María's new white shirt, stretching the translucent material tight against her shoulders. The strap of a new lace brassiere crossed her back. When had she gotten it? There were many new things about this María, many things that Chino could have listed on a long piece of paper.

María's departure from Agua Amargosa had been a relief for Chino. He remembered vividly the last time, years before, that she sat upon his knee, and the last time they walked hand in hand. Those things had somehow stopped of their own accord, without anyone stopping them, but that had not been enough, and Chino had been relieved when she went to live with the profesora.

But now, the once naked child had completed her sea change and she was returning to the place of her childhood. Chino looked away from her shoulders. He ignored the light, stinging touch of her hair on his hand as he gripped the tiller and steered the panga directly toward the Devil's Anvil.

Abundio's voice boomed so loud it almost made him lose his balance.

"*Mijo!* Look outside, you drunken jackass!"

Chino dropped his thoughts and raised his eyes to the horizon, searching the quadrant where Abundio was pointing. Scattered whitecaps marched northwards in the steady wind and their tops were blowing off and streaking the water everywhere. Then he saw it, a tight cluster of several hundred sea birds, just visible in the hazy distance, wheeling and diving into the water, then climbing and diving again and again.

"Sorry, amigo."

The birds were ahead of the boat, Chino's area of responsibility. They were lucky Abundio had happened to turn around and spot them. Chino applied a little pressure to the tiller. He eased the throttle down as they swung into the eye of the wind. The panga pounded and jumped and sent spray flying over their heads as Chino punched it through the swells.

Abundio spread his feet wide to steady himself. He readied the two short lines of heavy monofilament that they kept rigged with bullet-shaped metal heads, red-and-white chicken feathers, and stout double hooks. Abundio tied the lines to bicycle inner tubes attached to the gunnels, and he tossed the metal heads into the water.

María looked back at the lures. The lines held them at the edge of the wake, three boat lengths back, and they swam smoothly through the water, dipping beneath the swells and rising to the surface whenever a trough passed under them. She turned and pointed ahead to the frenzied birds working on the horizon.

"Is it dorado, papá?"

"No, daughter. *Atún.* Many, many *atún.*"

"How can you know, papá?"

"Under the birds, María. Do you see the splashes?"

María scanned the sea all around them, looking for signs of tuna. The water was covered with streaks of foam rolling off the backs of the whitecaps.

"But, papá... there are splashes everywhere!"

"No. No. Under the birds. The small splashes that go out quickly. Like sparks in the dark."

It took María several more seconds to realize how large the area was. The flock of diving birds was only a few hundred yards across but the school of tuna beneath it seemed to be almost limitless. Fully a quarter of the horizon now held not only the long rolling streaks of the whitecaps but also the quick splashes of the leaping tuna.

Now, María also saw the black outlines of the fish themselves as they arched out of the water, overshooting bait fish. Everywhere, hundreds of tuna were flying into the air and splashing back down again.

Chino brought them close to the feeding school, then turned the panga suddenly and ran just outside the edge of the agitated water. He seemed to be steering away from the tuna at the most critical moment and María whirled around and shouted at him.

"Chino! Where are you going!?"

Chino made a diving gesture with his hand as his eyes sought to discover the general direction of the school's movement.

"If we run over them they will go down! Besides, the biggest ones are just outside the edge."

Both feathers were hit as Chino spoke. The inner tubes absorbed the shock and kept the heavy monofilament from snapping as the fish were jerked from their paths and forced to follow the boat.

Chino cut the throttle, and he and Abundio hauled the lines in hand-over-hand. The tuna were swung into the boat, black-backed and silver-bellied, like oversized footballs. They were small schooling fish, about twenty-five pounds each. They landed in the shallow pool of water in the bow, where their tails shivered and beat a steady tattoo on the hull and sent a shower of droplets into the air. Abundio removed the feathered lures and tossed them back into the water as Chino gunned the motor and chased the school again.

"Four more, mijo."

"Right."

María was not accustomed to the fact that the fish buyer no longer came to Agua Amargosa.

"Why so few, papá?"

"We need only enough to eat. For ourselves and the others."

The birds had moved farther outside. Chino circled the school for another half hour and they caught three more tuna, but then the fish went deep. The splashing on the surface died away as quickly as it had begun and the birds disappeared as if by magic. In the aftermath of the feeding, the lures were struck by a few sierra mackerel, which they kept, but there were no more tuna, so they gave up and Chino turned the panga toward the flaming orange sunset above the Devil's Anvil.

Abundio bailed the bow out and María wrapped the bag around her legs for the run into the caleta. The whitecaps had grown larger during their hour outside. Now the panga was running crosswise to the waves, and Chino was forced to reduce speed in order to avoid broaching. They cruised slowly in toward the coast, quartering away from the wind, with the whitecaps kicking at the port gunnel and the panga's bow dipping deeply into each trough.

Abundio shouted into the wind.

"Mijo! Remember, we need to get some *cochis* for Socorro."

"Right."

To lighten the bow, Abundio moved back and sat beside María. She rested her head on her father's shoulder and they held hands as the panga rolled and pitched toward shore.

"María, do you remember the first time we came to the caleta?"

"Sí, papá. It was rough. Just like today."

Abundio watched the coast beneath the Devil's Anvil, waiting for the four islands of Agua Amargosa to appear. With the swells so large, their first sign of the caleta this evening would be the high columns of water thrown into the air by the fourth island, the pinnacle of red stone that stood like a sentinel at the outer end of the channel.

"There, María!"

She had seen it too, the distant flash against the gray, shadowed coastline. A few seconds later, it rose again, and then the coast sank from view as the panga settled into a valley between two large swells. When they came up on top again, they caught sight of the island itself. Then, one-by-one, the rest of the Four Horses rose above the water and Chino steered them straight in.

Abundio looked at the thin golden sandals on his daughter's feet. A few drops of fish blood, already darkening, had stained the cuffs of her new white pants.

"María, do the horses still dance for you?"

She looked at him questioningly.

"What do you mean, papá?"

"The *caballos*. On that first day, you said the horses danced and jumped over the sea."

"You remember *that*, papá?"

"I remember, María. Perhaps not the exact date, or even the year. But the colors, the sounds, the smells, the things we felt. Those things are all very clear to me."

And Abundio remembered especially that first arrival at the caleta, with María so small and helpless, clinging to the gunnel, her dark eyes wide in terror, as he and Socorro rowed for their lives.

They had set out from Isla Coronado in the early dawn two days before with both pangas very heavily loaded. Ramón had been in front, towing Abundio's motorless skiff at the end of a long rope, running his fifty horsepower Evinrude slowly to avoid overheating it, and they had crept south all day with diminishing hopes of making Agua Amargosa by nightfall.

In the late afternoon, the north wind had come up, driving a steep swell against the transoms that threatened to broach and capsize them and they had tried to run back to Las Ramalitas. But with the weight of Abundio's panga behind him Ramón had been unable to make headway against the wind, and they had turned south again and veered away from the cliffs, planning to drift all night and find the caleta in the morning.

During the middle of the night, at the worst possible time, the wind had risen to a near gale, with breaking waves. The stress of the rope tore the bow ring off Abundio's panga. Ramón circled and circled their wildly pitching boat and—with reckless skill—he actually jumped across once in the dark. He successfully retied the rope to the front thwart of Abundio's panga but as he jumped back into his own boat a wave threw them together, catching his thigh and smashing it painfully.

They drifted until dawn, constantly struggling not to bump each other, and at first light Abundio recognized the two peaks, El Yunque del Diablo and El Martillo de Dios, just beneath the solid gray clouds.

With their pangas surfing on the crests of the waves, Ramón took them landward at full throttle but they overshot the entrance to the caleta and he was forced to turn north again, into the wind. Then the strain of pounding head-on into the waves tore the front thwart out of Abundio's panga, taking the tow rope with it.

Ramón circled them within sight of the Four Horses, and he threw the rope again and again, but they were not strong enough to hold onto it and there was no place left to tie it.

Ramón shouted for them to abandon the old panga and jump into his boat, but Socorro refused to give up her things, her marriage things. In great pain from his discolored and swollen leg and unable to do anything further, Ramón passed them his oars and ran ahead into the caleta, where he could unload his panga on the beach and return for them.

With two sets of oars, Abundio and Socorro had rowed desperately toward the gap in the reefs, all the while urging little María to keep bailing with her toy bucket. The cold winter sun had already gone behind the cliffs when they finally made the safety of the channel, totally spent, and met Ramón coming out alone to find them.

Had they missed the entrance, they would have been smashed against the cliffs. Abundio had never told his daughter how close they came to disaster that day and her memory of it had always been of the spectacle of the swells crashing over the islands, turning them into dancing horses.

To Abundio, the islands had always looked more like camels, or perhaps turtles, anything but horses.

But she had seen horses, real, dancing horses that turned and leapt over the water. And there had been a few times, through the deceptive veil of moonlight refracting over a great distance, when Abundio thought that perhaps he too had seen the horses, with their heads bobbing up and down, their tails flying over the sea, galloping and leaping, playing like colts on a fine summer day.

Abundio wondered if María had been the one to give the islands their name, Los Cuatro Caballos. It seemed that her vision of horses had been a coincidence, but he was not sure, and he decided he must ask Fra Nacho or Pablo Santos about it sometime.

Now, with Abundio watching carefully for rocks, Chino steered the panga past the outer island and turned left into the caleta. The first lanterns had already been lit. María put her arm around her father's thickly muscled shoulders and she leaned against him.

"It has been good for us here, hasn't it, papá?"

Abundio felt the shroud of sadness settle over him. Yes, it had been good, he supposed, although he was not one to judge good from bad, but now it was ending, improperly, prematurely, in a way he had never expected. His reply was in a voice without hope.

"Ramón says the road will never be fixed. They are spending the money for sidewalks and new streets in Loreto."

"Then what will we do, papá?"

"You, my daughter, will finish with the profesora. Do your studies go well?"

María hesitated a moment.

"Yes… papá, of course. But… what will you and mamá do?"

"We are thinking of staying in the caleta."

"But papá, there is no way to live here."

"Fra Nacho lived here for many years with no road."

They swung past the second island. Immediately, the wind died and the swells flattened out to the glassy calmness of the inner caleta. Chino turned the panga toward the landing beach. The lanterns winked and glowed like big fireflies hiding among the palms.

"Your mamá, she swears she will never go back to the ranchos."

"Couldn't we move to Las Ramalitas?"

"And live on the rocks, like lizards?"

"Or Loreto… or La Paz?"

"Chino and I do not use the nets. Neither will Ramón."

"Couldn't you learn, papá?"

"That is not the question, María! We are fishermen! Not killers of every innocent thing that swims!"

Abundio thought of Ramón Ochoa, waiting in the dunes of Las Ramalitas for the news that would never come. Like himself and Chino, Ramón had decided years before that he would give up fishing rather than become a mere scavenger of the sea, spreading the deadly gill net and accepting the killing of everything that swam into it as the price of also catching marketable fish. Abundio had seen enough to be sickened by the gill net's power to destroy all life, the stilled multitudes of juvenile fish that would never have a chance to grow up and reproduce their kind, the wasteful trashing of fish with low market value, the decomposing bodies of innocent birds and seals and any other thing that became entangled in the nets and drowned.

Still, Abundio did not resent the nets. Nor did he scorn the men who used them, for they too had families to feed, did they not? Neither did Abundio resent the massive seining ships that wrapped up whole schools of yellowtail and tuna at once, or even the rusty trawlers that scraped their nets over the bottom, destroying not only the living things in their path but also the place where those things lived, making it impossible for new generations to replace them.

As a commercial fisherman himself, Abundio could not resent those things. Did he not himself use every trick at his command, every day of his life, to catch as many fish as possible? How could he argue that others should not do the same?

Still, he knew that once the nets came to Agua Amargosa, the old ways would follow the fish into oblivion, and all of them would be caught in a maelstrom of change that would engulf them and send them spinning into an uncertain future.

In the caleta, several fishermen had recently begun talking of nets. Once they began to use them, the caleta's catch would quickly be reduced to the point that Abundio, Chino and Ramón would be faced with the choice of either using nets themselves or quitting the business altogether.

But if they left the sea, what then?

For Ramón, the choice was clear. He would relocate his family to one of the ranchos or they would move north, perhaps cross the border, and find work on the land. For Socorro, the choice was equally clear. She detested the ranchos and said she would *never* exchange her life for a daily plate of beans and a shred of meat. The fact that her life in the caleta consisted primarily of just that seemed to have no effect on her. Socorro would eat palm fronds and lizard dung before she gave up her happy home beneath the trees.

And for himself? Abundio had no idea how to straighten out this mix of opposing forces, the rains of the previous spring, the stupid officials in La Paz, his stubborn wife, the gill nets' inevitable ending of a life he had led since before the days of El Tecolote Terrible. For Abundio and Chino and Ramón, the future seemed to offer nothing good. In fear of it they took refuge in the present as much as possible.

CHINO SLOWED THE panga between the middle two islands and tilted the motor half up without killing it. Abundio replaced the feathers on the short lines with wooden lures shaped like small fish. The lures had flat lips on their front ends that made them dive and wobble through the water, and they put them in and trolled them very slowly over the reef. María and Abundio held the lines while Chino stood at the tiller, searching the black water ahead for rocks.

"How many cochis does she want, amigo?"

"Ten or twelve. She will want to make *burritos* for everybody."

"With levanta muertos?"

Abundio stuck out his tongue and crossed his eyes.

"Ayyy!"

A sixteen-inch leopard grouper struck María's lure. She pulled it aboard the still moving boat and Abundio removed the hook from its mouth and threw it back into the water. A few moments later, María caught another one, then another and another, and Abundio released them all by grabbing them behind their heads and slipping the hooks from their mouths with his fingers.

Chino looked doubtful.

"Maybe no cochi tonight, amigo."

"Try a little deeper. Away from the rocks."

The panga glided slowly away from the reef. The sandy bottom became visible and Chino crossed back and forth between the rocks and the sand. They were fishing for cochis, or "little piggies," as they called the slab-sided triggerfish, with the strange smelling, gray leather skin and the face that, in profile, looked like the wild pig's. Despite its grotesque appearance, the triggerfish's firm white flesh had the flavor of crabs or lobster when cooked, and it was Socorro's favorite dish to poach it with sugar and then flake it and fry it until it was almost leathery. To this, she added a bit of the spiced sausage called chorizo and she rolled the rich mixture in warmed tortillas. Socorro's triggerfish burritos, or "little burros," were the Rodríguez family's favorite and most frequent dinner.

Tonight, however, in honor of María's visit, Socorro would be sure to add an especially potent measure of levanta muertos peppers to her usual blend.

Abundio released more line into the water, allowing his lure to swim deeper and farther back from the boat, and he was rewarded with a sharp strike as they crossed over the edge of the rocks. The fish pulled strongly and Abundio was forced to give it some line and ask Chino to stop the boat.

"That's one for Socorro, mijo."

Chino readied the gaff and the long-nosed pliers as Abundio brought the fish beside the panga.

In the dark water, they saw the electric blue lines on its head and on the edges of its wavy fins, signs that it was indeed a mature, good-sized triggerfish. Chino gaffed it through the back and held it high while he used the long pliers to remove the hook from its powerful, clicking teeth. Then he turned the panga around and circled the same area of the reef, looking for enough little piggies to fill Socorro's frying pan.

The mountains above the caleta had turned to jagged black silhouettes against a dull orange sunset. A few small, brightly glowing clouds clung to the highest peaks, like a family of swans coming to rest after a long flight. The evening breeze faded to nothingness, and on the caleta the lone panga circled and paused, circled and paused, with three people in it.

Some time after the stars had come out, but while a few orange reflections still swam on the black water, the panga turned toward the beach and its bow slid up against the sand.

The large man in front jumped out with the anchor. Then the younger man jumped out. He turned and took the woman's hand as she placed a foot on the gunnel to steady herself. But as she jumped, her foot slipped, and she cried out in the dark and fell into his arms.

Socorro was at the inside table, sharpening her best knife by the light of the kerosene lantern.

"Mamá!"

There's María with another silly crab or shell to show me. *Madre!* Why is she outside so late? Too busy for her now. She'll be here in a second anyway.

"Mamá! Are you there?"

Socorro dropped her knife and whirled to face the open doorway. Outside, the edge of the lantern light caught a pair of golden sandals and a pair of pure white pants. María's voice came laughing out of the dark.

"Mamá, look! I'm home!"

Socorro did not answer. She turned away from the door and stood against the corner of the cot, with her apron raised to cover her face. María came into the house. She put her hands gently on her mother's shoulders. But Socorro ran outside, to the back of the house, and hid, with the apron over her eyes.

María followed her mother outside and again touched her shoulders.

"Mamá... "

"Please... give me a moment."

"Of course, mamá."

When Socorro came back into the house, María was clearing off part of the table. She had laid out her gifts from Loreto. Socorro's eyes went first to the scarlet red ribbon, then to the peppers, then to the unfamiliar clothing of her only child.

"Thank you, María. I... I... did not expect you."

María, nearly a foot taller than her mother, bent down to look closely into her face.

"Mamá, are you all right? You look a little... tired."

Socorro rubbed her elbows. She stood stiffly, with her head lowered.

"I am a stupid old woman!"

"No, mamá! You are *not!*"

Now, Socorro let the tears come and María held her tightly, and they sat on the cot, laughing and hugging, as the moths dashed themselves against the lantern and its yellow light flowed out through the open door and the cracks in the walls.

After a while, Socorro stood and went to the table. With satisfaction, she counted the levanta muertos. She touched the wrapped sausages.

"Chorizos?"

"Sí, mamá. And we caught enough cochis for a nice dinner."

Socorro tied the red ribbon in her hair. She sorted the lumpy, shiny-skinned peppers, selecting the twelve biggest, and she picked up the long knife she had been sharpening. With a smile on her face that one who did not know her might have taken as almost malicious, she looked sideways at her daughter and spoke in a low, conspiratorial whisper.

"We'll set their butts on fire tonight, eh, María?"

DOWN ON THE beach, the men had helped Abundio and Chino pull the old panga out of the water. As they scurried in the dark to help the partners unload supplies, they kept their ears alert for the *"clink"* of glass that would tell them someone had grabbed a case of beer.

The telltale clink came once, twice, three times... a total of six cases! A truly excellent and worthy run to Las Ramalitas!

With the work done, Abundio and Chino made some desultory stabs at rearranging the supplies in piles. After a while, Abundio turned to the circle of men.

"We have fish."

"Oh, yes. Good. You have fish."

"It is tuna."

"Oh, very good. Tuna."

Chino hopped into the panga and began throwing the fish onto some palm leaves spread on the sand.

"We need the cart."

"Manuel! They need the cart! Get the cart, for God's sake!"

Manuel ran to get the handmade, bicycle-wheeled pushcart that served as Agua Amargosa's primary means of transport. In this case it would be used to distribute tuna to the families and haul supplies up to the Rodríguez house.

Abundio sat on the corner of a crate. He calculated the number of men standing around him, the strength of their thirst, and the number of bottles contained in six cases of beer. Steeling himself to the result, he drew a long breath and wiped his nose. He spoke to the sand between his bare feet.

"Would anybody like a beer?"

The circle of men closed in with a concert of clinks that could be heard far back in the palms.

Manuel returned, out of breath, pushing the cart to its limits. Accompanying him was a tall, thin boy with a shock of hair hiding part of his face. The boy sought out Abundio, who was sitting on his crate, trying to claim his share of the beer before it disappeared.

"Hola, Bundo."

"Ah... Joselito! Did Socorro give you the flour and water this morning?"

"Sí. Thank you, Bundo."

Abundio finished his bottle and opened another for himself and one for Chino. He took a full case and crossed his legs over it. Joselito Medina stood waiting silently at his elbow.

"Ah, listen, Joselito. We saw your father today... "

The boy leaned against Abundio, bumping him and almost making him drop his bottle.

" ...and he is not quite ready to have you come to Las Ramalitas."

Joselito shook Abundio's beer drinking arm.

"Why not?"

"Well... he is still working on a house for you. It is almost ready."

"But it has been over two months!"

"Sí, sí... well, he is busy, you know. Fishing every day."

"Why doesn't he send us food?"

"Ah, well... he thought you still had enough. But he sent food today. Look here!"

Abundio opened the sack Ramón Ochoa had given him. There were some new bags of flour, some oil and salt, a few onions and potatoes, and as many levanta muertos as Abundio had been able to divert from María's shopping bag without her noticing.

Abundio added two bottles of beer to the sack and handed it to Joselito.

"Your father asks that you stay here and take care of your mother just a little longer. He promises he will call for you the minute the house is ready."

Joselito clutched the sack to his chest, smiling brightly.

"I understand, Bundo."

"Take a fish, Joselito. Your father says he will send food with Chino every week from now on."

Joselito put a hand through the gills of a tuna and tried to drag it, but with the bag of food, the load was much too heavy for him. Abundio threw everything onto the cart.

"Here, Joselito. Bring it back when you are done."

The boy started into the trees, then left the cart standing and came running back.

"Bundo. Is he catching a lot up there?"

Abundio thrust out an oversized hand and mussed the boy's hair roughly.

"Of course, Joselito! Your papá is one of our best fishermen! And the price in Loreto is very good right now."

Joselito's eyes shined through his long, black hair. He ran to push the cart up to his mother's house, and quickly now, the night closed over the beach.

The sky became crowded with stars, and they reflected and jiggled on the black caleta as Chino and Abundio sat among the pangas with the other men, talking of the news from Las Ramalitas, of the weather, of fishing, of women they claimed to have known, or wished they had known, or wished it to be known they had known.

After a while Joselito returned with the empty cart and it was loaded with fish and supplies and taken from house to house and the smoke of frying tuna drifted lazily through the palms. The talk of the men died away to an occasional whistle or giggle as the beer and the hour dulled their thoughts and their fears of the days ahead.

For Abundio, the cloak of sadness settled over his shoulders once again, as it always did with beer in the evenings, and his thoughts returned to that long ago day when María had seen the dancing horses.

Those first years in the caleta had been the best. He and Socorro had dug the post holes and trimmed the palm leaves together, and they put up the roof of their house with Ramón's help. Then they had built a larger house for Ramón's family, and the waters of the caleta had been very full of life, just like Loreto or La Paz in the old days.

But then the fishing had gotten harder and Abundio could no longer keep up in his motorless panga, even with Socorro helping on the oars. He had tried fishing with Ramón again, but by then there were too many mouths to feed with only one boat, and no matter how hard he and Ramón worked there seemed to be no way to reverse their diminishing fortunes. Until, one afternoon in the early fall, a stranger had appeared on their porch, a tall, very lean young man with curly hair and a narrow face, who had a serious manner about him and an Evinrude motor, brand new he said, that he had left down at the fish shed.

For some reason Socorro had taken an immediate dislike to Chino Zúñiga. Perhaps it was because his laconic manner seemed to mock her own habit of revealing her feelings only to those closest to her. Or perhaps, as Abundio had always suspected, it was also because Chino reminded her of the son she had never borne. After María, no more children had come to Socorro and Abundio and they had felt the lack ever more sharply as Ramón's family had increased year-by-year and Socorro's time of child bearing had slipped away much sooner than expected.

But whatever the reason for her original objections, Socorro had quickly reversed herself when the new young man proved to be both a loyal friend and exceptionally strong in the boat. Soon, Socorro came to regard Chino not only as her husband's partner but also a stalwart member of the household. In fact, Socorro—although she would never admit it—considered Chino to be her lost son, delivered to her on a platter, as it were, by the fish buyer's truck, and she had become his chief advocate, defending him vociferously on those early occasions when he had found it necessary, at the cost of a few broken noses, to gain the respect of the village bullies, and also when Abundio had complained of Chino's reluctance to speak of his past life. "None of your damned business," was what Socorro had told him and Abundio had always left it at that.

Chino's arrival at Agua Amargosa had given the family two legitimate, working pangas to fish with and they began to do well enough over the seasons to feel that their lives were settling into a predictable routine. Even the loss of Chino's Evinrude during their ill-fated trip to the southern islands had not been catastrophic, for they had by then saved enough money to buy a replacement in excellent condition.

And for Abundio, Chino had become something even more important than a surrogate son, something richer and far more complex, a thing so mysterious and valuable that Abundio often thought of it in the mornings when the old rooster woke him too early to go down to the boat, and he lay awake in the dark, listening to the faint sounds of the night and watching the stars rise slowly in the doorway.

Abundio knew there must be a better word to describe his feelings for Chino—perhaps he would ask Fra Nacho about it one day—but the best word he had been able to think of during his pre-dawn broodings was the uncomfortable one of "love."

Was this an acceptable word to use with another man? Especially one who seemed perfectly capable of existing without the companionship of women? The mere thought of the word embarrassed Abundio and he could hear the whistles on the beach if he were ever to say aloud in the presence of the other fishermen that he *loved* Chino.

Yet, the two of them suffered and laughed together as one, and they shared what they had without counting, and they respected each other's faults and forgave without reason or words being necessary, and Abundio knew in his deepest heart that either of them, if called upon, would not hesitate to risk his own life in order to save the other.

If that was not love, what was it?

But then the endings had begun.

Two years ago Chino had moved out of their house and built a shack for himself in the sand dunes, not explaining except to say that he needed more time to himself. They still took their meals together, and of course they fished together as always, but the old closeness was gone and Socorro insisted that Abundio not question his partner about it.

Then María had left to take courses and get school papers from the profesora, far away on a rancho north of Loreto, and the house of Abundio and Socorro Rodríguez had grown suddenly quiet and lonely.

And then, of course, the spring rains had cut the road, making it impossible for María or anyone else even to visit the caleta except by sea.

And what of the beautiful young woman that his daughter had so suddenly become? María's future, at least, seemed to hold promise. She had always been quick to understand the meaning of things, just like Socorro, and now she would complete her education, perhaps attend university in Guadalajara or even México City. Abundio felt his heart move as he tried to imagine the places his daughter's life might take her, the wonderful, unknowable things that might someday befall her.

That is, if she didn't make a foolish mistake. Such as that old trick of falling off the panga into Chino's arms. Abundio had seen his daughter's foot planted firmly on the gunnel and he had seen her body turn as she fell so her breasts went into Chino's hands. Just an accident? Or was there something going on between those two? The sight of that brief contact had instantly taken Abundio back to the night on Isla Coronado, twenty years before, when Socorro had pulled that very same trick on him. And from the same panga!

God! What was it with these women!?

Abundio remembered the electrifying effect Socorro's young body had on him the night he caught her and how he had thought of nothing else until she had finally given herself to him a month later. The impact of that first meeting on the rocky slopes of Isla Coronado caused a stirring within him as he sat in the dark, scratching his back against a palm tree.

Well, anyway, María would have to wait a while longer before she took a man. She would finish her education first. Then she would choose a man of importance, not some smelly fisherman with nothing to offer.

But on the other hand, was not María already older than many women who were married with several children? Older, in fact, than poor Margarita in those long ago days on the beach of La Paz? Was it fair to María, after all, to expect her to remain alone during the years when her body yearned so strongly for the comfort of a man?

Abundio opened another bottle. He let his head wobble back and forth, leaning his shoulder against Chino's.

And you, mijo… what is going through *your* mind at this moment, as you sit on the sand beside me, helping me finish the last of our beer? Are you thinking of María's firm young breasts? Of the smell and taste of her? Of how she would spread her legs and ride you like one of her dancing horses and scream as you filled her with yourself?

And you, mijo… would you *really* be such a bad choice for her? After all… I like you well enough myself, don't I? And doesn't Socorro, our most severe critic, already consider you her son?

So who am I to hold it against you that you are a fisherman like me?

So… why should it not happen? I don't know… *Madre!* Perhaps it already has! I better talk to Socorro about this immediately….

Abundio tried to focus on his partner, but Chino's head was moving about too much to get a clear view of it. Then Chino's narrow face came out of the dark, with its teeth shining in a big smile and its eyes slightly crossed. Chino's cheeks puffed out and he blew a beery blast of air into Abundio's chest and fell across his legs onto the sand.

As Abundio and Chino slept beside their panga, María Rodríguez picked her way up the arroyo to the darkened shack of Father Ignazio Bertogna, who was neither priest nor even Mexican, but a one-legged former sailor of the Italian merchant marine.

Fra Nacho, or simply Nacho, as most of the villagers called him, had lived to such an advanced age that even he, at times, had difficulty in keeping track of exactly who he was. But he was not senile. It was just that he had outlived so many stories and had seen so many generations pass through his life that he had given up trying to keep them all straight and he felt at liberty to mix and match them freely to suit his purposes.

The confusion this created in the villagers' minds caused them to suspect either his sincerity or his sanity at first, but as they got to know the old man, his eloquence in the Spanish language and the entertaining twists of his intellect gradually won them over, and Fra Nacho had come to be regarded as an odd but highly prized leavening element in the day-to-day affairs of the village.

Socorro was the first to recognize that there was more to Fra Nacho than the crippled, half-demented old hermit that he appeared to be. The day after her arrival in Agua Amargosa she had stumbled upon his shack while surveying the arroyo for possible house sites.

It was the smell that attracted her attention. She followed it up a side branch of the trail, almost to the cliffs that walled in the arroyo, and she found him hanging salted fish to dry from the rafters of his porch. They were trash fish gleaned from the beach, too small to sell, and he had hung scores of them from the thatched roof, like holiday decorations. He was seemingly oblivious to the flies and smell.

Fra Nacho sensed someone watching him and he turned around suddenly. Socorro cried out when she saw his knotted beard and the broken mouth full of gaps. He had brilliant blue eyes, the first she had ever seen. He pointed a long fingernail at her and he used recognizable Zapotec words that she had not heard from anyone but herself and Ramón since childhood.

"Good morning. Zapotec woman."

Astonished, Socorro had blurted out in her ancient Indian tongue that, yes, she was indeed Oaxacan, and she began to ask him how he had known and how he had learned the language, but he waved his finger at her and switched to Spanish.

"Sorry, that's it, sister. Never got past first grade in Oaxacan."

In gestures, Fra Nacho indicated that she was to help him hang fish, which they did in silence. There were all manner of undesirable fish, grunts and small needlefish and even a few of the poisonous pufferfish, or *botete*, whose offal was known to be capable of causing death when eaten. Socorro asked him why he was preserving such fish.

"What do you do with these fish?"

"Eat them. Yum, yum."

"Even the botete?"

Fra Nacho waved his finger again and he spoke in ungrammatical Spanish as he loved to do when making a point.

"No eat botete, Zapotec woman. Eat botete, go bye-bye."

He bit down on his finger and pointed skyward, then tilted his head sideways and made an agonized rasping sound from his wide open mouth. Socorro shied back from the horrific sight but then realized that Fra Nacho was *intentionally* making a spectacle of himself. She was captivated by the old hermit.

"If you don't eat the botete, why hang them?"

"For the flies."

"What do you mean?"

"Flies touch botete. They go bye-bye."

They stood looking at one of the fist-shaped botete. It was covered with flies, just like all the fish. They didn't seem to be dying.

"Is it true?"

Fra Nacho grinned his almost toothless grin and used a finger to pull down the corner of one of his pure blue eyes.

"I don't think so. But you never know. It is probably a matter of faith."

It was Socorro's first experience with irony in any form and it sat for just a moment in the basement of her mind and then jumped up and awakened an aspect of herself that she found she enjoyed. From that day on, her house would always have a dried botete hanging under the porch roof and woe be it to anyone who dared doubt the fish's ability to kill every fly in México. Because no tangible evidence of its potency was ever offered, Socorro's botete came to be regarded by the villagers as a putative adjunct to the story of The Last Judgment and they imagined the reconstituted fish rising up beside Christ, sending the flies to damnation while He busied himself with the human sinners.

By the time the Rodríguezes came to live in the caleta, Fra Nacho was already an old man of sixty-nine, missing half a foot and too feeble to go out in the boats. He lived by fishing along the beach and scavenging what he could. He had conditioned himself to the unwholesome water from the well in the arroyo and his few other needs—for an occasional pair of pants or a frying pan or length of string—could be satisfied from the castoffs of others or by trading salted fish with the goat people, the quiet ranchers who sometimes watered their flocks in the mountain valley high above the head of the arroyo.

It was Socorro who first began calling him "Father Ignacio," partly because he had once actually studied for the priesthood, but mostly because of his tendency to speak in riddles and pontificate on matters that seemed to be of little consequence. Although the villagers soon shortened this humorous nickname to the diminutive Brother Nacho, or Fra Nacho, and finally, just plain Nacho, or even Fracho, they held the white haired old man in high regard as a *curandero*, or medicine man, a shaman who used herbs, dried rattlesnakes, and sophistry to treat their physical and spiritual ailments. Fra Nacho's open front porch was at once an informal forum for the resolution of the people's minor disputes, a twenty-four hour per day pharmacy, and a rustic confessional where he heard the results of their daily struggles with the forces of good and evil.

As his condition deteriorated over the years, María and Socorro had become Fra Nacho's caretakers, seeing to it that he was not abused and that he had enough water and food. The mother and daughter made daily pilgrimages to his shack in the arroyo and María would listen to his intertwining stories for hours. She loved to hear him tell of his boyhood adventures in the southern Alps, the things he had seen in the great palazzos and cathedrals of his native country, and his adventures high in the masts of the tall ships.

Fra Nacho was the third son of the fifth generation of a family of lithographers who had a business engraving exquisite illuminated typographic borders onto the heavy stone slabs used in commercial printing. They specialized in creating empty borders that could be reused over and over, for advertising posters, and they lived comfortably in the town of Treviso, near Venice.

One brilliant October afternoon, when the powdery blue of the vineyard copper spray had begun to contrast so beautifully with the dark red leaves of the grape, Fra Nacho had an epiphany of sorts. He was pulling a wagon of used slabs to the basement, where they would be stood against the wall with hundreds of their forebears, when he saw that his one life on earth, should he remain in Treviso, would be as vacant and unfulfilled as the empty frames his family etched into the heavy stones.

Fra Nacho begged successfully for release from what seemed to him an unimaginably tiresome life of scratching inverted curlicues to be used mainly in the promotion of skin ointments and ladies' underwear.

He was sent to a seminary in Milan and he studied diligently for three years. But he decided that he was irredeemably a creature of the present world, not the next, and he again begged successfully for release, this time into the offices of an uncle who owned a shipping company in Genoa.

For a time, Ignazio maintained a relationship with an impossibly beautiful and cultured young woman from the city of Udine, whom he had met on the beach of Lignano one summer, and gradually he came to realize that he was unofficially engaged to her.

But he soon thereafter discovered to his own amazement that he was as strongly attracted to the woman's brother as to her, a situation he found abhorrent and frightening. He fled his uncle's offices in favor of work aboard ship, seeking in adventure an escape from his dilemma.

Ignazio made his maiden voyage on a Genoan ship that rounded the Cape of Good Hope and eventually reached Japan. He sailed all the great seas of the world and visited all the great ports. Somehow, he never got back to Italy.

In his early-forties, he was working on a derelict Mexican freighter, hauling goat skins from the islands near La Paz to the port of Mazatlán, from whence they were taken to France and Italy to be made into gloves.

He jumped ship in La Paz in order to be near a beautiful boy he had fallen in love with and he became, in effect, a Mexican, finding work on Isla Cerralvo as a goat skinner and returning to La Paz every other weekend. But the cruelty of the work, of ripping the animals' skins away while they struggled, revolted him, and he found a job as cook on a trawler that plied the waters between La Paz and Mazatlán.

It was then that he lost part of the foot that was eventually to cost him his leg. The trawler had been fully loaded one summer, sixteen miles out of Mazatlán, and it had sprung a huge leak and had gone down in a matter of minutes, taking twenty-four tons of ice and half-frozen fish with it. As the crew swam about in the soupy-warm water, the hatches of the sunken ship had sprung open beneath them, and the dead fish and ice came up in a mass, six feet thick, all around them. They climbed up on it and watched in horror as the sharks began to devour the edges of their raft, and the heat of the sun began to melt it.

Fra Nacho saw his captain and another shipmate sink through the paralyzing slush before he and ten other survivors could be picked up by another trawler. He had been forced to kick at the frenzied sharks as he sought to hide himself in the thickest part of the ice and he had lost the majority of his cold-numbed right foot to their teeth and rough skin. After that he had been unable to find another job, and the young man in La Paz would have nothing more to do with him, so he began drifting through the fish camps, helping on the pangas.

It was in the horrible summer of 1944, during the worst of the suffering and the disgraceful occupation of his native Italy, that Fra Nacho decided his needs were much fewer than he had always thought, and he settled in a place he knew of where he felt he was least likely to be disturbed by news of the outside. He gathered his few things together and he built his shack in a hidden little bay tucked away on an inaccessible part of the desert coast between La Paz and Loreto.

The quarter century, more or less, since Fra Nacho had cut himself off from the world had been a time of peace for him. He had truly enjoyed his solitude and, in the waning tide of his life, he had finally become friends with himself. As a gaunt shell far removed from the acanthus leaves, the rich polenta, and the young merlot of his boyhood, Ignazio Bertogna had gradually and willingly become an inseparable part of the rocky arroyo of Caleta Agua Amargosa.

Now, under a veil of darkness, María Rodríguez walked up the arroyo, relying on memory to avoid stubbing her toes on the rocks sticking up in the dry, sandy streambed.

A transparent black curtain—closely hung with stars—stretched over the sky. She watched a meteor blaze a trail of embers across it and disappear behind the cliffs. Quick shadows darted among the palm trees, turned and flitted silently among the stars, bats, catching things that flew in the dark, and María shuddered as she thought of their horrid faces and the impassive killing and chewing going on all around her.

The bats had never bothered her before. But they did tonight, and as she dug her toes into the cool sand, María felt a certain unease, an unsettling residue of the day's events. She was aware for the first time of how large her father's stomach had grown and how much he sweated, and during their ride south, she had noticed for the first time how thin the hull of the old panga had grown and how it flexed in and out with the swells. And Chino's hand? He had not moved it from the touch of her hair in the wind and she was sure he had caressed her for just an instant as she fell into his arms on the beach. How could she fall from the old panga like that? She had put her foot on that gunnel ten-thousand times and she had never slipped like that until tonight, and the force of Chino's powerful grip, the hardness of his arms, and the gentle touch of his fingers had made her burn and tingle in a way she still found very troubling.

María turned right, leaving the streambed to climb a narrow path to the base of the cliffs. There was no light showing from Fra Nacho's shack, but she had expected none, and she called out as she reached the level spot at the top.

"*Tío!* Are you there?"

Fra Nacho's cot creaked as he shifted on it. He was somewhere outside, under the porch roof, but María could see nothing in the dark. He coughed twice before answering.

"Nice pants, María."

"Can you see them?"

"I am not that senile yet."

"I meant... it is so dark."

"No moon tonight. Just stars and mosquitos."

María held out the bag from Las Ramalitas and she felt his dried old hand take it.

"They are batteries... from Uncle Ramón."

"He is an angel of heaven."

"How are you, tío?"

He shifted on his cot.

"Less troubled than you, María. What on earth are you doing here?"

"It is a problem, tío. Do you have a moment?"

He laughed, coughing wetly.

"Hah! For you, daughter, I hope I will always have a moment or two."

He took some batteries from the paper bag and bent over to get the flashlight from beneath his cot. She heard him unscrew the cap and drop the batteries in. Her eyes were dazzled as the light leapt in her face.

"Ah! Sorry, María!"

Fra Nacho stuck the flashlight into a glass jar wrapped in layers of old fishing line and he set it on a wooden box beside his cot. He seemed even thinner than before and his pure white hair and beard were even more disheveled than María remembered. He looked as though he might have been in a terrible explosion.

His eyes, though, were sharp and blue as always. He lay on a cot made from the bottom cushion of an old car seat, balanced on a platform of flat rocks. His back rested against a suitcase padded with carpets and his white dress shirt was tightly buttoned at the neck and sleeves. His right pant leg was rolled closed and pinned just above the place where the knee would have been.

Fra Nacho poured the batteries out of the paper bag and counted them gleefully.

"So many! Please thank Ramón for me."

"He had no further use for them."

Fra Nacho looked up. María's face told him the news from Las Ramalitas was not good.

"Is Ramón leaving us?"

"He has decided to look for work on a rancho. Tío, this is not yet known by the others."

Fra Nacho sat looking into the glass jar. Some very small moths had flown into it and were clinging to the hot flashlight lens.

"Perhaps that would be best for all of us, except for me of course, and you."

"Tío. I have... left the profesora."

"Ah! And *that* is the problem."

Fra Nacho reached under his cot and brought out a battered, dusty record player wrapped in a plastic bag. It had been bought in La Paz by Pablo Santos for his complaining wife. Pablo had also bought her a fair-sized collection of popular and classical records but most of them had been broken one night during a fight overheard by the entire village. The next day Pablo had given the machine and the surviving records to Fra Nacho, who loved music and could sing entire operas in an incredibly loud voice, much to the amazed delight of the villagers.

Unfortunately, the record player consumed batteries like a school of tuna feeding on baby flying fish, and Fra Nacho got little use from it. He begged batteries from everyone, and when he got some he accepted them with the perfect humility and grace of a saint.

He put some new batteries into the record player and held up a pair of dusty disks.

"Mozart or Tchaikovsky?"

"No Beatles?"

"Armies of them. Big ones, little ones, black ones, brown ones, pretty red ones that give you blisters... Have you ever wondered why God made all the nasty things that torment us in the dark?"

María smiled. Since childhood, she had been playing these word games with the old man and she knew the kind of response he wanted.

"Do you mean like nightmares?"

"Exactly, María! And the special awareness of our mortality that comes in the night. The demands of our flesh and the remorse we feel for our misdeeds, the fear of those things we know must exist but that refuse to reveal themselves clearly. Why did God *make* all those goddamned things?"

"I do not know, tío. But isn't it mainly our fear of those things that makes us different from the rocks and animals?"

"I suppose."

Fra Nacho put a record on. He extinguished the flashlight and settled back on the cot with María beside him in the dark.

The scratchy music began. It was his favorite, the Tchaikovsky piano concerto. María listened happily, feeling the powerful brass, the uplifting strings, and the driving piano chords. She had heard the piece many times and she knew Fra Nacho would turn if off after the first three minutes, at the point where the music suddenly changed and lost its power.

The music stopped—right on schedule—and Fra Nacho's familiar, slightly accented Spanish came out of the dark.

"Have you told papá?"

"No!"

"In the end, he will understand."

"He wants me to have more than... a shack on the beach."

"And you?"

"This is my home! I only want to live here!"

Fra Nacho's voice became measured, cautious.

"Since you were young, María, we have all known that you do not belong here. There is something special about you, in addition to your rare beauty."

"That is an annoyance! I *hate* the way I look!"

Fra Nacho listened to her unsteady weeping. He thought of the wild goats of Isla Cerralvo, of how they shuddered and how the life hissed out of them as the first cut was made. And he remembered a young girl with beautiful, almond-shaped eyes who shuddered like that and left her tears on his bare chest the night he told her he could not love her in the way she deserved.

Gently, Fra Nacho pulled María's hands from her face.

"María... are you in love?"

"I don't know, tío."

"Is it someone from Loreto?"

"No. It's Chino."

Fra Nacho was taken aback.

"Do you mean... our Chino Zúñiga?"

"Yes."

"You find him... attractive... as a man?"

"Yes."

"And you have come back to be with him?"

"I think so."

"María, when did this happen?"

"In Loreto... I felt terribly lonely... unsuited. I heard Uncle Ramón was at Las Ramalitas and I have been coming on Fridays."

"To see Chino?"

"I realized how much I missed him."

"And your parents know nothing of this?"

"Nothing."

"And how does Chino feel?"

"From the first day, he had true feelings for me."

"How do you know?"

"A woman knows, tío."

Fra Nacho considered why, of all the children of the caleta, María Rodríguez should be sent away. Just because she was beautiful and capable? Surely that was not enough. But there was another reason for her to leave.

"María, there is no future here."

"I really don't care."

"And when Chino leaves?"

"I will go with him! Can't you understand, tío? I have nothing else!"

Fra Nacho thought of the girl with the almond eyes. She had loved him in this way. Could he have made her happy after all? Perhaps they would be together still, here, in this night. Had she found someone to share her years? Or had she, too, grown old and alone?

"María. Forgive me. But, is there a reason... a physical reason, you have no other choice?"

"No, tío."

Fra Nacho felt the bite of remorse. The girl with the almond eyes had not been so lucky.

"I will speak to your parents, María."

"Thank you, tío."

"But... you and Chino must work this out for yourselves."

"Will he accept me, tío?"

Fra Nacho tapped a place in the corner of his mouth where an eyetooth had once resided.

"With *those* pants? Believe me, Chino's fate has been sealed!"

María laughed and kissed Fra Nacho's sun-blotched forehead. He turned on his flashlight.

"Please stay, María."

"I must get back. Mamá is making burritos."

"With levanta muertos?"

"Just a few. Would you like to come down?"

"No, no. I will rest here."

"Then I will bring you some."

"And some water, please."

Fra Nacho shined his flashlight on the path until she was gone. Then he turned it off and lay back on his cot and let his eyes adjust to the dark. His vision was sharp and he sought out the fuzzy patches and cloudy areas of the night sky, the small clusters of faint stars that always caught his interest. He could see the bats clearly against the spangled void, cutting and twisting back and forth between the walls of the arroyo.

He thought of the old man in the open market of Treviso. "*Due Lire! Due Lire!*," the ragged war cripple had rasped over and over again. Two lira each for half-rotten artichokes no bigger than a hen's egg. Or broken melons with black fuzz already showing in the cracks. The old man always sat flat on the paving stones, with his crutches beside him and his pant leg pinned up, between the stalls of the egg lady and the flower lady, and people gave him coins but no one ever bought from him. As Ignazio's mother pushed him past the old man's place, the boy had always looked politely at the worthless gleanings and had greeted him with a friendly "*Buon giorno*," but the old man never answered. Instead he rapped the end of his crutch on the stones and repeated endlessly, "*Due lire! Due lire!*" One morning Due Lire was not there and he was never there again. After that, whenever Ignazio visited the busy, crowded market with his mother he stared at the vacant stones between the egg lady and the flower lady and he wondered what had happened to the old man.

As he lay looking up at the brilliant stars of the Baja California desert, Fra Nacho began to suffer from a familiar sensation, a feeling that he was growing larger and larger and very massive, as though he had drawn the entire universe into his soul and only he was left, perfectly alone, in the sterile blackness of eternity. He gasped and filled his lungs as deeply as he could and he tried to comfort himself, but he knew he would not sleep that night.

Halfway down the arroyo, María paused as the triumphant opening chords of the Tchaikovsky concerto reached her. It was unusual for Nacho to turn his record player up so loud. She turned and looked up the path. Far up, above the tops of the palm trees, the faint rays of a solitary flashlight played against the darkened cliffs.

CHUNK!... CHUNK!... CHUNK!...

Socorro was behind the house with the short-handled axe, working on the old camper shell.

She wanted some of the two-by-threes in the framework and she was making the wood splinters fly off into the dark as she chopped away the interior paneling. Pushing back the yellow insulation, she whacked a dozen pieces loose and threw them out the back.

"María! After you cut the fish, empty some ashes."

"Sí, mamá."

At the outside table, María quickened her pace on the heap of trigger-fish dripping in the lantern light.

One after another, she used a razor-sharp knife to separate the fillets from the skin and backbones. She cut the meat into small cubes, piled them in a cast-iron frying pan, and tossed the skins and carcasses into a five-gallon bucket on the ground.

"Mamá! I am through with the cochis!"

Socorro's voice came from behind the house.

"Empty the ashes."

The cooking barrel was full to the rim with cold ashes. María emptied two buckets on the pile behind the house. When she returned, Socorro had already put some two-by-threes and smaller sticks into the space and had thrown in a quarter-cup of raw gasoline.

María grabbed a towel and stood ready while Socorro struck a match and tossed it in. The flames burst up with a loud "whoop" and licked at the dry thatch of the porch roof. A few of the threadlike tips began to glow and spark, but María swung the towel at them and kept putting them out while the fire in the barrel settled down and Socorro put the grate over it.

A large, heavy-bodied spider, black with bold white stripes on its back, had been hiding in the palm thatch. It scurried out to evade the heat rising from the barrel and it tried to crawl to safety but lost its grip and fell to the ground. It made a crunching sound as Socorro stomped it with her bare foot and used her big toe to flick it away into the night.

"Don't you hate those things, mamá?"

"What things, my lovely?"

Socorro was busy heating the cubed fish, water, and sugar in the large frying pan. When the liquid had disappeared, she added oil, plenty of peppers, a chorizo, some onions, and a big pinch of salt. The aroma of the spicy sausage and the nutty, crab-like triggerfish filled the air as Socorro browned the contents of the pan and cooked it down to a chewy toughness.

On the table, she ground a handful of fresh tomatoes and peppers into a thick salsa, using a traditional mortar and pestle. Socorro loved her *molcajete*, which was carved from volcanic stone in the shape of a three-legged bowl with the head of a piglet projecting from one side. It had been bought in Guadalajara especially for her by a cousin of the fish buyer and it was the only one like it in the village.

While Socorro cooked, María mixed enough flour dough to make thirty-two tortillas. She divided the dough in half, and then divided each half again, and then three more times, until she had thirty-two balls of equal size. Then she began patting the dough between her hands into thin, round sheets, which she cooked one at a time on the cast-iron disk.

Socorro remembered how she had taught her daughter, as a young girl barely taller than the barrel, to divide the dough into halves.

"You have never stopped making tortillas that way."

"It is a habit, I guess. I like to make them come out perfectly."

Socorro finished the fish. She took the pan into the house and put it on the table to cool. She came back outside, dragging a chair, and she sat watching as María cooked the tortillas. There was a long silence, and then Socorro spoke with a kindness in her voice, mixed with concern.

"What is wrong, *mija?*"

María scorched the side of her thumb as she lifted a tortilla from the cooking iron.

"What do you mean?"

Socorro scooted her chair closer to the barrel.

"Listen, María. Your father and Chino will be here at any minute. Is there something you want to talk about?"

María concentrated on the light brown spots appearing on the bottom of the next tortilla. She grasped its hot edge quickly and flipped it over.

"Mamá... I am not going back to Loreto."

Socorro pressed her lips together, nodding.

"Too many lies?"

"It's not that. I enjoy school. But I want to have a family... like you and papá and Uncle Ramón. I want children and someone to love."

"So, that is why the tight pants and the red toenails?"

"Sí, mamá. I guess so."

Socorro went into the house and began setting the table with plates and forks from a heavy wooden shelf built into a corner of the front wall. From the shelf she also brought a large pot of beans and salt pork, still warm, which she had been cooking since morning, and a jar of candied fruits which she had saved from the last run of the fish buyer's truck. María came in with the tortillas and they sat down at the table waiting for the men to arrive. Socorro patted her daughter's smooth, slender hands.

"Your father will be very, very disappointed, but I will make him understand."

"Mamá, what about you? Do you approve?"

Socorro searched her daughter's eyes. She recalled the lonely years on Isla Coronado, years of such emptiness. And she thought of the windy afternoon when Abundio Rodríguez had come floundering onto her beach. With his arrival, even Socorro's body had sensed that her time had come at last. She had felt the changes, and in her distracted state, Abundio's fragile panga had seemed like a magic carpet that would carry her beyond the sea. The mundane realities of the past two decades made Socorro's passion of that time no less valid and no less apposite to the feelings of the eager young woman who sat beside her now.

And Socorro remembered the day her brother had returned to their beach with the strange new girl in his panga. So quiet and shy. From the ranchos. Knowing nothing of the fisherman's life she was about to share. Nothing of the fisherman's children she would bear on that lonely island. The two women had hardly spoken for the first year, but then they had become more than sisters, and now Emilia Ochoa, the only person Socorro had ever confided with on the subject of what it meant to be a woman, was gone from her life, probably forever.

Socorro looked at her beautiful daughter.

"María, you are of the caleta, but you are not one of us."

"That is what Nacho said tonight!"

"Nacho is right."

"But mamá... who *am* I then?"

Socorro looked downward. She pressed her hands on her lower belly and rubbed slowly from side to side.

"I don't know, my love. At the ranchos, María, I felt something break, here inside me, and it dried up and died. But somehow it swelled up again, just one time, for the miracle that was you. María, you are truly something rich and strange, something new and beautiful that grew out of your poor parents."

"I wish I didn't look so different... from you and papá!"

"Truly, that is what most people notice about you, María. Especially men, who are so blinded by it, and you must learn to ignore it. But, there is something more. You were always the child to ask puzzling questions with no answers, to gather more shells than you could carry, to create unnecessary problems for yourself. Do you know why we have always spent our afternoons at Nacho's house?"

"Why, mamá?"

"Many years ago, when you were young, he asked me to bring you. He said he would teach you the numbers and reading and writing, and pour into you all of his memories of the places he has been."

"But why, mamá? Why me?"

"He said that he saw something in you. He said I would understand one day. And I do. We all do."

María thought of the endless, pleasant afternoons she and her mother had spent sitting in the shade of Fra Nacho's porch, listening to his stories, answering his wandering questions, and drawing figures in the sand with sticks. Somehow, in a time before she could remember, the figures had become words, first in Spanish and then Italian, and somehow she had formed pictures in her mind of the people who spoke those words and the things they thought and felt. María could see the pigeon droppings and the turquoise patina on the bronze horses high above the piazza of San Marco in Venezia, feel the sting of the hoarfrost on the benches outside the train station of Milano. She knew the sounds the halyards made as they cracked against the masts of the ships in the great chubascos born off Acapulco, and the strange smells of the foods eaten by the Chinese and Philippine seamen. These and a thousand other things had come to her as she and her mother sat with Fra Nacho in the drowsy afternoons, swatting flies and waiting for the pangas to come in.

María saw, in the soft lantern light, that her mother's eyes had filled with memories and tears.

"Mamá? Did you dream of faraway places? When you were young?"

This was another of María's difficult questions, full of mirrors and hidden stairways, but Socorro understood its meaning. She reached around her daughter's slim waist and pulled her close.

"I know our table has not always been full, María. But I thank God for your father and especially for you, whom I love in ways I do not even wish to understand. We are women, who must be content with what is possible. And I am content to know that you wish to live your life as I have."

María lowered her face into her hands. Socorro gently stroked her daughter's rich black hair.

"But there is a problem, María. Very soon now, we must all leave this place."

"Perhaps the road will be repaired."

"That is not what I mean. The fish are almost gone. Not just here, but everywhere. In a few years, at most, we will have to make nets. Soon after that, there will be nothing. We will wander from place to place... like the people of Salina Cruz."

María thought of the destitution she had seen in Las Ramalitas and Loreto, the immature fish thrown back as the nets were pulled each morning.

"What will we do?"

"Ramón will return to the ranchos. Chino is capable of anything he sets his mind to. But for your father and me... I don't know."

María pressed her face into her mother's neck and held her tight. The streaks of gray in Socorro's hair were wider than she remembered. The bones of her mother's shoulders felt sharp beneath the thin, used up muscles.

"Mamá, we will think of something. Chino and I will always take care of you."

"You... and Chino?"

Socorro's mind skipped back and forth to complete a puzzle that had been assembling itself for years. From the beginning, she had entertained occasional thoughts of María and Chino together, but they had always been pushed aside by one thing or another. María's youth, Chino's preoccupation with the affairs of the day, Abundio's determination that his daughter should find a life off the beach. But now María had dropped the final piece of the puzzle into place and Socorro saw the picture that she had always suspected might be there.

"So! It is *Chino* you wear the pants for, eh?"

"Is it wrong, mamá?"

Socorro sat quietly and let the image form, as her Indian mother had taught her, the memories of things that had not yet happened. In the flickering yellow light, in the angled shadows of the room, she saw María grown old, older than herself, with children and grandchildren of her own. But try as she might, Socorro could not see the face of the man who stood in the shadows behind her and she could not tell if her daughter was happy.

"Chino is a good man."

"Don't you think he is very intelligent and handsome, mamá?"

"Well, he is definitely quite intelligent. But I don't know if he could be thought of as... handsome."

"Chino has many ideas, mamá. He thinks we can start a tourist business here. He says there are many tourist gringos in Loreto right now. He has heard the men at Las Ramalitas speaking of it."

Socorro was startled by the ripeness of these strange new ideas. She realized now why Chino had been so eager to make the weekly supply runs—alone—to Las Ramalitas.

"And... have you... given yourself to him?"

"No, mamá. But I kissed him once."

"And... ?"

"He took my shirt off... "

"Oh! Dios!"

" ...and then he turned away and told me never to do it again."

Socorro reflected a moment.

"And... was that when he built his house in the sand?"

"Sí, mamá."

ON THE EMPTY, darkened beach, two men stood up slowly. They clapped themselves all over to knock the sand from their pants. They looked up and down the shoreline and turned around several times and they set off, stumbling slightly, in the wrong direction.

A hundred feet later the men found their path blocked by a dense cluster of palms and brush growing at the edge of the high tide. They discussed this unexpected obstacle at some length, exchanging a few insults as to each other's intelligence and parentage, and then they reversed their course and began walking in the opposite direction.

Most of the lanterns had been extinguished for the night and a dead calm had settled over the village. Had they been listening, the men could have heard, even from as far away as the beach, the wicked giggling and cackling that came from the shack that was their destination, for within it a mother and daughter were enjoying a rite of passage, a discussion of things they had never discussed before and that were never discussed in the presence of men.

And had they overheard that conversation, the two partners would have become hot with interest, for the mother and daughter were discussing certain, very personal aspects of none other than themselves.

"So, mamá, does the size make it more enjoyable?"

"Well, he *is* huge, you know, in more ways than one."

"I remember the day he peed over a panga and won a hundred pesos from the fish buyer."

"Hah! On Isla Coronado, it used to be *three* pangas!"

"Does it hurt, mamá? You are so small in comparison."

"Sometimes, in a way… but he really only hurt me once."

"How, mamá?"

"It was my first time. He didn't know and he gored me like a wild bull."

"Oh! Was it his first time also?"

"I don't think so. He was quite… well… skillful."

"But he gored you like a bull!"

"Well… I mean a little later, when he did different things to me."

"Oooo! Like *what*, mamá?"

"Well… I don't want to say, exactly. But I can tell you there were times when I lost control of myself and he had the hair blown off his sweaty forehead!"

"Oh, *mamá!*"

ABUNDIO AND CHINO left the beach and followed the new gully toward the only house still showing a light. Abundio stumbled and was pulled to his feet by Chino, who then also stumbled, and the two men steadied themselves against each other as they pressed toward the doorway glowing in the distance. The women's voices came from the house intermittently, more subdued now.

"His is much shorter, also a lot thinner, but with a big head. We know that."

"Yes, it is smaller, but he is very strong, mamá."

"They are all strong at that age, daughter. But don't worry. I really don't think the size is so important after all. You can't feel much way up inside anyway."

"Then what *does* make a difference?"

Socorro did not answer. She rose from the table and went out to the cooking barrel, and she stood there, looking down at the glowing coals, bright orange flickers beneath the ashes.

What makes the difference? Socorro truly did not know. She stood there, thinking of herself, on her back in the little house on Isla Coronado, and of the times when the magic carpet did carry her, soaring and power-less to resist, beyond the sea. *I am a man of infinite passion and romance.* That promise, too, her Abundio had fulfilled, many times, but Socorro really could not say what made the difference. There had also been many times when she had been sure the carpet would come, when everything was right and he had done all the right things to make it come, but it had not. Socorro could think of nothing that *made* the miracle happen. Yet there were still times, even now, when it did happen, stronger than ever, and although she wished she could tell her daughter how or why—and make it happen for her too—Socorro knew she could not explain it. She could say nothing that would ease her María's way in this. It was something her daughter would have to discover for herself.

She went back inside and sat down.

"I suppose, what is most important is how you feel about each other. Are you in love with Chino?"

"I think so, mamá. But it is so hard to know."

"How does he feel about you?"

"He has always noticed me, but he keeps himself at a distance. What is *wrong* with me, mamá?"

"There is nothing wrong with *you*, my daughter. Chino is a very serious type of man, perhaps too serious, who sometimes... "

"*Peee... haw!*"

Chino's powerful arm slammed the outside wall so hard the whole house rattled. His long, grinning face came into the lantern light and he gripped the doorway with both hands for a moment before twirling around and sliding into a sitting position on the dirt floor.

Abundio was right behind him, cradling five bottles of beer in his arms. He nearly fell as he stumbled into Chino's outstretched legs.

Abundio kicked out a bare foot.

"Get up, you drunken jackass! You almost spilled our last beer!"

"Heee... heee... heee... "

Chino sat giggling and smiling around the room while Abundio stepped over him and carefully balanced the bottles in the middle of the table. Abundio then bowed deeply to Socorro who was still seated in her chair beside María, drumming her fingers on a stack of cold tortillas.

"Ah, Señora Rodríguez! As you can see, I have delivered to you this day, our daughter, María Guadalupe, who, because of the excellent results of her studies, has been granted a short vacation by her profesora, who says that she will soon, one day... soon... one day... very soon... "

"Enough, husband! Please sit and eat."

María rolled the spiced triggerfish in tortillas while Socorro opened the beers and brought some glasses to the table. Abundio and Chino each took a bite of burrito. They grabbed for their glasses and made sideways glances at each other. Socorro took a large bite, then another, and smiled inquiringly at the men.

"Too hot?"

"Oh, no! Just right actually. Not bad at all."

"Good."

Socorro examined her husband's face. There were some crusts on his forehead and his upper lip had been split. He had a dark puffy spot under his left eye.

"Did you get in a fight today?"

"No. Why?"

"Your face. It looks like the seagulls have been working on it."

"Ah... that. Well, a bush scratched me this morning when we were bringing the motor from Chino's house."

"What about your lip?"

"Ah... well, we had a little fútbol game this afternoon... in Las Ramalitas."

María rolled another round of burritos. She reached out to take her father's big, fat arm.

"Mamá! You should have seen him play today! In La Paz they used to call him El Tecolote Terrible."

Chino went around to stand behind his partner. He shook Abundio's shoulders and bent his narrow face into the lantern light.

"Socorro! Your husband may not be such a young man anymore, but today he showed them the meaning of true strength and courage. Like the bull!"

María and Socorro nearly choked on their burritos but neither of the men noticed and Chino continued.

"Abundio did not merely defeat them. He *destroyed* them! They had to take their best man to the *clinica* in Loreto."

Socorro seemed deeply unimpressed. She put two burritos into a paper bag and pushed the cap back on her bottle of beer, which she had not poured. She put the bottle in with the burritos, along with some pieces of candied fruit.

"María, Nacho hasn't eaten. He needs water, too."

"Sí, mamá."

María started out with the bag and a full water bottle. As she reached the door, Socorro put a hand on Chino's arm.

"Chino? Would you mind going with her? It is very dark in the arroyo tonight."

"Sí, Socorro."

As they went out the door, Socorro called after them.

"María! It is late. I will leave a blanket on your bed."

María's lilting voice came back from the darkened palms.

"Thank you... mamá."

Socorro placed a pillow and blanket on María's cot in the corner of the room. She lowered the cloth over the doorway, untied the new red ribbon from her hair, rolled it carefully, and put it on the shelf. Then she turned the wick of the kerosene lantern off.

In the dark of the dying flame, Socorro untied her woven red and blue belt and stepped out of her skirt. She pulled her blouse off over her head and went to the table, and she took Abundio's hand and led him to their cot. As he lay down beside her, she held his face and kissed him softly.

"Terrible owl, I missed you this morning."

THE HOUR OF the winter warrior had come. While the village lay entombed in its midnight shroud, Margarita Santos opened the door of the pink house and she rose up and soared among the stars to find him.

Orión! Orión! Orión! Are you there!?

She spread her arms, swirling high above the cliffs, searching for the lion hunter, the wielder of the club and shield. But she could not find him anywhere in the midsummer sky.

She rose higher and higher, circling upwards like the twin-tailed frigate birds above the islands and she flew north to Loreto and beyond, searching for the prince. She flew back to the village and searched up and down the beach, but she could not find him, and so she returned to herself. She found the pink house and sat on the edge of the concrete porch, breathless from her journey.

After a while, Margarita stood up slowly. She raised her eyes to the starry summer night and looked up to the scorpion and sighed a heavy sigh, and then she began to walk up toward the arroyo. She paused a moment outside the house where Abundio and Socorro slept and she looked for the pair of boots that usually hung on the porch. But the boots were not there and Margarita took the path leading up the arroyo, up to her secret place among the rocks.

Beneath the southern wall of the arroyo, she stopped at the abandoned well. She sat in the cool, damp sand beside the ancient ring of stones and she pushed back the heavy shawl that covered her head.

THE WELL WAS very old. Its open pit had first been dug in some timeless time, before the fishermen and their families, before the goat ranchers, before the steel helmeted man-gods on their floating islands.

The well's water was so salty and bitter even the animals drank it only when they could find nothing else, and it had been the source of the village's current name, for when a wandering Sinaloan panga fisherman discovered its bad taste he began referring to the place as the *caleta de agua amargosa*, the cove of bitter water, and the name had stuck.

But as unfit as the water was for people and animals, it was rich with the nutrients that plants required, and the area around the well grew lush with shrubs and trees. A huge old olive tree, gnarled and extending more sideways than up, grew a little way back from the ring of stones. It was the last survivor of a grove of date palms, olives, oranges, and lemons that had been planted in the arroyo long before anyone remembered, and the knobby roots of the vanished orchard could still be descried in the sandy soil, here and there, marking the intersections of a ghostly, long forgotten grid.

The well was now nearly filled with sand and gravel washed down the arroyo during heavy rainstorms. Only the uppermost ring of stones was visible, and in it, a shallow pool of thick green water bubbled up and overflowed slowly onto the sand.

And hidden in the bushes, where no one saw it, the remains of an old stone corral stood, decorated with the skulls of generations of burros that had lived out their lives on the shore of the caleta long before the fishermen had come.

IN THE WOMB-LIKE warmth of the summer night, Margarita Santos found a tall glass bottle stuck on the branch of a tree. She knelt beside the well and filled it, and poured the water carefully over a cluster of daisies that she had planted. Nearby, a small, white cross had been driven into the sand. Margarita sat beside it. She pulled the ribbon from her hair, letting it fall over her shoulders. She raised her eyes to the stars and swayed slowly from side to side and began to sing.

"Up to the sky... he flew... up to the sky... he flew... all wet and red... the little prince flew..."

Margarita raised both hands to the midnight blackness above her and she pointed her fingers at the swirling bats, turning them into stars. She rose up among them, became one of them, and they called to her, called her by name.

"Margarita!"

She answered the chorus of high-pitched, child-like voices.

"I am here!"

"Margarita! Come look what we have found!"

"What is it?"

"You must come and look!"

"Where?"

"Up, up high! Come up here! Follow us!"

Margarita picked a daisy and put it into the pocket of her skirt. She followed the voices up the arroyo, past Fra Nacho's darkened shack, to the end of the path, and then beyond it, up a steep slope of shattered rock. She climbed from rock to rock, nearly a third of the way up the cliff, until she came to a sandy, level place between two sheer walls.

Here, she found the small rock ferns, growing in profusion within the cracks, and descending from higher up, the wide, flat root of the *zalate* tree, the giant fig, covering the face of the cliff in a solid curtain of gray bark as high as six men.

Margarita found a small opening in the root and she crawled into the tunnel-like space behind it. She felt along the wall until she came to the fish and whales, and the deer with antlers, and more animals she did not know. She felt her way deeper into the cave, where the strange hoofprints and checkerboard patterns were, and then she entered the secret place itself, a rock-walled room whose sides sloped upwards together until they met somewhere high above.

Margarita crept along the wall until she found a box of matches. She struck one. In its flickering light, high up on the wall, leaning over the ceiling of the cave, she saw the painted figures of a man and a woman, etched in black and red, their elongated bodies spread-eagled across the stone surface. They did not touch, but they leaned toward each other as if trying to overcome some invisible force keeping them apart. Floating sideways above them, a smaller figure in black, childlike, seemed to reach out to the woman.

Margarita's match went out. She struck another and held it up.

Below the man and woman, someone long ago had painted a doorway into the rock wall. To Margarita, at least, it seemed to be a doorway. But within the waist-high arch there was no passage. Only solid rock. It was an illusion, laboriously fashioned by someone, that led nowhere.

On the sand beside the doorway was a collection of things from the village—a rosary, old toys, glass bottles, a ring of keys, some shells in a metal cup, some small animal bones, many other things.

The second match went out and Margarita lit another. She took the daisy from her pocket, along with a coiled piece of fishing line and some hooks, and she put them on the sand with the other things. She let the match go out, and she whispered to the chorus of voices.

"Is this what you want to show me?"

"Yes, Margarita! No, Margarita!"

"What do you mean?"

"Outside! Come outside and you will see!"

Margarita felt her way back to the opening in the root. She waited but the voices did not come.

"Where are you?"

There was no answer, but she thought she heard, very faintly, the cry of an animal in the arroyo below her. She called out in a loud whisper.

"Are you there?"

Still, the voices would not answer.

She heard the cry again, and then another time, and she climbed down to the streambed and turned to her left to follow the sound. It came again, louder, as she passed the cutoff to Fra Nacho's shack. She stood still to find its direction.

It came irregularly, from within a cluster of dry brush beside the trail, a low, rhythmic moaning sound, and then a sharper cry and more moaning. She came upon them, saw the glow of the new white cloth on the ground beneath them, the man's pale, untanned buttocks straining rapidly up and down, and the woman's slender fingers tearing at them, pulling him in.

In the dark, Margarita approached slowly. She stood over them, with her head tilted slightly, looking down, with her hands held folded against her chin. Over the man's mass of curly hair, the eyes of the woman were closed tight. The corners of her mouth pulled down hard as she cried out again and again, and then lay back, sobbing and kissing the man's hidden face.

The woman opened her eyes, a little at first and then wide with fear when she became aware of Margarita standing above her. They stared at each other as the man finished and lay gasping unevenly.

Silently, Margarita raised a finger to her lips and turned her head from side to side. A frightened María Guadalupe Rodríguez recognized the black figure outlined in the stars above her and she understood the silent, woman's gesture. She sighed deeply and nodded, and she wrapped her arms around Chino's neck and pulled him tight as Margarita backed away and the bats wheeled and skidded in the night.

THE MORNING SUN had risen high off the water and the shadows of the houses were short and narrow. Socorro hummed softly to herself as she warmed tortillas at the barrel. She had already cooked a pan of eggs with levanta muertos and tuna.

A plaid blanket covered María on her cot. Her hair stuck out at one end and her feet at the other, sand still clinging between her toes.

Socorro rolled half a dozen burritos and sat on the edge of the cot.

"Mija."

María's muffled voice came from beneath the blanket.

"Sí… "

"Hungry?"

"Sí."

"Come and eat."

María was still in her clothes from the evening before.

"Where is papá?"

"At Nacho's. The men are having a meeting."

"Why?"

"Some of them want to try clearing the road."

As María came to the table, Socorro pointed to the collar of her shirt.

"Your buttons. They are uneven."

María refastened the buttons. As she unzipped her new pants to tuck her shirt in, she caught Socorro staring at her panties. They were on backwards.

Socorro put a burrito on her daughter's plate.

"So. That is the new style in Loreto, eh?"

María did not answer. She left her underpants to fend for themselves, and they pinched uncomfortably as she seated herself and ate.

Afterwards, Socorro put the dishes into a bucket with a sponge and a squeeze of detergent. She stood behind María's chair with her hands resting lightly on her daughter's slim shoulders.

"Would you like to come and help me?"

"Sí, mamá. Then, let's walk down the beach."

"Excellent! We have plenty of water. Later, if you like, you can wash yourself."

"Sí, mamá. I think I will."

María tried to get up from the table but Socorro held her down with a force that was almost startling.

"But first, daughter, I want to get your opinion about something."

"Of course, mamá. What is it?"

María tried to turn around but Socorro held her in the chair and bent over to whisper closely into her ear.

"The size. Do you think it makes any difference?"

María shrieked as she leapt to her feet and threw her arms around her mother's old shoulders, laughing.

"*Ayy,* mamá! How did you know?"

Socorro was laughing too, but with a tear on her cheek.

"María! You must be kidding!"

THEY TOOK TWO buckets of dishes and pans and started down to the beach. María stopped at the new gully. It was wide enough to hold a panga and it crossed between the houses where there had once been flat ground.

"Mamá, you must have had some very strong rain here."

"It happened all on one night, in the first week of March."

"It must have been terrible."

"It wasn't too bad here. Most of the rain fell in the mountains during the afternoon. Then, in the middle of the night, a river came out of the arroyo... and did this."

Socorro waved an arm to indicate the path of the erosion. The soil was a loose mix of sand and broken shell, easily moved by water. A tremendous amount of it had been cut away during the two-hour flash flood. As they reached the beach, María saw a new tongue of dry sand projecting fifty feet into the caleta.

"Was anybody hurt, mamá?"

"In the morning Margarita was missing but we found her up near the well. She was wandering outside when the river came and she couldn't get back to Pablo's house."

They carried their buckets to the end of the new peninsula and began washing dishes at the edge of the water. María used the coarse, damp sand to scour the pans, then rinsed them in clean seawater and returned them to the buckets. She started on the dishes.

"Was she mourning her bastard in the moonlight?"

"What do you say, daughter?"

"In Las Ramalitas, Lupe said when Margarita goes out at night she is mourning her bastard baby in the moonlight."

"Ah... so now you know of that too."

"What does she mean, mamá?"

"Hmmm... I suppose it is time for you to learn the story... at least as much as I know of it."

"Tell me everything, mamá!"

They sat beside their buckets at the tip of the new peninsula, two small figures dressed in brilliant white, surrounded by the turquoise water of the caleta, and Socorro related to her daughter what she knew of Agua Amargosa's only recorded scandal, the story of Margarita Santos' dishonoring by a lover whose identity she refused to reveal even to the present day, the mysterious loss of her child, and her subsequent descent into the refuge of shadows and dreams.

"It happened before we moved here, when Margarita was a young girl in La Paz. They say she was normal in those days and very good looking.

"She got pregnant but her boyfriend refused to acknowledge her so she ran away. She came here to live with Pablo.

"There was almost nobody else here in those days. Pablo was one of the first to move here after they opened the road. That must have been five or six years before we came.

"Anyway, Pablo couldn't stand his sister's embarrassment. María, you must never, never speak of this to anyone.

"One night Margarita and Pablo had a terrible fight, in the house, and he beat her and almost killed her. But she ran up the arroyo and she had her baby there that night, alone. They say it should have been old enough to live, but it didn't, and she buried it somewhere."

María thought immediately of the old cross by the well, the flowers that Margarita tended in the night, long after the village had gone to bed.

"Her baby is buried by the well, then!"

"No. But that is where they found her in the morning. They thought the baby might be alive and they looked for it everywhere. They dug everywhere she could have buried it, but they never found it."

"And was that when she went crazy, mamá?"

"In a way, daughter. After that, they say Margarita grew old very quickly. She stayed inside the house and she has kept to herself ever since. But I don't think it is proper to say that she has actually lost her mind. Often, she seems perfectly normal. It is just that her memories are sometimes too painful and she needs to get away from them for a while."

María looked toward the village. The Santos house was hidden in the palms, but she could imagine Margarita sitting there, pale, with her head always covered, brooding over the memories of her lost lover and child.

"Was it a boy or girl, mamá?"

"Nobody knows. She has always refused to speak of it. And to this day, she has never named the father."

Abundio Rodríguez paused in the sand dunes. He bent over and pulled on his ankles to stretch his lower back, which, along with every other part of his body, felt as stiff as a dead horse. For a full minute, Abundio stretched himself. Then he resumed the climb to Chino's shack, walking slowly and cringing with discomfort at every step.

Ayy... Ayyyy! Legs, how can you object so much to a little game of *fútbol*? And butt, you too? You have *never* been sore before, butt. You are definitely getting old and soft. Ah... well, I am sure the Diagonal Stripe has more to worry about than we do, eh? It will be a while before he forgets El Tecolote Terrible!

Abundio found Chino sitting on the bench, doodling figures in the sand with a sharpened stick. Chino noticed his partner's awkward limp.

"What is it, amigo?"

"Pah! Just a little soreness from the game yesterday. It has been too many years."

"Where did you learn to play like that, amigo?"

"Well... here and there. You only need one or two tricks but you have to do them well and make it look real or there will be nothing but fights."

Abundio handed a paper bag to Chino, who held it at arm's length as though it contained a live snake.

"Highway flares?"

"She said not too many muertos."

"That's what she always says, amigo."

Chino tried a burrito. It was torrid with peppers. Chino ate half and closed the bag, shaking his head.

"Whew! How does she stand it?"

Abundio looked closely at his partner's face.

"Mijo, are you feeling all right? You look a little tired... or maybe sick?"

Chino cleared his throat. He spit out a piece of tuna skin and wiped his mouth.

"Ah... well, no, amigo. I am fine. Very fine, actually. It is just that I didn't sleep too much last night. In fact, Abundio... "

Chino stood up, facing his best friend.

" ...there is something we must talk about."

"Of course, mijo. What?"

Abundio was bent over, pulling on his feet and massaging his calves. Chino looked down at the big man's rounded, deeply tanned shoulders. Although he could not see Abundio's face, he knew the familiar expression on it, and he knew how completely unprepared Abundio would be for what he was now honor bound to tell him. What would be the best way to put it? My dear Señor Rodríguez, last night I, Chino Zúñiga, your most trusted friend and a luckless fisherman like yourself, with no present income and no probable future, violated your incredibly beautiful daughter. I removed her pants and had my way with her in the sand five times. Well, three, actually, and then she had her way with me twice. Anyway, the child you have loved and sheltered for the past nineteen years is no longer yours. Poof! Gone forever! But don't worry, amigo! I am prepared to make an honest woman of her! Unfortunately, that means she will never be anything more than the companion of an ignorant, unpromising nobody, namely me.

Abundio looked up.

"Well... what is it, mijo?"

There. There it is. That same expression you always wear, amigo. Trusting, optimistic, Abundio Rodríguez, never expecting the pie that is about to hit you in the face.

"Mijo... ?"

Chino cleared his throat. He sat down on the bench and began doodling again with his stick.

"Well, the thing is... Bundo... is... well... "

"Yes?"

" ...have you ever thought about getting into the tourist business?"

"Very funny."

"No, no. I don't mean selling Chiclets at the border."

"What, then?"

"You know how the *americanos* come to La Paz? They are coming to Loreto now, in airplanes, to go fishing."

"But mijo, there are no fish left in Loreto."

"To them it seems like a lot. A dozen small cabrilla or a few yellowtail or pargo makes them very excited. They like to catch anything. Especially marlin and sailfish."

"Why?"

"They think of it as fun. It is a sport to them. Like fútbol. And they pay plenty to go out in a panga."

"How much, mijo?"

"From what I've overheard in Las Ramalitas, they pay as much as thirty or even forty dollars for a day of fishing."

"*Madre!* For one day!?"

"That is what I have heard."

Abundio took a stick and began making his own doodles.

Since boyhood he had been aware of the wealthy Americans on the big yachts that anchored in the harbor of La Paz, or the few who arrived in their own planes and fished from the hotel boats. He had stood at the edge of the sidewalk in front of the Hotel Perla, watching them drinking and smoking cigarettes in the shade of the afternoon. And as they strolled the Malecón in the evenings, he had almost brushed against their women, so rich and glamorous and unattainable. He could not imagine them in the caleta.

"Chino. Those people are presidents and movie stars. They would never go out in a shitty panga with us."

"No, Bundo. These new fishermen are just regular people. Almost all men. There is an American who flies an old plane from the war. He brings many clients and they fish here, or they go over to San Carlos and fish in Bahía Magdalena. Many others come in their own planes and hire pangas for themselves."

Abundio considered this upside-down concept of fishing as something so pleasurable that one would actually *pay* to do it, even fly somewhere in an airplane to do it, even to a place where there were not so many fish anymore.

"And these gringos pay hundreds of dollars a day, just to catch a few worthless fish?"

"I said thirty or forty dollars. It is becoming a good business, amigo. Much better than fishing ever was."

"Hmmm… "

Chino snapped his stick in half. Dammit! Why should it be so hard to tell a man you love his daughter? Abundio rose abruptly from the bench, rescuing Chino from his determination to confess.

"Come, mijo! It's almost noon. We need to get to Nacho's place."

"Right."

They walked inland along the base of the cliffs, taking a path toward the arroyo. After skirting the sand dunes for a hundred yards, the path met the old cliff road where it touched the floor of the valley.

Abundio tried to imagine earning money by taking tourists fishing in the panga. The sight of the old cliff road reminded him of the American man he used to fish with, Señor Pete, who was also the only *americano* Abundio had ever known.

He had first met Señor Pete on this very spot, and as he thought about it, Abundio realized that his old friend had probably been an example of what Chino was talking about, someone who fished not for profit or even for food, but for the pure sport of it.

They had met in the old days, when the road was still closed and Abundio was about ten or perhaps a few years younger. Abundio and his father had been camping out of their dugout sailing canoe for most of the summer, set-lining shark and diving the caleta for pearl oysters, but not finding any, and one afternoon while they napped under the palm trees the sound of Señor Pete's old Ford pickup had come rumbling down the cliffs.

The tall, half-naked boy heard it first and jumped to his feet.

"Papá! A car is coming!"

"Impossible, mijo. Nothing can make it down that road."

"But I heard it! I am sure I heard a car!"

Abundio had run to the base of the cliffs as fast as his lungs would take him. He stopped and listened and it came again over the sound of his breathing, the racing of a motor somewhere high, high above, then silence. Someone had discovered the old road and was trying to break through to the caleta.

Abundio climbed a large rock beside the road and he waited like a lizard in the sun for the rest of the afternoon, hearing the motor a dozen times more. But by dark the car had not arrived and he returned to their camp under the trees. He lay awake all night in fear that whoever it was, sweating and straining up on the cliff, might have given up and turned back to the main road.

He got an early start. He took a bottle of water and began the long hike up the road, planning to meet the visitors and perhaps help them.

But before he could begin climbing, he caught sight of it, glinting in the yellow rays of sunrise, high up on the cliff, a dull gray pickup with something big tied on top of it.

Abundio sat on his rock all morning, keeping his eye on the pickup, listening to the sound of its motor as it would start, move a few yards, and stop again while a man got out and worked with the pick and shovel.

It was past noon when the pickup came around the final turn and Abundio leapt down in front of it, startling the driver and nearly getting run over for his troubles. Señor Pete tromped on the brakes and the pickup slid to a halt sideways on the sand. He shouted out the window in the worst Spanish that Abundio had ever heard.

"Hi, me boy. What number is it?"

"Mande?"

"Your number, amigo, what is your number?"

"Mande?"

"Your number! My number is fart. What is *your* number?"

"Mande!?"

They went on for quite a while in this manner, and finally, Señor Pete became exasperated and motioned for Abundio to hop in beside him. In those days the village had not yet been built and the road simply ended where it met the sand dunes at the base of the cliff. Señor Pete floorboarded the truck and they bounced and swayed through the dunes all the way to the beach. He turned off the engine and went to the back and opened up a heavy chest wrapped in canvas. It was full, absolutely full, of ice and bottles of soda and beer and Abundio's eyes had opened wide at the sight of the frosty treasure.

Señor Pete motioned for Abundio to help himself. The boy grabbed two sodas and two beers, thrilling to the icy coldness in his hands. He rubbed the bottles against his face and he licked the bits of ice clinging to them.

Señor Pete frowned at the beers, but the boy quickly pointed to the south end of the caleta and explained.

"They are for my father. He is over there, diving for pearls."

"Goat stew is not good for thee."

"Mande?"

Señor Pete pointed at the beers again, shaking his finger.

"Goat stew. It makes very bad for girl babies."

Abundio realized Señor Pete meant the beers, which he had referred to as *birria*, the word for a kind of salty stew made with goat meat.

"Ah, señor, these are *cervezas*! Birria means something else."

"Oh, oh! What birria mean?"

"It is a dish, señor, made from the meat of the goat."

"Meat of goat?"

"Sí, señor, the goat."

"Oh! No! Beer me fart no bueno españole!"

Wisely, the boy had decided to let that one pass.

Señor Pete opened two beers for himself. Then he opened both of Abundio's sodas and they sat on the ice chest together, feeling the wonderful coolness of the drinks in the afternoon heat.

Señor Pete was in his late twenties and he was in excellent physical condition, deeply tanned and muscular. He wore a small mustache of the same dust yellow color as his hair, which he was already starting to lose. Despite his barbaric Spanish, Abundio sensed the stranger possessed a certain intelligence, an empathy and understanding beyond anything he had encountered before. Furthermore, Señor Pete treated him as an adult, as a comrade, and Abundio's heart pounded with the excitement of making his first real friend.

Late that afternoon, as he helped Señor Pete make camp under the palm trees, Abundio stood and pointed a finger at himself and spoke in slow, clear Spanish.

"Bundo. My name is Bundo."

Señor Pete returned a wide smile and pointed to his own chest.

"Fart."

The man confirmed repeatedly that his name *was* "Pedo," or fart, in Spanish, and that was the way Abundio introduced him to his father later that evening.

Abundio and his father accepted the man's unfortunate name as something tragic that he bore with courage and grace. It was the second or third day before they determined with great relief that his name was really Peter, and that what he was saying was not actually Pedo, but *Pedro*, horribly mispronounced in Spanish so the normally rolled "r" was almost silent. Abundio corrected him one morning as they sat fishing the inner caleta in Señor Pete's small boat.

"Señor Pedro, it is very important to pronounce the 'r' in your name."

"Because?"

"To prevent misunderstanding, señor."

Señor Pete's Spanish-English dictionary did not contain *"pedo,"* but he was made to comprehend the meaning of the word, first through polite circumlocution, then frank explanation, and finally, gestures and sound effects.

Once he understood, he slapped his high forehead and laughed like a madman and after that they just called him Señor Pete.

Señor Pete stayed for a month and he returned for at least a few weeks every summer for the next six years. He and Abundio fished together every day in his small, square-ended boat, which he brought to the caleta tied upside down on his pickup. The boat had a toy-like outboard motor and the resonant name of "MASTER-BAITER," which he had painted on the transom in large black letters.

Señor Pete explained the joke twice, on separate mornings, about five years apart. The first time was when Abundio asked him why he never actually fished with bait, but only with small feathered hooks that he tied himself, using colored threads and bird feathers and bits of fur that he kept in a box in the back of his camper.

"Well, it sort of means a *maestro de carnada*, a master of fishing with bait."

"But Señor Pete, you do not use bait."

"Bait is for amateurs and meat fishermen, Bundo."

"We always use bait. Live bait, if we can get it."

"And that's good for you. You make your living from the sea. You will always catch more with live bait."

"So, why don't *you* use it, señor?"

"I feel closer to the fish if it hits something I made myself."

"And... that is important to you? To be close to the fish?"

"Yes, Bundo. I don't know why, but it is very important to me. It means something to me."

"The name of your boat... it is a joke, then?"

"Yes, Bundo. It reminds me not to take myself too seriously."

With constant use of the dictionary, Señor Pete's Spanish gradually improved to the point that he and the boy could be fairly comfortable together and they spent more and more time in each other's company.

Señor Pete cast his nearly weightless feathers over the reefs of the caleta, using a very long thin rod and a thick line that he let run through his fingers when he caught a fish. He always released his fish unharmed, never even keeping one for dinner, and he loved nothing better than to discover a new type of fish that he had not caught before. When this happened, he wrote down the date and the temperature of the water, the tides, and other details in a thick, hard-covered notebook that he kept in a waterproof bag.

Señor Pete was a high school teacher from Los Angeles. He was alone, although he said that once before he was to have been married. Abundio sensed a sadness in his friend, as though something about that experience still colored his everyday relationship with the world. Once, Señor Pete said that he expected he would go to hell for something that had happened to him, although he never said what it was.

Each summer, once he had set up camp on the beach, Señor Pete would plop down beside his ice chest and begin drinking beer in a great rush. He drank bottle after bottle, night and day. It would take him two days to finish it all, and when he was done, he would sleep for another two days before he felt like himself again.

Once he dried out, Señor Pete did push-ups and ran on the beach every morning before they launched the boat. The third year, Abundio began to run with him, just a little at first, and then farther and farther before dropping back.

One morning, as they jogged along, Abundio's eyes fell on the peculiar scar on Señor Pete's lower back. It was clearly visible just above his belt. The scar was about two inches long. It was a vivid pink and was raised in a narrow, undulating welt, shaped like an uneven letter "Y," tilted slightly on its side.

"Señor Pete, how did you get the scar on your back?"

"A piece of metal went through me."

"All the way through?"

"Yes, Bundo. It was in a car accident. It went in my side and came out through my back."

"It is lucky you were not killed."

Señor Pete stopped jogging and waited for Abundio to catch up. With his feet stationary in the sand, he slowly twisted his upper body back and forth and he looked at the boy with a strange smile.

"It's best not to need that kind of luck."

Two years later, Abundio's father went north in the canoe, leaving the young man to camp alone under the palms. Señor Pete arrived on schedule and he and Abundio fished the caleta until Abundio's father returned in late August to take him back to La Paz.

Abundio had begun his career as El Tecolote Terrible by then and he could easily outdistance Señor Pete on their morning runs and beat him at arm wrestling. In those days the water from the old well ran sweet enough to drink, even in mid-summer, and life in the caleta was easy. They fished every day. In the afternoons, they sat under the palms, talking and carefully rationing the enormous supply of canned food, flour, hard salami and cheese that Señor Pete always brought in the back of his pickup.

In the late summer of that year, when Señor Pete felt that Abundio had grown old enough, he explained the second meaning of the name of his boat and where he had gotten it.

"A guy from Montana gave me the name. I thought it was funny."

Abundio was sixteen years old by then, as tall as Señor Pete, and fully immersed in the Mexican cult of *machismo*, the masculine code of conduct that admitted none but the most straightforward use of the male genitalia. He was shocked by the second meaning of "MASTER-BAITER," and he couldn't understand how any man, especially such a fine man as Señor Pete, could permit a name like that on his boat. Abundio's skin crawled with shame at the thought of it and he refused to fish with Señor Pete for the remaining two weeks of the summer.

On the last morning, Señor Pete sought out Abundio on the beach. He removed his wristwatch and gave it to the young man.

"Bundo, take this gift. We may not meet again."

They had talked many times that summer of the news from a place called Pearl Harbor, on an island far away, somewhere in the middle of the Pacific Ocean. But Abundio still could not understand why there should be a great war. Was it because of the pearls in the harbor? Could they be so valuable that armies of men were willing to die for them?

Nor could Abundio understand Señor Pete's determination to enlist, to give up his rich, secure position as a respected *profesor*, and to risk his life for a cause that seemed so distant from their world in the caleta.

"Señor Pete, why must you go to this war?"

"I don't know, Bundo. Something inside is calling me."

By then, Abundio's anger over the boat had dissipated to mere embarrassment and he tried to apologize for his churlish behavior.

"Señor Pete, I am sorry… about the boat… "

"It is nothing, Bundo! Please, don't forget me."

"I will never forget you, señor."

Señor Pete had already tied his boat on the pickup. They sat on a palm log for their last two sodas of the summer, talking of the deteriorating road, of the Tecolotes, of a pretty girl Abundio planned to see when he got back to La Paz. Señor Pete spoke of his love of the caleta and of the magic way the fish seemed to come to his feathers of their own will. Then, he grew quiet and he said his final words in his halting, still awful Spanish.

"Bundo, always remember, the object of life is to try to live each day with honor and not let your disgraces destroy you, for *none* of us is perfect. In the end, the most we can hope for is the knowledge that, although we are failed, we have made the attempt in good faith."

Abundio flicked a pebble toward a hermit crab struggling with its shell at the edge of the water.

"So, the name of your boat, señor, says... in a joking way... that you acknowledge faults in yourself?"

"Yes, Bundo. And we must forgive ourselves, and each other, every day."

"I understand, señor. And I will not forget."

They stood and shook hands on the beach, in the American style, and Señor Pete waved out the window as his truck began the long climb up the cliff road. That was his last summer in Agua Amargosa.

By the following year, the great war of the Pacific had begun. Abundio brought the canoe up from La Paz alone, but Señor Pete did not appear, and Abundio returned to the city in the fall without seeing his friend. Twice more during the war, Abundio came to the caleta, and once he continued up the coast as far as the hidden cove ten miles south of Santa Rosalia, inquiring about the solitary American and the battered, twelve-foot boat named "MASTER-BAITER." But he never saw Señor Pete again.

Later in La Paz, a friend noticed Señor Pete's watch, which Abundio always wore on his left wrist, removing it only for soccer matches. The friend jokingly asked Abundio where he had stolen it and he was greatly surprised when Abundio said an *americano* had given it to him.

"Do you know what kind of watch that is, Bundo?"

"Is it a good one?"

"Christ! Bundo, it's a Rolex! A solid gold Rolex! It is easily worth more than any five pangas on this beach!"

Abundio took a good look at the watch. He noticed the tiny crown on its elegant, rectangular face and he studied the minute letters engraved on the back.

"Peter J. M. Grayson III, Providence, R.I., Mom & Dad, 1932."

To confirm the watch's value and get a translation of its inscription, they took it to a trusted jeweler in La Paz, an uncle of one of the Tecolotes.

Abundio had never worn the watch again. He had always kept it wrapped in an oiled cloth, buried in a mayonnaise jar a foot beneath the fire barrel, and of the present inhabitants of Caleta Agua Amargosa only he and Socorro knew of its existence.

As Abundio climbed toward Fra Nacho's shack, with Chino just ahead of him, he looked up to the multicolored cliffs shimmering through the heat waves and he thought of Señor Pete's gold Rolex. There had been several times in the past when he had come close to selling it, but somehow, somehow, it had never actually come to that, and he was proud that he had been able to hang onto it. Often, as he lay beside Socorro, waiting for the first signs of dawn to appear, he felt warmed by the knowledge that a man as strong and brave as Señor Pete had entrusted him with something of such great value, and he would remind himself to try to live that day with honor, and forgive his own shortcomings and those of others, and above all, not to take himself too seriously.

" ...So, Chino, do you really think they would come here?"

"Who, amigo?"

"The tourists. The sport fishermen. Do you think they would really come?"

Chino's mind was not on tourist anglers. They had entered the arroyo and come almost to the spot. From the corner of his eye, Chino scanned the brush beside the trail. Yes, this was the place. God! Look at all the footprints! I hope he doesn't notice. *Madre!* Her sandals!

Chino shifted to the opposite side of the trail and gestured with his hands, trying to sustain the conversation.

"Ah... what did you just say, amigo?"

Abundio gave his partner a curious look. Chino seemed distracted. Perhaps he was just tired or perhaps just a little hung over.

"I said, do you really think tourists would come to the caleta?"

"Well... it might be possible. We would need to fix the landing strip, for their planes."

"Ah yes, *la pista...* "

The people of Agua Amargosa had no idea who had cleared and leveled the piece of ground behind the village they called "la pista," or the landing strip. Probably, it was the same people who had built the original road many years before. No plane had ever landed there that Abundio knew of, and in fact he was not sure if the irregular, rutted strip of dirt between the village and the cliffs had even been intended for that purpose. The pista was about a third of a mile long and fifty yards wide and it stretched along the right side of the trail where they now walked.

" ...that would be difficult, mijo."

"Yes. Very difficult."

The landing strip sloped gradually up toward the arroyo and ended almost against the cliffs. It was crisscrossed by footpaths and spotted with sparse, woody desert shrubs. The winds had blown away most of the original sandy surface, leaving behind a field strewn with scattered cobbles and boulders. Worse, the rains of the previous spring had cut through the middle of the strip, bisecting it with a ragged gully deep enough to conceal a small house.

Chino continued, as they walked along the south side of the pista.

"We would need lots of gas and supplies."

"What supplies?"

"Well, rich food... chicken, beef and pork, and vegetables and soft bread. Many Americans dislike eating fish."

"But mijo, would they not be coming here to catch fish?"

"Catch them, yes. But they will want to eat something else. They dislike strong flavored fish especially. They like fillets of mild fish, with butter or sauces to cover the taste. The more it seems like chicken, the better."

Abundio stopped to stretch his calves.

"Hmm... what else, mijo?"

"We would need things like ketchup. Fresh milk. Sodas and beer. The Americans drink a lot of beer. Ice. Lots of ice and lots of fresh water for washing. Soap. Clean towels and toilet paper."

"Hmm... no magazines, eh?"

"No magazines. They want things to be nice."

"All that would be expensive, mijo."

"They will pay double or triple for everything. But it has to be nice. They dislike anything old, and they are easily offended by flies and especially garbage. They can't stand the sight or smell of it, or even the thought of it. It must be burned, or buried, or hidden, or taken away somewhere."

"They sound difficult, mijo."

"Many Americans seem stupid and loud, but they are really basically about like us. The difference is that even the coarse, ignorant ones, completely lacking in dignity, are wealthy and powerful."

Abundio thought of Señor Pete. It was true that he had never eaten the fish he caught. But Señor Pete had not been stupid, loud, or coarse.

"Hmm... how do you know so much about the americanos, mijo?"

"I used to live up there."

"Ah... "

They passed the end of the landing strip and turned up the hot, rocky side trail leading to Fra Nacho's shack. The sun bore straight down into the arroyo and the air grew still and silent. Here, few plants hazarded a show of foliage during the long dry periods between storms, and only brittle twigs and stunted cactus hid between the boulders. Big black lizards basked in the harsh light, stretching their legs to hold their bodies off the griddle-hot rocks. The men climbed slowly, feeling the heat in the soles of their bare feet, and Chino's thoughts turned, as they often did, to his private, bitter memories of his life in the United States.

CHINO WAS BORN to a loose-knit clan of Chinese-Mexican farm workers who lived on the southern edge of the dusty Baja border town of Mexicali. One of his grandfathers had come from Shanghai in 1934 to work first on the canal that brought water from the Colorado River and then in the American-owned vegetable fields on the Mexican side of the border. When Chino was six the work gave out and his family climbed through the international fence to labor in the fierce heat of the Imperial and Coachella Valleys. The boy learned early that it was useless to cry as he stood with a hoe taller than himself at the edge of a field so wide he could not see the other side of it.

By the time he was fourteen Chino had attended half a dozen schools on the U.S. side of the border, off and on, as well as several in Mexicali, and he had seen enough lettuce and tomatoes and strawberries to last a lifetime. He had also acquired a profound hatred of being called a wetback kid and he was well known among the whites, from El Centro to Palm Springs, as a bad one, to be left alone, for whatever the odds and whatever the punishment dealt him, they knew the narrow-faced youth with the curly hair had a crazy burning rage inside and could not be defeated in a fight unless they knocked him senseless.

From the beginning, Chino rebelled against the bovine passivity of his parents, brothers, and sisters, who seemed not to mind their low standing on the American side of the border. After work in the fields, Chino listened carefully to the radio, and he read comic books and old newspapers to teach himself proper English. He tried his best to keep up in school, despite the constantly changing faces of his teachers and classmates and the urging of his parents to join the labor gangs.

He hated the squalid anomie of the field camps, the having to keep his good clothes in bags and putting them on just before school in the mornings, the stealing of chickens and the baking of them, feathers and all, in balls of mud placed into the campfires. He ranted at his family and screamed that he was ashamed of them. But they reacted by ostracizing him and eventually he understood they no longer considered him to be one of them.

Chino left his family before he began to shave. To support himself, he dropped out of high school a month before graduation and he began to work full-time in the fields. He worked hard and honestly. Because of this, and because of his ability with English and with his fists, he was made foreman of a large truck farm just outside Brawley at the exceptional age of eighteen.

He shared a warren-like apartment with two dozen other men. He bought a derelict Chevy pickup and rebuilt the motor and transmission in the driveway after studying the Chilton repair manuals in the El Centro library every night for six months.

Friendless and alone, Chino found comfort in working as many hours as possible. He hoarded the money he earned in the sweltering fields and he borrowed many, many books from the library to improve his knowledge of English, for he had no goal in life other than to be taken for an American. He kept out of trouble. Indeed, he had no time for trouble. His days were filled with the numbing routine of the furrows, and his nights with dreams that he never remembered in the cold, dark mornings when he started his pickup and left for the ranch.

To make extra money, Chino found a second job working nights at a gas station in El Centro and it was there that he met Elizabeth Archer. She came through the station several times a week, with her parents or on dates with a regular group of boyfriends, and Chino fell obsessively in love with her.

For Chino, there had been a few girls from the camps, and once, a prostitute from the station wagons that parked in the canebrakes on Saturday nights, but Elizabeth Archer was something different.

She was peppy and blond and she was a songleader at the high school and very popular. Her father owned an established dry cleaning business in town.

Chino found out her last name and where she lived.

Late at night, after closing the station, he would cruise slowly by her parents' brick-veneered house, hoping to catch a glimpse of her. Once, when he slowed way down to watch her necking in the driveway, she recognized his yellow pickup. For the briefest instant, they actually made eye contact in the glow of the streetlight on the corner, and Chino had wanted to die.

But then she began to exchange a few words with him at the station. After she got her driver's license, she began to come through by herself, bringing her parents' car around for gas or to have the tires checked.

During Christmas break, she stopped by the station one night just to say hello. She touched the sleeve of Chino's khaki uniform and she gave him a small white box tied with red ribbon. It held a brushed steel tie clasp and a pair of matching cuff links with pearls. Chino thanked her for them, and after she drove off, he went into the station and asked the owner what they were.

As he lay down on the floor that night, surrounded by the mattresses and the snoring bodies of his roommates, Chino drew the little box out from under his pillow and took a final look inside. He noticed the corner of a small piece of paper peeking out from beneath the satin liner. He withdrew it and read it in the dim light of the forty-watt bulb hanging in the middle of the room. In pencil, she had written her phone number and the words, "Call Me, Dummy!"

Chino did not sleep that night. During the following weeks, he held the station phone a hundred times in his icy hands, but it was almost Easter before he could summon the courage to dial her number. Her younger brother answered the phone and shouted for her.

"Hey, Beck. It's the guy from the Chevron Station."

She came to the phone. He would pick her up Saturday night for movies.

Chino went to a men's clothing store on Main Street in downtown El Centro. He bought himself a striped tie to go with the tie clasp, a pair of narrow black pants, and a long-sleeved white shirt with holes for the cuff links. Also, black shoes and a pair of red-and-yellow argyle socks. He got a short haircut, a flat-top with fenders and a DA, and he bought a jar of heavily perfumed, pink Butch Wax from the barber to make his curly hair stand upright.

At noon Saturday, after work at the ranch, Chino drove to the station and washed the pickup. He installed a shiny chrome ball on the floor shift lever and he put the truck up on the rack and loosened the muffler clamps until he got a good exhaust tone, nice and loud but still legal.

He hurried back to the apartment and found an S.O.S pad. He scrubbed out the black-streaked tub and took a good, long bath, followed by a shot of cologne borrowed from one of the other men. At six o'clock, he shaved twice and brushed his teeth and put on the new clothes, taking a good while to figure out the cuff links and a longer while to get a proper knot in the tie.

He went to the refrigerator and took out a clear plastic box containing a lavender orchid. The huge, turgid flower was stuck into a rubber-capped tube of water and tied with a ribbon and long hat pin, also lavender. Attached to this corsage, which Chino had bought with reckless disregard for the expense, was a gold-bordered card on which he had carefully penned a message in block letters: "To Bethy Archer from your friend always Robert Zúñiga."

Since picking up the corsage Thursday night, Chino had agonized about adding the word "always" to the inscription. He had also worried about the diacritical tilde over the "n" and the accent over the "u" in his last name.

He had made two trips to the stationery store to get more cards. One version did not include his last name at all, but later he reinstated it as a matter of defiant pride in his Mexican origins, which there was no point in trying to hide from Bethy anyway. He had compensated by removing the final "o" from his first name, Roberto, which was the name she knew him by, for he had not yet become "Chino." That nickname would be given to him in another life by the daughter of an unusually big fisherman far to the south.

Chino read the gold-bordered card one last time and went out to the pickup with his plastic box. His headlights pierced a swirling, slowly drifting ground fog as he growled down the two-lane highway and turned off onto the perfectly flat grid of residential streets that formed El Centro.

He parked in front of her house. The joints in the flagstone walkway felt strange through the soles of his new shoes. He checked his fly. The musical chimes of the doorbell rang softly. He caught his left knee trying to buckle. Muffled voices came from deep within the house and then stopped. He waited but the door did not open. He rang the bell again.

At last, the door moved. It was her father, who smiled and said something as he held the screen open and invited Chino into the living room. She was there too, all made up and looking beautiful in a gray, pleated skirt and a white lamb's wool sweater with borders of tiny pearls embroidered at the neck and cuffs. She introduced them.

"Dad, this is Roberto."

They shook hands. Her father said something complementary about his ·
English. They were about to leave when Elizabeth excused herself for a
moment and then returned, smiling brightly.

"Roberto, come. I want you to meet my mom."

She took his arm and led him to the kitchen. Her mother stood at a
counter, washing dishes with her back to them.

"Mom, this is Robert. I've mentioned him."

Her mother did not turn around.

"Mom!"

Chino's hands began to tremble. He felt the floor curving strangely up
all around him, the walls leaning crazily into the room. They went back to
the front door. Her brother was there too. Chino gave Elizabeth the
corsage, after first removing the gold-bordered card. While she pinned the
lavender orchid to her sweater, he crushed the card in the palm of his hand
and dropped it into the pocket of his new black pants.

THAT SUMMER THE owner of the gas station offered Chino a permanent
job as manager and was surprised when he declined it.

"What's the problem, Roberto? Not enough money, eh? Okay, I'll fix
that."

"No, no. Doug, thank you very much for the offer. But… I'm going
away. I'm leaving El Centro."

"Back to México?"

"Hell no."

"Then where?"

Chino stood gazing out through the station's large front window. He
watched the heat waves ripple and blur the cars coming down the
highway.

"I don't know, Doug. Any suggestions?"

The station owner was a former Marine, nearly as wide as he was tall,
who had once lifted the engine block of Chino's pickup in his bare hands
and carried it from one side of the station to the other. He laughed
suddenly and gave Chino a slap on the back that almost knocked him
through the window.

"Hah! Now I get it! Roberto! I wish I was your age! Goddammit, I'd
kiss this place good-bye too! I'd come with you!"

The station owner paid Chino an extra two weeks' wages and the field
manager of the ranch did likewise. Both of them left him with standing

offers to come back any time. Together with his savings, Chino had almost a thousand dollars, plus his pickup. He packed his things, paid his share of the rent to the end of the month, and pulled out onto the highway, heading west towards San Diego.

But as he passed through El Centro, something stopped him. He turned off the highway. For two hours, he drove aimlessly around the familiar blocks south of Main Street, circling closer and closer to the house of Elizabeth Archer. Finally, he drove right past it. Then he parked his pickup across the street and sat in the oven-hot cab, staring into the shadows behind the sheer white curtains. He reached into the glove compartment and took out the little white box and held it for a while without opening it or looking into it.

Then he started the pickup and pulled back onto the highway. But this time he turned south, toward the international border crossing at Mexicali. He drove straight through the middle of Calexico to the quiet, single-lane gate.

The uniformed Mexican guard came out of a kiosk and stopped the yellow pickup. He rested his hand on the door handle and asked Chino where he was going.

"*Adónde vas, amigo?*"

"Mexicali."

The guard took his time looking Chino over, guessing correctly that the young man was coming back from a stay in the U.S. with money and no papers. He lifted the edge of the tarp covering Chino's belongings in the back of the pickup. The tarp was brand new, still creased from being folded in its bag at the surplus store.

"No guns?"

"No, sir. No guns."

The guard walked slowly around the pickup. His toe tapped Chino's almost brand new tires, a gift from the station owner. He stuck his head in the passenger door window and eyed the things on the floor of the truck, smelling dollars. His tongue flicked out, dressing the lower edge of his greasy mustache.

"Maybe we take a look, eh?"

Chino had prepared himself several blocks in advance. He held a ten dollar bill toward the window, rolled so the figure "10" in the corner was clearly visible. The guard grabbed the bill and waved him through with a flourish of the same hand.

Chino had only the vaguest idea of where he was headed, but he knew that even if he had to sleep on the bare ground for the rest of his life, he would never again stand trembling and speechless in the kitchen of a strange house, pretending not to notice while the walls closed in on him.

He drove south through the busy downtown section of Mexicali, then off on the dirt street leading to the neighborhood of his birth. He parked beneath an enormous date palm in front of the old house. It was a low, flat-roofed structure sheathed with weathered gray boards and pieces of sheet metal cut from wrecked cars. Some children were playing in a mud puddle they had made outside the front door. Although he sat for an hour, Chino didn't recognize any of the children nor any of the adults passing in and out of the house, and he knew that none of them would recognize him or even his name.

It had been a very hot day. He started the pickup and found the paved highway going south to the gulf coast fishing village of San Felipe. He drove toward a range of purple mountains, past the last houses and fields, leaving Mexicali behind.

Some time after dark, he crossed the great dry lake bed of Laguna Salada. A few miles later, he decided to turn off onto a lonely dirt road that he assumed would loop west through the rocky valleys all the way to San Felipe. He slowed the truck to a walk in first gear as he hit the deep, sandy washboard that he would follow for the next sixty miles.

He was in the second range of mountains when his radio began loosing contact with the English language stations north of the border. He turned the volume up higher and higher. By midnight he was getting nothing but static, even with the radio turned all the way up. He parked his yellow pickup in the middle of the deserted track and he searched the dial to be sure there were no stations left. Then he spread his tarp on the bed of the truck and he stretched out to sleep, looking up at the big desert stars. He would not hear English spoken again, or speak it himself, for a long time.

CHINO ARRIVED IN the quiet seaside settlement of San Felipe on the evening of his second day in the desert. It had been frighteningly hot. He was very thirsty and desperately low on gas.

He had become lost in a maze of wandering, sandy trails, and he had gotten stuck twice. He had driven most of the way in first gear to avoid damaging his pickup on the rocks and stiff washboard.

Within twenty-four hours of his arrival, Chino knew that he had grossly overestimated the employment opportunities of a fishing village with one semi-official gas station, no farms, perhaps two-hundred fishermen, and about six declared whores. He was at a loss for ideas on how to support himself.

He took to sleeping and sitting on the beach with the other unemployed men, kibitzing with them over the launching of the pangas in the mornings, the weather, the unloading of the fish in the afternoons, and the availability or unavailability of ice for their beer.

Unaccustomed to such idleness, Chino felt awkward among his more practiced companions so he went out of his way to buy them beers and tacos and give them rides in his truck, and before long he considered himself one of them.

But he was not. As an outsider with apparently limitless dollars, he was being closely watched by a small group of fishermen from the mainland who had recently arrived in San Felipe themselves, bringing with them a worldliness foreign to the sleepy Baja California village. One Sunday night, as he walked back to the beach alone from a visit to the baseball field, they took him by surprise in the dark streets at the north end of town. He woke in the morning beside a heap of discarded roof tiles, with a long cut just above his left ear and his money gone.

Chino's pickup key was still in the ignition where he always left it. He tried to report his loss to some officials in town, but that came to nothing since he had no money to get their attention with. In fact, he had no money at all, nothing for food or even gas for the truck. He drove to the beach where he usually slept and he parked the truck permanently, meaning that he rolled up the windows and took the key out of the ignition. As a precaution, he also unscrewed his chrome shift ball and hid it under the seat.

That afternoon he waited on the beach while the pangas came in. He talked to each fisherman in turn, arguing and bargaining until he had struck a deal. By that evening, Roberto Zúñiga, the lean, curly-haired young man from the farms of El Centro, had become a *panguero*, a commercial panga fisherman, albeit one who would work for half pay and who had never in his life touched any fish, dead or living, or set foot in any kind of boat.

Chino's new boss, whose grandfather had been German, was a squat old man, almost black from the sun, with the unusual name of Alejandro Weeghman.

Alejandro spoke very little, and when he did, it was in a hoarse whisper so low it was hard to hear him above the sound of the panga. He lived with his wife and children in a spacious stucco house, thickly covered with bougainvilleas, on a low hill below the ice plant. Usually, Alejandro fished alone around the north end of the bay for turtles or the south end for corvina. Sometimes he went straight outside, twenty miles, to the large rock that stood on the horizon like a white sailboat. There, he fished for corvina, or sierra, or the huge totuava, some weighing over a hundred kilos, that he cut open for their air bladders, which he dried and sold for the Chinese market.

It was a totuava that rescued Chino from pending starvation, for Alejandro had torn a shoulder muscle when one of the long, dark fish twisted just as he was pulling it into the panga, and he needed someone to help him until he healed.

Chino took readily to fishing, which he found much easier and much more interesting than farm work. He enjoyed the long rides out to the island and he was amazed by the beauty of the ever-changing sea and the elaborate wheel of life that it contained.

From the smallest bit of floating jelly to the largest shark, Chino saw that every living thing was locked in a desperate struggle for survival from the moment of its conception, and within a few minutes or even seconds of its weakening, it would be consumed by something else. Yet, even as it died, it became the essential giver of life to another struggling thing and the spectacle continued unabated.

Even the great whales died eventually, and their smelly carcasses, covered with open pink ulcers, were flayed by the birds and torn apart as they drifted, or they sank to the bottom, together with the bodies of lesser fish, their scales and excrement, their spines and tails, and all of it formed a rich ooze of death in the dark abyss.

As they visited Alejandro's regular places in the waters around San Felipe, Chino saw that the life of the sea was not evenly distributed, as he once might have guessed. In fact, most of the sea had little in it. The fish were concentrated where the currents brought the richness of the bottom ooze to the surface. It was in these places—around the islands and points and underwater cliffs—that the sun and nutrients consorted to create the humble, floating creatures that began the cycle anew.

Chino also enjoyed the tranquility of his new employer. He was fascinated by the quiet, patient Alejandro, who endured from day to day, and who accepted with equal temper whatever fortunes or misfortunes the fates dealt him.

As a boy, Alejandro had paddled south with his German-Mexican father in a dugout canoe, all the way to San José del Cabo, looking for possibilities, but they had found none. The father and son had returned to San Felipe, a round trip of over twelve-hundred miles in an open boat. They had built the house and planted the bougainvilleas and neither of them had ever gone anywhere again.

In Alejandro's company, Chino began to feel at ease with himself. He began to feel that he was part of something, not a wanderer as he had been in El Centro, forever suspended between his past and his future like a piece of taffy pulled thin.

In four months, Alejandro's shoulder was healed, but the fishing was good so he kept Chino on the boat, and gradually, without his realizing it, Chino forgot that he had known Elizabeth Archer, and he forgot that he knew English, and the farm boy became a Mexican panguero in heart as well as fact.

Late one September afternoon, Chino and Alejandro had beached the panga with their catch and they were waiting for the truck that would tow their boat, sled-like, above the high tide line for the night, when Alejandro pointed toward some fishermen two-hundred yards to the south.

"Roberto, look! Those must be the cabrones who hit you on the head."

Chino looked down the beach at the group of shrimpers from Guaymas, who had come to San Felipe shortly before he arrived in June. The strangers had kept to themselves while they waited for their ship to come and they were now uncrating a new Evinrude motor and were preparing to mount it on their yellow-and-blue panga.

"How do you know, Alejandro?"

The leather-faced panguero hissed as he looked down the beach with his eyes almost closed.

"They were broke six months ago and they haven't been working. Where do you think they got the money for that motor?"

Chino knew his boss was right. In a town as small and interconnected as San Felipe the list of suspects was short and the shrimpers had been at the top of it anyway. Chino also knew he had no hope of recovering his money. Compared to members of the shrimping cooperative, any bribes, or mordida, he might be able to offer the officials would only be laughed at. If justice was to be dealt, it would have to come from his own hand.

The rust-eaten Army surplus truck arrived and dragged their panga up the beach and they threw their fish through the barn doors of the buyer's truck. Chino spoke as his boss counted their money.

"Listen, Alejandro, can you pay me off tonight?"

Alejandro had been thinking the same thing. But he had not mentioned it. He had come to value Chino's help in the boat. And the price was certainly right. He had never given Chino a raise, even though the novice fisherman well deserved it.

"What are you going to do, Roberto?"

Chino's eyes were on the shrimpers.

"Amigo, it is better if you don't know."

"They are of the cooperativa. No one will believe your story. If you try anything, Roberto, they will put you in jail."

"I know."

"Roberto... this is good-bye, isn't it?"

"Sí, amigo."

Alejandro counted out a full week's wages and gave it to Chino. Then his conscience got the better of him and he impulsively added another week's worth of pesos.

He had a fair idea of what Chino was thinking. The young man was quick and very strong and his quiet manner suggested a certain confidence in these things. But Alejandro doubted that Chino would be able to exact revenge from the shrimpers without waking up beside a trash heap again, or maybe worse.

"Roberto, please tell me what you are going to do."

"I am not sure, amigo."

"There are four of them, Roberto. We could get help. I have friends who would come."

"Thank you, amigo. But it is better if you do not involve yourself."

Chino drove his yellow pickup to Alejandro's place. They filled water bottles and Alejandro gave him a large plastic carboy, half-full of gasoline, and a length of rubber hose to use as a siphon. Alejandro's wife brought out a bag of smoked fish and tortillas. When everything was loaded and tied down Alejandro put his arms around Chino and gave him the abrazo. It was the first time anyone had done it to him. Chino was embarrassed, but hugged Alejandro back.

"Alejandro. Thank you... for everything."

"You learn quickly, Roberto. You are a panguero now. You have become one of us."

"Perhaps, amigo. I think I would like that."

Alejandro pointed toward the sunset. The western peaks climbed above the desert floor in overlapping purple triangles and the evening sky glowed pure yellow and cloudless.

"Roberto, you must not go north or try to cross the border. They will be waiting for you in Mexicali."

"Right."

"Take the road south to Bahía Gonzaga. It is plenty rough, especially after Puertecitos. Take it easy. Use the pick and shovel. Be patient. Unload the truck if you have to. You can make it."

"Right."

"In two or three days, you will come out to the main road at a small dry lake. The ruts are deep and filled with dust, but you can make it. There is a rancho there, Laguna Chapala. They are good people, but do not stop. Avoid the main road. Keep to the side trails."

"Understood."

"It will be hot in the mountains, Roberto. Hotter than anything you have ever felt. Conserve your water. There is danger. If the pickup breaks itself, you will be in real trouble."

"Right."

"Don't buy gas or stop at any ranchos until you are past Loreto. Keep heading south."

"What then?"

"Try the hidden canyons and the side roads to the beaches. There are many places with just a few ranchers or hermits, places where no one will look."

Chino climbed into his pickup. Alejandro reached in through the open window and gripped his arm tightly. He looked into Chino's eyes.

"God rides with you, Roberto."

THE LIGHTS IN the tiendas were just coming on. Chino filled the pickup and carboy with gas and drove down the darkened beach to the camp of the four shrimpers. He backed his truck over the sand until his rear bumper was only a few feet from the stern of their yellow-and-blue panga and he left the engine running and hopped out.

Two of the shrimpers were young, about the same age as Chino. The other two were hardened fishermen with thick hands and tendons working under their dark skin. They all wore new clothes, including new tennis shoes. They had hung the Evinrude on the panga's transom but had not yet tightened the mounting bolts. Chino waved a cheerful greeting.

"Hola, amigos! Wow! What a nice new motor! Mind if I take a look?"

They watched silently as Chino passed through their midst. He patted the cover of the motor with his open hand as if it were the head of a dog.

"Sure wish I had a motor like *this!*"

One of the older shrimpers picked up a large crescent wrench and held it in the shadows behind his body. Chino stood with his hands hanging at his sides, pretending not to notice.

"But you know what happened… ?"

Another shrimper sat on the edge of the panga with his hand on the gunnel where a gaff lay hidden in the dark. Chino pretended not to notice that either.

" …some *pinche cabrones* took my money… "

Chino caught the glint of the wrench swinging in an arc toward his head. He had been waiting for it. He used both hands to seize the shrimper's fingers and clamp them more tightly around the handle of the wrench.

Holding his arms stiff, Chino deflected the blow and swung the wrench, man and all, into the face of the fisherman with the gaff, who fell backwards into the panga and lay gasping.

Still holding the wrench-swinger by his hand, Chino raised his knee twice into the man's groin and grabbed his hair and drove his face down on the gunnel of the panga. There was a dull thump and the man went limp, leaving part of a tooth embedded in the wood. Chino grabbed the seat of his pants and dumped him into the panga with the other shrimper.

He pointed the wrench meaningfully at the two younger men.

"Let's don't be stupid tonight, *muchachos.*"

One of them had an oar. They shifted left and right, looking for an advantage. Chino backed them toward the groans of the two fishermen in the panga. Crouching low, he pointed the wrench at the one with the oar.

"Put it down, now."

The young shrimper didn't yield. Chino gave him one last chance, speaking slowly and deliberately.

"You get it first, amigo."

The shrimper hesitated another moment, then dropped the oar and possibly saved his own life in doing so, for Chino had planned to make a rush at him, duck under the oar, and bring the heavy, fourteen-inch wrench to bear against the side of his head.

Prodding with the wrench, Chino forced the young shrimpers to face the panga. He hobbled their knees with rope and ordered them to put the Evinrude in the bed of his pickup. Then he tied their hands behind their backs and dumped them into the panga with the others.

"Stay quiet, *pendejos*, or you will not be walking for six months. *Comprenden?*"

The two young men nodded, as their companions rolled and moaned in the bottom of the boat. Chino emptied their pockets, taking all their pesos and over two-hundred U.S. dollars. He cut fifty feet from their anchor line, doubled it into a stout cable, and tied one end to the rear bumper of his pickup and the other through the bolt holes in the stern of the panga. As he tightened the final knot, one of the young shrimpers barked nervously.

"Hey! What are you doing?"

Chino turned and smiled.

"Have you ever been to El Centro, amigo?"

"Sure! Lots of times!"

Chino's teeth shined in the dark like a row of luminescent pearls.

"I bet you haven't been there in a panga."

"Hey, you son-of-a-bitch!"

Chino jumped into his pickup and raced the engine above the angry shouts of the shrimpers. He popped the clutch, showering them with sand and throwing them to the bottom of the panga as the truck jerked the boat and began dragging it backwards up the beach.

Chino floorboarded the pickup and his tires smoked and churned.

When he reached the hard-packed dirt of the beachfront street his tires let out a shriek and the pickup shot forward with the panga close behind. Chino flashed his headlights and waved as he passed the shacks of the amazed pangueros and the other men, women and children who were strolling on the beach or bedding down for the night.

The street was dead flat along the beach. The panga skimmed over the hard dirt in a smooth skittering motion, swaying just a little from side to side with hardly a bounce, even though Chino was going more than fifty miles-per-hour as he approached the sharp left turn at the end.

Just before the turn, though, Chino's pickup hit a section of pavement bridging a small tidal stream that ran out from a gully at the north end of the beach, where boats were pulled up for repairs.

The edge of the concrete slab was about two inches higher than the road surface, no problem for the pickup's rubber tires. But when the panga hit it backwards at about forty miles-per-hour there was a loud bang and

Chino caught an eye-level glimpse of the boat in his rear view mirror. It dropped out of sight again with its horrified occupants still in it.

Later, it was determined that the concrete had sheared off the lower three inches of the panga's transom and had continued on through the hull, neatly removing a two-foot-wide swath of the bottom. It was an interesting effect no one had seen before.

Chino barely made the left turn at the end of the road, almost losing the panga against a shack, and he swerved off onto the dusty streets leading up the hill to Alejandro's house. The shrimpers, now able to see the dirt passing beneath them, were engulfed in a storm cloud of grit and gravel as their boat began to disintegrate.

Chino honked his horn as he neared Alejandro's place. But he needn't have. Against Chino's wishes, Alejandro had assembled several friends who owed him favors, and they were standing in front of the house, debating on how best to assist Chino in the coming fight, when the pickup-panga combo went flying by.

Taken aback by the strange sight, Alejandro and his friends watched as the pickup whipped around at the end of the street and came back for another pass. Then they recognized what was left of the yellow-and-blue panga and they saw the stricken, bloody faces of the shrimpers, staring helplessly over the gunnels.

Alejandro's pangueros ran into the street and shouted and threw their hats into the dust-filled night as Chino floorboarded the pickup again and fishtailed down the hill.

Chino drove straight through the center of San Felipe, to the cheers of the children and the wonderment of their parents, and he circled the empty police station twice before speeding north towards the border with the panga still behind him.

Two miles out of town, Chino stopped and cut the rope, leaving the shrimpers and the remains of the panga to be found in the morning. He continued north on the highway to Mexicali for another five miles, and then switched off his headlights and turned onto a darkened, dirt side road.

He doubled back all night, skirting around San Felipe and somehow getting past the section near Puertecitos in the dark, and by first light of morning, he was all alone in the wilderness.

The heat of the interior mountains was all that Alejandro had promised and more. The nights, if anything, seemed worse than the days. Hour by hour, Chino would lie on the hot metal bed of his pickup, swooning in a purgatory of fatigue, pressing his eyes closed to force the sleep that refused to come. Finally, the silhouetted peaks would appear in the starry-blue morning sky and he would resume his southward journey.

The road in many places was just a pair of tire tracks squeezing between boulders and cactus. Sometimes it disappeared over shield-like stretches of solid rock and Chino would get out and walk to make sure it continued on the other side.

He found the rutted, crackled mud of the Chapala dry lake and what he assumed was the main dirt road south. Despite Alejandro's warnings, Chino feared to go farther without replenishing his water supply. He stopped at the small cattle rancho at the eastern edge of the lake bed, near two big trees, and he asked the family who lived there to fill his bottles with cloudy brown water from their well.

During Chino's afternoon at the rancho, not a single vehicle emerged from the mirages and dust devils hovering over the dry lake. He decided to risk the main road south. He passed through the scattered mining settlement of El Arco, and a day later he discovered the beautiful palm covered oasis surrounding the old mission village of San Ignacio. He stayed two nights, concealing himself near a shady pool outside the village.

The main road went directly east from San Ignacio and Chino followed it to the top of a mountain pass that offered a splendid view of a group of beautiful volcanic cones, and beyond them, the blue Sea of Cortez.

The road descended a very steep, almost impossible arroyo and came down to the shore. There, Chino caught sight of the ugly, blackened buildings, the slag heaps, and the ocher smoke rising from the smelter of El Boleo, the French mines of Santa Rosalia. Repulsed by the size and malignant aspect of the town, and fearful that there might be police on the lookout for a stranger with a stolen Evinrude, Chino pushed his yellow pickup back into the mountains, hoping to find a way around.

But all the trails ended in blind arroyos and Chino was forced to turn back to the palm shaded village of San Ignacio. He broke a pickup spring while crossing a rocky streambed and an old woman, leading a burro almost invisible under a load of fagots, gave him directions to a house where she said a blacksmith would be able to help him.

Chino was amazed to discover not only a blacksmith but a complete mechanic's shop run by an old man and his son. They had scavenged dozens of leaf springs from the wrecks of the desert and they kept them categorized by length against a sunbaked adobe wall, like pickets on a fence. From their collection they quickly found a pair that were an almost perfect fit. With skill, they fabricated new brackets and shackles of scrap steel and in less than three hours the family had fed Chino and sent him on his way. They refused to accept payment for their hospitality or labor and Chino wondered how they stayed in business.

Immediately upon leaving the village, Chino discovered that his new springs handled the rocks and boulders much better than his old ones. He found a very rough trail leading southwest and he followed it all the way to the Pacific Coast. He skirted a series of windy, mangrove-lined lagoons and continued south for six more days, eventually ending up in the very remote tropical valley surrounding the abandoned mission of La Purísima.

Here, Chino ran out of gas, water, and smoked fish almost simultaneously. He was forced to go into the village of San Isidro for supplies, his first contact with anyone since the family of the friendly mechanics of San Ignacio, a hundred and fifty very difficult miles to the north.

The people of the La Purísima valley spoke an accented Spanish and had little contact with the outside. Chino was able to fill Alejandro's plastic carboy by siphoning a little gas from nearly every pickup and car in the village. He paid dearly for the gas, but he was able to buy a tall stack of tortillas and a burlap bag of dried fish and beef jerky sticks for almost nothing. To this, he added a good supply of mangos, avocados, and some tropical fruits he had not seen before.

From La Purísima, Chino pushed his yellow Chevy pickup eastward over the rocky spine of the Baja peninsula and he encountered the roughest roads yet. He passed windrows of stones lining both sides of the old trail and he wondered who, in this empty wilderness, would have devoted so many years of his life to making a road that led from nowhere to nowhere else.

Without knowing it, he passed one night within a few yards of the old mission of San José de Comondú. Then he descended the steep eastern escarpment of the Sierra de la Giganta mountain range, avoiding the ranchos, working constantly with the pick and shovel, marveling at the multicolored layers of rock that climbed to the sky all around him. Finally, he reached the crystalline blue Sea of Cortez at the mission town of Loreto. He filled his carboy with gas and bought fresh supplies and he began to pick his way south again down the dusty, bumpy roads.

But he had gone less than fifty miles when his engine screeched and seized so suddenly that his rear tires locked up and nearly turned his pickup over. He ended up shaken but unhurt in a boulder-lined ditch.

The pickup's hood had come off and a fender was pushed up. Its frame was twisted badly. It sat in the ditch like a wounded lion with one paw raised in the air. Chino crawled underneath to take a look. The oil pan had been cracked in the descent of the Sierra de la Giganta and the engine had slowly run itself dry.

Chino climbed up to the road and looked in both directions for help that he knew would not be there. He had seen no one going in either direction since leaving Loreto. Working against the rocks and the awkward slope, he wrestled the Evinrude and his other things up to the road and he settled down in the shade of his tarp to wait for someone to come along.

No one came that afternoon or during the night, but about nine o'clock the next morning Chino heard the sound of a truck approaching. It swung into view, a battered five-ton truck with a hand-painted sign over the cab that said *Mariscos Tres Estrellas,* "Three Star Sea Foods." Above the words were some crudely painted pictures of a smiling octopus, a jumping marlin, and some creatures that were unmistakably marine in origin but otherwise unrecognizable. It was a fish buyer's truck making the rounds.

The truck stopped and the driver looked out over Chino's head, sizing up the salvage value of the wreck. He took note of the California license plates and new tires.

"What happened?"

"The motor is no good. I need a ride."

"Where are you going?"

"La Paz."

The fish buyer pointed his thumb at the road behind his truck.

"La Paz is back there. You're headed in the wrong direction."

"Really? Where does this road go?"

"Just a stinking fish camp."

"Fine! What is it called?"

The buyer jumped out and unlocked the rear doors of his truck. Stepping around a puddle of melted ice and fish juice, he tilted his head down the narrow dirt track in the direction Chino had been driving.

"Agua Amargosa."

They opened the back doors and spread Chino's tarp on a pile of shaved ice and fish reaching halfway to the roof.

In addition to ice and fresh fish, the truck was full of salted shark, groceries, magazines, clothes, gasoline and fresh water, and a brand-new American wheelbarrow someone had probably special ordered. Besides handling seafood, the fish buyer did business as a *falluquero*, an itinerant trader who visited the remote villages with essential supplies.

They lifted the heavy Evinrude and the rest of Chino's things into the truck. When they were done, the buyer got out his tools and started down to the pickup. Chino asked him what he was doing.

"We need to get the tires and battery."

"Why?"

"They won't be here when we get back."

They put the tires and battery into the truck. Chino also took his keys and chrome shift ball. They rolled up the windows and locked the doors.

As Chino hopped on the running board of the fish truck, the buyer went back to the pickup one last time. He removed the license plates from the front and rear bumpers. Then he used the palm of his hand to write a row of twelve-inch high letters in the dust on the pickup's side, "3 ESTRELLAS, HNOS. REYNAGA, LA PAZ."

It began to occur to Chino that he no longer owned a pickup.

"What is that for?"

The fish buyer shrugged.

"Maybe nobody will touch it."

Nothing in his previous life had prepared Chino for the beauty of the final seventeen miles into Caleta Agua Amargosa. Perched high on the fish truck's stiff, bouncing bench seat, Chino marveled as the rocks became more colorful with each passing minute. The tops of the cliffs were lined with patches of vegetation that looked like tufts of bright green moss. Between the cliffs, the intense blue sky was heaped with mounds of perfect cumulus clouds.

The road wound through a forest of tall cactus for eight miles. Then it climbed a long slope to a gate-like gap in the rocky crest overlooking the coast. When they topped the final ridge Chino could see almost straight down, a thousand feet, into the transparent Sea of Cortez. The view literally took his breath away.

"God! Stop! Stop the truck!"

The fish buyer slammed on the brakes and braced himself for the hidden washout, the boulder on the road, or the falling rock he assumed Chino had spotted. But there was nothing. Gripping the wheel, he turned to his passenger with a confused, anxious look.

"What!?"

Chino was already out of the truck. He went to the edge of the cliff and looked down.

The white crescent beach was partly hidden under an almost solid layer of palms, and there were houses nestled in the shade. There were fences running here and there, women and children at the edge of the water, and seven pangas pulled up above the high tide line.

Halfway to the horizon, beyond a row of four small islets, two more pangas sped landward, leaving V-shaped wakes behind. Every feature of the sea bottom was clearly visible. Even the shadows of the pangas could be seen scurrying over the reefs as the two boats cut inside the outermost islet, side-by-side, and ran towards shore.

Chino stood transfixed by the blue world spread below him. He began to notice smaller details. Just barely discernible as black specks moving above the surface of the water, hundreds, no, thousands of sea birds, wheeled and turned in dense flocks. Frigates and gulls and pelicans and other kinds cruised back and forth, sending their shadows down to race among the reefs.

There were differences in the color of the water itself. It was light turquoise where the bottom was sandy, especially near the beach. The lighter areas extended out toward the islands in long milky swirls, gradually darkening to a rich ultramarine, and everywhere, mottled red-blue patches showed where the reefs lay.

Finally, Chino saw that some of the darker patches were moving and there were shadows moving under them, slowly, along the bottom. They were not reefs, but schools of bait fish and the predators, the jacks and sierra and barracuda, that chased them. The schools of fish were moving everywhere in the caleta, swirling about each other in a chaotic ballet. The sea here was full of life, fuller than Chino had ever imagined anything could be, and he wondered what his friend, the ever-patient Alejandro Weeghman, might say if for just a moment he too could see through the eye of God.

The brilliant sun pressed down on Chino, on the road, on the truck, on the sea below him, flattening him to nothingness, and the hot breeze rising up the cliffs buffeted him, tugged at his hair and shirt, beckoned him to come out of himself, to leave himself behind and come down to rest beneath the shady palms.

As he gazed down at the village and the perfect sea, Chino began to feel that he knew this place. He could imagine the faces of the people down there, the timbre of their voices. It seemed he was waking from a long dream he had never been able to remember before, and he covered his face with his hands and fell to his knees at the edge of the cliff.

"Listen! What is it? What do you see?"

The fish buyer had gotten out of the truck and was standing beside Chino, looking all around, wondering what the problem was with his odd passenger. He thought that perhaps Chino had seen a vision, perhaps of The Virgin of Guadalupe, and that he had suddenly been overwhelmed by an urge to kneel and pray.

Chino recovered himself and rose quickly to his feet.

"It is only that I have never seen anything so... so beautiful as this place."

"Beautiful? It is just hot, amigo. Come on! I need to get going."

"Sí. Sí. Sorry."

They started down the cliff in compound low gear. The road narrowed to a single lane and dropped dangerously down a series of hairpin turns just wide enough to let them pass. The village disappeared beneath the sheer overhangs and then reappeared farther down.

As they crept down the cliff, backing up when necessary on the sharpest switchbacks, Chino saw that the houses were very poor, just shacks and lean-tos. There were no streets, or lights, or other physical improvements. Goats and chickens ran free. The fences he had seen from higher up guarded tiny vegetable gardens no bigger than a panga.

"What did you say the name of this place is?"

"Agua Amargosa."

"It is just a fish camp?"

"That's it. The road ends at the beach. I'm about the only one who comes here."

"And who lives here?"

"Maybe two dozen pangueros. I don't know. They come and go. Some of them have their families here. There's no water. No cooperativa. They're so poor they can't even afford nets. I tell you, amigo, I wouldn't come here myself, except they buy supplies and water from me. I make more off the tee-shirts and *Playboys* than the stinking fish."

"And how is the fishing?"

The buyer gave Chino a look.

"They have never used nets here. For a panguero with a hook and line, it is the best fishing left in Baja California, better than La Paz and Loreto used to be, better than Mulegé."

"But they are poor here?"

"They need nets and bigger pangas. They need an ice plant and a proper fish house. But the government money will never come as long as there is no water and the road is so bad. There is even one poor bastard here who still fishes with no motor. He lives off his Indian brother-in-law."

Chino was quiet as the truck completed the final, bone-jarring bend off the cliff and pulled onto the smooth sand. From his open window, Chino surveyed the arroyo behind the village, with its floor of palm trees and its rocky walls, stepping back in multicolored layers, blending with the cliffs and mountains above. The truck rattled through the village and stopped at the small ice shed on the beach. They hopped out and looked around but saw nobody. Chino spoke as they opened the rear doors of the truck.

"What's his name?"

"Who?"

"The panguero you mentioned. The poor bastard with no motor."

"Him? He's... ah... Bundo... Abundio Rodríguez. You can't miss him. He's *real* big. Everyone calls him Bundo."

"And where does he live?"

The buyer pointed toward a small shack nearly hidden in the trees. It was one of the poorest shacks in the village. Behind it, a very short, very dark woman was chopping wood, and a younger woman was helping her gather sticks and bring them to the front. The fish buyer poked a finger in the direction of the house.

"Over there. That's his wife and daughter."

Chino watched them work. Even from this distance, he could tell the young woman was tall and elegantly proportioned. She moved with a kind of grace he had never seen in El Centro or Mexicali.

"What's *her* name?"

"María Guadalupe. She's a beauty, but she's only twelve, and you'd better watch it. Her mother. Socorro. She's an old Indian witch who'll cut your liver out."

With the fish buyer's help, Chino lowered the freezing cold Evinrude and his other things to the ground beside the truck. He shook the buyer's hand.

"Listen. Thanks for the ride."

"You staying here?"

"Yes."

"What about your pickup?"

Chino reached into his pocket. He handed some bright, shiny objects to the buyer. A chrome shift ball and the keys to the wrecked Chevy.

"It's no good to me now. You keep the tires and battery. Look in the glove compartment. There's a little white box. It is all yours, amigo."

Chino took his California license plates and sent them spinning out over the caleta. As some men approached to open the ice shed, he came back to the buyer and smiled.

"Amigo, do me a favor. Don't tell anyone you brought me in here for a while."

Then Chino left the dripping cold Evinrude on the sand and he walked up through the trees, heading straight for the palm-thatched house of Abundio and Socorro Rodríguez.

Now, as he followed Abundio up the rocky trail to Fra Nacho's place, Chino knew that the great wheel of life was moving again. The part of his life that began with his arrival on the fish truck, seven years before, was coming to an end, had in fact already ended.

If nothing else, he and María had seen to that the previous night.

But there was more to it than the simple indulgence of two people in the dust, for that was written in dust, and that would end, some day soon enough, in dust. No. There was more to it. More than a freak spring rain. More than a simple decline in the number of cabrilla within range of their pangas.

After seven years of lying fallow, beneath its cloak of time, the wheel of life was moving again, and where it would take them Chino did not know. He feared for himself, and for Abundio and Socorro, and Ramón, and most of all for the beautiful María Guadalupe Rodríguez, whom he loved in a way he could not explain.

Where did such strength of feeling come from? Chino did not know, but he knew that he loved María and he knew that he had loved her from the moment he first saw her, chopping wood behind the house. From that first day, Chino had known María was intended for him, that she would someday entrust herself to him, and this distant, sustaining love for a thing of such perfect beauty had been a salvation, for it had cooled the fire of self-loathing within him.

It was obvious that María took her quickness from her mother, for Socorro easily had the sharpest mind of anyone Chino knew, sharper even than Fra Nacho's, or in fact, María's.

And from her father, the great, sweaty Tecolote, María had acquired the strength to follow her life without complaint and the courage to smile at whatever pies might hit her in the face along the way.

And what of that incredible face? Not to mention the rest of her. The long, clean limbs, her natural grace. Her perfectly flat stomach and her tight little rear. These things did not come from her mother's Indian blood, and they certainly could not have come from Abundio's! As he followed his partner's broad back up the arroyo, Chino could only conclude that the unlikely miracle of María had come to him as an unearned gift, straight from God, and he resolved to love her as fully and as long as possible.

PABLO SANTOS AND several other pangueros were waiting for them in the shade of Fra Nacho's porch. There were eight of them in all, in addition to Fra Nacho, who reclined on his cot as usual.

Abundio and Chino seated themselves on five-gallon oil drums. They listened as Pablo and the others debated the idea of clearing the road by hand. Pablo was doing most of the talking.

" ...so I say, we should at least try. How do we *know* it is impossible unless we try."

Chino handed Fra Nacho the bag containing Socorro's burritos. Fra Nacho peeked inside and rolled his eyes silently. As they listened quietly to the pros and cons, it seemed that Pablo was the only one in favor of trying to clear the road. The other men were unanimous in their objections.

"I have seen the rocks!"

"There is no way we can clear them."

"That's right!"

"The rocks are big and loose. It is much too dangerous."

"It can't be done without a *Caterpillar*."

"Why don't they bring equipment up from La Paz? It's their responsibility to keep the road open."

"They don't give a damn about us!"

Pablo stood and waved his hands through the busy cloud of flies that always hovered beneath Fra Nacho's porch roof.

"All right! Listen! *I'm* not giving up! Tomorrow morning, *I'm* going up there! And anyone who wants to can join me!"

Pablo pointed a finger at the two partners.

"How about you, Bundo? And you, Chino. Are you two willing to do something? Or are you just going to sit on your butts like the rest of these guys?"

Pablo stared down at Abundio with his arms folded across his chest.

"Well... what do you say, Bundo?"

Abundio was always uncomfortable when called upon to make a statement in the presence of others. He cleared his throat and waited for Chino to say something, but Chino's mind seemed to be somewhere else. After an awkward silence, Abundio finally spoke, but he directed his comments to Chino rather than Pablo.

"Ah... well, we don't know, do we, Chino? We haven't been up as far as the rockslide. Have we, Chino?"

Disappointed, Pablo turned to Fra Nacho, who lay, propped up on one elbow, on his cot.

"What do *you* think, Nacho?"

Fra Nacho's lips whistled silently and his fingers tapped on the edge of his cot to the rhythm of something only he could hear. He stilled his hand and addressed the group as a whole.

"This much is clear. You must immediately either fix the road or leave the caleta. If you stay any longer, you will be broke and without options."

Pablo Santos paced back and forth, speaking first to one person, then another.

"Nacho is right! We must either do something or leave! Right now! I am willing to make the decision! We go up there tomorrow morning! I'll see all of you at six!"

Pablo turned on his heel and left. The other men continued the argument as though he were still present.

"It's too dangerous!"

"Forget it!"

"Right! Why should we risk our necks?"

"Pablo you're crazy. You just want to act like a *jefe*."

The meeting broke up with no clear resolution of its agenda. As the fishermen drifted away from the porch, still shaking their heads and arguing, Fra Nacho gestured to Abundio.

"Say, Bundo. Could you stay a minute? I need some rattlesnakes."

"Sure, Nacho."

Chino rose to go, winking at Fra Nacho and wishing him a pleasant lunch.

Fra Nacho waited until they were alone.

"Listen, Bundo, I need to talk to you."

Abundio was mildly surprised by the old man's request for rattlesnakes. The serpents' severed heads were dried and ground into a rough powder said to be useful for headaches and nervous disorders of all types, but Nacho hadn't shown much interest in the curandero trade for some time and Abundio thought he had given it up.

Actually, it was Socorro who had "taken the fun out of being a curandero," as Nacho referred to the dangerous and painful episode of his life, a decade before, when his partial right foot had become infected and had threatened to kill him. As the leg swelled and blackened all the way to the knee he had limped over the hillsides searching for the yellow flowered stalks with the ruffled, thorny leaves that he hoped would stop the spreading putrefaction of his flesh.

But he could not find the plant he needed and Socorro had lost patience with his methods. She had literally pounded her hard little fist on the top of his head, demanding that he allow himself to be taken to the clinic in La Paz, or stop whining and lie down to die, but goddammit, cut out the useless bullshit in between.

Fra Nacho was by then nearly lost in a haze of fever and pain but he had summoned the presence of mind to fend off his Indian tormentor and remind her that she, of all people, should understand his faith in the wisdom that far antedated man's dependence on pills and needles.

In the end, his heart had begun to fail and the leg had been taken off just in time to save his life, not at the clinica in La Paz but by kerosene lantern light on the table of the Rodríguez house, and his savior had been none other than Socorro herself, assisted by a tearful but brave, nine-year-old María. None of the others had possessed the stomach for the hideous work.

With only the crudest tools, half a bottle of tequila, and the hot fire of the cooking barrel, Socorro had done a credible job and Fra Nacho had survived once again, albeit after a bout of fever that lasted another month.

Afterwards, Fra Nacho loved to claim that his leg had been bitten off by a female crocodile and he often complained to Socorro that she had left him with an unattractive stump, ruining his opportunities for satisfactory relations with the opposite sex. To this, Socorro would retort that she should have taken off his worthless balls for good measure and she would offer to finish the job whenever he liked, and the two of them would laugh and laugh, like a pair of witches over a bubbling cauldron.

In truth, Abundio knew that his dark-skinned Indian wife valued Fra Nacho's company as much as his own, and he too felt a sort of protective loyalty toward the old man, as well as gratitude for the mentoring he had given María. Socorro had never attended school and Abundio had gone no farther than fourth grade. The Rodríguezes were well aware that their clever daughter's future owed much to her afternoons with the demanding but ever-patient tutor she had grown up calling "*tío*," or uncle.

So, if it was rattlesnakes Fra Nacho wanted, Abundio was happy to provide them, even though he had not hunted snakes in the arroyo for years.

"No problem, Nacho. I can get Joselito to help. How many snakes would you like?"

"None."

In his mind, Abundio had already decided that a concerted, early evening effort by himself, Joselito Medina, and possibly Chino, would probably net them two or three rattlesnakes before it got too dark to see. It would be useless to hunt for them any earlier since they would be hiding from the heat of the sun.

"Would twenty be enough?"

"I said none, Bundo. I don't need any snakes."

"Then... why hunt for them?"

"Actually, I just wanted to talk to you, Bundo."

"Ah... of course."

Abundio used the outside of his foot to flip a milk crate over and push it close to Fra Nacho's cot. The crate made a loud cracking sound as Abundio settled on it.

Fra Nacho raised his hand in a gesture that looked as if he were holding an invisible pebble between his thumb and first finger, the Mexican sign to be patient for just a second.

He cleared his throat and began a little speech as he brought his record player out from under his cot and put a disk on.

"Old friend, you have heard this music before. But *por favor*, listen to it one more time. It is by the great Russian composer, Peter Tchaikovsky, who died when I was a young boy. It is called his Piano Concerto Number One in B-Flat Minor. He was about thirty-five, I think, roughly in the middle of his creative life, when he wrote it."

Abundio, like everyone who came to sit under Fra Nacho's porch roof, was very familiar with the romantic, soaring chords of the Tchaikovsky, and like everyone else, he knew Fra Nacho would either turn the music

off after the first few minutes, or move the needle back to the beginning
and play the opening measures again and again.

As the rich harmonies floated through the hot, still air of the arroyo,
Fra Nacho looked earnestly into the big fisherman's eyes.

"Abundio, what do you see?"

"Well... I see the record turning. I see you... "

"No, no! Close your eyes. Listen to the music and tell me what you see
in your mind."

"Ah... "

Abundio closed his eyes and listened intently. Fra Nacho stopped the
record and replayed it. On the third playing, the remembrance of a day,
a time, a moment of the past, came to Abundio. He wasn't sure if the
vision was his or not, but it was clear, quite clear.

"I see... the water. A panga, running fast. Toward the morning sun."

"Yes! That's it, Bundo! What else?"

"There is a long swell on the water, very smooth. It is glassy smooth.
The boat runs over each swell powerfully and smoothly... "

" ...and beautifully?"

"Yes, it is very beautiful. Thank you, Nacho. I think I understand."

Now, for the first time, Fra Nacho let the music continue past the
opening section. The two men listened as the concerto's lush imagery
faltered and made an awkward transition into a series of light, plinking
folk melodies.

"What do you see now, Bundo?"

"Nothing."

"Nothing at all?"

"Well... people walking, or perhaps dancing?"

"In a grand ballroom?"

"No. Nothing like that. Just a few people. Outside. Just simple people,
like us."

Fra Nacho stopped the music and tucked the machine beneath his cot.

"It stays like that, Bundo. All the way to the end. The rest is nothing
but trivial tunes and folk dancing."

"But Nacho, why would Señor Tchaikovsky begin his concerto so
beautifully and then ruin it with stupidities?"

"I don't know. It seems unforgivable, doesn't it? That he would first
make us weep and then abandon us. That he would breathe life into us,
arouse our hopes and passions, and then cut us off without an

explanation. Such brilliance! Such promise! All for nothing!"

"Do you suppose Señor Tchaikovsky just made a mistake?"

"Perhaps. He was a great artist and I am sure he thought he knew what he was doing. Nevertheless, it cannot be denied that the result is a disappointment, at least for the two of us."

"But how could a great artist make such a mistake?"

"Perhaps it is not a mistake, but a masterpiece beyond our understanding. We can never know for sure."

Abundio settled deeper into his milk crate. He gazed over the palms covering the floor of the arroyo. High above, a pair of hawks circled in the currents of heated air rising up the cliffs. He knew Fra Nacho had something important to say.

"Ignacio. What is it?"

"I had a serious talk with María last night."

"And?"

"She asks your permission to return to the caleta."

"But she is already here."

"She means permanently. She wishes to leave the profesora."

Abundio squeezed his big hands together and shook his head from side to side. His fragile dream, that María would make a successful life for herself, had helped sustain him since the rains of the previous March, and Fra Nacho had just driven an iron harpoon into it.

"But Nacho! You know better than anyone! There is *nothing* for María here!"

"She wants only to take her chances with the rest of us."

"María is special. You have said so yourself!"

Fra Nacho nodded.

"Yes. She learns so effortlessly. And the night Socorro cut my leg off, María stayed, even as I cursed her and tried to break the cloths that held me. She is a wonder."

"Ah… "

Abundio's sigh became a long groan. He was not really surprised, for he knew that his daughter and wife were as similar in their thoughts as they were different in appearance, and he knew that Socorro had little use for the insincerity and material trinkets that found their way down the cliff road. He supposed that, despite his dreams for her, María had always held those same sentiments in her heart of hearts.

"She shows such promise."

"Perhaps it is best to be satisfied with the miracle of herself, as she was originally conceived, and not try to stretch her, farther and farther, until she becomes something weak and meaningless."

Abundio clasped his hands above his head. His legs ached powerfully from the pounding they had taken in the soccer match. As he rocked back and forth, stretching his bulky muscles, he noticed that the milk crate under him was bulging at the sides and making cracking, splitting sounds, threatening to collapse from the weight bearing down on it.

Then, Abundio looked at the record player, wrapped in its dusty plastic bag, and he stood and nodded to his old friend, who had lived alone among these rocks for as long as he could remember.

"Weak and meaningless… like the second part of Señor Tchaikovsky's piano concerto."

"Yes."

ABUNDIO STRODE QUICKLY down the arroyo, ignoring the complaints from his knees and calves. As his feet kicked up divots of sand behind him, he formulated one plan after another and discarded each in turn.

María's decision to leave the profesora had brought their situation to a crisis, for Abundio loved his daughter, future or no future, and he felt he must see to it that she had a proper life.

But how? The days were gone when he could simply hop into his panga and row away from his problems, trusting fate to provide an answer, or at least a different set of problems. Abundio had asked much of his body during his forty-two years and the mere thought of pulling across the open sea again set his deeply grooved joints to aching.

Besides, there was no place to row to anymore. And why row, anyway? They had two Evinrudes, hadn't they? Plus Ramón's. Besides, nobody rows anymore, anyway...

Around and around Abundio's thoughts went, and the conundrum always came circling back like a persistent mosquito.

In a few more weeks at most their money would be gone. Abundio doubted his wife would really want to remain behind once all the others had left. Certainly, she would never permit María to languish as she herself had on Isla Coronado. Nor, Abundio supposed, would she permit Fra Nacho to remain behind.

No. Once their money ran out, Socorro would admit defeat and they would surely cross the reef of Agua Amargosa for the last time.

Abundio imagined they would load what they could into the panga and run it to the outskirts of La Paz or Loreto. There, they would sell their motors and build a shack for themselves among the other poor families. He and Chino would beg work, sweeping or carrying somewhere. Socorro and María would compete with the other women for wood and whatever else might be scavenged from the beaches and trash heaps. Abundio knew the probable outcome of that chain of events. They would descend gradually into the insensitive melancholy of hopelessness. Eventually, they would forsake each other and themselves as well, each seeking his own escape, regardless of the cost. At some point, the family that had created itself from nothing would return to the nothingness from which it had come.

"No... "

The word swelled in Abundio's belly. He drew in a deep breath and clenched his fists, and he tried to send it echoing up the cliffs. But his voice was a quavering, half-choked croak.

"No... no... "

ABUNDIO FOUND THE house deserted. Socorro's net bag for dirty laundry was gone from its peg. Her five-gallon bucket and bar of yellow soap were also missing. She had probably gone to do her washing at the well, which was shaded at midday by a rock overhang projecting from the south wall of the arroyo.

Abundio skirted around the back of Pablo Santos' pink house, heading for a path that would take him through the middle of the village and up to the well.

One-by-one, the houses of Agua Amargosa had been built on the level ground at the mouth of the arroyo, despite Fra Nacho's warnings about the flash floods he had seen in the days before the road was reopened.

Abundio, too, thought he could remember a summer, many years before, when he had paddled into the caleta with his father to find a swath of palm trees missing and a new curve on the beach made of gravel carried from far back in the mountains.

But the best launching area for the pangas was in the middle of the caleta. The beach at the north end was soft and difficult to reach because of the sand dunes, and the south end was too steep and blocked by rockslides and boulders. In the middle, the sand was coarse and firm, with just the right slope into a rock-free bottom. And the shade of the palms was deepest and coolest here and the trees grew right up to the water's edge. Here, the land was also fairly level and free of underbrush.

So it was here that the village of Agua Amargosa had been built. The only structures apart from it were Chino's shack, way off by itself in the sand dunes, and Fra Nacho's, perched on the rocky slopes a short distance up the arroyo.

There had not been a full *chubasco*, or summer hurricane, in this part of the coast for several decades. In fact, during the fourteen seasons that Abundio and Socorro had lived in the caleta, there had been only one storm strong enough to cause a flashflood, the one of the previous March, and the damage to the village had been minor. It had amounted to nothing more serious than the new gully through its middle and even that had missed all the houses.

BEHIND PABLO SANTOS' bright pink house, Abundio threaded his way through an accumulation of vehicle parts scattered under the trees. In the middle of this junk sat the bare chassis of a pickup with a kitchen chair wired on top of it. Grass grew up through the truck's rusty metal skeleton, partially hiding it from view.

Pablo's was the only working vehicle in the village. Originally a 1949 Ford, the pickup had gradually lost its identity over the years as Pablo extended its life with parts from a number of cars, trucks, and even boats. He had also cut away most of the rusted body, piece-by-piece, so that in its current avatar the Ford consisted of little more than a drivetrain, a naked backbone, and a steering column.

To provide extra flotation on soft beach sand, Pablo had salvaged four big truck tires, and he had wired these on top of his pickup's originals. Pablo could drive his lightweight, stripped down creation anywhere in the caleta, even over the sand dunes, or a considerable distance into the water at low tide.

But in truth, there was nowhere much to go and Pablo's pickup usually remained parked in its place next to the outhouse, except when it was needed to carry a large fish to the ice shed or when a panga had to be dragged off the beach for some reason.

Abundio left the skeletal truck slumbering in the dappled light beneath the palms and he bore slightly to his left to pass by the deserted house of his brother-in-law, Ramón Ochoa.

Ramón's light blue house was big and solidly built of adobes and boards. Although the front porch was thatched, the house itself boasted a roof of corrugated sheet metal that eliminated the irritation of insects dropping from the ceiling. In front, bright red geraniums and purple bougainvillea mingled with a stand of cactus, nearly hiding the house from view. A row of yucca trunks planted in the ground had sprouted leaves to form a tight, hedge-like fence.

The house was stripped bare to the walls.

Needing space in the panga for basic necessities and seven children, Ramón and his wife had left behind most of their belongings during the move to Las Ramalitas. But week by week Chino had run everything north, including five of their sixteen goats. Like most of the dwellings in the caleta, Ramón's house now stood empty except for the chickens that wandered in and out looking for scraps that were no longer there.

Abundio glanced in the open doorway and noted that everything appeared to be in order. Socorro had come every few days to bring a gallon of well water for the flowers. Aside from that, there was really nothing else to be done.

Abundio turned sharply to his left, following an overgrown, little-used trail that went straight to the southern wall of the arroyo. As he pushed through the tall bushes surrounding the old well, he caught sight of Socorro's bright red ribbon fluttering up and down among the twigs like a curious bird. She was in the narrow band of shade beneath the cliff, on her knees at the ring of stones, elbows locked, throwing her weight into her work with a rhythmic kneading motion.

Abundio sat near her and stretched his aching legs on the sand. The air was hot and close and it vibrated with the steady hum of a panga running somewhere on the caleta. A dragonfly, slim and metallic, darted in and touched the stagnant green water in the basin of stones.

Socorro had pushed her skirt above her knees. She worked steadily, dipping the clothes and rubbing them on the stones with a little soap, paying no attention to the sweat that ran down her face and dropped off her nose and chin. As she finished each piece, she wrung it out and spread it to dry on a black boulder made almost too hot to touch by the noontime sun.

Margarita Santos' rough little cross stood beside the boulder, surrounded by the yellow daisy plants she tended each night. The cross was wired together from the slats of an old whiskey crate and painted white. The wood was weak and brittle and the sun had bleached the paint to the purest, most brilliant white imaginable. Surrounded by the rich green of the carefully pruned and watered daisies and the black mass of the rocks, Margarita's little garden was the only thing in Agua Amargosa that the villagers thought of as a purely aesthetic creation.

Virtually every other artifact in the caleta had as the reason for its presence some specific purpose, whether practical, merely decorative, or even spiritual, as in the case of the framed saints that hung on at least one wall of every house. When any object no longer served its intended purpose, it was recycled to another use, and when that was no longer possible, it was discarded on the trash heaps or burned. Nothing escaped this utilitarian process. Even the magazines, after being thumbed for years, eventually wound up in the outhouses where, page by page, they surrendered their existence even as they served their final purpose.

But here, hidden away in the arroyo, where few ever saw it, stood this little garden with these carefully trained plants, each with a border of egg-sized stones surrounding its watering basin. It was a lonely tableau that graced no house, fed no chickens, caught no fish, saved no souls, and served no useful purpose whatsoever in the minds of the villagers. It seemed to the people of Agua Amargosa that Margarita's lonely composition was nothing more than a token of sentimentality and aesthetic self-indulgence—incomprehensible in their desert of practical necessity—and they largely ignored it.

For Abundio though, this place beside the well held a significance that had bedeviled him secretly since the tempestuous night, fourteen winters before, when he and Socorro had first rowed their panga into the caleta.

Exhausted from their narrow escape in the windstorm, they had pulled the panga up on the sand beside Ramón's and in the dark they unrolled their seawater-soaked blankets and made camp between the two boats.

They had not eaten since the previous day, having lost their food in the wild boat ride, and they had nothing for supper but salt and plain tortillas which Ramón's wife made for them. María filled her little belly without complaining and fell asleep, trembling from cold and hunger, sensing the tension in her parents.

Sometime, very late in the night, Socorro had jabbed Abundio's shoulder and hissed in his ear.

"Husband! Husband! There is someone walking around the boats."

The beach was bright with a gibbous moon floating high over the caleta. A strong offshore night wind had come up, whipping the surface of the water into sparkling sheets that scurried out from shore. Abundio sat up but could see no one in the cold blue light.

"Where is he, Socorro?"

"Over there. He walked right between us and went up the beach."

"It is just someone from one of the houses."

Socorro pushed with both hands, trying to make Abundio stand up.

"What is he doing in the middle of the night?"

"The wind. He is probably just checking his anchor."

"All the boats are on the beach!"

"Ah... "

The caleta was no longer deserted as it had been during the summers with Señor Pete. There were now perhaps half a dozen houses under the palms, perhaps more. Nevertheless, Abundio doubted that anyone in the small community would see much profit in disturbing their camp.

On the other hand, why should anyone be snooping around in the middle of the night? With Socorro hissing and shoving, Abundio rose to his feet. The cold wind made him shiver. He wrestled on a sodden sweatshirt that made it seem even colder.

Ramón groaned as he rolled over on his swollen knee.

"Mmmm... what is it, Bundo?"

"Nothing, brother. Go back to sleep."

Abundio looked around but there was nobody to be seen. Then, in the moonlight, he found a line of footprints cut sharp in the smooth-washed sand just above the ebbing tide.

Curious, Abundio followed the tracks for a distance north along the beach. Whoever had left them had wandered left and right, sometimes entering the water, sometimes making a complete circle, before heading north again.

Abundio had concluded that he was tracking a drunken panguero who had become lost in the dark, and he had just decided to turn back when he saw the woman.

She was sitting on one of the three rocks that protruded from the sand at the high tide line, rocks that Abundio knew very well, for he and Señor Pete had used them as turnaround markers on their daily jogs up the beach.

Abundio did not immediately recognize the form in the moonlight as something separate from the rock, for the woman's head and body were covered by a long, black shawl that hung down to the sand. Washed in the chiaroscuro shadows of the night, the woman appeared to be a part of the rock on which she sat, making it seem taller than Abundio remembered.

As he approached almost close enough to touch her, Abundio was still unaware that he had discovered the maker of the footprints. He was thinking that the currents and winds must have lowered the beach here, exposing more of the rock to view.

Then she turned her head into the moonlight and her stark white face stared straight into Abundio's like a mask of death. Abundio gasped, imagining a witch was about to devour him. The skin on his neck thrilled and tightened. He fell back and would have fled, but at that moment the lips of the impassive mask opened and she spoke to him in a low, cool voice.

"Have you seen the prince?"

The cold night wind whistled out of the arroyo, ruffling the edges of her shawl and driving grains of sand along the beach that pricked Abundio's ankles.

She was an old woman but her voice was youthful, very deep and sonorous, and the sound of it transported Abundio back to the Malecón of La Paz, back to the time of El Tecolote Terrible and a sweltering spring night in the back seat of a friend's battered Buick.

A voice such as this had soothed his nervousness that memorable night as for the first time he had been undressed with a woman. Fearful of discovery, he had insisted on keeping the windows rolled up tight and the doors locked and she laughed as she sat on him and jerked herself from side to side to bring him quick pleasure. After, she kissed the sweat from his face and drank it, and he drove her back to her uncle's house at the west edge of town.

They returned to the Buick many times that summer. She was the most popular girl on the Malecón, wild and unpredictable, and she had enchanted every boy who saw her. But for some reason she had chosen the big, awkward Tecolote, and with tenderness she had overcome his surprising shyness and lack of experience.

Abundio had already prepared the panga for a long trip north, a trip from which he knew he would not be returning. He could not say why but since the death of his father he had grown uncomfortable in La Paz and he would not be dissuaded from his plan to search for the old places.

So he had left her on the Malecón on a hot, overcast morning in late July and in the middle of the bay the breeze had come up and he had stepped the sail and set his course northward toward Punta Mechudo.

During his long voyage up the coast, as he rowed hour after hour in the hot doldrums, or sailed in the southeast wind, listening to the distant rumble of the mountain thunderstorms, Abundio often thought of the girl, of her intense seizures of ecstasy and her sudden moods, the sometimes incomprehensible things she uttered, and especially, her low, rich voice.

It was that same voice, resonating across a sea of time, that came from this moonlit mask, now, on the shore of Caleta Agua Amargosa, and although she had been only eighteen when he last saw her, weeping on the seawall of the Malecón, Abundio knew that this shadowy, black-draped crone, regardless of how improbable it might seem, was the girl of the Buick.

"Margarita? Is it you?"

Hearing her name called, Margarita Santos came back from the far side of the world, where she had been sailing a ship made of pearls. Like a black butterfly, she settled down on a rock, under the gaze of the shivering man who had spoken her name.

"Have you come to see the prince?"

He took a step forward, looked closely into her face.

"Margarita...? It is me... Abundio Rodríguez... from La Paz...."

She seemed not to recognize him, but reached out and grasped his hand. At her touch, a current of recognition surged out of Abundio's past. It *was* true. This *was* Margarita.

She tugged his arm, trying to lead him up the beach, but he pulled away, repelled by the thought of what she might have in mind. Her unblinking eyes looked through him as though he were an open window.

"Do you wish to see him?"

"Who, Margarita? See who?"

"The little prince. He flew up to the sky."

"Margarita! My God! How have you come to this! What has happened to you!?"

He let her lead him up the path to the old well. He knew it from his summers in the caleta. On many mornings, he had run up there to fill water bottles and check for the tracks of the animals that came down to drink in the night. There were always coyote and bobcat tracks and twice he had seen the enormous wide paw prints of the mountain lion.

She led him to the old ring of stones and they stood leaning into the cold wind howling down the arroyo. There was a small cross he did not remember from before. There were some very old graves, of Indians or Spaniards perhaps, up near the cliffs, but there had never been one at the well.

The moon was straight overhead now. Its pale blue light flooded the arroyo, turning the path to an incandescent river flowing between banks of shadowed boulders. To Abundio, it seemed they were at the bottom of the sea, looking up at the sun obscured by a hundred fathoms of water. Or perhaps this was what the moon itself was like, blocked with rugged, unscalable cliffs and wandering arroyos that lead nowhere. Yes, this arroyo must be exactly like the moon, an *arroyo de la luna*. A place of mystery, always changing, appearing and disappearing, an alluring world of dreams and illusion...

Abundio's mournful contemplation was interrupted by a rustling in the bushes. What mystery was this, hidden in the moonlight? The bush moved. Abundio found a large stone and raised it over his head with both hands. He was about to bring it crashing down when the bush sent out a loud scream, a long, piercing shriek that froze him like a block of ice.

"Cock-a-doodle-doo!"

A family of chickens came out of the bush and crossed to the well in single file. They took their places on the ring of stones and filled their beaks.

Abundio checked the eastern sky for signs of morning. Strange that chickens would be out at this hour, easy prey for the owls and coyotes. Weren't they supposed to be blind in the night? Apparently not. Perhaps the moonlight brought them out.

The white cross beside the well glowed as though it had a life of its own. Margarita knelt beside it and pointed up to the stars at the head of the arroyo.

"The prince... the little warrior... came here... all wet and red. But he flew up... up there. He is up there."

"What prince, Margarita?"

"The son of the feathered serpent! Don't you know?"

"Of... of the devil?"

"No, no! Silly! El Tecolote Terrible is no devil! But he went away too. They both went away."

El Tecolote!? She remembered him after all! But what was she talking about? Abundio could not begin to understand her meaning. He held her by the shoulders, those same slim shoulders, and he shook her and spoke in a desperate whisper.

"Margarita! It is me. Bundo. What is this prince? This warrior?"

Her face was lined and shrunken, but her teeth were still perfect, just as they had been when she threw back her head and laughed in the lights shining through the Buick's pitted back window.

She smiled and her eyes cleared. Those same eyes.

"*Mi amor!* You have come back!"

Abundio hurried before he lost her again.

"Margarita! How have you come to this place?"

"Oh, Bundo! I missed you so much!"

He squeezed his big fingers around her arms.

"Margarita... tell me! What has happened to you?"

"Our son, he flew up to the sky, Bundo. I am sorry! I am sorry! I could not stop him! I swear!"

She had used the Spanish formula *"voló al cielo,"* literally meaning "flew up to the sky," but also meaning "went to heaven," when engraved on the headstones of infants or children who died at a young age. Abundio looked down at the handmade cross. In the moonlight, he saw that the plants around it were trimmed and that they had been watered.

"My God... Margarita. I never knew of this... "

But before he could finish, her eyes changed again. She pulled the shawl off her head and unraveled her hair and let it fall down her back, and she picked a yellow daisy from one of the bushes. Without speaking again, she turned away and took the path up the arroyo.

He let her go and hurried back to the makeshift, first night camp between the pangas. As he slipped beneath the blankets, Socorro murmured.

"What was it, husband?"

"Nothing of importance."

SINCE THAT NIGHT long ago, Abundio had gradually learned the events of Margarita's sad life after La Paz, including the violent confrontation with her brother that was thought, tacitly, by the villagers to have caused the death of the infant and the madness of its mother.

The story had come to him in fragments, from offhand comments by the other fishermen, or from Socorro, who would sometimes pass along a bit of gossip from one of the other women.

Margarita herself had been of little help, partly because of her imperfect recollection, and partly because Abundio was reluctant to exchange more than pleasantries with her. He was appalled by the path her life had taken and by his role in it. Each night, as he fell asleep, he mulled over their time on the Malecón, and he thought he could remember signs even then that Margarita's vision of the world about her would sometimes blur and darken. But he wasn't sure.

He had never mustered the courage to reveal his secret to Socorro. What good would that do? To make his wife share his shame and misery, just to lessen his own? Nor would it have helped poor Margarita, a victim of the light and dark of life itself, of the moonstruck madness that came from God knows where.

Surreptitiously, Abundio had seen to it in the first weeks that he and Socorro built their house close to Pablo's, and for the past fourteen years, he had kept a sorrowful vigil over Margarita Santos, the most popular girl on the Malecón, and he had watched over her as she descended deeper and deeper into her lonely world of dreams.

And he had listened, as the screams of the Santos family had shattered many nights in the caleta. Pablo Santos hated his sister and blamed her for the troubles he had with his wife. Many times, he had tried to send Margarita back to La Paz, but she always refused to go.

As he sat between the well and cross, watching Socorro wash clothes, Abundio considered their present set of problems. He was still wondering which to discuss first when Socorro wrung out the final shirt with a sharp grunt and flung it through the air. It spread itself out on the hot rocks like a casting net.

She came over and sat in the sand with her legs folded and her skirt wrapped beneath her. She combed Abundio's hair with her fingers and picked off a gnat that had become caught on his sweaty shoulder.

"So, husband, what has been decided about the road?"

"Pablo is the only one in favor."

"Why?"

"The others think it is too dangerous."

Socorro wiggled her little feet.

"What do *you* think, Bundo?"

They sat with their arms braced in the sand, watching the dragonflies hover around the well. Against the far wall, a stand of bright green papyrus nodded in the shade. To their right, Margarita's daisies drooped in the heat of the afternoon sun.

As they watched the dragonflies, Abundio used a fingertip to draw a figure-eight on the back of Socorro's hand.

"Last night, María told Nacho she wishes to leave the profesora."

"Really...?"

"She said she wants to come back here."

Abundio loved dragonflies. He admired the deep metallic blue of their bodies and the skillful way they flew just above the surface of the water. He tossed a pebble and watched them dodge it.

"Have we asked too much of her?"

Socorro reached a toe over to scratch the side of Abundio's big leg.

"You have not been at fault, husband. But perhaps it was the wrong thing for her."

There were many dragonflies now, hovering over the bubbly green scum of the well.

"The money would have run out anyway."

"Yes."

A bubble rose up in the water. It held a moment, then burst silently,

sending a spray of pinpoints an inch into the air. Abundio rubbed his
wife's back and shoulders.

"Socorro, do you think there could ever be anything... between María
and Chino?"

"What do you mean?"

"You know... as a man and a woman."

"They are both young and attractive."

Abundio reached for his feet and stretched his calves. He scratched the
back of his neck.

"Do you really think of Chino as attractive?"

"In his own way, he could be attractive to a woman."

"How, Socorro?"

"Well... he is a man of dignity, a man who can be trusted. And he is
strong and confident of himself... like the bull, eh?"

Abundio considered the idea of Chino and María together. If his
daughter really was going to live in the caleta she would need a man, a
panguero, to provide for her and give her legitimacy. María's desirability
as a woman was obvious and had been since she was ten, no matter how
much Abundio had tried to close his eyes to it. He could understand why
a man like Chino would be attracted to her. But the idea that his daughter
might see a suitable mate in Chino was still a novelty to him. Although he
respected and trusted his partner, Abundio could see little in him that
would make him a prize catch for any woman, especially a woman like
María. But then, what did he know of these things?

"Chino is no better at fishing than I am."

"And... has that ever made a difference between us, husband?"

Abundio tossed another pebble at the dragonflies. No... Socorro had
never once complained about his lack of success in the panga. They had
sometimes gone weeks without chicken or meat, just barely making
enough to buy drinking water and gas for the boat, and she had never even
seemed to notice.

And somehow, each night, as she lowered the cloth over the doorway
and led him to their cot, all that had never seemed so important after all
and it had never even occurred to Abundio to think of himself as a failure.

But this was different. He could not expect his daughter to live like
that. María should at least have a real house and a man with a pickup
and a decent panga, and those things would not be possible unless
something drastic were to change. Without realizing it, Abundio had

come to a watershed, a turning point that would determine the course of their lives for the foreseeable future.

"Socorro, I think the time has come to sell the Rolex."

"To what purpose, Bundo?"

"We could buy nets and lines and a good panga with a big Evinrude like Pablo's. We could join a cooperativa."

"Would there be enough for that?"

"I think so."

"And you and Chino. You would pull net and fish shark?"

"Yes."

"Would you really be willing to do that, husband?"

"I will do it."

Socorro knew her husband had reserved no recourse for himself.

If Abundio said he would finally sell the watch—the gift that had always been such a strange combination of blessing and burden to him— if he said he would give up his baited hand-lines and become a gill netter, he would do so, and he would pull net for the rest of his days if necessary. He would become a gill netter and a set-line shark fisherman, salting the shark's fins and its flabby white meat for *machaca*, the fish jerky used in tacos for which there always seemed to be a good market.

During their twenty years together, Abundio had committed himself this way only a handful of times. Once, on Isla Coronado when he asked to fish with Ramón. Again, on the night he nervously asked permission from Ramón to build a house for the two of them. Again, when they took Chino in. And finally, a year ago, when he had dedicated their entire savings, including Señor Pete's gold Rolex if necessary, to pay for María's education.

With the road and their income gone, even the Rolex could not allow María to continue with the profesora. They would need it to relocate themselves. Socorro wondered how long her daughter had known, and she realized it was no coincidence that María had come home almost at the exact week when their cash reserve would run out.

Now, Abundio had laid out a plausible course for their future and Socorro knew that if she allowed him to take it, her man would follow it, even to the end of his life, without complaining.

But she also knew what it meant for Abundio to give up the feel of the baited hand-lines, for him never again to watch as the mysterious, living color manifested itself in the void.

Abundio loved fishing with a purity and simplicity she would never fully understand. The sea held an unexplainable significance for him. Socorro knew that for her husband the strike and the struggle of the fish— and its fearless, staring death—somehow served as a link to the invisible life-spirit that lay at the foundation of everything.

Socorro's heart filled with love for her husband, for she knew he had just offered to sever himself from that essential, sustaining force. He had offered to pull and pull on the heavy, endless nets, until he died, if necessary, for her benefit and for María's.

She squeezed his thick arm.

"Husband, what if we *could* clear the road?"

"With no Caterpillar, it would be very dangerous."

"But *might* it be possible?"

"There is always the possibility, I suppose."

"Would it not be worth trying, at least until it becomes clearly too dangerous?"

"And then we would stop?"

"Yes. At the very first moment it seemed the rocks might fall."

The idea of clearing the road by hand had been considered and rejected months before. The village pangueros were well acquainted with the annual routine of prying and pushing fallen rocks off the road and sending them over the cliff, hopefully all the way to the bottom. Sometimes the rocks would land on the road again farther down and they would have to be pushed over the edge a second time, and occasionally a third. It was a difficult way to keep the road open, but it was the only way, and it was accepted as part of life in Agua Amargosa.

But after the great March storm, the first men to go up the cliff had come back shaking their heads, saying that the new slide had not only blocked the road but had completely buried it for twenty-five meters in either direction, leaving nothing to be seen but a steep slope of jagged boulders.

It was across this unstable field of rubble that Pablo Santos, and now Socorro it seemed, were proposing to build a new road by hand. They would have to move enough rock to make a ledge as wide as the fish truck. The greatest danger was the possibility that their digging might trigger another slide, burying anyone in its path.

Abundio considered the idea as presented by Socorro. What harm could come of it? None, if they did as she suggested and stopped at the first sign of danger. And if the idea worked, everything would be returned to the way it was before. Abundio leaned back on his hands.

"The others don't like it when Pablo tells them what to do."

"You and Chino must convince them."

"But how?"

Socorro tossed a pebble toward the well. With uncanny accuracy, she hit a dragonfly square on its back and knocked it momentarily into the water.

"Tell them… María and I will come too."

"What?"

"Why not?"

"But Socorro. There is danger."

She stood up and grabbed Abundio's thick hair in both hands and pulled his face to her stomach. Looking down at the top of his head, she spoke to him softly.

"But not just for you, husband. Go. Talk to them."

THE INVISIBLE MOON on the far side of the world had pulled the tide to its afternoon high.

Chino sat perched on the tallest of the three rocks that marked the path to his lean-to. His feet and ankles were bathed in the warm, lapping sea. María stood behind him with her white pants rolled up to her knees. She had taken off Chino's shirt and she dipped her hands into the water and gently patted the scratches on his back.

"I can't believe my nails could cut so deeply."

Chino had María's golden sandals in his lap. He smiled.

"You should have seen the marks all over the sand. It's a miracle he didn't notice them. He almost stepped on your shoes."

"We need to tell him, mi amor."

"Sí, and mamá too."

"Mamá already knows."

"Oh... ?"

Chino raised an eyebrow, and looked south toward the village. At this distance, the houses under the trees were obscured by heat waves. No one watching would be able to recognize them, even with binoculars.

"You know, María, when I moved up here, I had no idea how handy this place would be."

"Shhh!"

María slapped her hand across his back.

"Ayyy! Hey, that hurts!"

"That's for all your girls in El Centro!"

He grabbed for María's long legs, but she was off running up the beach, splashing through the shallow water, cutting back and forth to evade him. She was surprisingly fast. She got all the way to the big rocks at the north end of the caleta before Chino brought her down in knee deep water. They rolled over and over, laughing and gagging on the salt, stirring up clouds of sand and butter clam shells, and then they sat facing each other, up to their armpits, with their legs tangled between them. Chino leaned forward and cupped María's perfect face in his hands. He kissed her slowly and very softly and his eyes saddened and he spoke in a strange, high-pitched voice she had never heard before.

"María Guadalupe Rodríguez, I was born at the moment I looked down the cliffs at this beautiful place and I saw you, chopping wood with mamá. From that day, I never loved anything but you."

María's eyes, too, grew serious. She squeezed Chino's rough, work-hardened hands tightly between hers, and she spoke in a whisper, with drops of seawater falling from her chin.

"Chino, why... why did you wait so long?"

"Your papá. On that first day, he made me swear I would never touch you."

"But I was only twelve!"

"He was very clear. He meant for always."

"But, Chino, why would he do that... to you!?"

"He loves you so much. He wants you to have someone... something better."

"So you allowed him to imprison you? All this time!"

"María. I was alone... lost. He saved me. He didn't have to."

"He wanted your Evinrude!"

"Not really. You know him. He needed a motor, but only to buy your way out of here."

María tightened her grip on Chino's fingers. This outrageous story must be true, just as he described it. For despite all his strengths, Chino was still just a fisherman, a panguero like the rest of the men, and Abundio had always made it clear she was never to get involved with a panguero.

"But, Chino, why have you changed your mind now?"

"You came back to us. In a strange way, our bad luck has forced you to come back... to settle... for me."

"Chino. I swear, I would have come back anyway."

María fought with herself. Was that really true? As much as she wished to, she could not feel the kind of passion she sensed in Chino's strong hands.

But she knew that she did love him in her own way and she knew that for her that kind of love would be enough. Yes, she would settle for that and make it last. And it was *not* true that Chino was like the rest of them. He was very different. Of all the people María knew, only Chino seemed always dissatisfied with himself, always eager to consider things in a new way. And had he not grown up among the *norteamericanos*? Had he not taught himself to read and write and speak both English and Spanish, each as well as the other? And was he not, in his quiet way, the strongest, the most truly *macho* of any man she knew? María was sure these things were true, and she was sure that if her father could let her return to Agua Amargosa, he could also accept her choice of Chino.

"Amor, we must tell him immediately. He will understand."

"I don't think so, María. In the boat, he speaks of his dreams for you a hundred times a day. He will not give up easily."

María stood and pulled Chino out of the water. She unbuttoned her shirt and held herself against him, her nipples erect.

"He has no choice, amor. I will never let you go."

Chino felt the passion returning. The wet hairs between his legs pulled painfully.

"All right, María. But let me speak to him myself."

"Agreed, as long as you do it soon. But before we go back, mi amor, I think I would like to visit our little house in the sand again."

He lifted her across his arms and turned into the dunes.

IN THE SHADE of his front porch, Pablo Santos sat working the greenish-blue fishing line with a wooden hand shuttle.

The shuttle was carved from a single piece of bamboo. It was flat like the blade of a throwing knife, about an inch wide and as long as Pablo's hand, and it was pointed at one end and square at the other. There was a rectangular hole through the middle of the shuttle. A free-standing spike of bamboo extended from one end of the hole almost to the other, and Pablo had wound his monofilament line over the spike and around the square end of the shuttle over and over until it was shaped like a small football.

Pablo was making a gill net.

Quickly and mechanically, he passed the loaded shuttle through a hole on the edge of the net, and he made a knot. Then he moved to the next hole and made another knot. He worked his way along the edge of the net, unwinding more line from the shuttle when necessary, and when he reached the end, he reversed his direction and started another row.

Pablo's legs were covered up to his thighs by the billowing, bluish-green folds of his net. The pile extended all the way across the porch and spilled off the other side. Every so often the shuttle ran out of line and Pablo stopped to reload it from a large spool beside his chair.

Pablo had been working on his net, off and on, for nearly two years, but since the rains of March he had spent more time on it. The net was now twelve feet wide and fifty yards long, and Pablo planned to work on it until he had added another fifty yards.

Then he would splice his net to another he had found at sea, cutting through the exposed vertebrae of a dying porpoise. When the gill net was finished, it would contain more than fifteen miles of monofilament and a quarter of a million knots, and it would make Pablo Santos—by a very wide margin—the most productive fisherman in Agua Amargosa.

The net would be strung out across the invisible paths that the fish were known to take each day as they followed their food in the tides and currents. The upper edge of the net would be suspended with floats and the bottom edge would be weighted down with sinkers so it would hang in the water like an invisible curtain, ready to entangle the gills or spiny fins of any fish that tried to swim through it. Once caught, the struggles of the fish would only entangle it further, and it would die and remain there until Pablo pulled the net up and removed it.

Since there were fewer and fewer large fish around the caleta, Pablo was making his net with a small, three-inch mesh. In the old days, four-inch, or even five-inch would have been better, and the line would have been much heavier. But for this net, he needed only light monofilament, about like kite string, and a small mesh. The net would catch many incidental fish of no market value, but that could not be avoided, and Pablo was prepared to move to another area after it had taken so much that there was nothing left nearby. In the meanwhile, he would spread his net among the reefs around Agua Amargosa and he would enjoy the temporary surge in his income that it provided.

Pablo's eyes were on his knots and he was thinking about the best place to try his new net. He didn't notice Abundio standing in the sun just outside the shade of the porch.

After a while, Abundio cleared his throat and shifted his bare feet to raise a little cloud of dust. Pablo's hand jerked and his shuttle fell into the net.

"*Ayy!* Bundo! You startled me!"

"Sorry, Pablo. I just came to tell you Chino and I will join you on the road tomorrow."

"Well, that makes three of us. Better than nothing."

"Five, actually. Socorro and María are coming too."

"What? Women? It's too dangerous for them."

"They can take care of themselves, Pablo."

"I won't be responsible for them."

"Nobody asked you to."

Pablo pushed his hand into the net and retrieved his shuttle. He tied a terminal knot in the end of the line, and he bit it off with his front teeth and kicked the pile away.

"Three men isn't enough, Bundo. Even if we use my pickup."

"I know."

"Then what's the use, Bundo?"

"I will talk to the others."

"Bundo! I've already done that!"

There was a brittle edge on Pablo's voice that he reserved only for Abundio Rodríguez. As Agua Amargosa's top fisherman, Pablo felt only justified in claiming leadership in the affairs of the village. Except for Fra Nacho, he had lived there longer than anyone. He owned the only pickup and he lived in the largest house. Day after day, season after season, his panga brought the most cabrilla and pargo to the fish truck, and he never hesitated to point out that his success was due not to luck, but to his endurance in the boat, his diligence, his knowledge, and his skill in reading the water.

Pablo's panga was always the first one out in the mornings and the last to return in the afternoons, and he would launch into the wind on days when no one else cared to. He was teaching his two sons everything he knew. The older boy, at ten, was already more skilled than half the men in the caleta, and the younger, only eight, promised to be the best of all.

It galled Pablo Santos that he was not the headman of Agua Amargosa.

And it galled him even more that the crown of leadership had fallen by default to this thickheaded mountain of flesh who now stood sweating in the sun at the edge of his porch. Abundio Rodríguez, a poor man, married to an Indian that gave him no sons, who still lived in an open shack after all this time, who risked his life in a panga too old even for clamming, and who was often skunked on the fishing grounds, even during the spawning seasons when the cabrilla and pargo came in so thick you could almost walk on their backs.

Ridiculous!

Why do they love him so much? Why do they prop him up every time he folds over like an undercooked tamale? Pablo had to bite his tongue each time the fish buyer shook his head and blamed bad luck for Abundio's poor catch. He could never understand why the people of the village deferred to Abundio and not himself when a decision was to be made. *Madre!* Sometimes the men would actually ask for Abundio's advice on *fishing*! With himself standing right there! Looking like the court fool!

Even Margarita, his lunatic sister, was caught up in this worship of idiot pretenders to the throne. Long ago, she had invented this game of coaxing him to tell her the best spots, and then giving them to Chino on the sly. Why? Why them?

What a joke! Pablo remembered when he first suspected and gave Margarita a false spot he knew to be empty of anything worth catching. Those dumb bastards had sat there for two weeks before they realized what was going on! *Two weeks!* How could anyone be so *stupid!?*

And when he confronted her, Margarita had actually threatened to kill herself! Why would his own sister care so much for strangers?

But what galled Pablo Santos most of all was that Abundio seemed indifferent to the responsibilities that had befallen him. The man never asserted himself and he always went running to his wife, or Chino, or Nacho when he had to make a decision about anything.

The present situation was a perfect example. Had it not been for the long suffering Pablo Santos, the idea of clearing the road would never have come up in the first place. Now, Abundio would steal his idea and talk to the other men, and they would follow *him* up the cliff and *he* would get all the credit!

Pablo stared at Abundio, daring him to say something. But the big fisherman hesitated because of the harshness in his voice. Abundio stood just outside the edge of the porch, in the full heat of the afternoon sun, with beads of sweat rolling down his stomach. He drew a small circle in the dirt with his big toe and he made a kissing sound with his lips, and finally he spoke without looking up.

"Well... Pablo. Ahh... Socorro. She thinks it might be worth talking to the men one more time."

Pablo used his fingers and thumb to pat the corners of his thick mustache. He flipped the bamboo shuttle end-over-end, burying it deep in the pile of netting.

"Fine. Go ahead then."

DESPITE WHAT HE had promised his wife, Abundio had no intention of speaking to the other men himself. He hated making speeches, and besides, that would not be necessary. Instead, he planned to make use of the messenger service that distributed news around the caleta better and faster than telephones ever could.

Abundio walked to the beach. Way down at the south end, past the pangas, some children were turning over stones in the shallow water. Abundio went toward them until he was close enough to be heard. He stuck his fingers into his mouth and whistled, and several of them looked up.

He cupped his hands and shouted.

"*Jo-se-li-to!* Joselito! Come here!"

Joselito Medina put down his jar of shells and shouted back.

"What?"

"I have a job for you! Come here!"

When they heard the word "job," the children threw down their shells and buckets and they came running as fast as their feet could carry them. The day had been boring, like all the days since the pangas had stopped going out and their playmates had begun leaving the caleta, and Abundio Rodríguez was their favorite adult.

They came racing toward Abundio, staying down on the hard packed sand at the edge of the water, and the smaller, naked ones began to loose ground. They fell farther and farther back as they tired, but they kept coming. Some of the smallest ones began to cry for fear they would be left out.

Long-legged Joselito Medina was in the lead. He stayed down on the wet sand until he was almost opposite Abundio and then he cut square away from the water. In his rush, Joselito ran right past Abundio, who reached out and grabbed the boy's arm as he went by and swung him around like a tether ball.

"*Híjole!* Joselito! Where are you going?"

Joselito went sprawling on the sand, but he picked himself up quickly and stood in front of Abundio, panting, with his hands on his knees. He stayed bent over, sucking and blowing, with his long hair hanging down.

The other children ran up, equally out of breath. They crowded around Abundio, who stood with his arms folded, waiting for the smallest to arrive. He had planned to make some jokes, but as they caught their breath and stood up, he saw the deadly seriousness in their faces. There was not a smile among them.

They stood waiting for his words with their eyes fixed on him, silently, not like children at all. Even the smallest ones stared with a hardness that reminded Abundio of the eyes of the coyotes who would sometimes slink to the well in broad daylight when it had not rained for a year.

Abundio thought of the circle of men around the fish buyer's truck in Las Ramalitas. They had looked at him in the same way. These children, at such an early age, already had that same fear in their eyes, of lives thrown into the winds of an uncertain future.

Abundio decided this was not a time for jokes. He knew he must do something to help these children forget themselves, even if it was only for a while. He stretched his long arms out over them, like the branches of a tree, and he shouted above their heads.

"All right! Everybody sit down!"

Abundio waited until they were all sitting cross-legged in the sand. He backed up and stood facing them with his arms folded across his chest and he spoke in a deep, commanding voice.

"All right! Everybody listen carefully! Juana... can you hear me?"

Juana, a black-eyed girl of seven, was partially deaf, so the question carried some sense of legitimacy, although she could easily have heard Abundio's booming voice from fifty feet away. The other children all nodded for her and Abundio continued.

"Joselito! Come here. Sit in front. You are the oldest. I need you to take charge of this."

Joselito Medina scuttled forward like a crab. He elbowed two of the other children aside, basking in the protection from retaliation he enjoyed under the aegis of Abundio's overhanging belly.

"All right! I have a very, very important message for your parents. You must give it to them immediately and without mistakes. Does everyone understand?"

They all nodded.

"All right! Tell your parents we are going to clear the road tomorrow!"

The children bounced up and down on their little butts. Some of them began to chatter and squeak but Abundio's voice roared out again.

"*Quiet!* I need everyone up there at six with shovels, bars, and wheelbarrows. The work may take several days. Any questions?"

Joselito raised his hand.

"Who do you want to come?"

"Everybody, Joselito. Everybody who can work."

"Even us?"

"Well... do you think you can be of help?"

They all answered together.

"Yes! Yes! We can!"

"Then I want to see *all* of you at six! And don't forget your shovels!"

Now came the smiles, the expectation, the giggling and laughter. They leapt and danced around Abundio, playing their favorite game of pinching his huge, gourd-shaped love handles and running away before he could catch them. But this time he ignored them and sent them scattering with his final words.

"One more thing! Socorro and María are also going! Now, get to work! Tell everyone!"

With Joselito Medina barking orders, Agua Amargosa's messenger service disappeared into the palms like a swarm of angry bees.

In the moonless, pre-dawn dark, Abundio's feet made a steady crunching sound on the gravel path in the arroyo.

He ate as he walked, breaking pieces of smoked tuna from a slab that he carried in a paper bag, and every third piece he tossed to a small, black-and-tan shepherd dog following timidly a few steps behind.

She was a young dog and she had just given birth. Her soft belly skin hung heavy and thick. Abundio had not seen her for several days, perhaps as much as a week. He stopped and squatted down to pet her but she would not let him approach. He tore off a piece of fish skin and held it out, and while she tugged, he stroked her head. He sat down on the gravel, making a circle with his legs, and the dog came into it, wagging her tail and shivering with happiness. She put her front paws on his chest and tried to lick his face.

Abundio felt the emptiness in her flanks.

"Ah... my *perridita*, you have dropped your little ones. Where do you hide them? Somewhere in the rocks?"

He called her "perridita," a word made up from the word for a female dog, *perra*, and the word meaning something that is lost, *perdido*, and it was the closest thing she had to a real name.

No-Name had been nursing her pups beneath a flat boulder in the arroyo for three days, but weakening from lack of food and water and feeling the life beginning to leave her, she had consumed them early on the morning of the fourth day and she had returned to the village.

Neither her confinement nor her reappearance had been noted by the people of Agua Amargosa, who attributed little in the way of feelings or emotions to dogs or other animals. No-Name had been born beneath an overturned panga, and she had learned to eat fish scraps and find water before her teeth had come in. She was the only survivor of her litter and she lived on the edges of the village, moving silently through it like a shadow, keeping herself as inconspicuous as possible in order to avoid trouble.

She came often to the Rodríguez house because the gentle, quiet man who lived there always left a piece of fish for her under the porch bench. But she came only in the darkness of the night, after she was sure the woman had gone to sleep, because the woman had no use for her and would chase her with the broom or even throw the frying pan at her.

Each morning Abundio checked under the bench for No-Name's furry body, and if she was there they would go down to the beach together to meet Chino and launch the boat. But she had not been there for the past week, and Abundio had forgotten about her until she appeared on the path in the arroyo.

Abundio tore off another piece of fish and placed it into No-Name's mouth. She took it carefully with her front teeth, and she held it there until she felt him release it. Then she swallowed it in a single gulp.

"What good manners you have, perridita!"

Abundio held No-Name's head and belched into her face, blowing his breath up her nostrils. Her nose twitched as she analyzed the sudden rush of odors, but there was nothing new so she pulled her head free and began to nuzzle the paper bag. Abundio held her back.

"Ayyy... perridita. You would not steal the breakfast of an old one-legged man would you?"

Abundio stood up, closing the paper bag, and the dog slunk off a few yards, unsure of his intentions. Abundio started up the path again, but looked back after a few steps. The eastern sky had begun to lighten. In the last dark of the receding night, he could see No-Name's black form outlined against the sand. He tore off a large piece of tuna, almost half the slab, and threw it to her.

"Ha! Perridita! Nacho is getting too fat anyway, eh?"

The side path was still in deep shadow. Abundio left No-Name tearing at her slab of fish and he climbed to Fra Nacho's place, cursing a rock he should have been able to avoid. As he reached the level spot, a flashlight came on. Fra Nacho was already awake on his outdoor cot.

"Buenos días, Bundo. You are up early."

"Buenos días, Nacho."

Abundio seated himself. He pointed his thumb down the arroyo.

"The rooster. Did you hear it this morning?"

Fra Nacho pressed his thumbs and fingers together into a pointed cone and he shook it like a rag.

"*Ohhh!* It's getting worse and worse! Why doesn't someone twist that damned bird's neck?"

"It is truly *loco*."

"It destroys the tranquility of the village."

Abundio gave Fra Nacho the paper bag. The old man shined his flashlight into it.

"Atún?"

"Socorro smoked it all night. With mesquite wood."

Several burritos lurked beside the still warm pieces of smoked fish.

"Levanta muertos?"

"She insists."

"How many more has she got?"

"Only a few. And those she will save for herself and María."

"Thank God."

Fra Nacho was very hungry. There were times, especially in the months of the heat, when he lost his appetite for days. But then his body would suddenly demand great quantities of food, as if to make up for its over-sight, and he would lie on his cot waiting for Socorro or María to bring him relief from the fire in his belly. These swings in Fra Nacho's appetite were a constant source of friction between himself and Socorro, for when he was not hungry, she insisted that he eat just the same, and when he needed more than usual, she refused to indulge him.

Fra Nacho tore the bag open and spread it on a crate. Ignoring the burritos, he broke the savory smoked tuna into bite-sized pieces.

"Do you want some, Bundo?"

"I had some on the way up."

Fra Nacho sprinkled the chunks lightly with salt. He ate them slowly, washing them down with water. By the time he was finished, the sky had lightened and the rich green of the palm trees was showing on the floor of the arroyo.

"Thank you, Bundo. I will eat the burritos a little later."

"*De nada*."

Abundio used the automatic Spanish phrase, "of nothing," to say that

Fra Nacho was welcome to the favor. The literal meaning of the words hung in the air between the two old friends. Abundio cleared his throat.

"We are going up to move the rocks today."

"Who is?"

"I'm not sure. They don't like Pablo."

"Pablo is an empty fool, Bundo."

Although he was loath to argue with Fra Nacho, and so said nothing, Abundio did not consider Pablo Santos to be a fool. Pablo did have faults, the worst of which was probably his intolerance for his tormented sister, but over the years Abundio and Chino had uttered Pablo's name in gratitude too many times to consider him a fool. There had been many days when one of Pablo's spots saved them from coming in with nothing. And Pablo had been the one to propose clearing the road in the first place, and it was Pablo's pickup, paid for honestly with the sweat of his brow, that would be used to move the biggest rocks. No, there *was* a difference between being a fool and being an obnoxious asshole, and Abundio felt that although Pablo probably deserved to be called by that name, he was certainly no fool.

But Fra Nacho held no such reservations. He had seen many fishermen come and go, and he considered Pablo to be one of the worst kind, a man who would just as soon be skinning goats if that paid better, a rapacious, purely instinctive predator who cared nothing for his prey, except to kill it and count his money.

The sea was always an uncertain master, always cracking the whip of misfortune over those who worked on it, and so they all caught as much as possible each day they launched their boats. In this sense, Pablo Santos was no different from the rest of them.

But what Pablo lacked was humility. He was never grateful for the bounty that came to him, but only scornful of those less fortunate than himself. Over the years, Pablo was known to have caught well over two-hundred-thousand tuna, dorado, cabrilla, yellowtail, pargo, shark, and other types of marketable fish, and it had not once occurred to him that any power greater than his own may have had something to do with it. No, Pablo Santos held nothing sacred, and therefore nothing profane. And that made him a fool. A complete and irredeemable fool.

Fra Nacho ate the burritos slowly, taking frequent sips of water.

"Are you worried about leading the men, Abundio?"

"I don't know what to tell them."

"Let Pablo do the talking. But don't let him do anything stupid. He has no restraint when he wants something."

"What if the road cannot be cleared?"

"Then, you must accept your defeat and lead your family away from here. They only wait for you to make the decision."

"We will end up pulling shark."

"There is no shame in it, Bundo! After all, the Twelve Disciples of Jesus were basically pangueros, you know."

"Really, Nacho? Do you suppose they pulled shark?"

"Of course! Why wouldn't they?"

The sky was light now. The work party would soon be gathering at the base of the road. Abundio needed to get back, but before he went, there was one more thing to ask his old friend.

"Nacho, do you think there is any attraction... between María and Chino?"

"Yes. And there has always been."

"Always?"

"I'm afraid we have been the last to see it, Bundo. Will you allow her to stay in the caleta?"

"Socorro feels it is best."

ABUNDIO HURRIED DOWN the arroyo beneath a copper dawn sky.

He was near the village when he caught sight of the people waiting at the base of the cliff, where the road met the floor of the canyon. They were standing in groups of twos and threes, leaning on their shovels in the horizontal, yellow rays of the morning sun. Socorro and María were with them, as was Chino.

The messenger service had done its job well. Except for Fra Nacho and Margarita Santos, the entire population of Agua Amargosa seemed to be waiting for him, including all the women and children. There were about forty in all.

Pablo Santos' vestigial pickup was on the road, smoking and coughing. The big wooden box in back held a wheelbarrow, heavy rope, some picks and shovels, and some freshly cut mesquite limbs. Pablo sat perched on the chair that served as the driver's seat. His voice carried above the percussive hammering of the engine.

"Put your things on my truck. I'll drive them up the hill."

Nobody moved. Pablo glared at them and jammed the transmission into gear with a loud ratcheting noise and the truck started up the road on its oversized tires. He shouted back.

"I'll be waiting up there! Don't take all day!"

Joselito Medina spotted Abundio and came running. His feet kicked up puffs of dust in the orange-yellow light cutting across the road.

"Bundo! Look at all the people we got!"

Abundio ground a knuckle into the top of the boy's head and tweaked his nose playfully.

"Good job, Joselito! I can always depend on you."

The boy wrestled free and tossed his hair aside, grinning. He stood at attention with his chin out and his arms held straight.

"What shall we do first, Bundo?"

"Well... we need to carry everything up the hill."

"Will we clear the road today, Bundo?"

"Of course, Joselito! With this many strong backs? How can we fail!?"

"And... my papá will come home?"

"With certainty, Joselito! And everything will be just as it was before."

Socorro and María were waiting with Joselito's mother. Ana Rosa Medina was a very heavy woman in her late-thirties who had borne too many children. She had given her husband, Luis, two sets of twins and nine other children, thirteen in all, of whom eight had lived, and she had gained weight with each confinement until her body was almost globular in shape.

Nevertheless, Ana Rosa Medina remained as buoyant in spirit as her lively brood and she seemed quite capable of bearing another thirteen children if it was God's will to give her husband the strength for such a feat. As they reached her, Ana Rosa cuffed her oldest surviving son and reproached him in mock anger.

"Lito! You worthless jelly fish! You should be watching your brothers and sisters."

Joselito hid behind Abundio and pleaded with his mother.

"But mamá, I am helping Bundo move the rocks today!"

Ana Rosa Medina hitched up her wide, gathered skirt and turned to Abundio.

"Bundo, thank you for the tuna, and for bringing our supplies from Las Ramalitas."

"De nada, Ana Rosa."

She bowed slightly.

"I respect your decision, Abundio. Is my lazy son old enough to be of help to you today?"

Abundio looked down into Joselito's imploring eyes and his skinny, bare shoulders. He doubted the boy could even lift one of the iron bars they would be using to pry the rocks. Yet, Joselito's messenger service had fulfilled its end of the bargain.

"Ana Rosa, I am not as quick as I used to be. I was hoping you would let me have Joselito today... to... ahh... carry messages to the others."

Joselito jumped at his mother and almost pulled her blouse open.

"There! Do you see? He needs me! I told you!"

"All right, Lito, you may do what Abundio asks. But you must not get in his way. Is that clear?"

"Sí, mamá!"

Joselito grabbed a shovel and ran off to join the other children.

Socorro had brought the high-topped combat boots. Abundio pulled them on and stood.

"Thank you, Socorro. Shall we go?"

"All right, husband, if you think we are ready."

They all started up the hill. Chino and María walked in front of the others, with Chino pushing a wheelbarrow and María carrying a pair of picks crossed behind her shoulders. She wore a wide-brimmed straw farmer's hat that Abundio recognized as Chino's.

The rest of them strung out in a long, loose line, trudging slowly upwards with their picks and shovels and iron bars. Everyone carried something, a bottle of water, a bag of lunches, an infant slung in a shawl, and they rounded the switchbacks, one-by-one, and ascended the cliff.

Abundio and Socorro were at about the middle of the line. They each carried a shovel in one hand and a heavy, six-foot bar in the other. Abundio's boots began to grind the tops of his bare toes. His legs were stiffer than ever from the soccer game two days before.

Straggling far behind, Ana Rosa Medina followed with the children of the village, scolding and urging them up the steep road like a shepherd driving a flock of uncooperative sheep.

They climbed past the first big turn, to where the road began a long, almost level run back into the canyon. Below to their left lay the pista and village, and beneath the trees Abundio could see the light brown palm thatch and cardón wattle of their house. Beyond it lay Pablo's house, bright and pink, with Margarita sitting alone in the darkened room.

They paused long enough for Abundio to remove his boots and hang them around his neck. When they resumed, Socorro took both the iron bars, leaving the shovels for Abundio. With his feet unfettered and his load much lighter, Abundio made better progress up the steep road.

The morning air in the canyon was almost painfully hot. No one spoke. Accustomed to laboring in tropical conditions, each person in line set an individual pace that would allow him or her to reach the landslide, work all day, and return to the village by sunset without becoming too exhausted to repeat the process the next day, and the next, if necessary. Each person expended the precise amount of effort that would allow work to continue indefinitely. Whether the task was merely to sit in the shade mending clothes, or to swing a heavy hammer in the noonday sun, the people had learned from experience that the amount of effort expended per unit of time must never vary. Any violation of that rule, any slowing of the pace, or any sudden outburst of energy, would prevent the task from being completed in the shortest possible time.

As they climbed higher, the road gradually turned to coarse gravel mixed with dirt and rocks. It reversed itself and made a long run back toward the sea. Then it began a series of short, climbing switchbacks above the sand dunes. They reached a spot where they could look out over the water, and here Abundio and Socorro paused to rest and enjoy the grand view of the Sea of Cortez. The day was clear and windless. On the horizon sat the low, bluish-gray outlines of Isla Monserrate, and farther out, Isla Catalán. The greens and blues of the sea ran toward the islands in marbled sheets.

Socorro threw down her iron bars and climbed into a hollow in the cliff that gave some shade. Abundio followed her and they sat together looking out at the water.

Abundio patted his wife's knee, admiring her ability to find hope in things that seemed impossible. That was the woman's special courage, Abundio thought. The man is impulsive and impatient. He is made for fighting, for making things and destroying them, and that takes courage too. But if the fight is lost, the man despairs.

Abundio looked at Socorro's gray hair and her leathery dark face. She seemed so small, almost frail. Yet she was able to carry the heavy iron bars without help. That is the woman's special strength, he thought. The woman is actually stronger than the man. She is patient, and she finds a way to endure, to preserve and nurture that which remains to her, no matter how difficult the task or how many times she is defeated.

Several of the others passed them. Ana Rosa Medina came into view one switchback below. Two of the smallest children had grown tired and Ana Rosa carried one of them slung on her back and the other in her arms.

Socorro had not spoken in some time. Abundio stirred a hand through the infinite blueness of the sea and sky.

"It is a beautiful day, is it not?"

"Not bad."

"What makes you so quiet, Socorro? What are you thinking?"

"We are out of fish."

"Ahh! Chino and I will go out this evening! Would you like cochis?"

"Whatever."

"We will catch you some nice cochis. And Chino will dive for scallops and clams and we can have soup. I will ask Joselito to find some crabs for it."

"María loves soup."

"Yes, she will enjoy it."

They rose to resume the climb and Abundio gave both shovels to his wife.

"I will take the bars. My legs feel much better now."

"Are you sure, husband?"

"Yes. I am fine now."

BY THE TIME Abundio and Socorro reached the rockslide, the early arrivers had already begun work.

Pablo Santos' pickup had been attached by a long rope to a goat-sized boulder in the middle of the road. The rockslide had come down a small arroyo at the apex of a tight, V-shaped turn in the road. By dragging the rock down one leg of the V, Pablo planned to pull it over the edge of the cliff. The others were working with wheelbarrows to clear away smaller rocks.

Pablo had taken the slack out of the rope and was about to drag the rock over the edge when Abundio arrived and held his hand up to stop him.

"Just a second, Pablo!"

"What?"

"I will look to make sure no one is in the way."

Pablo waited impatiently while Abundio pulled on his boots and climbed over the rocks to the clear section on the far side. Abundio continued another twenty yards to a projecting point on the road that gave him an unobstructed view of the cliff below.

What he saw chilled his sweaty back.

Far below, directly in the path of the arroyo, waddled Ana Rosa Medina, surrounded by a dozen small children. She had fallen very far behind and had not even begun to climb the last series of switchbacks. A landslide now could bury them all. Abundio ran back to where Pablo could see him and he waved his arms and shouted.

"Pablo! No! Don't pull yet!"

Pablo could not hear above the loud rattle of his pickup and he assumed Abundio was giving him the all-clear signal. He put the pickup into gear and gave it full throttle.

The rope tightened and the big rock flipped on its back and slid off the road. It stood upright for a moment and then slowly toppled over and began to skip down the face of the cliff, gathering speed as it went. Abundio ran to the edge of the cliff. He leaned out as far as he could and cupped his hands and shouted.

"Ana! Ana Rosa! Look out! Look out!"

The white circle of Ana Rosa's skirt continued to roll rhythmically back and forth with her steps. She had not heard him and she continued up the road holding the hands of two children. Abundio looked to his left and saw the rock turning slowly through the air and coming down. A spray of flinty chips flew from it as it struck the cliff and leapt out again, followed by a shower of stones and gravel.

The slide grew as it went, loosening larger rocks now. Abundio looked down to the place where it must fall and he recognized the figure of a thin, long-haired boy on the road, thirty yards ahead of Ana Rosa. The boy carried a shovel over his shoulder and he was trotting alone ahead of the group. Abundio had time to shout once more before the falling dust and rock obscured them all from his view.

"Jo-se-li-to!"

Ana Rosa Medina heard her son's name come from the sky above her just as she looked for him to make sure he had not gotten too far ahead.

Joselito heard his name called too, and thinking it was his mother, he turned back to her at the same moment.

Their eyes made contact, and they understood that neither had called the other, and they looked up to see where the voice had come from. A cluster of black boulders, some bigger than a truck, came churning down through the brilliant blue sky, and there was no time to run from it. They looked to each other one more time, mother and son, locked in the embrace of that eternal bond, and Ana Rosa stood watching as the rocks seemed to slow down, slow down until they were hardly moving, until they had almost stopped in mid-flight, as if by magic. But the first rock, the size of a fist, came down, and it struck Joselito's outstretched right hand, and then a larger one struck the middle of his back as he bent away from them, and then Joselito disappeared from her view.

On the cliff, Abundio could see nothing but the rising cloud of yellow dust that marked where the rocks had gone over the edge. He turned and ran back to the blocked part of the road and scrambled across it on all fours, shouting.

"Chino! Chino! Chino!"

Socorro and María understood that something was very wrong and they came running toward Abundio and met him at the edge of the rubble. But he ran past them without stopping to speak.

Chino had already guessed what had happened. He moved over to Pablo Santos' truck and stood at attention beside it, hands dangling loosely at his sides, waiting for his partner to reach him. He shouted as soon as Abundio was close enough to understand.

"Ana Rosa?"

Abundio's eyes were glazed with fear and tension. His voice shook.

"I think it is Joselito."

Chino looked up at Pablo, who sat uncomprehendingly on his chair, pumping the throttle of his pickup to keep the engine running. Chino spoke quickly and distinctly.

"Get down."

Pablo did not move. Without speaking again, Chino stepped up on the frame of the pickup, grabbed Pablo around the shoulders, and hurled him through the air.

Abundio threw a bar and shovel into the wooden box on the back of the pickup. He grabbed a machete. With a single blow, he severed the rope tied to the truck's rear frame member. Then he scrambled into the box himself as Chino jammed the pickup into gear and floorboarded it. Abundio clung to the sides of the box and shouted to the others as they sped away.

"Joselito has been buried! Come quickly!"

The pickup bounced and twisted down the switchbacks as fast as Chino dared push it. As they came out of the last turn, they saw the cloud of yellow dust curling slowly away from the base of the cliff and then the new pile of boulders covering the road where they had walked only an hour before.

Chino stopped the pickup and they climbed around the rock pile. On the far side, they found the other children huddled together in a group, staring at Ana Rosa Medina who was in the middle of the road tearing at a boulder with her fingers.

Ana Rosa stood against the face of the rock, making small birdlike noises and ripping her nails across it as if to scratch it. Abundio came up behind her. He waited for a moment and then placed his hands gently on her plump arms. She stopped and leaned her forehead against the rock. She had ground off the ends of her fingers. Without seeing him, she knew who had touched her.

"Bundo… "

"Sí, Ana Rosa."

"My Lito… "

"Sí."

"Bundo… there must be many spaces… between the rocks."

"Chino is looking."

They stood there until Chino's head appeared at the top of the pile. He signaled silently for Abundio to join him. Abundio stroked Ana Rosa's shoulders and whispered gently to the back of her head.

"Ana Rosa, I must go to help Chino now. Please, sit with the children."

Ana Rosa Medina left her hand prints on the face of the rock. She gathered the children about her, as Abundio climbed around to meet Chino in a place where they would not be seen. Chino was covered with scratches and cuts from wedging himself down into the dangerous spaces between the boulders. He handed Abundio the bloody, splintered shaft of a shovel and whispered.

"Joselito is dead."

"Did you find him, mijo?"

"A small part of him. The rest is under a rock."

"Where?"

"At the very bottom, on the other side."

Abundio looked out over the wide Sea of Cortez. There was hardly a ruffle on it anywhere and the subtle light and dark streaks made by the currents were sharp and clear. On the far horizon, groups of pelicans and seagulls were working bait fish. It was the season of the tuna.

"Mijo, we must try to dig him out."

Chino shook his head.

"Impossible, amigo. These rocks are too big, even for the pickup."

"It is our duty... to Ana Rosa."

"A gesture, then?"

"Yes, mijo. A gesture."

The people of Agua Amargosa worked all through the morning, clearing the smaller rocks and burrowing themselves between the larger boulders in hopes that Joselito Medina might be found alive somewhere beneath the landslide.

The women shaded Ana Rosa with their scarves, comforting her as best they could, and only Abundio Rodríguez and Chino Zúñiga knew the dreadful secret, and they saw to it that no one dug at the far end of the slide where Joselito lay entombed.

They took lunch in shifts. When their turn came, Abundio and Chino joined Socorro and María in the broken shade of a palo verde tree beside the road. Socorro handed Abundio a burrito and watched him unroll it part way to check its contents.

"No levanta muertos today, husband."

She pointed toward Pablo Santos, eating alone in the shade of an enormous, overhanging boulder. Pablo had worked more than diligently throughout the morning, volunteering repeatedly to descend into the most difficult parts of the rubble. No one had spoken to him.

"Pablo feels bad."

"It was not his fault. It was an accident. An act of God."

"He is in much pain. He landed on his hip when Chino threw him off the pickup."

Abundio grunted.

"That was an accident too."

The flies and sand bees, desperate for moisture, soon discovered the four of them sitting beneath the palo verde tree, and the insects swarmed to the sweat of their skin and clothes. Their burritos became covered with the biting pests, which refused to flee when swatted at and would cling and prick and drink thirstily even as they were smashed.

Chino and María tried standing in the sun, but the insects followed them, so they took their burritos and walked back to the slide. Abundio and Socorro remained in the shade of the tree. As they ate, they waved their hands constantly over each other to keep from being bitten. Abundio was particularly sensitive to insects, especially mosquitos in the evening. He made a rare complaint as a sharp bite hit the back of his shoulder.

"It is like hell here. Hot and miserable."

In Abundio's recollection, his wife had never been bitten or stung by any insect. Perhaps her Indian blood protected her. Socorro waved her little hands protectively around him, but she seemed unconcerned for herself. Abundio tried an experiment. Briefly, he stopped waving his hands over his wife, and he observed the flies and bees closely to see if they landed on her. He was right. The insects buzzed very close, and sometimes they just barely grazed her skin, but they didn't land or bite. Abundio was fascinated.

"Socorro. Do you know that flies do not even land on you?"

"Yes."

"I wonder why."

"It is a state of mind. My mother taught me."

"How do you mean?"

"You form a picture of yourself, deep in your mind, and it becomes true."

"Do you mean... a picture with no flies?"

"Yes."

Abundio decided to try it. Over the years, his wife had surprised him many times with her Indian ways. If this trick with insects worked it would be a miraculous deliverance indeed.

"What do you mean by deep in your mind?"

Socorro kept waving her hands over him.

"I am not sure, husband. It is difficult to explain. It is a calm feeling, a feeling that is both large and small at the same time."

"Do you do it all the time, or only when the flies come?"

"All the time... I think."

"Even at night? When you are asleep?"

"I suppose so."

"Are you doing it right now?"

Socorro thought a moment.

"Yes."

Abundio closed his eyes. He imagined a place somewhere in the middle of his head, directly between his ears, and there he visualized a tiny image of himself, standing in a panga way out at sea, with the air about him free of insects.

"Socorro, in the picture, does it matter if you are sitting down or standing up?"

"I don't think so."

Abundio kept his eyes closed tight. He concentrated on the image, trying to fill in as much detail as possible. He felt ready.

"All right, Socorro. You may stop waving your hands now."

"Are you sure, husband?"

"Yes. I am confident that I am doing it correctly."

Socorro withdrew her hands. After a short moment she spoke hurriedly. "Bundo?"

"Yes, Socorro."

"There is a big one on your neck."

"I am sure it will not bite."

"Can you feel it?"

"Yes, but... *Ayyyy!*"

Abundio slapped the side of his neck and looked with contempt at the bloody horsefly crushed between his fingers. He rose to his feet, swatting himself all over, and he thought of the brittle pufferfish Socorro always kept hanging on their front porch.

"It works no better than Nacho's botetes."

"Perhaps it is matter of faith, something one learns as a child."

Socorro used the Spanish word *niño*, or masculine child, and it reminded them both of the doleful charade they had been playing out all morning. The word "Niño" also referred to the Christ Child, and Abundio thought of the Sunday mornings of his own boyhood in La Paz, of the smooth, cool, wooden benches in the church and the pungent smell of the ball-shaped censers that were kept in the sacristy. He thought of poor Joselito under the rocks and he tried to remember the consoling words of the priests. He hoped, for Joselito's sake, that at least some of the words were true. And he hoped that the priests' faith worked as well as Socorro's. Then he felt the need for relief from his burden of knowledge and he spoke to his wife.

"Joselito is dead."

"Of course."

"No. I mean we *know* he is already dead. Chino found him this morning, under the rocks."

"We know."

"Did Chino tell you?"

"We knew from your face that Joselito died when the rocks fell. We knew there would be no miracle today. No levanta muertos, eh?"

"Then... why have you said nothing?"

"We understand. It is something we can give to Ana Rosa."

Abundio looked up the road. Chino and the other men were on the rock pile, throwing small pieces down. A little distance off, Ana Rosa Medina sat waiting with the other women and children in the edge of the afternoon sun. Soon, the shade of the cliff would cover them.

"Does she also know?"

"She has not acknowledged it. But she knows."

"And... the others?"

"All of them, husband. How long shall we continue?"

Abundio looked out toward the distant islands, yellow and flat in the afternoon light.

"Socorro... I don't know what is proper."

Three hours later, the shade of the cliff finally touched the people of Agua Amargosa, and they welcomed its coolness at first. But then their spent muscles chilled and stiffened, and their tools grew heavy.

In the late afternoon, the children were taken back to the village. But the men and women continued to work as the sun fell into the mountains.

In the early evening, when the shadows had crept out over the inner reefs and the rich sunset had turned the distant islands to mounds of gold, Abundio dropped his iron bar and sought out Ana Rosa. He found her sitting alone on a low rock by the side of the road with her heavy legs wrapped beneath her.

"Ana Rosa... "

Abundio's eyes were dark smudges in the rock dust that covered his body. Ana Rosa was looking out toward the golden islands.

"Did he suffer, Bundo?"

"No, Ana Rosa. He did not suffer."

"Thank you, Bundo."

Her ankles were swollen and white from lack of movement. She braced herself with one hand. With the other, she touched the ragged cuff of Abundio's black trousers.

"Every night, he practiced the knots you taught him. He never forgot the times you took him in your boat."

"He was... a very fine boy."

"Bundo, would you please help me up?"

Abundio held Ana Rosa under her arms and slowly lifted her up. He steadied her until she could stand by herself. Then he waved for Socorro and María. At this signal, all the others also stopped working, as though he had given a command. They dusted themselves off and gathered their things, and in the deepening twilight they passed by on their way to light the evening fires.

Ana Rosa Medina stood at the edge of the road. To each person she gave a word of thanks and they took her hand and nodded silently.

Pablo Santos was the last to come.

"Señora Medina... "

"What will be, will be, Pablo. It was an accident."

"Yes. An accident."

He limped slowly toward the village.

Chino and Maria arrived with the wheelbarrow. María had broken a sandal strap and she had worn a hole through the knee of her new pants. Her hands were roughened from handling the stones. Abundio threw his shovel into the wheelbarrow.

"Mijo, we need something for supper. Are the oars still in the panga?"

"Right."

"We need some clams and scallops. Also crabs. Socorro wants to make a big soup tonight."

"No problem, amigo."

María took Chino's arm.

"I will row for you."

"Right. We need to hurry."

They left the wheelbarrow and set out toward the beach at a half trot. It would be dark by the time they got the panga out but they could guide themselves by the lights of the houses. They could gather clams and get some cochi or pargo in the rocks near shore. Someone would help them pull the boat out of the water.

Ana Rosa Medina had gone back to the rockslide and she was standing alone, looking out at the darkening sea. Socorro went to her.

"Ana Rosa, it is late. I could use some help with the cooking tonight. Would you mind?"

"Thank you, Socorro."

AFTER DINNER, ABUNDIO and Socorro walked Ana Rosa Medina and her children home, and then they took the dark path up the arroyo to Fra Nacho's place.

His record player was sending its scratchy music into the night as they reached the level ground in front of his shack. His batteries were nearly gone and he apologized for not lighting their way.

"Sorry, Socorro. Batteries almost bye-bye now."

They sat down beside his cot and Socorro gave him a heavy, grease-saturated paper bag. He opened it with a smile as the nutty aroma of fried snapper and garlic surrounded them.

Socorro cleared off the top of a crate, and put a fork and plate on it.

"Chino caught a very big pargo in the caleta tonight. They said the strike almost pulled María out of the boat."

"Socorro, your generosity keeps an old man alive."

They sat in uneasy silence, listening to the music. Fra Nacho had the record player turned all the way up, but the sound was distorted and full of static.

Abundio listened closely. It was not Señor Tchaikovsky's piano concerto número uno. At least, not any part of it that he recognized.

"What is this music, Nacho? I have not heard it before."

"It is by Wolfgang Amadeus Mozart, a German who died about two-hundred years ago. He is considered by many to be the greatest composer, perhaps even the greatest genius, ever produced by the human race. This is one of his last compositions, the Symphony Number Thirty-Eight in D Major."

"Thirty-eight symphonies! He must have been a very old man."

"Actually, he was only about thirty when he wrote it. And he died only a few years later. He was a child prodigy."

They listened as the lively strings of the first movement gave way to the measured rhythmic dissonances of the second. Fra Nacho's finger waved in time to the music.

"Do you see anything, Bundo?"

"Ahh… !"

Abundio sat up straight and cleared his throat, concentrating on the music. The third movement began and seemed to split into two voices, one harmonious, birdlike, and the other dissonant, like a chaotic, powerful storm, with each energetically battling the other for dominance. Time and again, the storm seemed victorious, only to have the bird jump up and rejoin the struggle. Then the voices intertwined into the most dramatic conflict of all, and just as it seemed inevitable that one or the other must win out, they suddenly combined into one, and the symphony ended unexpectedly, on a high, piercing note.

Abundio waited for another movement, but there was none.

"Is that all of it, Nacho?"

"Yes, Bundo. Did it make you see anything?"

"No."

"No swells or pangas?"

"No. But there is something."

"Yes, Bundo?"

"Señor Mozart's symphony is a thing of absolute perfection, is it not?"

Fra Nacho leaned forward, beckoning.

"How, Bundo? How is it perfect?"

"It is not like the Russian Tchaikovsky's piano concerto at all. Every part of it belongs to every other part. Even when it seems the German's notes must be wrong, a little later you see that they were perfect and necessary after all. The last note requires the first."

Fra Nacho's eyes shined in the dark.

"That is wonderful, Abundio."

"But Nacho, there is one more thing."

"Yes?"

"The German's symphony is very beautiful and perfect, but I prefer the Russian's piano concerto."

"Why, Bundo? Why do you prefer the Tchaikovsky?"

"When I hear the Russian's music, I ride the sea and my heart is happy."

"Even if the ride lasts only three minutes?"

"Yes."

"And... you know it will end unsatisfyingly?"

"Yes."

"And... even if you can never know why Tchaikovsky wrote it that way?"

"Yes."

The night cast a spell over the three old friends and the uneasiness returned, making them reluctant to speak further, and they sat silently until very late, surrounded by the impenetrable shadows, feeling each other's presence in the dark, recasting the day's sad events in their minds again and again. Faint children's cries came from somewhere near the village. In the distance, a watery boulevard of light led straight out to a moon just coming over the horizon.

Abundio rose to leave.

"Nacho... Ana Rosa asks that you come up the road tomorrow. She asks that you say a prayer for Joselito."

"I am no priest, Bundo."

"She requests a favor. Just a few words."

"Well... Bundo. I don't know."

Abundio turned to face them from the head of the path. His voice was suddenly hard, strange, different.

"I ask it also! As a favor! For me!"

Nacho's voice answered, much smaller.

"I will do what I can."

"Thank you, Nacho. I will go for Luis early in the morning."

Socorro began gathering the dishes together.

"Husband, I will stay a few minutes and clean up."

"All right."

They watched Abundio's dark silhouette disappear down the path. Fra Nacho shifted on his cot.

"He is... upset."

Socorro was standing now, looking in the direction of the path, with her hands folded in front of her.

"He was very fond of Joselito."

"He is usually so quiet. It is easy to forget what strong feelings he carries inside himself."

"Yes."

Socorro emptied the rusted steel bucket into the outhouse behind the shack, and she rinsed it with a little water from the well and put it back under the cot. She stood in the dark with her hands on her hips.

"Nacho, you must take better care of yourself."

"It is difficult."

"Does the leg bother you?"

"A little. I tell you, Socorro. Sometimes I feel like a one-legged man in a butt-kicking contest."

"Still, that is no excuse for living like a pig. In the morning, María and I will come and wash you. We will help you get dressed."

"Thank you, Socorro."

She sat down.

"Nacho, I have always wondered why you studied to be a priest, but never became one."

"The Holy Spirit would not come to me."

"Why not?"

"I felt... unworthy."

ALL DURING THE night a high, thin overcast crept up from the south, gradually blotting out the moon and the wheel of stars turning above the caleta. In the hour just before dawn, the village was so dark a hand held out was not visible, and Abundio Rodríguez stubbed his toes twice before reaching the old panga.

He groaned softly as he put his shoulder to the bow, lifted and swung it around a few inches, and then went to the stern to repeat the process. Slowly, using all his weight and strength, he seesawed the boat down the sandy slope until it touched the water and floated.

He walked the panga into the lukewarm sea, shuffling his feet to warn the sleeping stingrays of his coming and give them time to scurry away. As his hands moved along the familiar, worn-down gunnel of the old boat, he thought of his father and their happy times together.

Well, papá, our boat may be old and it may be scarred from many honest battles on the sea, but it is a faithful boat and it weighs very little. A man may launch it even if he is alone. And if the motor does not work? A boat such as ours serves quite well enough with oars... or even paddles. How many men does it take to launch Pablo's panga? At least seven or eight! Who would want such a boat? Not us!

Abundio swirled his free hand through the black water, and it left a glowing wake as the phosphorescent plankton flashed and subsided. He slapped his wet leg and saw the shape of his hand writ in the dark by the sparkling sequins of the warm summer sea. The phosphorescence was unusually strong, perhaps the strongest he had ever seen. Abundio thought of another year like this, when La Paz was little more than a village and he fished with his father from their dugout canoe.

Do you remember our old *canoa,* papá? You watched them carve it from the trunk of a tree in Mazatlán. And you sailed it alone across the open sea to La Paz. You were such a man, papá! I am not ashamed to tell you I could *never* do such a thing! I remember how we cooked our dinner on the beach in the evenings and how hard and rough your hands felt as we walked home. Remember how I always carried the gaff for you? Papá, there are some mornings I still miss you so, and I wish you had not died. But I know you could not help it.

Abundio put both hands on the gunnel and spilled himself headfirst into the panga. He used the long gaff to push himself away from the beach, and he got the old Evinrude started and left it half tilted up as he steered toward a line of scattered, purple and orange clouds just starting to show in the eastern sky.

Working mostly by feel and memory, Abundio threaded his way carefully out through the reef. The tide was about at its midpoint and there were many rocks that might strike the whirling propeller. The rocks were invisible in the starry-black water ahead, but Abundio watched several of them pass by in the panga's bubbly, phosphorescent wake.

When he saw the needle of the fourth island, standing black against the dawn, he steered past it and lowered the Evinrude for the run to Las Ramalitas. The sea was level and still. The warm wind and the growl of the motor were the only indications of motion as Abundio opened the throttle and pointed the bow toward the North Star.

ABUNDIO SKIMMED INTO the bay of Las Ramalitas and headed for the cluster of lean-tos that marked the colony from Agua Amargosa. The beach in front of Ramón's camp was deserted, with not a single panga on it.

He had made excellent time. As he drew near the beach, Abundio saw the flat morning sun just touching the tops of the hills behind the lean-tos. Schools of silvery bait fish shot into the air, chased by barracuda and jacks in the midst of their morning bite.

Abundio spotted Ramón on the beach, but as he cut the motor and tilted it up, he sensed that he had arrived at a troubled moment. Ramón, whose face was typically as impenetrable as Socorro's, looked worried and nervous. He gave Abundio the abrazo.

"Bundo, why have you come today? It is only Monday."

"I need to get Luis Medina. Joselito was killed by a rockslide."

Ramón shook his head sadly.

"Luis is gone."

"Where?"

"He would not tell us. He just loaded his panga and left."

They went up to camp. Ramón had gathered a big pile of supplies for them. Their carburetor—a brand new one still in its cardboard box—lay on top. There were also many things that did not belong there, extra food, boxes of clothes, and things that belonged to Ramón, including his fishing lines and spare hooks, and even his oars and gaffs.

Abundio realized why the scene on the beach had seemed so strange. Ramón's panga was not there! It was the first time since that hope-filled day sixteen years earlier, when Ramón had brought his panga home to Isla Coronado, that the man and his boat were not together in the same place. Abundio searched way up and down the beach.

"Ramón... where is your panga?"

Ramón shook his head.

"There is a truck coming for us. Tomorrow night."

Abundio stared at the stocky, round-headed man who had become his brother. At last he understood the meaning of the things in the pile.

"I will bring Socorro and María. They will want to... "

But Ramón interrupted sharply.

"No, Bundo! I don't want to see *anyone!*"

"But Ramón, why not? Why didn't you tell me!?"

"I am... I am... "

Ramón could not finish. Abundio put his big arms around him.

"Oh, Ramón!"

"I am so frightened, Bundo. With so many to care for... I... I don't know if I still have the strength for the ranchos."

"Where do you go?"

Ramón turned away, looking beyond the curtain of thin gray clouds hiding the northern sky. Then he showed Abundio a letter containing an important looking card punched with strange rectangular holes.

"This is a kind of money, Bundo. Dollars. From the americano post office. Miguel and Isabel sent it. They have jobs up there."

"Where, brother?"

"They say there is a place called Encinitas, about thirty miles north of San Diego. They have ranchos covered with glass and clear plastic where they grow flowers."

"Flowers? That's all?"

"Yes. There are ranchos just for flowers and they need many workers. Every family has a car or pickup. There are schools for all the children and special buses that come to the villages to pick them up in the morning. There is free water that comes out of pipes in every house."

They sat on a hump of sand, looking out over the bay. Ramón examined the printing on the card as he continued to recite from memory the contents of the letter that had been written and forwarded to him on behalf of his eldest son and daughter.

"Miguel and Isabel say the work of the flowers is very difficult to learn, but not heavy. They say that on these ranchos an older man could be just as valuable as a young one, if he were to apply himself."

Ramón reached into his back pocket and gave Abundio a greasy paper bag folded into a packet and tied with string. Abundio opened it.

"What is this, brother?"

"It is half the money from the panga. When I have found work, I will send more. I promise it, Bundo."

There were pesos and U.S. dollars in the packet. Also, an elegant pendant of polished black stone, carved in the shape of a reindeer head and hung on a thin gold chain. Ramón touched the exquisitely detailed obsidian, which Abundio had not seen before.

"It was our mother's. Socorro will know it."

Abundio tried to give the money back.

"This is not necessary, brother. Remember, I have my gold watch."

Ramón's voice was sharper than Abundio had ever heard it.

"Forget that watch! It has made you lazy!"

"What do you mean, brother?"

"In all our years, you have never really applied yourself to anything because of that watch."

"It was a gift of friendship."

"Yes, but you never earned it. In the end it… castrated you."

"But… it was given in friendship."

"The intentions of the watchmaker are irrelevant! It is the result that counts."

Abundio let the pendant swing back and forth on its chain. Castrated? How could something given in sincerity do such harm? Surely, Ramón must be wrong.

"But brother, if that is true, how can I accept this money from you?"

Ramón smiled at the big man.

"This gift, Bundo, you have earned a thousand times over."

Ramón looked at Abundio's wide, comforting face, and he preserved an image of it to take with him. He would keep this last portrait of his brother-in-law beside the images he had already stored in his heart for the long journey north. Socorro waving good-bye from the beach, María so elegant in her golden sandals, the wake of his panga as it disappeared across the bay in the hands of its new owner.

Ramón held his face in a tight smile to conceal from his brother-in-law the pain of the other, older images in his heart. The hopeless, empty market of Salina Cruz, the cruel trek north, the peace on the faces of his parents and brother and sister as they were wrapped in their clothes and buried. He remembered how shockingly worn and old Socorro had looked on the day she left the ranchos and joined him on Isla Coronado. And he remembered how he and his sister had come to believe their loneliness would never end and how easily they had accepted it as their fate.

He stood and gave Abundio the abrazo.

"Abundio Rodríguez, I leave you my house, the animals, everything. Love my sister and care for her as you promised to do many years ago."

Abundio had never been farther north than Santa Rosalia. No one that he knew, other than Chino, had ever crossed the border into the United States. He tried to imagine Ramón's family on their journey to *El Norte,* the unknown.

"How will you get to San Diego?"

"We have sold everything. The truck takes us as far as San Ignacio. After that...."

"The Indian way."

"If necessary."

ABUNDIO'S MIND WAS crowded with thoughts of Ramón and of Joselito Medina as he pushed on the tiller and pointed the panga toward the high gray point. He scanned the base of the cliffs for the white rocks he knew should be visible just beneath them.

Two small boys sat facing forward on the seat in front of him. Their long hair fluttered like black ribbons in the slipstream coming over the bow.

The panga weaved unsteadily left and right as it neared the cliffs. Abundio was searching for the rocks but could not find them and the older boy turned around and looked at him questioningly.

"Bundo, are you looking for the bait fish rocks?"

"Yes, Rubén. Do you see them?"

"We passed them five minutes ago."

"Ah... well in that case, we are just about where I want to be."

Abundio pushed the panga north again, right along the base of the cliffs. He focused his eyes on the shoreline ahead, trying to remember the exact spot where they caught the big grouper. They had drifted quite a distance south of the rocks, he knew. They had been about a mile south of them, or perhaps it was two miles.

The panga rounded a bend in the cliff and the white rocks popped unexpectedly into view only a hundred yards ahead. Abundio turned the panga around and headed south again. The older boy frowned at him, puzzled.

"Bundo, what are you looking for? The new garropa spot?"

"Yes, Rubén. It was right around here someplace."

"It is a mile south of here. Between the third and fourth arroyos."

"Ah... "

Abundio began counting the narrow arroyos that cut the shore every quarter mile or so, partitioning the cliff into large, pyramid-shaped faces.

The panga had just passed the third arroyo when Abundio suddenly realized it was not possible for Rubén Santos and his younger brother to know the location of the new grouper spot. It had been only three days since he and Chino discovered it and the boys had been with their mother in Loreto during that time. Abundio chuckled to himself. He shouted forward.

"Eh, Rubén! This is a new spot. You don't know about this one."

They looked back with sly grins on their little tanned faces.

"Oh yes we do!"

"Ah? How is that possible?"

"Papá caught two more big fish there! He told us when he came to give the clothes and money to mamá."

"Your papá came to Loreto? When did he do that?"

"Saturday, in the morning."

So! Pablo Santos had gone fishing early Saturday morning!

And he had said *nothing* during the meeting at Nacho's place! Or that afternoon while working on his gill net! He must have taken the fish straight up to Loreto, and then rushed back to the caleta with his big Evinrude howling like the end of world! *Caramba!* What a fisherman that Pablo was!

Abundio slowed the panga to idling speed. With four big fish taken from the area in less than a week, maybe this stop was a waste of time anyway. As his eyes sought a familiar landmark on the rocky shoreline, Abundio wondered what had happened with Lupe Santos. Why had she brought the boys back to Ramón's camp?

"Eh... Rubén. Why did your mother bring you back to Las Ramalitas?"

"She's a bitch."

"Well... ah... where did she go?"

"She's a bitch."

Abundio did not question the boys further. He tried to remember what the shore looked like where he and Chino had caught their big grouper, but the rocks all appeared about the same to him. He steered the panga south, very close to the cliff, with gradually diminishing hopes of finding the spot again.

Rubén and Mario Santos, meanwhile, concentrated their attentions on the patterns of color and texture in the green water passing between the panga and shore. They were searching for subtle signs invisible to Abundio, signs that might lead to other grouper holes and even bigger grouper.

"Hold it! Bundo! Drop a bait here!"

"What?"

Abundio cut the throttle and stopped the panga by putting the motor momentarily into reverse. The boys pushed the bags of food aside to get at the winding boards. Quickly, they cut a dead mackerel into pieces, baited two lines, and threw them back toward a submerged, house-sized boulder under the face of the cliff. There was a swirl of activity in the water and they pulled in a yellow snapper and a tremendous, tremendous hogfish.

Abundio watched as the boys baited up twice more and caught three large spotted cabrilla and another hogfish. He smiled in proud admiration of these young sons of Pablo's. In twenty minutes, they had filled the bow of the panga to near capacity with fish that he would have missed.

The boys wound the lines carefully onto the boards and used the stone to resharpen the hooks. They tucked the knife into its spot between the front thwart and the hull and they replaced the bags of food and clothes. Without a word, they took their seats. Rubén gestured over his shoulder for Abundio to put the motor into gear and resume their run south to Agua Amargosa.

There was only the hint of a southern swell on the light blue sea.

Abundio leaned back thoughtfully on the end of the tiller as the panga rose up and flew over the water.

Now… how did they do that? What—exactly—did Rubén see down there? A big boulder? *Madre!* There were thousands of big boulders between the white rock and the caleta, and Abundio knew that he and Chino could throw mackerel at them for a month and never catch fish the way these two sons of Pablo Santos had.

Perhaps Ramón was right after all. Perhaps he and Chino really didn't care strongly enough, in the way Pablo and his sons did, whether they caught fish or not.

But on the other hand, Abundio knew he saw many things that Pablo and his sons missed. Just now, for example, he had seen the lightning bolts spiraling down to the endless depths.

The lightning bolts were only visible if you looked directly away from the sun, at the shadow of your own head in the water. It was an unusual sign to see them in summer, especially with the nighttime luminescence so strong now, and especially so close to shore.

Abundio loved to watch the lightning bolts that sometimes surrounded his shadow in the clear, cool offshore water of winter, because it reminded him of the pictures of Jesus and the Virgin and the other saints, and when he saw the halo surrounding his head, he fancied himself as one of them, a creature of the mystical and infinite, the mysterious depths known only to God and the fish.

But Abundio had never noticed the lightning bolts so close to shore in the middle of summer. And Pablo's sons had missed them completely.

He shouted forward to the boys.

"Eh!… Rubén, did you see the lightning bolts back there?"

"The *what?*"

"The lightning bolts, when you look at your own shadow in the water."

"Oh, that? Sure. There are lots of places like that. It's because clear water comes from way down deep there."

"Ah… "

"A<small>NA</small> R<small>OSA</small> M<small>EDINA</small>, we have come today to share your sorrow for the tragic loss of your son, Joselito… "

Fra Nacho grabbed at the supporting arms of Socorro and María. He had risen from the fish cart but his hard-soled dress shoe had rolled sideways on a pebble and his crutch had nearly slid out from under him. He regained his composure and continued his address to the small congregation gathered on the cliff above the sea.

"So young! Joselito flew up to the sky, alone, to a fate that we the living can only surmise.

"What can we poor, blind creatures know of Joselito's present circumstances? How can we know if his life was part of God's grand design, or just a meaningless ripple on the endless sea of time?

"And what can we know of Joselito's way of passing from this world? Was it a cruel blow struck by jealous evil? Was it an accident of random fate? Or was it, also, the deed of a God that deigns not to reveal His purposes to us?

"We can never know the answers to these questions. Nor can we even know why we wish to ask them… "

Fra Nacho bent over and coughed for half a minute as María pounded his back, and then he continued.

" …Ana Rosa, all we can know with certainty is that we loved Joselito, as you did. The pain of his passing burns in our hearts, sharp and undeniable.

"And it is in our pain that we know Joselito lived among us once, and that, despite our blindness, we ourselves are truly alive, and our lives were once illuminated by the beauty and goodness that was his."

Fra Nacho bowed to Ana Rosa. Aided by Socorro and María, he seated himself on the fish cart and sat there looking up at the others, obviously finished, waiting for someone else to speak.

Socorro pressed a finger into the back of Abundio's white dress shirt. He did not move, so she pinched his waist hard enough to make him lurch forward.

"Oh!"

As everyone looked, Abundio scratched his eyebrow and cleared his throat.

"Well... ah... on behalf of Ana Rosa, I would like to thank everyone for coming here today, and especially Nacho, whose words are always so... interesting. Now... ah... Ana Rosa has a memorial for Joselito which she would like to put beside his... ah... well, his final resting place."

Ana Rosa was surrounded by her children. She wore a satin blouse and a wide, gathered skirt. Her head was covered by a black scarf tied under her chin. Her black, high-topped boots were fastened by a double row of buttons reaching from her toes almost to her knees.

Chino waited at the handles of the wheelbarrow. In its center, a wooden cross stood three feet tall, like the mast of a small sailing ship. The cross was held upright by a heavy base fashioned from a steel tire rim. It was completely encrusted with a faceted, jewel-like veneer of beer bottle caps nailed into the wood, and it was decorated with bright pink and yellow plastic flowers. Attached with wires to the center of the cross was a framed color picture of The Virgin of Guadalupe. A card inserted under the glass bore a hand-lettered inscription: *"José Antonio Medina... Voló al Cielo..."*

On a signal from Abundio, Chino began pushing the wheelbarrow around the rockslide. He was followed by Ana Rosa, her children, and the others, who formed a short procession in single file.

They reached Pablo's pickup, still trapped on the far side of the slide, and Chino was looking for an appropriate site for the cross when his eye caught the gleam of polished metal, almost hidden in the dry weeds beside the roadbed. He kicked aside a bush to reveal a small, footed metal cup mounted on an ebony base.

"What is this?"

The old-fashioned cup was low and wide, with a handle on each side. Its polished brass surface was hazy with the passage of years. It was half full of water in which floated a loose cluster of stemless yellow daisy heads. In the middle of the water, standing up to its knees, was a child's toy cow, carved in wood and very old, with its faded paint nearly gone and some long-grown toddler's tooth marks visible all over it.

Chino looked to Ana Rosa. She shook her head to tell him she knew nothing of the metal cup or its contents. The others gathered about, pressing close. One of Ana Rosa's daughters reached out for the toy cow and had her hand rapped sharply back.

Abundio arrived, pushing Fra Nacho ahead of him in the fish cart.

When he saw the old cup, Abundio instantly recalled the fourteen other cups—identical to it in every way—with which it had once formed a glistening row on a felt-covered table beneath the palms near the Casa de Gobierno of La Paz.

Abundio felt the strength of his youthful legs on that sparkling, winter day, when he had stood so proudly with his hands clasped behind his back, in the center of the second row, as the Tecolotes had their photograph taken for the newspaper and the trophies were handed out, one-by-one.

Abundio had put his cup in the back window of the old Buick and everyone who saw its polished sheen in their headlights as he cruised the Malecón in the evenings knew its significance.

But he had not thought of the cup for many years and he knew he had not taken it with him when he rowed the panga north. As he helped Fra Nacho get up from the fish cart, Abundio was wondering how the cup could have come by itself to Agua Amargosa.

Chino's voice interrupted.

"Whose work is this? And what is the meaning of the cow?"

Abundio was about to reply, but an uneasy feeling stopped him, and he was relieved when Fra Nacho answered for him.

"It does no harm. Perhaps one of the children put it here."

"Well, all right. Ana Rosa, would you like to put the cross here?"

"Yes. Thank you, Chino. This will be fine."

Chino, assisted by Pablo Santos and his sons, lifted the cross and its heavy base out of the wheelbarrow and placed it in the weeds a few feet off the road. With its faded plastic flowers, its tilted picture of The Virgin of Guadalupe, and its gaudy sheathing of bottle caps, the cross managed to look both sad and cheerful at the same time.

Ana Rosa and her children gathered around it, and they held hands and prayed silently for the soul of Joselito Medina. Then, Ana Rosa left her children and went to Fra Nacho. She bowed and shook his hand. Her eyes welled with tears.

"Señor Ignacio, thank you for coming so far from your home and for speaking on behalf of my Lito today. But would you mind? There is something you said that I do not understand."

"Of course, Ana Rosa. What is it?"

"I just want to be sure I understood you correctly, señor. You did say... didn't you, señor... that my Lito has gone to heaven?"

Fra Nacho tottered slightly forward, and he was steadied in Abundio's arms. He felt the massiveness coming, the universe falling, pouring itself into him, disappearing into a pinpoint of nothingness, the void within the void.

Ana Rosa's round, smooth face was pinched with the fear that Fra Nacho felt for himself. She tugged on his hand.

"Señor Ignacio?"

He caught himself just in time, just as the void was about to close.

"Yes... Ana Rosa. Of course. Joselito now sleeps in paradise, in the arms of God."

Ana Rosa Medina sighed with relief. She helped Fra Nacho sit down on the fish cart and she walked beside him as the procession returned to the village. They reached her lean-to, and Ana Rosa counted her children and was about to take them inside when Abundio stopped her.

"Ah... Ana Rosa, you know, Ramón's house is empty now. Would you like to use it for a while?"

The sturdy house of Ramón Ochoa was second in comfort and appearance only to the tile-roofed home of Pablo Santos. It stood in the distance, bright blue in the afternoon sun, lovely with its canopy of bougainvillea and its fence of living cactus and yucca. The two large clay pots on the porch were brilliant with the red geraniums now tended by Socorro.

Ana Rosa could have made good use of the house. In the village, the lean-to that Luis Medina had built for his large family was second in its poverty only to the listing, ramshackle dwelling of Abundio and Socorro Rodríguez.

But, she was surprised by the offer.

"Abundio, why don't you and Socorro live there?"

"Ah... well, Socorro is used to things as they are."

Ana Rosa looked out over the cobalt blue caleta. The Four Horses were sharply etched in the channel, each trailing an almost invisible wake of lighter blue in the southern current.

"Luis is not coming back to us."

The children were already running up to the lean-to. Ana Rosa followed them, laboring up the short slope of packed sand. Abundio called after her.

"And the house, Ana Rosa?"

She turned and smiled and blew a kiss at the reluctant leader of the survivors of Caleta Agua Amargosa.

"Thank you, Bundo. But you have already done so much for us. It would be best—for the children—if we were to stay here."

MARÍA'S KNEE BRUSHED against Chino's as she leaned forward to distribute burritos made with a spicy, sea turtle *guisado*.

The pungent mix of chili, garlic, onion, and dark turtle meat charmed the space under Fra Nacho's porch roof, transforming it into an open air banquet hall spread with reassuring abundance.

They were all very hungry.

In the three weeks since Ramón's departure for the United States the supply runs to Las Ramalitas had taken several hours longer than before. Chino was now required to go from house to house himself to bargain for supplies. And for the past two weeks he had been forced to hire a pickup for the long, rough ride into Loreto.

On the present Friday, Abundio had accompanied him, but it had taken half the day to find a ride into town and the two men had returned late, over the darkened sea.

There had been no time for catching cochis, but luckily they had harpooned a basking sea turtle on their way north in the morning. The creature's rich, beef-like flesh had provided a good dinner for the children of Ana Rosa Medina, as well as the burritos the Rodríguez family now shared by starlight.

For the briefest moment, María allowed her hand to rest on Chino's. His knee moved against hers and she knew that he had smiled at her in the dark. As Socorro opened the beers and passed them around, María spoke to nobody in particular.

"Does anyone here know that Chino's real name is Roberto?"

Abundio's voice, slurred by guisado and beer, came from the shadows on the opposite side of the porch.

"Well... of course, María. Don't you remember? It was *you* who decided we would all have to call him Chino."

There were laughs from around the collection of wooden boxes and overturned buckets that served as their dining table, for during the first weeks after Chino's arrival in Agua Amargosa the twelve-year-old María had adopted her mother's hostility toward the newcomer and she had begun taunting him with the nickname "Chino," because of his abundant, curly hair.

It was only years later, when Chino revealed that one of his grandfathers had actually been Chinese, that they all realized how uncannily prescient María's nickname had been, for in Spanish the word "chino" held the oxymoronic double meaning of both "curly-haired" and "Chinese."

But for María, the story of how Roberto Zúñiga had been reborn as Chino Zúñiga was lost like a distant island receding in the mist of the morning sun.

María tore a tortilla in half and used it to wrap a bit of turtle meat. She wondered what other threads of Chino's life she had forgotten or missed. He spoke so little of his past. By gently pushing and prodding during their quiet moments together, she had learned something of how much he detested his family's self-destructive system of lies, their cowardly refusal to reveal their feelings to anyone, even to each other, their ludicrous, pathetic claims of superiority over people better than themselves, their spiritual impoverishment, so wrenching and profound that Chino could hardly bear to describe it except as a withdrawal from the world itself, an obscene self-denial, a wasting of sacred human life.

María also knew that Chino was locked in some terrible struggle within himself. In his deepest sleep, after they made love in the afternoon shade of their lean-to, Chino's fingers tightened into fists and his hard-muscled chest was wracked with sobs and half-formed expletives.

But what it was that haunted him remained a mystery, for he could never recall the demons that he battled in his sleep. No matter how much María questioned him and no matter how many hours they spoke of his life before coming to Agua Amargosa, neither of them could penetrate the veil he had thrown over his memories.

And for María, the consuming passion she sensed in Chino during their lovemaking was also something she could not fully understand, even after questioning her mother about it. The carnal, the animal component of that passion was comprehensible; she knew that she wanted Chino's strength inside her as much as he, and she lost herself in the ecstasy of their embrace, just as he. But afterwards, María was always left with a lonely feeling that she had missed something, a second component of the force that drove Chino forward, forward, always forward.

Was this merely an illusion? María did not think so. For it was her mother, Socorro herself, who had first taught her about the mysterious, motivating force that lay just under the surface of everything. In the villages, the flowers blossomed, the palms grew tall and shady, and the animals and chickens ran free among the houses. Children were born, grew old, and died. Each generation followed the last in orderly fashion. But why? What made the whole machine run? What kept it from stopping?

María chewed on the spicy turtle meat and she thought of her mother and Fra Nacho arguing this very point as the flies circled about their heads in the hot afternoons.

Socorro always insisted that the visible world was controlled by a greater, invisible force that she had been able to sense since the quiet moments of her childhood. Otherwise, she said, everything would soon fall to pieces.

And Fra Nacho would scoff that her arguments reminded him of Saint Thomas Aquinas' five proofs of God's existence, an exercise in wishful, unjustified assumptions, circular reasoning, and conclusions not supported by the evidence offered. "The light of Greek reason," he would say, with his finger stabbing skyward, "cannot illuminate the dark mysteries of Medieval mysticism."

And her mother would ask.

"Then, what *can* we believe in?"

And Fra Nacho would reply.

"When all the false arguments have been thrown aside, we are left with no choice but to trust in the pure, unsubstantiated faith that transcends reason. We are truly creatures of the dark, Socorro. We are created in the dark, in the mindless spasms of our parents beds, and we leave this world alone, in darkness. In between, we are drawn to the light, like moths, only to be dazzled by it."

"Then, do you trust in pure faith, Nacho?"

"No, Socorro. As much as I want to, I cannot. And for that, I envy you. I sincerely admire and envy you."

As María finished the last of her turtle meat burrito, Fra Nacho lit a thick yellow candle. The flame wobbled and flickered in the almost motionless night air of the arroyo. Chino was speaking at length about his idea for starting a tourist business. As they all listened, María admired his intelligence and manliness.

" ...This is not a new or untested idea. There are a number of successful tourist businesses already established whose clients arrive in their own small airplanes.

"At Bahía de los Angeles there is a small hotel operated by one family. There is another at Mulegé, another at Rancho Buena Vista south of La Paz, two more in Loreto, and a very large and luxurious resort called La Palmilla, near Cabo San Lucas."

Chino's hands cut left and right through the humid night air.

"All of these hotels have built landing strips for their clients' airplanes. They charge for sport fishing from pangas. They also charge for meals and rooms."

Abundio's voice came from outside the circle of candlelight.

"But mijo, how would these clients find *us?*"

Chino raised a muscular arm toward the stars. He passed it back and forth above his head.

"The *americanos* are flying up and down the beaches all the time, looking for places to land. We must make a big sign, easily visible from the air. We must repair the landing strip and outline it with white stones. The airplanes will come."

All of them, of course, were familiar with the small airplanes that buzzed the caleta once or twice a month before continuing on their way. And sometimes planes descended and circled the pangas as the men fished. Most of the planes carried the large American letter "N" with the numbers on their sides, as opposed to the Mexican "X." These were probably the planes carrying Chino's tourist anglers from the United States.

Fra Nacho now spoke.

"Chino, even assuming these pilots are looking for places to fish, there is no hotel here, no restaurant, no swimming pool, no tennis courts, and now that Ramón is gone we don't even have a panga suitable for tourists."

Chino's reply surprised them.

"Pablo has agreed to rent us his panga for ten dollars a day plus gas. Until the road is fixed, he has little need for it anyway. In Pablo's panga, we can take up to four clients outside for tuna, dorado and marlin. For fishing near shore, our panga can hold at least one or two clients."

They listened more intently now.

"As for the hotel and the swimming pool, they are not necessary. These new tourists are more interested in fishing than luxuries."

Chino lowered his voice as if there were spies eavesdropping in the shadowy rocks around Fra Nacho's shack. He whispered directly into their eyes, each in turn.

"One day last month—at Las Ramalitas—two American planes landed on the mud flat. I have overheard conversations about it. The Americans stayed for three nights, camping in their own tents. They paid for sport fishing in two pangas. When they left, they promised to return."

Chino allowed this revelation to have its effect. Las Ramalitas! *Already* with sport fishing clients! There was a long silence as each of them considered what steps would be necessary to start a tourist business in the caleta. Abundio's deep voice, serious and carefully measured, interrupted their thoughts.

"You have spoken of this before, mijo."

"Yes, amigo. It has been on my mind a long time."

"And you seem confident it will work."

"I think it is worth a try."

Abundio's voice became lower, almost somber, with a feeling of weariness they had not heard in him before. He came into the candlelight and sat beside Fra Nacho.

"The sun is setting on our little world, isn't it Nacho?"

"It seems so, old friend."

The candle burned while each of them wondered silently what the future held. What would the world look like when the new moon unfolded itself and its light returned to flood the arroyo and the mysteries of the night? And who would they be, what would they call themselves, in the hot light of the days that followed?

María and Chino went back to the house, followed shortly by Abundio.

As usual, Socorro remained behind to straighten up. When she had completed her chores she sat beside Fra Nacho and pulled a torn piece of paper from her skirt pocket. She unfolded it and gave it to him.

"What does it say, Nacho?"

The paper had been held against something with engraved writing on it, and it had been rubbed with a pencil. The letters were small and indistinct. Fra Nacho had difficulty reading them through the heavy streaks of pencil lead. He turned the paper toward the yellow candlelight and read aloud as well as he could.

" ...ECOLOTES ...CIPAL ...A PAZ ...194... that is all I can make out, Socorro. What is it?"

"Could the first word be 'Tecolotes'?"

"Yes... that could be it. Also possibly... 'La Paz' and a date."

"I ask a favor."

"Of course, Socorro. Anything at all."

"You must never speak of this. Never."

In the flickering candlelight, Fra Nacho saw that Socorro's eyes were not directed at him. He recognized the dreamy expression on her face from his time with the native people who lived on the edges of the port cities of southern México and Guatemala. Socorro's eyes were half raised to the star-filled night, and she wore the peaceful, distant gaze of the Indian contemplation of a place beyond death.

"As you wish, Socorro."

"It is a small thing, Nacho, that... "

He raised his hand.

"No explanation is necessary."

They sat for what seemed to Fra Nacho like a very long time. The sighing sound of a large snake, pushing its coils against the sand as it hurried through the night, came from the rocks behind the shack. Finally, Socorro spoke again.

"Nacho, this tourist business. Do you believe it is possible?"

"I have no knowledge of such things."

She winked at him.

"What about the pure, unsubstantiated faith that transcends reason?"

Fra Nacho choked and nearly fell off his cot and his candle went out.

"Hah! Socorro, you would mock a poor old man!"

They sat in darkness as Fra Nacho waited for Socorro to continue. He had known her long enough to respect her silences, regardless of the length. After an hour, she spoke.

"Nacho, did something draw you to the caleta? Or, were you chased here? I mean, would you have come here of your own free will?"

"That sounds like one of María's questions."

"Please."

Fra Nacho thumbed through the yellowed chapters of his life. There had been a time when he could have answered affirmatively that he had been driven to Agua Amargosa. Driven by his disappointments in the outside world. But now he was not so sure. Perhaps, like the moth to the flame, or the fish to the bait, he had instead been drawn by something he could not understand.

"Socorro, I am sorry. But I suspect, perhaps, they are the same thing."

"Do you mean, it makes no difference, whether one is drawn to something or driven to it?"

"Perhaps."

Socorro had already come to the same conclusion. It mattered not why she and her husband, and the two young lovers, María Rodríguez and Chino Zúñiga, found themselves on this uncertain shore. What mattered was that they were here. This was where their fates had brought them and they must find a way to make the best of it. Socorro rose to leave. She bent forward to touch Fra Nacho's shoulder gently.

"Thank you, Nacho, for our many evenings together."

"It has been my pleasure as always."

Socorro's voice came back from the head of the path.

"I have decided we will repair the airstrip. We will try this sport fishing tourist business."

Fra Nacho was surprised.

"Shouldn't you talk to Abundio? He seems doubtful."

Her high, childlike voice materialized from the night itself and Fra Nacho knew Socorro was smiling. She was smiling in the way she smiled when she served levanta muertos.

"Abundio may decide what is perfect. I will decide what is possible."

CHINO RAISED THE hood of the old Chevy, and he took his time surveying its contents for signs of life. A methodic perusal of the wrecked sedan gave little reason for optimism. Missing entirely were the generator, battery, voltage regulator, starter, coil, distributor, fuel pump, fuel tank and connecting lines, radiator and hoses, and all four tires. Loose wires dangled everywhere.

María brushed a bird's nest off the air cleaner.

"Chino! How can we ever get this car started? Half of it is missing!"

"I don't think it's as bad as it looks."

"*Mande!?*"

Apart from the missing pieces, the car appeared to be in good condition. The engine block, carburetor, and intake manifold were intact. The transmission had not been removed because, as Chino recalled, it had lost all its gears except reverse and had been the reason for the car's retirement several years before.

The Chevy's keys were also missing, and since no one could remember who its most recent owner had been, Chino planned to start it by crossing the ignition wires.

"First, we fix the fuel system. We need a clean glass bottle, the kind with a ring-shaped handle on the neck. It should have a cap."

María found a bottle and Chino filled it with gasoline and taped it to the middle of the Chevy's roof. He drove a hole through the cap just big enough for a rubber fuel hose which he clamped to the Chevy's carburetor with multiple passes of fishing line. Siphoning action and gravity flow would keep the engine supplied with fuel, and a kink in the hose would serve as an on-off valve.

"All right, now for the cooling system. We need a big barrel with no leaks."

María was intrigued by Chino's command of auto mechanics.

"How do you know so much about cars?"

"I read all the Chilton manuals in the El Centro library."

"*All* of them?"

"It helped my work at the station."

There was nothing in the Chilton manuals about glass bottles taped to the roof or gravity flow carburetors. In traditional Baja style, Chino was making things up as he went along.

María knew where to find a barrel. Two years before, they had bought an almost new oil drum to hold the cooking fire but they had never gotten around to cutting off its top. It was next to the crab traps behind the house.

They removed the Chevy's back seat, wrestled the barrel into its place, and filled it with water from the well. Two long hoses led from the barrel, one to the Chevy's water pump, and the other to the nipple on the engine block. Chino would be able to drive quite a while before the barrel overheated. Meanwhile, the weight of the water in back would give them extra traction on soft dirt.

The four missing tires posed a serious problem. Chino and María searched every wreck and trash heap in the village but they could find only two serviceable tires that fit the Chevy's steel rims.

What they did find, though, was a large pile of manila rope someone had towed in from the sea.

Chino pushed two oversized truck tires onto the Chevy's remaining rims. He coiled the rope around and around inside the tires until he had packed them as hard as possible. To keep them from spinning, he drilled holes in the rims and beads and wired everything together.

The Chevy's electrical system was fairly easy to reconstruct since most of the missing parts could be retrieved from the long-dead village vehicles to which they had been transplanted.

With a little guesswork, Chino quickly located the Chevy's original generator, voltage regulator, and distributor. An old Pontiac supplied a working coil, and Pablo Santos' pickup, sitting in lonely exile up on the cliff, contributed a fully-charged battery.

The Chevy's starter motor was nowhere to be found. Chino conjectured it was probably sitting in the bowels of some car or pickup that had suffered its final incapacitation somewhere in the desert. But he had neither the means nor the time to search for it and he decided they would push-start the Chevy.

Chino installed all the parts and tightened the belts and hoses. He cleaned the carburetor and filled it with fresh gasoline. Using experience gained in tuning the engine of his old yellow pickup, he set the point and spark plug gaps by eye and guessed at the ignition timing. Pablo's battery would at least give them a nice hot spark.

BY TWO O'CLOCK on the third afternoon, Chino and María had the Chevy as ready as it would ever be. Chino poured a little raw gas down the carburetor throat and closed the hood. He crawled under the dashboard and was trying to figure out which ignition wires to cross when his eye caught the shine of something hanging from the gearshift lever. It was a ring of keys. Car keys. Chevy keys.

"María! Where did you find the keys?"

Her clear, bell-like voice came from outside.

"What keys?"

"The car keys! They're right here."

"I didn't find them."

Chino tried a key in the ignition. The car radio came to life with a loud hiss of static. It had been left on. He showed the keys to María.

"They were on the gearshift lever. Who could have put them there?"

"Could they have been there all along?"

He shook his head.

"Impossible. We would have seen them."

"It is a miracle, then."

"Perhaps."

MARÍA ROUNDED UP some men from the beach and they pushed the Chevy out of the grass, backwards, with Chino steering. Through the dirt-smeared back window of the car, Chino caught sight of Margarita Santos on the front porch of the pink house. From a distance, she had been watching them work for the past three days.

When they reached the road, Chino put the transmission into reverse and they pushed the car backwards as fast as they could. Chino popped the clutch several times, and then got out.

"You have to push faster."

The men hooted and whistled. María, too, gave Chino a sweaty, dusty look that said he wasn't going to get more speed out of this pushing crew. Chino thought a moment, then snapped his fingers.

"I have an idea! We need Pablo's panga and a lot of rope."

They positioned the Chevy in front of Ramón Ochoa's house with its rear end facing the water, and they found enough rope to make a cable over a hundred yards long.

They tied one end to the back bumper of the Chevy. The other end they passed to Pablo Santos in his panga, floating in the caleta with its eighty horsepower Evinrude turning just fast enough to keep slack from forming.

Pablo was worried about his boat. He shouted to Chino, who was making final adjustments on shore.

"Eh, Chino! I'm not so sure about this! Have you ever done this before?"

Chino waved and smiled his biggest, toothy smile.

"Well, not *exactly*, Pablo. But I did something pretty similar once! One night in San Felipe."

"Well... I just hope it doesn't tear the bottom off my panga!"

"Me too."

Pablo couldn't hear above the noise of the Evinrude.

"Eh!? What did you say, Chino?"

Chino waved his hands and smiled again.

"Nothing, Pablo! Are you ready?"

With everybody pushing and Chino steering backwards, Pablo wrapped the rope around the Evinrude's mounting bolts and twisted the throttle wide open. The panga squatted in the water and foam churned up as it began to move away from the beach.

The Chevy picked up speed rapidly, soon leaving its pushing crew behind, and Chino steered carefully as he shot backwards across the packed dirt road. At a pre-arranged spot, Pablo released his end of the rope and Chino popped the clutch.

The Chevy chugged and chugged and lost momentum while Chino kept pumping the gas. Just as his heart began to sink, the engine roared to life with a puff of black smoke. It rattled and missed and just barely kept itself running while Chino threw up the hood and twisted the distributor back and forth to get the timing right.

At last, it seemed the engine would not die of its own accord and Chino was just closing the hood when María ran up and jumped into his arms, laughing like a child. She had outrun all the men.

"Chino! Chino! My God! We did it!"

HIGH ON THE cliff, directly above the old well, Abundio Rodríguez inched his way across the rock face like a fly on a wall.

In his left hand, he carried a paint brush and a half-empty can of white paint. In his other hand, a shovel.

Abundio had never climbed this high on the cliff before, even in the summers with his father. To reach this place, with its dizzying, almost straight down view of the palms, Abundio had followed a goat trail up the arroyo. Then he had turned left onto a narrow ledge formed where the wall of the cliff came down on a slope of loose rock. He had doubled back almost to the village again, crawling along the joint between the cliff and the steep slope below him.

"*Híjole!*"

A flat rock cracked and slid out from beneath his foot. He watched it spin down the slope and over the edge a hundred feet below. His shovel also rattled away but stopped before going over.

Carefully, Abundio retrieved his shovel on all fours. Then he climbed back to the ledge and resumed his slow, crab-like journey across the face of the cliff.

The afternoon shadows had covered the floor of the arroyo by the time Abundio reached the place where he planned to make the sign. From the pangas, the bare slope looked smooth and clean. It was about two-hundred feet above the palm trees, facing the sea from the south side of the arroyo. Pilots flying down the coast would spot it easily.

Abundio stood up slowly, letting go with his hands. The slope was rougher than expected. But it would have to do since he could go no further. The ledge ended in a pile of loose boulders a few yards ahead.

"Bueno. This must be the place."

Abundio used his shovel to clear an area of the slope about twenty feet wide. He collected some small rocks and arranged them into four-foot tall block letters which he painted white.

"Just wait until those Ramalitas bastards see this!"

Abundio sealed his paint can and sat down on his haunches to enjoy the afternoon view. Nestled against the far side of the arroyo, he could see the thatched roof of Fra Nacho's shack with its zigzag path leading up from the trees. On the road above the sand dunes, he found the new pile of rocks that held the sleeping body of Joselito Medina, and below it to the right, Chino's house hiding in the black shadows against the base of the cliff.

A wisp of silent, yellow dust rose high into the sky, like smoke from a campfire. Abundio searched the shadowed landing strip for the source of the dust and he caught sight of the blue-and-white sedan that Chino and María had been laboring on for the past three days.

"*Aha!* Excellent work, my children! Excellent work!"

During two weeks of making plans for the tourist business, there had been a fair amount of wagering on whether or not the cannibalized Chevy could be made to run, and Abundio had been among the few who expressed confidence in the near impossible. He smiled with satisfaction as he watched the resurrected metal beetle circling around and around, in reverse, on the landing strip.

Using his one good gear, Chino was repeatedly backing the Chevy up and down the pista. He had tied a wide wooden platform weighted with rocks to the Chevy's front bumper. As he dragged the platform back and forth, its leading edge simultaneously cut down high spots, pulled out small brush, and filled in holes. A long loop of anchor chain tied across the back of the platform added a final touch to each dusty pass. Gradually, imperceptibly, the landing strip was becoming smooth and clean.

Abundio picked out the white-clad figures of María, Socorro, and Ana Rosa Medina swinging machetes at the larger bushes. Several men worked with picks and shovels, digging out rocks. When the Chevy came by they piled the rocks and brush onto the platform and Chino dragged it over to dump it into the largest gully.

During one of the dumping stops, Chino left the car and walked over to María. While the couple talked, Abundio watched a whirling column of dust and dry weeds form itself on the far side of the pista.

The dust devil writhed and hesitated, twisted and danced to the left and to the right, and it seemed almost to have a will of its own. It crossed over the newly graded dirt and came up behind María, snatching her hat into the air.

"*Hah!*"

From his high, empyrean perch, Abundio's belly laugh echoed out over the arroyo. He watched as Chino and María scattered in mock panic, María swatting at the sudden swarm of flying sand and dust, and Chino leaping like a mad gazelle after her escaping hat.

It was near sunset by the time Abundio started back to the village. He followed a circuitous route that took him up the cliff road to the rockslide and Pablo Santos' abandoned pickup, sitting with its hood up and its battery removed. Abundio visited the bottle-cap encrusted cross with its picture of The Virgin of Guadalupe, and he found the metal cup hidden in the weeds, still containing the tooth-marked cow and the stemless daisy heads, now crisp and dry.

With a sharp stone in his hand, Abundio held the cup and looked for the inscription engraved on its side, but someone had already scratched it out. Strange. He was sure it was intact the day they found it.

EARLY THE NEXT morning, Abundio was on the face of the cliff again, inching his way along like a fly on a wall. In seven years of friendship, the previous hour had marked the first time that he and Chino had really argued. Abundio's angry words still buzzed in his mind as he climbed carefully out to his freshly-painted sign.

"What? Too small!? I can see it just fine."

"It is too small, amigo."

"But it is perfectly legible. Perfectly. I will *not* change it!"

At Abundio's invitation, the village had come out at first light to see the new sign. They had stood in the middle of the freshly graded pista and they had looked up at the cliff. The small white letters, just barely discernible between the rocks, slanted sharply downwards and trailed off into a crack.

Chino restated the case he had been making for the past forty-five minutes.

"The pilots will be much farther away than this, amigo. They will never be able to read such a small sign."

"Then they are blind, one-eyed horses' asses!"

María tried to mediate. She took her father's hand.

"Papá, perhaps you could make it just a little larger. And the letters, a little more straight."

Abundio bristled at Chino with his fists clenched and the veins in his neck standing out.

"There is nothing wrong with the sign! And that is *final!*"

"Papá!"

"*Come,* Socorro!"

Abundio had jabbed Chino's shoulder with his finger—very lightly—and he had commanded Socorro to accompany him as he stalked away. But Chino's calm, trusted voice stopped him.

"Amigo, there is something more serious wrong with the sign."

Chino looked at his feet, reluctant to speak. He kicked a broken stick away.

"It is misspelled, amigo."

They all turned to reexamine Abundio's sign. A hawk soared through the transparent air directly in front of it as their eyes traced over the white rocks forming the roughly spaced letters, "F IC HIN." Abundio's brow gathered into a series of horizontal furrows.

"But… it says "fishing" in English, does it not?"

"No, amigo."

"Then what *does* it say?"

"It says nothing, amigo. It is nonsense."

"Ah… "

Up on the cliff again, Abundio smiled ruefully to himself as he reached his letter "N."

The sign did seem smaller than it had the day before. Abundio sat just beneath it, facing the arroyo, and he carefully analyzed the pitch and curve of the rocky slope. He visited each of his letters and for each he tried to figure the shortcomings of angle, size, or alignment that had made his sign so difficult to read from below. He pulled a roll of heavy monofilament from his pocket and stretched it along the tops of the letters. They lined up perfectly.

How could the sign look so damned crooked?

He placed an eye at one end of the fishing line and sighted along the horizon. *Aha!* He had aligned his letters with the edge of the rock face. But the edge was not horizontal here. It ran downwards toward the head of the arroyo.

Abundio climbed back up to the ledge and squeezed himself under a rock overhang just large enough to shade half his body. He took a slow drink of water. Far below, in the full flood of the morning sun, the dust was rising from the pista again. Chino's work party had pushed an old panga and three junk cars into the last remaining gully and his rearward running beetle was putting the final touches on the dirt.

A long, rectangular border of rocks, spaced three feet apart, outlined the new runway. María, Socorro, and Ana Rosa Medina had already painted about half of them. White dots appeared like mushrooms on the desert floor as the women dipped their brushes into their single can of paint and leapfrogged each other down the line of rocks.

Chino would have their new landing strip completed by the end of the day. Their last remaining hurdle was to make a suitable sign on the cliff that would tell the American pilots of their new sport fishing business.

Seated in his shady niche, Abundio studied the rocky, vertiginous canvas sloping away from his feet. He unfolded a piece of paper and began to memorize the letters Chino had written for him.

For several minutes, he sat looking off toward the new rockslide on the cliff, thinking sadly of how much Joselito Medina had wanted to help clear the road.

Then he stood and unrolled his length of fishing line.

"All right, mijo. This time we do it right."

FRA NACHO SPREAD his hands, catching a double armful of the moonlight flooding his porch.

"So... he says he is all right?"

"He says he will not come down until the sign is finished."

"Why not?"

"He says it is a matter of pride."

"Hmmph!"

Only a few stars penetrated the milky bright light of the full moon. Across the arroyo, the cliffs rose in a wavy curtain of stark white pinnacles and folded black shadows. Somewhere up there, Abundio Rodríguez toiled alone.

Socorro pulled back an errant strand of gray hair and retied it with the ribbon María had brought from Loreto. Her face was lined with concern.

"He fought with Chino this morning."

"About the sign?"

"It was more than that. He felt foolish... helpless."

Socorro finished her chores and returned to the house to wash the dinner dishes. Then, she sat up in a chair as María slept in the corner of the room. Once, about midnight, Socorro felt someone approaching the house and she lifted the cloth from the doorway. But it was only the small black dog that came to sleep under the porch bench and she hissed it away and returned to her chair.

In the dark hours before morning, Socorro dressed and slipped out past the cloth. She walked barefoot to where the cliff road crossed the end of the landing strip. There, she sat down in the warm sand, facing the cliff where she knew Abundio must be. The row of new stones beside the runway glowed white in the moonlight. Socorro watched them slowly disappear, one-by-one, as the moon went down behind the cliffs and a deep, predawn shadow covered half the village.

Chino and María found her there in the soft yellow glow of sunrise. María shouted as they came running up to her.

"Mamá! What are you *doing* here? Papá is looking all over for you."

Socorro pointed over their heads to the top of the cliff and they turned to look.

The first rays of a sun that had not yet left the horizon were just touching the highest part of the cliff, setting it aflame in the indigo sky. A perfect circle, forty feet across, had been etched into the bare sloping spot above the well. The circle was outlined with a border of white stones.

Curving just inside the top and bottom halves of the circle were two rows of large block letters, perfectly formed and spaced. The top half of the sign said, "AGUA AMARGOSA," and below it in English, "GOOD SPORT FISHING."

But it was not the perfection of the circle or the lettering that held their attention.

For, as the first heat of the sun turned the cliff to burnt gold, they stood in the long morning shadows of the pista and gaped in amazement at Abundio Rodríguez's masterpiece. In the middle of the circle, just under the words "Agua Amargosa," was the lifelike figure of a leaping marlin, created in bas-relief from a mosaic of multicolored stones.

The fish's back was made of dark black rocks, shading to gray on its belly. Its eye was green and the inside of its mouth was red. Running along its flank was a distinct lateral line of yellow. Each stone of the mosaic was set with a flat surface turned outwards. Abundio's marlin caught the morning sun like a faceted diamond come to life.

Socorro tugged at Chino's shoulder.

"Chino. The words. They are correct?"

Chino nodded.

"And what do they say?"

"It says, 'Agua Amargosa, Good Sport Fishing.' "

"And this is what you wanted?"

"Yes, Socorro. He has done an amazing job. It is almost a miracle."

They were still admiring the new sign when Abundio came out of the trees and spotted them on the landing strip. It was the first time anyone had seen the name of the village displayed in writing.

"It is time, María."

"Mmm...."

Chino rose from the cot and began dressing.

There was a steady breeze blowing in from the sea, but it gave no relief from the heavy tropical air that smothered the dunes like a blanket.

Scattered drops of rain made pockmarks in the sand around Chino's lean-to. A rising mass of thunderheads, blinding white in the afternoon sun, churned slowly above the cliffs.

Chino listened to the distant rumbling that had awakened him. It was raining hard in the high passes, as it had done for the past three days. This evening the lightning would be visible over the mountains again and it would continue until well after midnight.

María pulled an oversized shirt around her shoulders and buttoned it. She sat on the cot with her knees pulled up to her chin while she watched Chino gather his things for the trip.

"Chino, are you sure the clothes still fit you?"

"I tried everything on this morning."

"Where will you sleep?"

"I should reach the top of the cliff tonight. By noon tomorrow, I should be on the road to La Paz, waiting for the fish truck."

Chino tied a short rope to the ends of his blanket roll. He slung the long, fuzzy tube across his back and walked around the shack to test its fit. Rolled tightly inside the blanket were his good clothes, a bag of tortillas and dried fish, a roll of pesos, and a hundred U.S. dollars.

Chino sat on the edge of the cot to pull on his socks and tennis shoes.

He would need them for the long hike out to the main road. As he bent forward to tie his shoelaces, María put her arms around his waist and dug her fingers into the bands of muscle across his stomach.

"Chino, your body is so hard everywhere."

"It has always been."

"Even when you were a child?"

"As far as I can remember."

María hopped up from the cot. She found a plastic bottle and leaned out the door to water a flowering geranium she had planted in a pot just outside. Chino watched her borrowed shirt pull up over her back.

"María, that is an... interesting... flower."

Still leaning out through the half-open door, María wiggled herself as she filled the pot to the rim.

"Oh?"

She had watered the geranium just for his pleasure.

"You fox."

María plopped herself onto Chino's lap. Her thighs were smooth and cool, and she moved for him as she sensed the places where he wished to touch her. Her eyes closed and the hollow of her back began to arch against his hand.

But Chino's mind would not be turned from the difficult eighteen-mile walk that lay ahead of him and from the unknown potential for success or failure that he might find when he reached La Paz.

Seven weeks. Seven full weeks, they had waited for a plane with an "N" on its side to touch down on their new landing strip, with nothing to show for it but one twin-engined plane that had circled twice and then opened its throttles and climbed away again.

Now they had reached the first week of September, and each morning, it seemed, another panga was missing from the beach, another panguero gone with his family and his few possessions, heading north or south, to any place where he might find a sheltered bay, a road that led to it, a fish camp that would allow him to sell to its buyer.

They had taken a head count a few days before. Of the nearly one-hundred people who had once lived and worked in Agua Amargosa, only thirty-six remained. Of these, only eight were able-bodied heads of households or single pangueros. The rest were women and children, and Fra Nacho in the arroyo.

The village, for all practical purposes, had ceased to exist.

The Rodríguez family and those who had helped level the pista continued to look to the sky each time the steady, far away drone of an aircraft engine intruded upon the solitude of the caleta.

But their hopes lessened with each passing day, and gradually Abundio's fine marlin, leaping over the cliffs in its circle of rocks, came to mock them like the carrion birds that had begun to hop around the edges of the village, even entering the empty houses, with their big black wings dangling above their heads.

Two families were suffering from sickness for they had tried to drink the unwholesome water of the well in order to reduce the need for supply trips to Las Ramalitas. For these families, whose money jars were nearly empty, the outhouses were almost continuously occupied by one member or another.

The Rodríguezes, thanks to the sale of Ramón Ochoa's panga, still had enough money for weekly runs to Las Ramalitas, and had thus far escaped the indignity of the outhouses.

But they had not escaped the entropy of their situation, the emptiness of a sky without tourist anglers, and the echoes of their own fears that they heard each night in the muffled screams and shrieks that came from the house of Pablo Santos.

And yesterday, they had been shaken from their somnolent vigil by an event that none of them had foreseen, the landing of an aircraft carrying not tourist anglers but a group of mysterious, arrogant Mexican officials from the mainland.

The unmarked, dark green DC-3 had come in low just an hour before sunset. It had circled the caleta twice with its two big engines rattling the palm thatch of the porches and they had watched as the landing gear dropped down from its wings.

Then the fat-bellied plane had flown out to sea again, and their hearts had dropped, but it circled back and came in straight over the Four Horses. The plane floated in past the beach. It just skimmed a palm tree and the roof of Ana Rosa Medina's house, and it touched down so close to the end of the landing strip that its wheels flipped over one of the new white painted rocks.

A makeshift welcoming committee, composed of Abundio, Chino, Pablo Santos and two other men, dodged the shower of dirt and gravel thrown up by the Gooney Bird's props as it taxied back and shut down. They reached the plane just as its gangway door popped open and its furious, red-faced pilot emerged at the top of the steps, ripping off his sunglasses and screaming at them.

"Who is the stupid prick responsible for this airport?"

The pilot's tight black pants, his epaulettes, his tone, and his exact choice of words, especially the Spanish word *aeropuerto,* created the instant impression that their simple landing strip, or *pista*, as they had always referred to it, was going to be a source of problems. The pilot pointed his finger at Abundio's bare chest.

"Goddammit, I asked you a question, you... "

The pilot stiffened to attention and stood to one side as a slim, baldheaded man in a dark suit came onto the landing behind him. The man looked around for a moment, then descended the steps, accompanied by two other men, also in suits. His Spanish was crisp and concise and he stood only three or four inches shorter than Abundio.

"What is the name of this place?"

Abundio found himself standing in front of a solid wall of pangueros. Unable to retreat, he answered the elegantly dressed man.

"Agua Amargosa, señor."

"It is not on the charts."

"I... we are sorry, señor."

The tall official swept his hand toward the village and then back toward the beach. His manner was sympathetic, condescending.

"There are many houses here. Why only four pangas?"

"The road, señor... it was buried by rocks."

The official sniffed and looked up toward the top of the cliffs, where Abundio's marlin sparkled in the last direct rays of the sun.

"You have sport fishing here?"

"No, señor."

"Then what is the sign for?"

"We hoped the planes would come, señor. But they have not."

The official walked to the tail of the DC-3. He dug the heel of his shoe into the dirt and he glanced at Chino's blue-and-white Chevy, parked just off the edge of the landing strip with its gasoline bottle still taped to its roof and its wooden platform still tied to its front bumper. He summoned them with a pushing motion of a hand held outwards.

"Come here!"

They approached to within ten feet of him and they stood in a group with Abundio in front as before. The official spoke in a level tone.

"This pista is very dangerous."

"I... we are sorry, señor. We did not expect such a large plane."

"Large or small, if there is an accident here, someone may go to jail for a long time. There is some kind of hole, or perhaps a soft spot in the middle that almost caused our pilot to lose control. You must fill it with firm soil immediately or remove the border of stones and place a large white 'X' across the runway."

"Sí, señor. We will fix it tomorrow, in the morning."

"Be sure that you do."

The man came over and almost patted Abundio on the shoulder, but stopped short.

"And how long has your road been blocked?"

"Since six months ago, señor."

"Hmmm... too bad. And do you have good water here?"

"No, señor. Just a salty well."

The official dropped his smile. He returned to the foot of the gangway, closely followed by his aides, who had not spoken. He addressed the pilot who stood waiting at the top of the steps.

"Victor, this place will not do. We will proceed to Las Ramalitas as planned."

The pilot saluted and answered as they climbed the steps.

"Sí, señor. However, it will be too dark to land by the time we arrive there."

"Then return to La Paz. We will see Las Ramalitas in the morning."

"Sí, señor."

Chino had been tempted to speak, but he had been too busy listening to do so. Now, just before the door closed, he took his opportunity.

"Sir! Excuse me!"

The door swung open a foot and the pilot's head popped out.

"What is it?"

"I have a question, please."

"Well?"

"Why are you going to Las Ramalitas?"

There was some discussion inside the plane. After a few moments one of the aides came to the door and spoke to them.

"There is going to be a new cooperativa established in this area. There will be an ice plant, a cannery, many pangas. There will be a pier for unloading seiners and trawlers, jobs for many families."

"At Las Ramalitas?"

"Perhaps."

The door locked shut and the big engines of the DC-3 whined and belched black smoke. They stood at the edge of the strip as the plane taxied to the far end and turned around, and its engines sent heavy vibrations through their clothes. It cleared the palms behind Ana Rosa Medina's house, banked slowly over the Four Horses, and pulled itself up into the evening sky.

CHINO TIGHTENED HIS arms around María and held her firmly to stop her movements. She understood. She tweaked his nose and rose from his lap to help him tie his water bottles.

"Mi amor, is it wise to drink water from the well?"

"I won't drink it unless I have to."

María connected a pair of plastic water bottles together with a length of rope just long enough to reach across Chino's shoulders and down to the hand on either side. The rope would help relieve the strain of carrying the bottles as he walked.

One of the bottles held a full gallon of good drinking water from Las Ramalitas.

The second bottle was from the well in the arroyo. It was tinted light yellow by algae and mineral salts. Chino would have preferred two bottles of good water, but the decision to go to La Paz had been made urgently the night before, just after the three government officials had taken off in their DC-3. The Rodríguezes' supply of drinking water was down to a few gallons and it was not yet time for a supply run to Las Ramalitas.

Besides, Chino estimated that his gallon of good water would be more than enough to last him the eighteen miles to the main road.

María adjusted the rope over Chino's shoulders. She watched him walk back and forth.

"Does that feel all right, amor?"

Chino smiled as he put the bottles down and stroked her sides.

"I have felt better."

She pushed his hands down. She had not been in favor of sending Chino to search for clients in La Paz. But the shocking news of a fish cannery at Las Ramalitas had catalyzed a bold plan that had been under discussion for weeks. Chino's knowledge of English, of Americans, and of the other sport fishing businesses made him the only choice for the trip. María wished she could go with him to see the hotel where the Americans stayed.

"Will you try the Hotel Perla first?"

"Yes. And after that, the other names from papá."

"And then?"

"I will wait for them on the Malecón."

"Like a taco seller?"

Chino held her tightly, leaning back and admiring her astonishingly perfect face. She seemed especially delicate in his oversized shirt. He bowed low to the most beautiful woman he had ever seen and he raised his voice to a shrill falsetto.

"Ah, *Señorita*, could I interest you in a nice *taco* and a nice cold *soda pop?*"

THE HIGH MOUNTAIN valley lay trembling hot in the noontime sun, and the figure of a man came into view on the trail running down its middle.

The man wore a straw farmer's hat. He walked with a steady pace, conserving his strength against the heat. His faded green shirt was stained dark with sweat under the blanket roll across his back.

In his arms, he carried a bottle, cradled like a baby, and the water in it was stained light yellow. The bottle was suspended by a rope that he had looped, noose-like, around his neck.

He walked, bent slightly forward, looking for shade among the rocks and the columns of cardón cactus rising on either side of the trail. He stopped and looked up at the cliffs, then lowered his bottle to the ground. He threw off his blanket roll and pulled down his pants and squatted in the full sun as the flies attacked the thin brown liquid that came out of him.

Panting, he stood and looked up at the sky again. The transparent black spots were floating, converging in the middle of his view, like birds circling high above him. He walked another thousand feet, another mile, and then he sat down in the hot dust with the bottle in his lap. For several minutes, he stared into the cloudy, yellow contents of the bottle. Then, he lifted it to his lips and drank deeply.

THERE HAD BEEN no fish truck.

In fact, there had been no one at all, and Chino had concluded by the previous evening that the thunderstorms must have cut the main road somewhere, perhaps in several places.

Wait for a truck to come through? Or start back immediately, before the water runs out? Chino had made a compromise, and that had been a mistake. He had mixed one-third of the yellow water with his good bottle from Las Ramalitas. He had taken shelter beneath the rusted, cut up hulk of his old yellow pickup, and he had spread his blanket to spend the night and wait the extra day that his extended water supply allowed him.

But within two hours the cramps had begun in earnest. By morning, all of Chino's good water had run through him, and his thirst was stronger than ever. He had started back to Agua Amargosa at first light, conserving half a bottle of the water that had poisoned him. As he pushed himself toward the safety of the caleta, he had run over and over in his mind the calculation of his chances that always seemed to come up a little short.

Sitting in the griddle-hot trail, Chino lowered the empty bottle from his mouth. The treacherous water had tasted falsely sweet. Even as he swallowed it, another cycle of spasms began to pass through him. He tossed the bottle away and rested for a while, letting his guts calm down, breathing deeply. Then he stood and resumed his careful, measured stride against the waves of superheated air pressing down all around him.

Time was the greatest enemy. Chino knew he must reach the caleta before the attacks drained all his strength, before he became too weak to stand.

He stumbled in the dry heat with his steps growing closer and closer together. He thought of the goat ranchers who sometimes watered their flocks in the canyons above the caleta. Did they ever come this way?

His legs seemed childishly short, and he felt the hoe in his hands, strangely long and heavy and awkward. He looked across an endless, burning field of furrows converging on the horizon ahead of him.

He began the long climb up to the cliffs overlooking the sea. It was dark. How was it dark? In the middle of the afternoon? And cold, so cold and foggy, as he stood in his hard new shoes, with the purple orchid and the keys to the yellow pickup in his hands.

"Mom, this is Robert. I've mentioned him."

As he staggered over the crest of the cliff, Chino came to the place where he had leapt from the fish buyer's truck, to look down at the caleta for the first time. But it was so dark now, and he was in his extremity, clawing toward life on his hands and knees, and he looked down and saw not the crystal sea, but instead himself, battling evil, black birds made of fire.

Chino saw himself in the kitchen, with the floor curving up all around him and the walls leaning in, and they stared at him as he broke the dishes one after another and swore he would never come back to that place, and her younger sister crying, and her father yelling at her mother to shut up.

And then Chino was running away from the endless fields, from his faceless parents and brothers and sisters, bent over in the endless rows, groveling, with their asses in the air like skunks. And his good friend Alejandro Weeghman was there, and they ran like the wind, down a mountain of rotten tomatoes and Evinrudes, across the perfect sea, so far away the dogs and the *migra* could never find them.

But as he ran, Chino stumbled and fell in the dark, hitting his head, and he rolled and rolled down the cliff road and across the sand dunes, letting himself go, leaving the burning demons behind. And in the dark, he dreamt he was in the arroyo, and he could go no further, wanted to go no further, and María was there with him. She held his head in her lap and she stroked his forehead and lifted a beautiful, crystal glass to his lips, and he drank deeply, and fell into a restful sleep, with the insistent voice of a rooster, calling his name, again and again, from somewhere far in the night.

MARÍA RAN UP to the house, breathless. When she was close enough, she shouted ahead to her mother.

"He was not there!"

"Where can he be then?"

Socorro was very worried. Chino's blanket lay unrolled on the table with its contents spread out. The pesos and the hundred dollars he had taken from the money jar were untouched. Only a few pieces of the fish had been eaten.

"He would not have left money like that."

María, too, could not imagine why Chino would drop his blanket roll beside the house and disappear.

"Perhaps he is in the boat with papá."

Socorro shook her head.

"No. Ana Rosa says papá went out alone this morning."

"Oh, mamá! Something terrible has happened!"

Socorro tried to comfort her daughter, but she could think of no logical reason why Chino's things should appear so mysteriously during the night. She pushed María in the direction of the arroyo.

"Run. See if Nacho knows anything. I will check the beach again."

"Yes, mamá!"

María's long legs took her bounding up the arroyo and up the path to Fra Nacho's shack. He was sound asleep on the front porch, with the sluggish, morning flies crawling over his blanket and white shirt. His eyes opened slowly.

"Ah… María… buenos días… What brings you up here so early?"

"Have you seen Chino?"

Fra Nacho sat upright and swung his leg to the ground. He was wide awake.

"What is wrong?"

"We found Chino's blanket and money outside the house this morning."

"Perhaps he left them there and went home."

"No, no! They were just thrown in the dirt. In the middle of the road. We can't find him anywhere!"

Fra Nacho's long fingernails picked at the edges of his beard.

"Margarita was here last night."

"Why?"

"I don't know. She took my water bottle. A little later she brought it back. Perhaps it has something to do with Chino."

"What time was it?"

"Just before the rooster began crowing."

"This morning?"

"No. It must have been a little after midnight."

"Thank you, tío."

María hurried down the trail. She had never actually had a purposeful conversation with Margarita Santos and she hesitated to attempt one now. Nevertheless, she turned onto the narrow side path to Pablo's pink house and she broke into a fast trot.

As she approached the house, her eyes scanned the beach. She saw with relief that Pablo's panga was not there. He had gone fishing and he had probably taken his sons with him.

Margarita would not come to the door.

"Please, Margarita. I need to talk to you. I need to ask you something."

"Is it about your prince?"

"My prince?"

"The prince you make love with… in the sand house."

María looked around. She whispered hoarsely.

"Where is he, Margarita?"

"He loves you. He called your name."

María hissed at the door.

"Margarita! Tell me where he is!"

"He was hurt. Something bad happened to him."

"Oh, God! Where, Margarita? Where?"

"He was thirsty. I gave him water."

María pushed the door open enough to see through the crack. She had not been in this house for many years. On the far side of the darkened room, a treadle-powered sewing machine sat against the wall with the letters "S-I-N-G-E-R" molded into its cast-iron frame. Margarita was sitting with her bare feet on the treadle but not working it. Her black shawl was on her head and her hands were folded in her lap. Her feet were coated with beach sand.

María backed away and pleaded through the narrow opening.

"Margarita! Please! Tell me where he is! Where is Chino?"

At the mention of Chino's name, Margarita stood and came to the door.

"He was lost. He was very tired."

"Please, Margarita! Where?"

"In the arroyo. Where you left your gold shoes after you… "

María flew back up the path. She must have gone right past him! She found him lying in the bushes exactly where Margarita had said. He stirred at her touch and she shook his shoulders.

"*Amor! Wake up!*"

"Mmmff… María."

"Chino! What happened to you!?"

Chino raised himself up on one elbow. He looked around, amazed and delighted to be alive, and he managed a weak version of his favorite, toothy smile.

"I ran out of soda pops."

THUS ENDED THE Rodríguez family's attempt to secure clients for its sport fishing business.

There had been scant confidence in the La Paz plan anyway, and after Chino's near disaster, Socorro made it very clear to everyone that the sport fishing idea was dead and irrevocably buried. The sleepy September days following Chino's recovery from his ordeal were spent mainly in discussing where the family would resettle on that proximate but as yet undetermined date when they would leave the caleta.

For Chino and María, the long afternoons in the sand dunes were a time of almost magical closeness, as Chino's past life in El Centro unfolded, layer after layer, and he opened himself to the healing embrace of María's love. They spoke for hours of his family, of the endless furrows, of Bethy Archer, of the broken dishes on the kitchen floor, and Chino understood at last the pain of who he had been, and he understood that he was no longer that person, and the beasts no longer came to him in his sleep.

And for María, the moments together in the lean-to became a time of closeness not only to Chino but also to her mother, for in Chino's loving arms María learned of her mother's secret magic carpet, and she understood the true power of her mother's love and strength, and why her mother had been unable to explain it, or even describe it to her.

But for the two lovers, an awkward duty loomed over every conversation and over every surreptitious appointment they kept in the dunes. For it seemed that of all the people of Agua Amargosa there was only one who had not admitted to at least implicit knowledge of their affair. And that was the one they most dreaded telling.

They were sure Abundio knew what was going on.

But the longer the subject was avoided, the more awkward and difficult it became to broach.

All parties concerned, including Abundio, wished that the air about them would simply clear itself somehow. And given time, that is probably just what would have happened. But the Rodríguez family did not have the luxury of time. Even with the sale of Ramón Ochoa's panga, the added expense of sharing food with Ana Rosa Medina and her children had caused their reserve of funds to run critically low again, and they knew they must make their decision and move before the winter winds came down from the north.

Socorro occupied herself with sorting their belongings into lots light enough for the panga. She decided to give up nothing, including the large grindstone bequeathed to them by her brother. With its wheelbarrow-like cradle, made from the fork of a mesquite tree, the upright, circular grindstone weighed over fifty pounds.

In the hot afternoons, Socorro's mind wandered through the house, separating her things into imaginary piles. She guessed it would take at least two-dozen round trips in the panga to move Ramón's stone, the Medina family, and all their belongings, but she was determined to take everything.

And each evening, she visited Fra Nacho, to take him his food and water, and to argue with him, for the old man had confirmed his intention of remaining in the caleta, preferring a lonely, struggling death, he said, to being forcibly returned to a world he had scorned for nearly a third of his long life. Socorro argued and argued, but in truth, she knew it was hopeless. In her hidden heart, she agreed with her old friend and she would gladly have stayed with him, were it not for her duty to María, Chino, and her husband.

Abundio's last days in the caleta were a time of neither worry nor sorrow. The new carburetor from Loreto had been a disappointment, for it had not solved their motor problems. But no matter. Abundio had already decided to sell the gold Rolex and use its proceeds to buy a large gill net, several long set lines, and the twenty-two-foot panga and eighty horsepower Evinrude necessary to handle them. Abundio saw himself pulling shark and salting the white, blubbery flesh for the machaca market, and he did not mind. He had looked into the mysterious first color of the sea enough times, he felt, and he did not mind pulling shark.

But he felt sorry for Chino, so young and full of possibilities, doomed to a life of picking dead fish from the nets. He hoped that Chino and María might find something better someday, perhaps something like the tourist business that had not worked out.

Chino himself refused to give up hope that a plane would land on their pista before the end finally came. And Abundio hoped for his partner's sake that one would, but he did not believe it. Even as he helped Chino dig the new outhouse, and even as they picked up garbage together and dumped it out of sight in the arroyo, he did not believe it.

ANOTHER WEEK PASSED, then another, as the Rodríguezes continued their final preparations for the move and Socorro spent more and more time at Fra Nacho's shack in the arroyo, trying to convince the old man that he must come with them. She even pounded her fist on his head, but he would not agree, and as long as he did not, Socorro refused to let them leave the caleta.

One sweltering-hot afternoon, she was on her knees, doing her laundry at the well, when she felt the presence of the invisible spirit behind her. It often came and watched her as she washed clothes and she enjoyed its company for it reminded her of her mother.

But then the spirit took the form of the all-seeing eye and Socorro felt it come spiraling down behind her. Startled, she dropped a shirt and sat in the sand with the loose gray hairs standing out on her neck.

She twisted around and looked up to the sky. She raised her hand to cover her mouth, and she left her wash and her bar of soap and ran down the arroyo as fast as her tired legs would carry her.

FAR ABOVE THE caleta, the slender, metallic bird came out over the edge of the cliffs. It turned slowly left, then right, so high its droning engine could not be heard, and it seemed to be searching for something as it floated like a silver leaf in the midday sun.

"Whoa! Check this out!"

"Oh yeah! It's paradise, guys!"

"In-*cred*-i-ble!"

"Look at those islands!"

The metal bird wheeled slowly above the emerald panorama, tilting its wings in the hot, whispy blue air.

"My God! Look at the colors in the reefs!"

"Is this the place?"

"It might be. It's hard to tell from the air."

The Rodríguez family heard the engine throttle down. They watched the plane drop its nose and make a lazy turn high above the Four Horses.

It slowed down and descended toward the beach.

"Lotta houses under the trees."

"Look at the kids come running out!"

"This can't be it."

"Why not?"

"There weren't any houses before."

"Look! There's a strip behind the trees!"

"There wasn't any landing strip, either."

As the plane crossed the beach and leveled off over the pista, the letter "N" was plainly visible on its shiny, white-painted flanks.

"Come on, Howard. Let's get down!"

"Okay, we'll take a look."

But the plane did not land. It dragged through the air two-hundred feet above the pista, then banked left and turned back out to sea. It flew by the face of the cliff, passing directly in front of Abundio's circle of white rocks.

"Hey, look at that!"

"Agua Amargosa. Good Sport Fishing."

"All right!"

"Check that marlin out."

"Whoever did that was a real artist."

"These Mexicans are geniuses with stone."

The plane buzzed the pista twice more, descending lower each time. On the last pass it came in very low with the flaps hanging down behind its wings. Then its engine moaned again and it banked sharply to avoid the cliffs.

"Can't get close enough for a decent look."

"It looks good to me, dad."

"Yeah, come on, Howard. There's bait all over the bay. This place is jumping."

"Okay. Hold onto your butts. There ain't gonna be no go-arounds."

This time the plane's engine throttled back until it was barely audible. The flaps dropped almost straight down behind its wings. It slowed until it seemed they could catch it by running after it, and it wobbled in low over Ana Rosa Medina's house. It touched down in the middle of the pista and bounced up into the air again before skidding around and stopping at the far end.

Through the heat waves, they saw the door of the plane pop open. Two men jumped out and looked underneath. Then they climbed back in, and the plane taxied toward them with its door still open.

María's finger jabbed Chino, pushing him to the front of the welcoming committee. She whispered in his ear as the plane's propeller shuddered to a stop.

"Remember what I said... Robert."

Four men, stiff from their confinement, climbed out of the door. Chino spoke in English to the pilot, who seemed upset about something. The pilot wore expensive-looking dark glasses. He was short and middle-aged, with a belly that pushed out beneath his belt. He was very light-complexioned and his pink, sunburnt face was flushed and dripping with sweat. As he continued to discuss something with Chino, Abundio's curiosity got the best of him.

"Chino, what is the problem?"

"He wants to know who is responsible for the pista."

Abundio thought of the red-faced pilot of the DC-3.

"Why?"

Chino pointed to one of the metal struts supporting the plane's landing wheels. It was pushed slightly out of alignment and the sheet metal skin near the door was wrinkled.

"He says we put too much dirt in the hole. It made his plane jump off the ground and it has been damaged. He cannot take off until it is repaired by a licensed mechanic."

Now Abundio recalled the tall official from the mainland and specifically his threat of jail time if the pista were not made safe. *Madre!* These damned kites were more trouble than they were worth!

Abundio wiped his mustache with the back of his hand. He eyed the little, pink-skinned pilot, sizing him up, and he decided what he must do. He stuck his face into the pilot's and his booming voice exploded in what he hoped was a convincing show of rage.

"Tell him... he is a blind, one-eyed horse's ass of a pilot! *None* of our other clients has any trouble landing here at all! In fact, this *aeropuerto* has just been inspected by México City!"

María's eyes rolled back. Socorro stared disbelievingly at the husband she thought she had come to know. Pablo Santos and his sons backed up two steps and awaited further developments. Chino's mouth dropped open and snapped shut again.

The pilot and his companions, taken aback by Abundio's sudden outburst, fell silent and waited for Chino to translate. Abundio knew any hesitation on his part would be fatal. He grabbed Chino by the shirt and shook him, roaring.

"Tell them! You drunken jackass!"

Chino began jabbering in very rapid English. There were some harsh words exchanged and there was much pointing at the bent strut. The talk seemed to go on longer than necessary but gradually Chino seemed to be winning out.

Abundio stood with his arms folded across his chest, glowering over the proceedings like a chained bear, as much to intimidate the men as to keep Chino from conceding any responsibility for the accident.

There seemed to be a breakthrough of some kind. The men were smiling at Chino. Laughing, even. The pilot slapped Chino on the back and pointed toward the beach. María and Socorro glanced at each other, greatly relieved.

Abundio kept his arms folded, just in case.

The tourists unloaded their things from the plane and the pilot taxied back to the far end of the pista to park it. The men drove long, crossed spikes into the dirt beneath each wing and they tied their plane down to keep it from blowing away.

Chino winked and motioned for Abundio to come close.

"Excellent, amigo! We take them fishing tomorrow."

"What did you tell them?"

"Exactly what you said. Also, that our licensed aircraft mechanic would certify the repairs to their plane."

"Mechanic? What mechanic?"

Chino smiled his big toothy smile and he whispered into Abundio's ear. "You, amigo."

"Ah… "

ONE OF THE tourists had wandered off to the beach alone. He was an old man, thin and bald, and he came back limping slowly with his shirt in one hand. The skin on his chest hung in loose, hairy folds.

As the old man bent over to pick up a duffel bag, Abundio thought he saw something on his lower back, a small bandage or a smudge of something white.

Abundio took one end of the duffel bag.

"May I help you, señor?"

The man responded in strongly accented Spanish as Abundio helped him lift his bag into the fish cart.

"Thank you. It is much heaviness."

Abundio stole a glance at the man's lower back. There was the mark, faded and thinner, almost lost in the folds of skin sagging over his belt, but recognizable as a small "Y" tilted slightly to one side. Abundio examined the man's face more closely.

"Have you ever been here before, señor?"

The man's voice was different, smaller, as though muffled under tarps. His Spanish was barely decipherable.

"I think... yes. Maybe. But much years. No people before. No houses. Everything much different."

The man pointed north.

"Up there... is three rocks on beach?"

Abundio stood with his long arms held stiffly at his sides. His eyes shined.

"Sí, Señor Pete. The rocks are still there. Shall we race to them?"

The old man took half a step back, struggling with the decades.

"Oh... Bundo... I thought maybe... is it really you?"

"Sí, Señor Pete. It is me."

Maríа wrestled with the second of two huge balls of tortilla dough. She pounded the rubbery mass flat with a dozen quick blows of both fists. Then she folded the dough over into quarters and threw her weight into it again.

At the fire barrel, Socorro stirred her largest pot with a long wooden spoon. The bubbling mix of salt pork and pinto beans had turned a rich brown. In another two hours it would be as thick as stew.

Ana Rosa Medina was in the house, feeding coffee beans into a cast-iron grinder attached to the post in the center of the room. She cranked the handle round and round, catching the coarse black grindings in a metal cup.

Outside, Chino sat backwards on a chair with his legs spread apart. He dangled his arms over the high wooden backrest as he questioned Abundio, who was sitting on the porch bench with his feet tap-tapping on the dirt.

"So, amigo, did you tell Pete the price or not?"

"Well... ah.... not exactly."

"What *did* you tell him?"

"Well... actually... mijo, I told him they could pay whatever they feel is fair."

Chino rose and paced around the table. He brushed past María, who was pounding her tortilla dough furiously.

"But amigo, I thought we agreed to ask for thirty dollars."

"Ah... well... I felt it was not polite... to ask for money that way."

"From an old friend?"

"I guess so, mijo."

Abundio looked over to Socorro at the fire barrel and he caught her eye. He thought of the mayonnaise jar buried in the sand beneath the barrel and he raised his eyebrows in a silent question, but Socorro quickly shook her head "no."

María punched her ball of dough so hard the table shook. Her arms were dusted white with flour up past her elbows.

"Maybe Chino can go talk to them."

Chino stood and rested his hand on the corner post of the porch. Through the palm trees, he could see the patch of sunlight that contained Ramón Ochoa's bright blue house, with its yucca fence, its canopy of bougainvilleas, and the newly dug outhouse in back. Three of the tourists sat in the shade of the porch, joining their fishing rods and reels together. Chino sighed as he looked toward the clients.

"Whatever they feel is fair… "

"I'm sorry, mijo."

"Well, it's too late to do anything about it anyway."

ON RAMÓN'S PORCH, the tourists were suffering from the heat and flies. The pilot had changed into swimming trunks and beach thongs.

He was using a wrench to attach a heavy, metallic gold fishing reel to a stout rod that he held between his legs. When the locking nuts were tight, he wrapped the heavy monofilament line around his hand and yanked hard. A yard of line came off the reel with a loud ratcheting noise.

"Shig, how tight should I set the drag?"

"Let me see."

He handed the rod to a heavily built man with Asian features who pulled off another yard of line and made some adjustments to a chrome knob and a lever on the side of the reel. Shig tested the drag another time and handed the rod back to the pilot.

"That's about right, Howard."

"Should I set them all the same?"

Shig glanced into the pilot's two large tackle chests. There were several flannel reel bags that had not yet been opened.

"How many did you bring?"

"Four."

"All the same size?"

"Yeah."

"All with eighty-pound?"

"Yeah."

Shig turned back to sharpening his hooks.

"Yup. Set 'em all the same, Howard."

For two hours, Howard and Shig sat in the shade of Ramón Ochoa's porch, rigging up their rods and reels and sharpening hooks. Then they were interrupted by the voice of a young man who had been sleeping on a cot pushed against the house.

"Hey... when do they serve dinner around here?"

Shig grinned as the young man rose from his cot and pulled off his tee-shirt. He was the tallest of the group and he carried the bulbous chest muscles of someone who did bench presses.

"I think Danny wants to meet that long-legged waitress. What's her name Dan?"

"I don't know, but she's got some *nice* tamales."

"She's a beautiful girl."

Howard found a spare file in his tackle box. He tossed it to his son, who was looking back toward the Rodríguez house, scratching his stomach.

"Here, Danny, why don't you sharpen some hooks."

"Okay."

"Anybody know where Pete went?"

Shig had attached his reels to several rods of varying lengths and he was busy sorting a pile of lures and feathers. He waved a hand toward the beach.

"Pete's down there. He's going fishing with that mechanic."

Danny, on the cot again, was at work with his file. He tossed a sharpened hook into the tackle box and laughed.

"That big fat guy? If he's an aircraft mechanic, we're in serious trouble."

"Robert says he's certified. Plus, he *owns* this village. And he's the best fisherman from here to La Paz."

"No kidding! What's his name?"

"Bumbo, or something."

Down on the beach, Peter Grayson paused to catch his breath as he and Abundio slid the battered, old panga into the water.

"The years have not been kind to your boat, Bundo."

"Nor to the two of us, señor."

"Hah!"

Abundio held the panga steady while Pete climbed into the stern. They left the balky Evinrude tilted up. Abundio took the oars and rowed them slowly east, about forty yards off the beach. The late afternoon sun was strong and both men were soon running with sweat.

"What are we after, Bundo?"

"Dinner. For tonight."

Pete threaded a piece of lead-core line through the guides of his thin fishing rod and he tied on a blue-and-silver streamer about the length of his middle finger. As they crossed over the first reef, he began casting his lure and retrieving it with quick jerks of his free hand.

"You still fish with the little feathers, señor."

"Yes, Bundo, but I haven't caught a fish in a long time."

A small leopard grouper struck Pete's fly with a splash, and he pulled it in and admired its vibrant, mottled bands of brownish gray. He removed the hook from the fish's mouth and released it, and it hung in the water for a moment and then shot away toward the bottom.

He began casting again as Abundio rowed slowly through the hot, humid afternoon.

"Bundo. Did you find your girl that summer? The pretty girl in La Paz?"

"Sí, señor."

"And?"

"Well… I am married now and I have a daughter of nineteen."

"A daughter? Bundo, you don't mean the tall young woman at the landing strip?"

"Sí, señor. Her name is María."

"She's beautiful! You must have a very beautiful wife, then!"

"Well… ah… "

Pete had just realized that the other woman at the pista—the dark, square-bodied one who stood in back—was probably the girl's mother, when his line suddenly tightened and then when limp. He pulled it in to discover his blue-and-silver feather gone, cut off cleanly an inch above the knot.

"Sierra?"

"Sí, señor. Do we follow them?"

"Yes! I haven't seen one in years."

Abundio rowed toward deeper water where the school of sharp-toothed sierra mackerel were flicking the surface, chasing small bait fish around the submerged rocks. As Abundio rowed toward them, Pete attached another streamer to his line, this time using a short leader of thin, brown, stainless steel wire.

A mass of bait fish thirty feet across began to boil on the reef, with sierra flashing all around it. When they were within range, Pete cast his streamer to the edge of it. There was an explosion of bait into the air, and a twenty-inch sierra took Pete's feather with a somersaulting leap.

Pete struggled to keep the darting, leaping fish from breaking his line or cutting him off on the rocks. He worked it to the side of the boat and Abundio lifted it up, gently and with respect. The sierra's perfectly proportioned, bluish-silver body, decorated with large golden spots, looked just as Pete remembered.

"Bundo. This fish is as beautiful as ever."

"More beautiful than the dorado, Señor Pete?"

Pete was delighted to hear the name of the dorado spoken here, on this water, where he had actually caught them so often, both in real life and in the dreams that lately were so difficult to distinguish from it.

"Are there dorado now, Bundo?"

Abundio beamed happily.

"Sí, señor. Many."

"Tomorrow?"

"Sí, señor. If you wish it."

They put the sierra into the gunny sack, along with a dozen others, and Abundio rowed toward shore thinking of that last summer in the caleta with Señor Pete. So much had happened since. He thought of Pearl Harbor and the wartime market and the easy money he and his father had made cutting out shark livers for their thick oil.

Señor Pete was so much quieter now, an old man, and Abundio wondered what had happened to him after that last summer.

"Señor Pete, did you go to the war?"

"Yes."

"Did you find the thing... the thing that was calling you?"

Pete looked at Abundio, not quite sure if he had understood the Spanish.

"What did you say, Bundo?"

"That summer, you said something was calling you to the war. Did you find it?"

Pete wound his line in and cut his feather off. He watched the palms moving slowly by, as Abundio rowed them back to the launching spot.

"I said something was calling me?"

"Yes, to the war. I have always wondered what it was."

Pete studied Abundio's face and he saw the strong young man who had been so angry over the name of his boat that summer. He tried to remember speaking of something that was calling him, but he could not.

"I'm sorry, Bundo. But I really don't remember."

On the beach, Socorro, María, and Ana Rosa Medina were washing their best dishes and drying them with towels. There would be important guests for dinner tonight, three sport fishing clients from the United States and an old friend of El Tecolote Terrible.

DANNY CAME DOWN the landing strip, rolling an old tire in front of him. When he reached Chino at the plane, he let the tire slap down onto the dirt and he pointed this thumb back toward the arroyo.

"Hey, Robert, who's the old one-legged guy in the shack up there?"

"That's Nacho."

"He's scary looking, man."

"He's harmless."

"He sounds *loco,* too."

"No. He's all right."

Chino squatted beside the tire. He licked his finger and rubbed the powdery dust off the sidewall lettering. Danny squatted next to him.

"Is this the kind you wanted?"

Chino nodded.

"Yes. Michelin. Was it hard to find?"

"No kidding! I bet I turned over a hundred tires up there. I found a rattlesnake, too."

Chino placed the tire on a low pile of rocks and broken wood. He poured a cup of gasoline on it and touched it off with a match. They stood back and watched the hot black smoke billow into the sky.

Danny wondered what they were doing.

"Why are you burning it, Robert?"

"We need some good wire."

"What for?"

"No fiberglass."

Chino had already opened the plane's door, and he had removed some panels from the floor of the cockpit, revealing the area where the landing strut was bolted to the frame. The metal was cracked, and it buckled back and forth, allowing the strut to wobble when any weight was applied to it.

Danny was shocked by the extent of the damage.

"Jesus H. Christ! Robert, do you think you can fix it?"

"Maybe."

"Can you get parts around here?"

"No... no parts."

"Looks like it needs a welder, and some angle iron, and long U-bolts."

"We don't have those things either."

Chino left Danny to tend the fire while he went to the village for tools. When he returned, he sifted through the ashes with a stick, pulling out the woven reinforcing wires that had been embedded in the rubber carcass. Taking his time, he separated the thin cables, cut them into lengths, and rubbed them clean with sand and a piece of leather.

With ropes, they forced the landing strut into alignment, and Chino climbed into the plane with a hacksaw, a pry bar, and a big, heavy hammer. He cut back the useless pieces and pounded the edges flat.

Then he wound a tight layer of old braided dacron fishing line around the frame and the base of the strut. On top of this, he placed a woven layer of wire cables, held in place with more dacron line. Then more wire and more dacron. He covered everything with a good soaking of the quick-hardening liquid plastic they used to repair the pangas.

They were waiting for the plastic to set when Howard and Shig arrived to check on the progress of the repair job. Howard poked at the wires and strings protruding from the thin, lightweight composite cast Chino had created around the damaged strut. He seemed skeptical.

"What do *you* think, Shig? You're the mechanical engineer."

Shig leaned into the cockpit and ran his hands over the plastic cast. He went to the little pyre of rocks and inspected the remains of the burned tire. Gripping his chin thoughtfully, he walked back to Chino at the plane.

"Steel belted radial?"

"Yes."

"And eighty-pound dacron?"

"Yes."

Shig leaned in again to look closely at the repair job. He analyzed the pattern of loose ends coming through the plastic cast and he tried to deduce the arrangement of wires Chino had created within it. He fiddled with his ear lobe, making rough estimates. Then he stood up, shaking his head. There was a broad smile on his face.

"I'll be damned."

ON THE DARKENED beach, Socorro grunted under a heavy load of pots and pans.

"So… this Danny, the young one, touched you?"

"Sí, mamá."

"When?"

"When I was serving him beans."

"So you spilled them on him?"

"Sí, mamá."

They knelt at the edge of the water and began scrubbing with handfuls of sand. At the south end of the caleta, Peter Grayson was casting his feathers onto the lavender reflection of the evening sky.

Socorro grabbed a pan streaked with refried frijoles, and she tilted her head down the beach.

"The old man is all right. But I don't like the others."

"Why not, mamá?"

"Too nice. You know what I mean?"

As she scrubbed the pan in the deepening twilight, Socorro raised the pitch of her voice in a singsong parody of Spanish badly spoken.

"Oh! What *wonderful* tortillas! And, Socorro, what wonderful *beans* these are! And the *fish!* It is *so* delicious! It is *fried,* isn't it? Oh, you *must* give me the recipe! And your house is *so* beautiful! You Mexicans are *so* fortunate to live in this *beautiful* place!"

María collapsed in a fit.

"Oh, mamá! That is cruel!"

THE KEROSENE LANTERNS had been cold for several hours when Capt. Peter J. M. Grayson III, USMC, drifted back into consciousness again. He found himself buried deep within the same tangle of splintered palm trees, and near his hand, his .45 automatic lay with its clip half empty.

He knew that he had been out for only a second. He could still hear the low, reverberating moan of the SBDs, and he caught sight of one through the torn leaves and smoke, banking sharply up and away from its bombing run. He tried to push the body of the faceless soldier off his chest, but as always, it was too heavy.

Beside him, the radioman lay face down beneath his heavy backpack. Far away, someone was screaming again and again in a frantic, high-pitched voice. He could not tell what language it was. And what did it matter now?

His orders had been to hold the isthmus until the rising tide brought reinforcements over the reef. At any cost, the radioman had said, staring at him blankly. Captain, we're ordered to hold the trees… at any cost. The enemy had come with an incomprehensible disregard for its own and the fighting had quickly gone hand-to-hand. In the end, with nothing to lose, he had called for the bombs on the narrow isthmus, on the enemy, and on his own men as well, and the Navy planes had made a big circle over the atoll and dived, one at a time, to their duty. At any cost.

Those who could had run into the thickets, mindless of who might already be there, as the sand danced up all around them and the black seeds fell from an infinitely clear sky. And jolly Considine, his radioman, and quiet Richardson, his corpsman, had been just behind him when he had stumbled into the cowering soldier and fired blindly. And then the seeds had blossomed all around them, and the silence had ended everything.

Their isthmus had fallen anyway, but their little, nameless island had held, anyway. And then, incredibly, they had abandoned it the very next morning.

Afterwards, the yes and no of it had blurred together, and there were medals, and speeches by those who had not been there, and he had taken up his life again. But on many nights, he woke with the unshaven soldier across his chest, and he heard the cries of young Considine and Richardson and all the others, and he wished, he wished with an endless pain in his heart, that they could come out of the smoke and trees, just for a moment, and forgive him.

PETER GRAYSON OPENED his eyes. He looked up at the stars above his cot, on the front porch of Ramón Ochoa's abandoned house, in the caleta of Agua Amargosa, Baja California, México. A warm onshore breeze was caressing the tips of the palm thatch above him, ghostly black fingers on a sparkling black sea. It would be dawn in a few hours. It was late summer, he knew, and the dorado were just out past the reefs. But he was sleepy now, and he rolled onto his side and pulled his blanket up over his shoulders.

ABUNDIO LOOKED UP and saw the blue-red eye of morning, winking in the star-filled southern sky. First, the purest blue. A few seconds later, a deep, rich red. Blue. Red. Blue and red.

Abundio did not know if the star was a planet, or some other heavenly phenomenon, or even if it was something made by men, but he loved to spot it in the indigo morning sky for it seemed to him that the fishing was always better on those days.

"Old friend, I would call your name, if I knew what it was. Please, bring us fish today. Of all days."

Chino was already at the beach. He had prepared both pangas for launch and he was sitting on the warm sand waiting for their clients.

Abundio sat beside him and they passed the time by watching the patches of ruffled water made by the minnows. Occasionally, one of the three-inch fish touched the surface, sending a ring-shaped ripple out a few feet from the school. And a splash, now and then, marked the instant when a minnow was suddenly inhaled by a leopard grouper or cabrilla and came to the end of its brief existence.

"Where do you take them today, mijo?"

"The pilot, Howard, wants to fish for marlin."

"Only marlin?"

"Marlin and sailfish."

A hot sliver of light appeared on the horizon behind the Four Horses. On the innermost island, a noisy flock of gulls and pelicans squabbled over scraps, rising into the air a few feet, and then settling down again as the first rush of warmth struck their feathers.

"And where do you take the old man, amigo?"

"We fish for dorado."

"Good, then you can catch dinner."

"Well... actually, mijo... he doesn't like to kill them."

"Why not?"

"He says they are too beautiful."

"Well, all right. Maybe we'll get some tuna."

"Sí, maybe."

HOWARD SAT UP the moment the yellow light touched his face. The two cots beside his were empty. Against the wall of the house, Danny was still asleep on top of his rumpled bag.

Howard shook his son's foot.

"Hey, boy. Time to get up!"

Danny yawned and stretched his back and waved away a trio of flies that tickled his legs.

"Man, how can they sleep on these hard cots?"

Howard had tied his fishing rods together into two heavy bundles. He handed them to his son and picked up a duffel bag and his two wooden tackle boxes.

"Come on. Pete and Shig must be down there already."

"What about breakfast?"

"They're supposed to have lunches for us."

Danny pulled on a tee-shirt and a pair of sandals. He shouldered the fishing rods, and they started through the palms. Howard labored across the gully with his heavy tackle boxes.

"Hot last night."

"Buggy too. Why are there so many flies here?"

Howard had an egg-sized mosquito bite on his forehead. He lowered his boxes to the sand, catching his breath.

"It's the garbage and fish scraps."

"Yeah. You should see all the garbage up in the canyon."

They resumed their hike to the boats. One of the pangas was already in the water. Near it, they saw Shig and Pete standing with two Mexicans.

"These bugs are really bad."

"Yeah."

Howard stopped for another rest.

"Did you get what the old woman said about the flies?"

"You mean the pufferfish hanging under the roof?"

"Yeah."

"I think she said it's to draw the flies."

"Why would they want to do that?"

"Beats me."

Several more Mexicans had appeared on the beach, and Pete and Shig were talking to them. The old woman and her daughter were there with the lunches.

"Well, at least the food is good."

"Yeah. That old woman can really cook."

A Mexican with a big, bushy mustache trotted over to them, accompanied by two boys. Without speaking, the man took the fishing rods from Danny's shoulders and motioned for each boy to take a box.

They put Howard's tackle with Shig's in the big panga. They had thought to cover a seat with rags to protect the finish of the gold-colored reels. The boys stood silently with their father, observing the americanos from a distance.

Robert, the thin one who spoke good English, came over and greeted them with a big smile.

"Good morning, Howard. Good morning, Danny. Everything is ready."

The smaller panga was floating twenty feet off the beach. In it, the big Mexican, the one called Bumbo, struggled and cursed as he tried to start his outboard motor. Peter Grayson had climbed into the boat. He sat facing backwards on the middle seat with his fly rod propped on one knee. He raised a thumb in the air and chirped.

" Morning, Howard! Fine day!"

Howard returned a cheerful wave, but then frowned at Chino.

"Say, Robert? What's going on here? You said Shig and I were fishing with Bumbo."

Chino stammered a reply as Abundio's starter rope broke and nearly threw him out of the panga.

"Yes, but… this panga is better for outside, for marlin."

"What's wrong with Bumbo's boat?"

"It's much smaller. And old. Very old."

Howard was unconvinced.

"Bumbo's the best fisherman around here, right?"

Chino stole a glance at Pablo Santos and his sons, who stood waiting to help push their panga into the water. Pablo noticed the look and raised his eyebrows in a question, but Chino waved him off as he answered Howard.

"Well... yes. Bundo is very good. But... "

Abundio had thrown the cover of the old Evinrude down in disgust and he was pushing himself back to shore. Shig broke in.

"Listen, Howard, let's check out the other boat."

"All right."

The bow of Abundio's panga nudged the sand with Peter Grayson still sitting on the middle seat. They walked over to take a look. As they reached the old boat, Danny noted it really was much smaller than Pablo's fiberglass model.

"Dad, this thing won't hold four guys anyway."

Shig went to the stern. He grinned at Abundio, who was attaching a new handle to the starter rope. The heavily corroded motor reeked of gasoline and neglect. Most of the lead patch on the lower unit had come off. The crack in the gear casing was clearly visible. Shig shook his head.

"Hey, Howard, this motor's a wreck."

Up front, Howard had already seen enough. The wooden strakes of the hull were rotted and beginning to separate and there was six inches of water sloshing around in the bow. More water was seeping through a tee-shirt driven into a hole below the water line.

Howard leaned over to Pete, who was still perched on the middle seat with his rod pointing into the air.

"Say, Pete, you're not going out in this thing are you?"

Pete smiled ingenuously.

"Is there room for me in your boat?"

"*In our boat...?*"

Pete raised a hand.

"Howard, don't worry about me! I'll just fish in the bay today."

They left Pete sitting there and went back to the big panga. Howard motioned for the rest of their things to be loaded and he winked at Chino.

"Okay, Robert. We're with you."

"Right."

Howard pointed his thumb toward Abundio, his eyes mocking.

"So, that's your best fisherman, eh?"

"Well... you see... "

He swatted the top of Chino's head and laughed.

"Hah! Don't worry about it, Robert! No hard feelings!"

They turned Pablo's panga around and slid it into the water. Socorro
and María brought the lunches in a cardboard box. As he took the box
from María, Danny caught her hand and spoke to her in English.

"Thanks! What's your name?"

María flushed. She pulled her hand free and looked for Chino.

"What does he say?"

Chino's hands hung loosely at his sides. His eyes were on Danny.

"He asked your name."

Now Danny gave Chino a leering smile.

"Does she speak any English?"

"No."

"What's her name?"

"María."

"María! Very pretty! Robert, can you tell her? I think she's very pretty."

Chino was composing a reply when he caught sight of Socorro's dark
face. His intended mother-in-law was standing rigidly, by herself, a little
distance back in the trees.

"A moment, Danny."

Socorro's eyes drilled through Chino. She had bitten her lower lip.
Chino came close and whispered.

"Socorro. What is it?"

"Chino, do they insult us?"

He glanced at the others waiting on the beach.

"It is just their way, Socorro."

"He touches your head... like a dog."

"He meant no harm... "

"They laugh... at my husband."

"Well... "

"They insult my daughter."

"Not really... "

Chino braced himself for the untimely demise of the Rodríguez sport
fishing business. Socorro's gaze was fixed over his shoulder, somewhere
beyond the sky, and he knew when she looked that way she was
unpredictable and unconcerned with petty, mundane details. And Chino
was sure that—in Socorro's way of thinking—the tourist business was a
petty detail, a dry burp in the greater scheme of things.

But then, very slowly, the anger on Socorro's round face faded away,
and her eyes took on the dusky sadness of The Virgin of Guadalupe. She

sighed as though she were very tired and she reached up to caress Chino's cheek with the backs of her rough fingers.

"Thank you, Chino. Good luck today."

THE EARLY MORNING sea at the Four Horses was as flat and slick as a millpond.

There had been a brief flurry of sierra mackerel, followed by uncounted barracuda. Then, a large amberjack, the *pez fuerte* with the bandit's stripe through its eye, had broken off at the boat after taking a foil streamer just under the surface.

Abundio handed the bailing scoop forward and motioned for Pete to empty the bow out. Pete tossed several gallons over the side and returned the scoop.

"Bundo, does your father still fish?"

"No, he died."

Abundio's sun-blackened Sonoran father, the shark fisherman and pearl diver who could never quite make ends meet, was still alive in the face and shoulders of his son. Pete saw the old man now, traced in the lids of Abundio's eyes, in the angle of his wrists, in the bones of his cheeks.

And Abundio looked sadly back at his old friend, so greatly reduced, so much changed for the worse, it seemed, since the seasons they fished together in the small, square-ended boat called *Master-Baiter*.

Señor Pete no longer drank beer at all and he ate very little. He was still alone. He had gotten married, he said, after the war, but his wife had divorced him and his children were grown. He had retired as principal of the same school in Los Angeles where he worked before the war.

Señor Pete's chest was now marked down its middle by a fresh pink scar, and by the square lump under his breast where they had buried the machine that kept his heart alive and allowed him to escape the prison that his life had suddenly become a dozen years before.

And, Abundio wondered, what keeps the rest of us alive? Why do we rise from our beds each morning? Is it just that we are hungry or have to pee? Would a simple battery in the chest serve just as well? Perhaps it is different for each of us. Socorro has her invisible spirits, Ana Rosa her faith in the priests, Fra Nacho his music and powdered snakes. But no. No, no, no. There must be something more. There must be a *reason* we wish to cling to those things in the first place.

Pete gestured for Abundio to take the panga out to deeper water. They ran slowly to a place about a hundred yards outside the third island. Pete tied on a small, curved metal lure with a red stripe down its outer side, and he lowered it to the bottom. He pulled all of the heavy line from his reel, then a few feet of running line, and he jigged the spoon up and down.

The rocky floor of the sea was visible, oddly magnified and tilted up by the refraction of the water, even though it was fifty feet below them. Abundio waited fifteen minutes before disturbing Pete's dreamy gaze.

"Do we fish for huachinango, señor?"

"Yes. For dinner tonight?"

"The water is very warm, señor. Perhaps a little deeper."

"All right."

Abundio ran the panga out another hundred yards and Pete dropped his line to the bottom again, this time twice as deep.

The lure sank slowly, with Abundio working the oars to keep the line straight up and down. When Pete finally touched bottom, his thin rod tip immediately whipped into the water and he pulled up a fat goldspotted bass. The fish was stiffened by the distended air bladder pushing out of its mouth.

Abundio stuck the bass into the gunny sack. They lowered the line again and tried several more spots, looking for the delicious, orange-eyed huachinango that Socorro would slash and fry whole in lard, salt, and garlic.

But all they caught were two more goldspotted bass and then the bite stopped completely.

"There is a good place farther out, Señor Pete. I will try to find it."

"Can I reach it with this rod?"

"Yes, it is very shallow, but small."

Abundio steered northeast to look for the *bajo*, or high spot. He ran the panga a quarter mile past the outer island, to where he could look back and see The Hammer of God riding just off the left-hand shoulder of The Devil's Anvil.

He circled an area two-hundred yards across, keeping his eyes on the peaks' slowly shifting parallax. But he couldn't remember the exact little dip on the mesa that The Hammer of God should be touching.

"I wish Chino was here."

"Do you mean your partner, Robert?"

"Yes."

"Is he a good fisherman?"

Abundio hunched his big, round shoulders.

"He is a good man."

Abundio gave up on The Hammer of God. He killed the Evinrude and rowed the panga in a wide figure-eight pattern. Every hundred feet or so, he lowered an oar straight down into the water and placed the upper end of the handle hard on his ear, listening intently to the wood.

"Bundo, what are you listening for?"

"Ah… little clicking sounds. Sometimes, it growls like a dog."

"No kidding! What is it?"

Abundio shrugged that he didn't know.

"My father said it is the crabs talking to each other."

They tried a dozen more spots, with Pete holding the oar to his ear and growing more skeptical with each attempt. The water was still glassy smooth, even way out here, rising and falling on a lazy southern swell, and the air was so motionless it seemed they were floating on the surface of a dream.

"Bundo, are you sure about this?"

"Ah… well… "

Then Pete heard it, a distinct, intermittent clicking, as though someone were tapping on thick metal with the tip of a sharp knitting needle.

"Bundo! I hear it! Right under us!"

Abundio looked again at The Hammer of God. He checked the alignment of two other peaks to the south. They were still about twenty yards west of the bajo. He rowed to the exact spot and stirred the oars.

"Here, señor."

Pete dropped his spoon over the side and began pulling out line. He touched bottom after only a few brazas had been pulled out and he immediately got a strike that jerked half his rod into the water.

"Whoa! Bundo! This ain't no huachinango!"

Pete fought the fish almost up to first color, but it sounded straight down when it sensed the boat and refused to come up again. The tip of Pete's rod stayed beneath the surface and its shaft throbbed rhythmically as the fish beat toward the bottom and then away from the bajo.

Abundio followed with the oars, keeping Pete's line clear of the gunnel, as The Hammer of God drifted off The Devil's Anvil and a light ruffling breeze moved over the water. After fifteen minutes, with no gained line to show for it, Pete was sweating heavily. He twisted his head around to look at Abundio.

"Another pez fuerte?"

Abundio nodded yes, maybe, another amberjack, or "strong fish," as it was called in Spanish. But he indicated with his hands that it must be larger than the one they had caught earlier.

"Sí, señor. *Pez fuerte… toro… atún… barrilete…* "

Pete considered the possibilities Abundio had recited… amberjack… jack crevalle… tuna… black skipjack…

"Or, a big cabrilla? A *cabrilla grande?*"

Abundio shook his head. He and Chino, Pablo Santos, and the others had long since taken any resident cabrilla from this bajo that might be capable of pulling so strongly. And this fish's determined run, away from the safety of the rocks, indicated it was probably a migrator, an open water swimmer with the bad luck to have visited the bajo at the moment Pete dropped his lure to it.

Pete held on for another quarter hour, but then began to weaken. He put the butt of his rod between his legs and clasped both hands high on the shaft, leaning back against the fish. He raised his ashen face toward the sky with his eyes tightly closed and his heart pounding, and he panted in shallow, painful breaths.

Abundio leaned close and whispered respectfully.

"Señor… we go outside for dorado. Let me break the line."

Abundio's small, pleading voice reminded Pete of the hot afternoon, many summers before, when the boy had jumped off his rock, spry as a coyote, almost under the tires of the old Ford.

Pete felt himself slamming on the brakes and leaning over the hot frame of the window as he shouted to the boy in Spanish.

"What's your name, boy? My name is Peter. Does this road go all the way to the beach? Speak up, boy! What's wrong with you?"

The boy's eyes shined under a mop of hair hanging down past his shoulders. He wore nothing but a pair of underpants and he had spoken shyly, afraid to look up.

"Do you go fishing, señor?"

"Yes! Are you a fishing guide, boy? *Una guía?*"

The chubby, brown-skinned boy had suddenly begun bouncing up and down on the balls of his feet.

"Sí, señor! I have great knowledge of fish! All classes of fish!"

Pete had looked for the boy's family. There was a single canoe at the south end of the beach. But no fish camp. He would need a guide for the first few days.

"*Cuánto cuesta*? How much?"

The boy had pointed to the elegant, rectangular gold watch on Pete's wrist.

"May I have your watch, señor?"

"Hah! No way! But how about a cold drink?"

He opened the ice chest and let the astonished boy help himself to all the sodas and beer he could carry off, and the bargain had been struck. The fishing had been good. So very, very, unbelievably good. They found thirty-seven species that first summer alone.

But now, Pete's chest was full of cotton and his hands were numb, and reluctantly he handed his rod off to Bundo the man. Pete watched with dissatisfaction and regret as Abundio wound the line over his hand and elbow and gradually increased the strain until the leader parted with a slow, empty looseness.

"Pez fuerte."

"Sí, señor. Pez fuerte."

"Maybe big cabrilla."

"Sí, señor. Maybe."

Pete sat recovering his breath while Abundio reeled in the empty line. Abundio's big hands nearly hid the narrow, aluminum reel, and his fingers slipped awkwardly on the stubby winding knob.

He wasn't wearing the Rolex. Pete wondered if perhaps he had sold it. He remembered the day his own father had given the watch to him. It was a fine, warm spring day. The quad on the hill above Providence was heartbreakingly green with the rush of new leaf and Pete's arms had fumbled inside his long, black gown as they stood beneath the big elm tree for photographs.

"Peter, have you thought any more about law school?"

"I can't see the point of it, father."

"What will you do?"

"I thought maybe I'd go west. Maybe take a look at California."

"Times are bad out there, too. Remember son, the firm will always be here for you."

"Thanks, father."

"And son... "

"Yes, father?"

"Try to remember, nobody blames you for anything."

They had walked down Waterman Street and gone up to the paneled offices in the Hospital Trust Building, where Pete was introduced to his new trustee and they signed some papers, and later, they all drove down to Newport for a dinner of lobster and clams and thick, creamy chowder.

Across the candles, they talked of Hoover and Roosevelt, and just what should be done to save the country, and Pete had tried and tried, but he could not see the point of it all. To him, they all sounded like first year law students, training themselves to argue both sides of any question with equal conviction, and Pete could hardly stand to listen to it. He could not shake his belief that after all the arguments were peeled away, like the layers of an onion, somewhere inside there *had* to be a kernel of absolute truth, an irrefutable right or wrong. Otherwise, what did their lives amount to but pointless, endless, self-deception that led to thinking you had done something when you really hadn't?

The next afternoon they drove to the train station and dropped off Peter J. M. Grayson III, twenty-three years old, out to change the world, or at the very least make some sense of it, with two bachelor's degrees, two Pullmans, and a fly rod case his only baggage.

Abundio held the rod out.

Instead of taking it, Pete tapped the big man's thick wrist.

"Do you still have it, Bundo?"

Abundio held the rod suspended between them.

"Sí, señor."

"But you don't wear it?"

"It is hidden."

Abundio set the rod down on the seats of the panga and they drifted on the gently rolling sea. High above, a shoal of thin, white cirrus clouds floated slowly north, like great bird's wings driven by the wind. Abundio's fingers stroked the varnished shaft of the rod.

"Señor?"

"Yes, Bundo?"

"Why did you give me something… of such great value?"

Pete smiled.

"You asked for it. Don't you remember?"

"Seriously, señor."

Pete looked back toward the Four Horses. A dark line of palms marked the shore of the caleta. The arroyo behind the village showed as a tan scar in the cliffs, and above everything, the high mountains rose into the sea haze, purple and rugged.

Pete thought for a moment that he could hear something like the drone of an airplane engine, beneath the sound of his breathing. He took a deep, easy breath, feeling the lightness return to his chest, and he passed his hands slowly along the shaft of his grandfather's shiny, bamboo rod.

"I didn't want it, Bundo. Somehow, I think I felt burdened by it."

FOR THE HUNDREDTH time, it seemed, Chino cut the throttle and slowed Pablo Santos' big panga down to idling speed. He lowered the plastic bucket over the side and filled it to the brim, and he poured five gallons of fresh seawater into the open space between the panga's front and middle seats.

A dozen languorous live baits swam dizzily in the shallow pool of water sloshing back and forth between the seats. The mixed school of mackerel, grunts, and small green jacks was kept just barely alive by Chino's bucket and by the drafts of seawater that flowed in and out through a hole Pablo had drilled in the hull.

Clever Pablo had sealed the floor between the seats with fiberglass, and the hole he had drilled admitted about six inches of water into the pool, no more. It was just enough to keep a few baits alive while he fished in the rocks for cabrilla.

But at trolling speed, about five miles-per-hour, the hull of the panga rose up enough to drain Pablo's baitwell almost dry, and Chino was forced to stop every few minutes to refill it with half a dozen buckets of seawater.

"All set!"

Chino twisted the throttle and resumed trolling straight east.

He gave a smile and a half salute to Howard and Shig, who sat facing backwards, side-by-side, on the forward seat.

They had taken off their shoes, and their bare feet dangled in the pool of water together with the slowly dying baits. Each man held a heavy fishing rod across his lap that he kept angled out over his side of the panga. At the end of each line, about three boat-lengths back, a semi-live mackerel with a one-inch hook in its nose trailed through the water like a dog pulled on a leash.

Howard's dreadfully seasick son, Danny, lay curled on his side in the bow of the panga with a gunny sack protecting him from the heat and harsh light of mid-morning. Danny's exposed legs were burned to a startling red and they appeared all the redder where the gunny sack had pulled up to expose another inch of skin.

Howard and Shig were also red, especially around their foreheads and noses and on the tops of their knees, and Chino made a mental note that they should make some kind of shade for their clients, something that could be raised and lowered to protect them from the sun.

And rod holders. Howard and Shig had complained all morning about the lack of rod holders. Chino imagined it would be easy to attach short tubes to the gunnels that would accept the butts of the clients' heavy rods and relieve their hands of having to pull against the drag of the baits.

Shig held up a grease-stained paper bag.

"Lunch, Robert?"

"No thank you, Shig."

The clients poked around in the cardboard box that Socorro had packed by lantern light early that morning. They unwrapped the foil from a package of fresh tortillas and some boiled eggs with salt and pepper. There were seven or eight eggs in the package. Chino grunted to himself in approval of Socorro's uncharacteristic extravagance. She had committed a full week's production of the Rodríguez hens to assure their clients a filling lunch.

As the men ate, Chino looked back to check their baits. The mackerel trailed just under the surface with a slight weaving motion. Now and then one of them flicked its tail and tried to turn away from the boat, but it was checked immediately by the hook through its nose.

Behind the baits, the purple mountains of the coast had long since faded from view. Chino knew the mountains were still there, real and solid, but they were concealed by twenty miles of sea haze, and the panga seemed to be surrounded on all sides by featureless, open water.

In the southwest, an enormous, single thundercloud rose high above the horizon, like the head and torso of a colossal giant standing behind the edge of the earth. Chino knew that beneath the cloud the rain was falling on the mountain passes, and water was collecting in the *tinajas*, the rocky pools where the goat ranchers tended their struggling herds. He wondered if the main road had ever been reopened, and if it had, if it was being washed out again today.

Howard turned around to his son in the bow.

"Fried chicken, Danny?"

"Ummm... no way... "

Chino chuckled to himself at Howard's joke of referring to their boiled eggs as fried chicken. It reminded him of Abundio's game of imagining that their usual lunch of burritos or plain tortillas had turned miraculously into a fantasy banquet of dishes they rarely tasted.

But Chino was amazed when Howard pulled a real fried chicken leg out of the aluminum foil and handed it to Shig. Then Howard took a leg for himself and offered another to Chino!

Three legs! At least two chickens! Socorro, it seemed, had sacrificed not only a week's worth of eggs, but the entire means of production as well!

Chino was reaching forward to take the chicken leg, when Shig's reel emitted a loud, rasping buzz and his legs went rigid in the pool of bait fish. Shig screamed.

"Hook uuupp…!"

The chicken legs went flying. Howard stood up in the pool, shouting, as the spool of Shig's reel spun and yard after yard of line pulled out behind the panga. Chino looked down and saw his chicken leg swimming around with their mackerel.

"Hook up! Hook up! Robert! Stop the boat! For Christ's sake, stop the boat!"

At last, Chino understood that Shig's bait must have been hit by a fish, a very large fish. In fact, a very, very large fish. Either that or he had snagged a turtle. Or perhaps a log floating just under the surface.

Chino cut the throttle and pushed the tiller hard over to turn back toward whatever had taken Shig's mackerel. The marlin came up directly abeam of the panga, headed in the same direction. It hurdled free of the water a dozen times, gaining distance with each leap, as it passed by them and crossed the bow with Shig's line pulling in the corner of its mouth.

"Madre…!"

It was the first marlin Chino had ever seen strike a trolled bait.

He was astonished by the fish's strength and fury as it leapt into the air again, this time straight up. Its sides flashed electric blue bars, and its long bill slashed the air left and right. Its sleek, black body flexed repeatedly through a high somersault and it landed sideways in a geyser of spray only twenty yards ahead of them.

Howard reeled in the other bait. Quickly, he buckled a heavy leather butt belt around Shig's waist and helped him snap a shoulder harness to his reel.

The marlin jumped no more. It sounded straight down, taking half of

Shig's line with it, before it leveled out at an incredible depth and the fight settled into a prolonged standoff.

The veins in Shig's neck stood out as he pushed the drag lever of his reel forward and pumped his rod up and down in short, rapid strokes. Each time his rod came down he whipped the handle of his reel half a turn and gained a few inches of line.

Danny had revived from his seasickness. He stood at the gunnel of the panga, searching the cobalt blue depths for signs of a fish that was still a quarter of a mile away.

"What kind is it, Shig?"

"A blue."

"How big?"

"Two-fifty, maybe three-hundred."

Shig regained about half his line. But then his arm muscles cramped and began to tremble. He stopped pumping. He tightened the drag lever as far as he dared and he sat leaning back against his bowed rod.

Half an hour went by. Then forty-five minutes. Then an hour, with no change.

Chino settled into the routine of shifting the Evinrude in and out of gear to keep the line straight for Shig. He felt relieved that the clients seemed to be enjoying themselves despite their sunburns and the dullness of the day. Since dawn, they had spent the first hour jigging for live baits, followed by two hours of fruitless, non-stop trolling, out of sight of land, and finally an hour of this fooling around with a fish that might be subdued in half that time with a heavy hand-line. All morning, their only relief from monotony had been the hectic few minutes immediately following the hooking of this marlin. Yet, the clients joked constantly among themselves, and they were obviously having a very good time. They seemed content to spend their entire day in the senselessly prolonged pursuit of this one fish. Chino made a mental note that he must try to gain a better understanding of the sport fishing business.

Throughout the fight Shig's line had been pointing down and away into the water. Now, Chino saw it swing in, close to the side of the boat, and then make a very slow circle, clockwise.

Shig saw it too.

"Robert. Get ready. Here it comes."

"Right."

Four-hundred feet down, the female blue marlin had finally tired and had begun to circle in a last attempt to stay away from the small shadow above it. But the quick pumping of the hook in its mouth now resumed, and the relentless pull of the line kept it from flexing its body fully. With each half-stroke of its tail, the exhausted fish lost a few inches of depth and half a degree of direction, and its circle became a little smaller. It pulled with all its strength, but it could not stop the shadow from coming closer. Now, the shadow took the form of a panga's bottom, black against the sky-bright surface, and the strange, muffled sounds of men's shouting mingled with the steady growl of the Evinrude. The long-handled hook swept through the water. It missed twice before sinking home in the great silver belly. And the marlin's sword was pulled out of the water, and the heavy club came crashing down, and down, and down.

"BIRD WORKING, BUNDO. Straight south."

Pete's rod drooped over the side of the panga. They had trolled around the Four Horses until noon, hoping for dorado, but they had caught nothing and had returned to jig over the bajo.

Abundio was half asleep. He shaded his eyes, scanning the afternoon horizon to the south, but he saw nothing.

"Are you sure, señor?"

"Yes. About two miles. We'll have to run to it."

Abundio studied the distant haze for a full minute. He searched for the bird in a wide arc between shore and the eastern horizon. He could not find it, but that was not unusual. He shipped the oars and went to start the Evinrude, turning to Pete as he took a grip on the starter rope.

"You still have the eyes, Señor Pete."

"Yes. That has remained."

The motor had grown cold. As Abundio pulled repeatedly on the rope Pete kept his eyes trained in the direction of the working bird.

"Bundo, do you think it's safe to go out so far?"

Abundio sat down for a break and snorted loudly.

"No hay problema, señor. Chino and I, we watch for each other."

The motor backfired with a puff of smoke that squirted out from under the edge of its cowling. On the next pull, though, it caught and Abundio popped it quickly into gear and swung the bow around to the south.

Pete sat facing forward on the middle seat as the panga picked up speed and climbed and fell against a smooth southern swell. He made a sweeping motion with his left hand for Abundio to veer a little to the east, farther away from shore. Abundio still could not see the bird.

"Do you see it, señor?"

"No. But it's there."

They ran a full mile south before Abundio finally caught sight of the bird, even farther to the left than Pete had indicated. It was a solitary, long-winged frigate bird, hidden by the distance and the humidity in the air. It was visible only in brief flashes when its wings caught the sun at just the proper angle. It had risen momentarily above the horizon and Abundio saw it turn and dive back down. It was definitely working on bait. Pete had been lucky to spot it.

The panga began to pound into the swells, so Abundio reduced throttle to smooth the ride for his passenger. Pete turned around and gave the "okay" sign with his thumb and first finger and they settled into the run out to the frigate bird. It would be another ten or fifteen minutes before they reached it.

Pete replaced his metal spoon with a six-inch streamer of silver foil and feathers of yellow and dark green. He held it up for Abundio to see.

"Our old dorado special!"

Abundio nodded with a grin. It was good to see Señor Pete so animated and he hoped the frigate bird had indeed found them a school of dorado. Up ahead, Abundio could now see that the frigate was not alone after all. It was accompanied by dozens of gulls and pelicans, all diving furiously on bait.

They were still a quarter mile from the birds when the slowly rising hump of a swell revealed a brownish yellow stain on the water, and Abundio's heart leapt. It was a patch of floating sargassum weed, right in the middle of the feeding melee, and they were likely to find dorado hiding under it. Pete saw it too.

"There it is, Bundo! Do-*rrra*-do!"

"Sí, señor! Mucho, mucho dorado!"

A dense school of dorado surrounded the weed paddy. The excited predators flashed brilliant greens and electric blues just beneath the surface as they cut into bait fish and drove them upwards to the diving birds.

All around the panga, schools of silvery bait fish shot hissing into the air, as though fired from cannon, and they fell inevitably back to the marauding dorado, only to be chased to the surface again a few seconds later.

Cautiously, Abundio steered just upwind of the fish and killed the Evinrude. He let the panga drift to the weed patch and become part of it. He used the gaff to hold the boat to the edge of the paddy while Pete stood up and began false casting his streamer through the air in big loops. Pete was beside himself. He had never seen so many dorado and he shouted to Abundio in English.

"Bundo! Is this a sure thing or what?"

Abundio grinned and nodded yes to whatever it was that Señor Pete had said.

With each false cast, the streamer flicked out farther and farther from the boat and the electric blue flashes showed constantly where it must touch down.

Pete needed as much distance as possible to allow for a decent retrieve through the thickest part of the fish. For his final cast, he pulled the fly back very hard and let the line stretch out full-length in the air behind him. He waited as long as he dared and then he drove his arm forward as hard as possible.

But before Pete's streamer could begin its forward flight, a brilliant, metallic gold and green fish, five feet long and flashing electric blue lines all over its body, shot a yard out of the water and snapped its vicious jaws.

"What the hell…?"

Pete was nearly tipped off his feet by the sudden pull from behind his back.

He staggered to maintain his balance as his reel screeched and the huge bull dorado turned a double flip, ten feet in the air, and then two more before greyhounding north. And Pete still hadn't seen it.

Abundio lay laughing in the stern of the panga. He made winding motions with his big hands and shouted in English to a confused Peter Grayson.

"Feesh! Feesh! Reel, señor! Reel!"

THE DEAD MARLIN'S long, black body curved tight against the outside of the panga. They had lashed the fish under the starboard gunnel and its weight made the boat lean to the right as they trolled.

"Danny… *por favor*… "

Chino waved his hand for Danny to move to the left side of the boat, and they ran a little more level.

Chino glanced over his shoulder to check the baits. Everything seemed fine.

They were headed straight east again. For the past hour, he had been looking for the current of clear, deep blue water that ran far offshore. When he found it, he would turn south and troll along the boundary between the current and the greener, near shore water in hopes of finding another marlin.

On the front seat, Howard and Shig sat holding their rods. They chattered back and forth and seemed quite satisfied and cheerful as they made jokes about the size of their fish and how long it had taken to reel it in. Shig seemed especially proud of his catch. He reached down over the side occasionally and patted the fish's back.

The clients' sunburns had become almost frightening. Chino wondered how they could be so oblivious to it.

"Piece of chicken, Robert?"

Chino shook his head. He looked down at his other chicken leg. Bloated and soaked to a pasty white color, it sloshed around in an oily pool of water with their now dead baits.

Suddenly, Danny bolted upright in the bow. He pointed northwest, past Chino's left shoulder, and shouted.

"Hey look! Jumping marlin! Back there!"

Chino's head snapped around in time to catch the last edge of the distant splash as it settled back into the water. It was another *manta raya*, leaping into the air with its mates, as they often did in the months of warm water.

For the past half-hour, they had been trolling through a very loose school of the ten-foot-wide, bat-winged rays. Chino had seen at least twenty or thirty of them jump out of the water and he thought the clients had seen them as well. He couldn't remember the English word for manta ray.

"It isn't marlin… "

Danny was adamant.

"Yes! I saw it! Dad, make him turn around!"

Chino looked to Shig for help.

"Shig, they're *manta rayas,* you know?"

Shig shook his head blankly. He couldn't understand the rapid Spanish pronunciation, *mahn'-ta-rye'-yah.* Chino spread his arms wide and flapped them like a bird.

"*Manta raya*, Shig. Like stingrays, you know? But real big."

"Ah!"

Shig's face broke into a wide red grin.

"He says it's a manta ray. They jump out like that too."

They settled back into the troll and Chino was able to point out another manta ray in time for them to see its diamond-shaped body flip through the air and come crashing down with a tremendous splash.

They trolled east for another hour, with their heads nodding in the heat, in the low growl of the Evinrude, and in the slow pitch and yaw of the panga as it quartered into a southern swell. Then, Chino looked up from a three-second nap and he saw the knife-like edge of the blue water current cutting across their path a tenth of a mile ahead.

He sharpened his eyes. He searched left and right for the vertical spike in the water that would mark the tail fin of a marlin on the surface. He thought he saw one, but when he approached it turned out to be nothing more than a small sea turtle, lolling in the swells with a flipper raised in the air.

When they reached the edge of the blue current Chino turned the panga due south, directly into the swell. He had Howard and Shig put on fresh baits.

But they trolled for another hour without seeing anything more. To be sure they were in the current, Chino looked over the side at the deep halo of light surrounding the shadow of his head. Silently, he cursed his luck and hoped the clients would be satisfied with their one fish. At least, the sea had been uncannily calm the entire day.

Chino was beginning to think about turning back to the caleta and about how fast Pablo's panga could run over such a flat sea when he saw the spikes.

"Shig! Howard!"

There were three of them. No. Six. No. More than six, swirling around in a tight school, a hundred yards off the port bow. Chino pulled the tiller over and eased the throttle open to hurry toward them. The trolled baits rose up and skipped over the surface in the panga's wake.

Shig tried to count the spikes. There seemed to be about twenty but there were too many to be sure. He had heard stories of marlin feeding in schools but in many years of fishing he had never witnessed it.

"Robert, are those *all* marlin?"

Chino grinned and nodded. He pointed to the spare rods.

"Shig. Two more baits. Quickly."

"*Jesus!*"

Shig clamped his trolling rod between his legs. He used his free hands to bait two more lines with dead green jacks. He put the two fresh rods down on the seats with their reels near Chino.

"Robert, can you handle a lever drag?"

Chino smiled and shrugged his shoulders. He had been watching closely all day to learn how the gold reels worked.

"Why not?"

Howard and Shig sat stiffly with their eyes fixed on the boiling water. Marlin tails, too numerous to count, lashed and cut the surface in an area fifty yards across. The fish were cutting up a school of juvenile dorado. Every few seconds, a one-foot lightning bolt of greenish gold came pinging out of the water in a series of long leaps.

Chino decided to run parallel to the edge of the feeding school. He pushed the tiller over, but before the panga could react, Howard's bait was hit, then Shig's.

Howard screamed as he reared back to set the hook on his fish.

"Wow! Double hook up!"

Two struck marlin leapt off in opposite directions.

Chino threw the big Evinrude into neutral. He cast a bait into the water and handed the rod off to Danny in the bow. Then he cast another for himself.

Within seconds, both baits were taken and began to pull out away from the panga. Chino waited for what seemed like two weeks and then threw his drag lever forward and struck his fish again and again. The hookup was incredibly solid and heavy. He had never felt anything like it.

Danny's bait was still running rapidly away from the boat, clamped in the mouth of his marlin. Chino shouted to him.

"Danny! Set your hook! Danny! Set your hook!"

Danny jerked back on his rod. But he had not tightened his drag lever. The spool of his reel spun around wildly, burning the end of his thumb and leaving his line an impossible tangle.

"Oh shit!"

"Here, Danny!"

Chino quickly switched rods with Danny, giving him the solidly hooked marlin just as it came out for its first jump. He cut off Danny's tangled line and laid the rod down on the seats, and the clients whooped and hollered as they bent to their work.

Chino leaned against the tiller of Pablo Santos' beautiful, smooth-idling

Evinrude. Occasionally, he popped it into gear for a few seconds to keep the clients' lines from crossing, and he reached for the box and helped himself to a big piece of fried chicken.

The sport fishing business seemed to be going quite well this afternoon.

THE BIG MALE dorado swam calmly beside the boat, exhausted but still flashing blue on its long dorsal fin.

Abundio leaned over the side as far as he could. He grabbed Pete's leader, pulling the fish close, and he used a pair of long-nosed pliers to twist the hook from the corner of its mouth and set it free.

The weight of the bull dorado's enormous, square forehead pulled its body downwards, and its tail flicked weakly back and forth as it sank and its image grew smaller and smaller. At a certain depth, it lost its shape entirely and became an electric blue leaf, undulating slowly in the blackness. They watched until they lost sight of it.

"*Uno más*, Señor Pete?"

"No. I'm finished, Bundo. Let's go home."

The bite had stopped anyway. During Pete's long battle, they had drifted several hundred yards from the weed paddy. The birds were nowhere to be seen. The sea seemed barren and spent.

Abundio got the motor started and pointed the panga toward the high gray point in the northwest. They quartered with the swell now, fortunately, for it had risen and lengthened during the afternoon, and it was now so deep the horizon was hidden from view each time they sank into a trough.

But it was a smooth swell and Abundio was able to open the throttle wide for the run back to the Four Horses. The panga soared over the water like a low-flying pelican, running up each wave and gaining speed down its back side before rising again.

Pete was enjoying the ride. He leaned against a gunnel with his rod pointing straight up and he studied the distant lightning flashes and the slow, moiling movement of a thunderhead that dominated the sky behind The Devil's Anvil and The Hammer of God.

"Bundo, your panga handles this swell very nicely."

"Sí, Señor Pete."

Abundio flexed his knees as they bottomed out in a trough and he stretched his body upwards as though to help the panga over the next wave. He opened the Evinrude's throttle even wider to increase the sensation of surging power, and he began to sway with the rhythm of the swells, as though he were dancing a slow ballet. He swept his free arm through the air like an orchestra conductor in time to music.

"Ah, Señor Pete! Do you know what this reminds me of?"

"What, Bundo?"

"The first three minutes of Señor Tchaikovsky's piano concerto número uno. Do you know it?"

Pete did know the piece. It had been one of his mother's favorites. He sat remembering it as the panga pushed up a long swell and dropped into the next trough. It was true. The timing and force of the ride over the waves was a very good match.

"Bundo, where did you learn that music?"

"From Nacho."

"Nacho?"

"He is an old Italian sailor. He lives in the arroyo."

"An Italian? Living here?"

"Sí, señor. Nacho has been here for many years. He came during the war, before they opened the road."

Pete gave the grown boy a curious look. An Italian sailor! There were always surprises with these people, just as in the fishing. Always a new aspect. He was glad he had let himself be talked into this trip. He had dreamed of one more dorado, just one, and now he had caught it after all this time. And he had come back to this magic place and slept under the palms again, and here was Bundo, all grown up and very overweight and speaking of concertos! *Agua Amargosa!* The hidden little bay even had its own name now! But these houses. All empty! What was happening to these people?

"How is the sport fishing business going, Bundo?"

"Ah... not very good, Señor Pete."

"Not much business, eh?"

"Well... actually señor... you are our first customers."

As the Four Horses gradually appeared in the distance, one-by-one, Abundio slowed the panga to trolling speed, and he told his old friend the story of the spring storm, and the road, and the fish buyer's truck. He told of how Ramon's blue house had become available for the clients' use, and of how he had climbed the cliff twice and made signs to attract the airplanes. He described how Chino had gotten the Chevy started and smoothed out the pista, and how they had waited for weeks and weeks for someone to land.

But Abundio left many things out of his story, things that he felt were not related to it, or that were unnecessary to the understanding of it, and so the day itself was diminished in a way that neither he nor Peter Grayson would ever be aware of.

Abundio left out Joselito Medina, the bright-eyed boy who had never once failed to meet his panga in the afternoons. He did not mention the painful sighs that Socorro sometimes made, very late, when she was sure he had fallen asleep, nor her dreadful, nightmare fear that Fra Nacho would refuse to leave the caleta with the rest of them. Nor did he speak of the hot winds that blew toward Isla Coronado in the early fall, nor of his daughter, María, for whom he had resolved to pull shark when the time came, nor of Margarita Santos and the old Buick and the unforgotten thing that would have become the next Abundio Rodríguez, had the wheel of life but paused or turned in a slightly different way.

As he neared the end of his story, Abundio looked down at his old friend. Señor Pete had fallen asleep in the late afternoon sun, with his stubbled chin resting on his chest. His fly rod lay across his knees.

They passed the outermost of the Four Horses and turned into the channel. Abundio stood tall at the tiller, watching carefully for rocks hidden in the slanting rays of the orange-yellow sunset. Absent-mindedly, he whistled an old tune that his father had loved to sing to him when the sky looked like this, in the early evenings, as they paddled home to dinner across the bay of La Paz.

...and you, my son... and me, my son. We'll row the boat together! We'll stop to dream a while, and we'll row some more... And you, my son... and me, my son...

They glided onto the flatness of the inner caleta. Abundio cut the throttle to idle and his eyes searched the dark shadows beneath the trees for the running, darting figure of long-legged Joselito and his rusty fishhooks. But then he remembered, once again, that the boy was no longer there, and he steered toward shore, looking for the yellow rock that was now visited by no one in particular. It was late, but Socorro still needed something for dinner. The evening tide was rising now and the little crabs would be floating over the reefs.

"BUMBO! YOU TOO!"

"Stand between Shig and Robert!"

"Come on, Danny and Pete! Get in here! Stand next to Bumbo!"

The flash on Howard's camera didn't fire the first two tries. He fumbled in the dark, got it going, and took a full roll of pictures of the happy, horrendously sunburnt group on the beach.

The evening lanterns had already been lit. Nearly everyone had left dinner on the table and had come down to see the tourists and their catch. Five long fish—a blue marlin and four smaller striped marlin—were laid out on the sand beside Pablo Santos' panga.

Chino was chattering with the clients in English while Abundio busied himself with unloading their rods and tackle boxes.

Unnoticed by the men, Socorro and María were checking the gunny-sacks in the two boats for eating fish. Chino's sack was completely empty. Abundio's held three mushy goldspotted bass, obviously caught early that morning.

Socorro shot a dark glance at Abundio, who shrugged his shoulders and opened his hands toward the early evening stars. The yellow rock had not come through tonight.

María went over to check the blue marlin. She pressed her finger hard into the brittle, sun-dried skin of its back. The fish cracked open where she pushed her finger in, and the dent in the flesh did not come out. She looked back to her mother and shook her head no.

Socorro waved a hand for María to take a look at the four striped marlin, which seemed to be in better shape. One was quite fresh. Chino must have caught it on the way in. María pointed at it and nodded yes to her mother. Then the two women stood back and waited with their arms folded.

Howard finished with his camera. He and Chino shook hands.

"Listen, Robert. I'd like to give our fish to the people of your village."

"Well… thanks… Howard."

"Of course, you take first pick! Which one do you want?"

Chino looked at the long black carcasses.

Unfortunately, the blue marlin had been caught first. After a day in the hot sun, with the seawater temperature at well over eighty degrees, its delicious white flesh would be soft and ripe. It would fall to pieces at the first touch of a knife.

Of the stripers, the smallest would be best. The damned thing had hit a tuna feather on the way home. Its tough, gray, sinewy meat would raise complaints from Socorro. But at least it was fresh.

"How about the small one?"

"Are you sure, Robert? Go ahead, take the big one! You earned it!"

"No… really, Howard… "

"Well, all right then."

After asking Chino to translate, Howard addressed the little gathering on the beach. He swept his arm over the marlin in a grand gesture.

"We give these fish to you friendly people of México! With our thanks for your hospitality! Robert, tell them they can have as much as they want!"

Chino relayed the message. The clients watched as María drew a rectangle on the side of the smallest striped marlin with four straight, shallow knife cuts. She peeled up a corner of the skin and ripped off a five-foot-long section of it. Then she cut out half a dozen blocks of the fish's firm, dark pink flesh and put them into a plastic wash tub.

As the women left with the meat, Howard again shook Chino's hand.

"Listen, we'll settle up at dinner, okay?"

"No problem, Howard."

"Robert, could you have her fix our marlin with garlic and butter?"

"Sure, Howard."

The clients left for Ramón Ochoa's house, with the Santos boys carrying their rods and tackle boxes. When they were gone, Pablo pointed his thumb at the dead marlin and raised his eyebrows in a question.

Abundio shrugged, shaking his head.

Chino grabbed the tail of one of the five carcasses and began dragging it toward the water.

"Help me launch the panga. I'll take them out and dump them."

ABUNDIO RODRÍGUEZ SAT on a fruit lug, fanning the money in his hands as María pinched the skin on his elbow and pulled it out to a sharp point.

"Papá! That can't be right! Explain again what they said!"

"Well... first he asked me how much they owed us."

"Who? Which one?"

"The short one... Shig."

"In Spanish?"

"Well... sort of."

"And what did you *say,* papá?"

"Well... I thought I said thirty dollars."

"And then... ?"

"He spoke to the older one, Howard."

"And... ?"

"They gave me this... "

Abundio spread the bills out, one-by-one, in the candlelight of Fra Nacho's porch. There were sixteen of them. All twenties. Three-hundred and twenty U.S. dollars. And the Rodríguezes were having a hell of a time figuring out what they were for.

Socorro had listened intently to her husband's account of his meeting with Shig and Howard. She suspected, as they all did, that this windfall could not possibly be what it seemed and she feared what unimaginable obligations they might have brought upon themselves.

"Husband. Could it be for two pangas? For you and Señor Pete also?"

"No. Señor Pete is a guest, a friend."

"But do they understand that?"

"Well... I think so."

Fra Nacho had said nothing during Abundio's interrogation. He had been ravenously hungry all day long and had concentrated his attentions on his bag of tough, striped marlin tacos. Now, he cleared his throat and spoke.

"Why don't we just wait and see what Chino finds out."

Chino, busy dumping the marlin, had missed both dinner and Abundio's encounter with the clients. Reluctant to ask Shig or Howard about the meaning of the money, he had gone looking for Peter Grayson, who was casting his flies under the stars at the south end of the caleta.

They heard the crunch of Chino's feet in the arroyo. A minute later he came out of the dark. He wore a reassuring smile as he pulled up a crate and sat down in the candlelight, not speaking.

María folded her arms across her chest.

"Well... ?"

Chino stood up again. He paced around importantly, enjoying the lime-light. Then he sat back down and spoke slowly and clearly, as he tallied the totals on his fingers.

"When Bundo said thirty dollars, they thought he meant thirty dollars *per person.*"

There was a brief silence. Then the Rodríguezes drew a collective gasp on Fra Nacho's dark porch.

"Ah... !"

"Therefore, *ninety dollars* is to pay for marlin fishing today in Pablo's panga."

"Híjole... !"

"They plan to stay here for three nights."

"Ah, so... !"

"Bundo told them to pay whatever they wished... "

"Oh... !"

" ...and they decided thirty dollars *per night* would be fair for the four of them... "

"No... !"

" ...for meals and for the use of Ramón's house. That's another *ninety dollars.*"

"Santa María... !"

"They paid us another *fifty dollars* for fixing the leg of their airplane."

"Jesucristo... !"

"And finally... "

Here, Chino paused for dramatic effect, but he got no satisfaction for the Rodríguezes had run out of gasps.

"The last ninety dollars is payment *in advance!* They... want... to... go... fishing... again... tomorrow!"

The stars and bats wheeled silently over the arroyo as five minds subtracted expenses from the grand sum spread out between Abundio's big fat knees.

They would have to pay Pablo Santos twenty dollars for two days' rental of his panga. *Hah!* No problem there! Gas? Call it another twenty at most. Socorro added two good hens which would have to be replaced, the last of her olive oil, the flour, beans, and rice, and half a kilo of goat cheese, bought with cash from the mountain rancheros. María remembered the garlic, the new bar of soap, and the many bottles of precious drinking water the clients had poured over their heads in bathing. Chino counted their time and effort, and the cost of the plastic resin and catalyst used to fix the plane. Abundio threw in the twenty-seven warm beers the clients had drunk since their arrival, and even the cost of the white paint used to line the pista and make the sign on the cliff.

No matter which way the figures were turned and kneaded, pounded and stretched, each of the Rodríguezes came to the same inevitable conclusion. They sat there staring at the money and at each other.

As they waited for someone to speak, Socorro heard a very low sort of sniffing sound that seemed to be coming from Abundio, as though he were weeping in his sleep. His belly began jiggling, ever so slightly, and his head began to bob up and down, as the sound grew loud enough for them all to hear.

Then the sniffing grew into a chuckle, and then a laugh, and finally a roar, as Abundio pushed down on his knees and jumped so high his head banged against the porch roof, unleashing a shower of dust and insects. Abundio thrust his big fists into the air, and threw back his head, and he sent an exultant jubilation echoing down the arroyo.

"Ayyyy! Yes! I say! Yes! Yes! Yes! *Yeeessss!*"

And then the candle fell over, and they nearly tipped Fra Nacho off his cot. Socorro was lifted off her feet, and she felt herself danced about like a rag doll, with Abundio's strong hands clamping her under the armpits. And in the dark, María found Chino, already coming to her. She squeezed his arms hard as he kissed her.

"How many dollars they have to spend!"

"It's incredible!"

"Chino was right after all!"

"But papá, what's so special about marlin?"

"It's sport fishing!! That's all!"

Fra Nacho found the candle and relighted it as the Rodríguezes debated ideas for the future sport fishing business. They would need a big panga! Like Pablo's. Hell! Bigger than Pablo's! With the biggest damned Evinrude ever made! And a real baitwell. And rod holders. And a sunshade for the clients. Flies. They must do something about the flies. But what? And a generator. There's a generator at Las Ramalitas. Agua Amargosa must have one too! How much does a generator cost?

THE HOUR HAD become very late. A steamy curtain of thin, high clouds had moved up from the south, obscuring the stars. Fra Nacho blew out his candle and turned over on his cot. He could hear the voices coming from below his shack, as the Rodríguezes picked their way down the pitch black path in single file.

"The problem is water and gas, amigo. If we go fishing tomorrow, we won't have enough water for the clients. And we won't have enough gas to get back to Las Ramalitas."

"Then tomorrow we go for water and gas. And we take them fishing the next day."

"Tomorrow is Sunday. We will have to go all the way to Loreto."

"In Pablo's panga, no problem."

"All right."

There was a pause as the Rodríguezes reached the floor of the arroyo and turned down the sandy streambed. Then Abundio's voice came through again, loud and clear.

"Socorro! Let's have a *big* party tomorrow night! With music!"

"No."

"Why not?"

"We are too busy."

"With what?"

"Cooking and cleaning. For your sport fishing clients."

"But the party will be in their honor! To celebrate our new business!"

"Well... "

"Fine! It is decided! A fiesta tomorrow night! Kill a pig. We'll get some chickens in Loreto. And cold beer for the clients! And ice! Mijo! Don't let me forget. How about some soda and candies for the children? And chorizo, eh Socorro? And how about some levanta muertos...? But not too many! And how about... "

The voices gradually became unintelligible and faded away into the night.

Fra Nacho smiled to himself. He had not seen the Rodríguezes so happy for a long time. He lay back on his cot and fell into a deep sleep, dreaming of a picnic, of lightning bugs and wild raspberries in the delicate late summer of the Alpine hills above Pordenone. Some time later, well after midnight, he heard the crunch on the path again. He felt the faint breath of air against his arm, and he whispered, "Margarita... " But the black-shrouded figure swirled under his porch roof and out the other side without speaking. Again came the crunching on the path, and he heard her turn up the streambed and climb higher and higher until the sound disappeared. As he fell back into his dreams, he wondered what Margarita Santos did on those nights when she went up the arroyo.

"WELL, WHERE THE hell are they?"

"Dad, I'll run up and check their shack."

"Okay. But where's their boat?"

"Maybe they're out making bait."

"Yeah, let's hope so."

Howard and Shig sat on their tackle boxes with the butts of their rods making holes in the sand. A shallow groove led to the edge of the water, showing where Pablo's panga had recently been launched into a rising tide.

The pre-dawn sky above the caleta was just beginning to show an advancing field of orange-edged mackerel clouds, neat parallel rows marching up from the south. It would be another hour before the sun came up but it was already hot and both men were sweating.

Shig skipped a rock over the shallows, and the black water flashed each time it struck the surface.

"Howard... did you see that?"

"What?"

"The luminescence. It's unbelievable."

Shig threw another rock, and Howard saw the little puddles of light.

"Hmm... what is it?"

"Phytoplankton. Pete said it was so bright last night he could see the fish hitting his line."

"Amazing."

"Yeah. This bay must have a lot of nutrients."

To their right, a patch of ripples betrayed the presence of a school of bait fish cruising just under the surface. Farther out, two V-shaped wakes marked the meandering explorations of a pair of predator fish, probably jacks of some kind.

As Howard and Shig watched, the predators and prey simultaneously sensed each other's subtle vibrations. The bait fish compressed themselves into a dark stain moving slowly toward shore. Their agitated surface dimples showed like black eyelashes, fluttering in the silver face of dawn.

The predators disappeared beneath the surface, then reappeared, much closer to the bait.

"What are they, Shig?"

"Jack crevalle, maybe. Or roosters."

The dimples grew larger and larger as the bait fish tried unsuccessfully to escape upwards through the surface. Gradually, the water seemed to come to a boil over an area thirty feet across, and within the boil, the glow of luminescent plankton showed like a floodlight inside a fountain of water. The dorsal fins of two roosterfish circled tighter and tighter on opposite sides of the school.

Howard and Shig heard the sound clearly in the darkened stillness of the caleta, a soft purling that grew into a loud, steady rumble. The surface of the water rose in a deep froth, with bait fish churning through it in all directions.

Then the froth exploded into a shower, four feet high, with trails of light streaking out from beneath it like underwater comets, and a few seconds later, another, then another, and another explosion hissed into the air as the roosterfish pushed the school against the beach and cut it to pieces.

The roosters' high, plume-like dorsal fins slashed back and forth as they tightened the circle and some of the bait fish hurled themselves onto dry sand. One of the roosters overshot the bait and stranded itself in inch-deep water and Howard ran over and grabbed its tail before it could flop back to safety. He held the thrashing fish up, and spread its big, spiked dorsal fin for Shig to see.

"Wow! A beauty! Shall we keep it, Shig?"

"Nah! Lousy eating."

"Can't be any worse than last night!"

"Oh yeah?"

"Worse than marlin?"

"Just as bad."

"Okay, you win."

Howard carried the struggling roosterfish out to knee-deep water. He released it with a big splash as Danny appeared on the beach with Peter Grayson, Pablo Santos, and his sons.

"Dad!"

"Yeah?"

"They're gone!"

"I can see that, Danny. Where did they go?"

Pete came down to the water with his fly rod already rigged. He had a black-and-silver streamer on the end of his leader. He pulled out twenty feet of line and began false casting as he called over his shoulder to Howard.

"What was that you just let go?"

"Roosterfish."

"Great! That would be a new species!"

Pete pulled more line out, sending his fly farther and farther.

"What did it hit?"

"Nothing. It stranded itself, chasing bait."

"No kidding!"

Pete's fly settled to the water and he began his retrieve. He pointed back to Pablo Santos and his sons.

"That's Pablo. He says our guys went to Loreto to buy gas."

Howard confronted the bare-chested panguero in English.

"But we paid in advance to go fishing today!"

Pablo kept his hands in his pockets, saying nothing, looking toward Pete for help. Pete's voice came from farther down the beach.

"He says the boat actually belongs to him."

Pete wanted a roosterfish badly. Over the years he had managed to hook three, but he had never landed one. He walked twenty yards farther down the beach and began false casting again.

"Pablo says he's throwing a big party for us tonight."

"But... what about fishing!?"

"He says tomorrow he'll take you out himself. He says he's the best fisherman around here."

"Oh, for Christ's sake!"

Shig motioned for the boys to take the rods back up to the house.

"Come on, Howard. Ain't no use fussin'."

"Dammit! Shig, we just got screwed!"

"Hey, if there's no gas today... we'll fish tomorrow."

Howard was adamant. He paced back and forth and pointed his thumb at Pablo's chest.

"With *this* guy!? What about Robert?"

"We can straighten it out when Robert gets back."

Still dissatisfied, Howard now aimed his thumb toward the houses.

"What about that shoe leather dinner last night?"

"Yup."

"And taking showers out of a goddamned bottle."

"Yup."

"And no toilet paper."

"Yup."

"And everything paid for in advance."

"Yup, yup, yup."

"Damn these Mexicans! I wish I could speak better Spanish!"

Pete's voice came from far down the beach.

"Hey, Howard! Don't feel bad. I called myself a fart down here for years."

PABLO SANTOS SQUATTED in the mid-afternoon shade of the palm trees, watching the old man cast his feather closer and closer to the yellow rock. The tide was going out now, and Pablo knew the rock would be barren. He smiled with satisfaction as Pete made a dozen casts all around it, caught nothing, and moved on.

Pete moved slowly east along the shore. He caught and released a leopard grouper and then disappeared behind a pile of rocks. Pablo smiled to himself again. On a falling tide, the old man would find nothing but small grunts there. Worthless fish. But they would give him a few moments of false hope.

The sun was dropping toward the cliffs by the time Pablo finally spotted his dark green panga outside the channel. Even a mile and a half away, Pablo could tell his boat was carrying a big load. It rode low in the water and disappeared from view when it sank into the troughs. He could see Chino at the tiller and Abundio in the bow, spotting rocks, as they crossed the Four Horses and turned in toward the launch spot.

The heavily laden panga approached the beach at half throttle, pushing a big bow wave ahead of itself. Pablo met them and began helping unload. Besides the usual supplies and water bottles, there were a dozen garbage bags tied closed at the top, and a huge amount of beer and sodas, at least twenty or thirty cases.

When he saw how much beer they had, Pablo pulled his cheeks down and nodded his approval. Chino jumped out with the anchor and stood wiggling his eyebrows up and down and smiling. Pablo spoke to him as Abundio rummaged through the bags in the boat.

"Eh... Chino... the americanos are pissed at you."

Chino was startled.

"What happened?"

"You didn't take them fishing this morning."

"We had to go for gas."

"They don't want to fish with you anymore."

Abundio had not overheard them. He was busy opening a double garbage bag containing twenty-four bottles of beer, buried deep inside a nest of precious, quickly-melting chipped ice. He dug out a cold six-pack, and he turned around with bottles for Pablo, Chino, and himself.

But his partner was gone.

"Where is Chino?"

Pablo was looking toward the village, in the direction Chino had run at top speed. He shrugged.

"Who knows?"

"Oh, well."

Abundio handed two bottles to Pablo and kept four for himself. He raised a toast to the hot afternoon.

"To all the marlin of the sea! May we catch every damned one of them!"

As they drank, Abundio grew serious. He sat down beside Pablo and pointed out to the horizon, past the Four Horses.

"Pablo, there is a big swell out there. Very big. It comes from the south. But there is no wind."

"I know."

Abundio was surprised. The swell had come up only during the last two hours, during their ride south from Loreto, and the caleta itself was perfectly calm. How had Pablo learned of it?

"How do you know, Pablo?"

"Look... "

Pablo picked up a small twig. He squatted down and waited a moment. Then he stabbed the twig upright into the sand, at the exact edge of the water. They watched as the water slowly receded a foot and then slowly returned to a point a foot higher than the twig.

Abundio snorted.

"Pah...! It does that all the time, Pablo!"

Pablo wrapped his arms tightly around his raised knees. The afternoon sky had taken on a brassy color and the horizon was pressed flat by a dark gray, horizontal cloud layer. Pablo pointed to the slow rise and fall of the water.

"Look how much it moves."

Pablo's hand chopped through the air, pointing to the south.

"There is a very big wind. Way down there."

"Is it a chubasco, Pablo?"

"Maybe. Maybe."

They drank several more rounds of beer in the afternoon shade while the tide turned and covered Pablo's twig, and Socorro and María hauled everything to the house in the fish cart.

They had just pulled the panga up when Chino came out of the trees, accompanied by Shig and Howard. Pablo's heart dropped when he saw the coldness in Chino's eyes.

"Eh, Chino... *qué pasó?*"

Chino's hands dangled loosely at his sides. Pablo had seen that enough times before, and he knew to take a precautionary step backwards. Chino closed the gap, just a little too close, and his voice was as hard as stone.

"Pablo... do you have something to say to our clients?"

Abundio watched silently, trying to figure out what was going on. Chino's eyes were fixed on a small spot in the middle of Pablo's forehead.

"Now, Pablo. Tell them."

Pablo stammered.

"But... I... don't speak English!"

"Then you have nothing to say to them?"

Pablo lowered his eyes.

"No."

Chino now extended an open hand.

"Listen, Pablo. We know ten dollars a day is not right. We will pay you thirty, plus gas. But you must not interfere. Is that agreed?"

Pablo reached out gratefully and shook Chino's hand.

"You are fair, Chino."

Now Chino turned his attention to the americanos, looking serious.

"Shig, Howard. I'm sorry we missed you this morning."

"We go fishing tomorrow?"

"Yes. I'm really sorry. It won't ever happen again."

Shig patted Chino's shoulder and smiled. There were deep, puffy wrinkles in the sunburnt skin around his eyes.

"You know, Robert, in San Pedro my family used to fish, just like you folks. You're doing just fine, and… "

From the corner of one eye, Chino saw Abundio and Pablo suddenly stiffen and look out to sea. Something unusual had caught their attention. But he felt constrained from turning to look as long as Shig continued his patronizing monologue.

" …you just need to learn how to run a business, how to deal with Americans, and… "

Abundio and Pablo were staring now, gaping almost, at something out near the Four Horses. Chino could stand it no longer. He raised a hand in Shig's face, silencing him.

"Thanks, Shig… but just a minute… "

Chino spun around. Three pangas, in tight formation, were coming across the caleta at full throttle. A fourth panga followed a hundred yards behind. The boats of the impressive little flotilla wore the numbers and the red-and-white colors of the cooperativa at Las Ramalitas and each held two or three pangueros.

The partners checked each other's eyes. Chino frowned, shaking his head in a question. Abundio held up a hand, rubbing his thumb and fingers together in the air, and Chino understood the gesture. They had been a little too obvious in Loreto that morning. Spent a little too much. Perhaps talked a little too freely to the men on the beach and to the driver of the pickup they had hired.

The pangas sped toward them at full throttle.

At the last moment the Evinrudes were killed and the Las Ramalitas pangueros threw out their anchors and hopped onto the sand. The tallest of the group, the one who had worn the diagonal striped shirt, had his eyes on Shig and Howard, who had gone down to look at their pangas.

Chino gave them a cheery wave.

"Hola, amigos! Do you have fish to sell? Our commission is only five percent today."

The tall one came over to the partners.

"Very funny, Chino."

He tilted his head toward Shig.

"Who is that?"

"Americanos."

"We heard you have sport fishing here."

Abundio's fists were clenched. He stood impertinently close to the Diagonal Stripe. He was a full eight inches taller than the man, and he seemed capable of pounding him into the sand, upright, like a tent stake.

"And *we* heard it is none of your goddamned business."

The Diagonal Stripe ignored Abundio, inviting a fight. There were ten of them altogether. He spoke to Chino.

"You have a pista here... with a hole in the middle... "

Chino remembered the DC-3 from México City. It must have landed at Las Ramalitas. He was preparing a reply, when Abundio's voice boomed out.

"Lies! There is no pista here!"

Abundio intentionally allowed his belly to brush against the arm of the Diagonal Stripe. The brief, grazing contact was noticed by everyone as though Abundio had struck the man full in the face with a brick. But the Diagonal Stripe did not take his opportunity.

"Then what is the place behind the trees, bordered with white rocks?"

Abundio's answer came so quickly Chino thought he must have prepared it in advance.

"It is a fútbol field! That's all!"

The Las Ramalitas men whistled all around Abundio's back, but at a safe distance. The Diagonal Stripe's eyes opened wide in mock amazement.

"A new soccer field! May we have a look?"

ABUNDIO FELT HIMSELF becoming angrier and angrier as he led the Las Ramalitas pangueros up the beach and past Ana Rosa Medina's house to the end of the pista. *Madre!* What a stupid situation! How embarrassing! Abundio felt as though he were marching to the gallows. He glanced at Chino and Pablo, who could offer nothing in comfort except a shrug of their shoulders. He braced himself for the ridicule that would be heaped upon him at the moment they reached the pista.

But as they passed Ana Rosa Medina's house and as he waved to two of her children at play in the doorway, Abundio remembered that he must not take himself too seriously. And he remembered how much he detested these Las Ramalitas bastards for what they had done to Ramón Ochoa and his family. Oh, poor Ramón! Abundio wondered if his brother-in-law had ever reached the flower ranchos where even the workers lived in fine houses and free water came running out of pipes. He wondered if it was really true that on those ranchos an older man could be as highly valued as a young one.

They reached the pista.

At the far end of the twin rows of rocks, stark against the shadowed cliffs, Howard's glistening white plane was staked down tight to the dirt. To their left, Chino's dusty Chevy sat with two flat tires.

Abundio had decided what he would do. He stood glowering at the Diagonal Stripe with his arms folded across his chest.

"Well? How do you like our new fútbol field?"

The Diagonal Stripe kicked at the dirt and eyed the slope of the runway. This pista was almost as good as the one they had made on their mud flat, six months before. He wondered how much the Amargosa pangueros were charging their clients. And, he wondered, did they have anyone who could speak English to the americanos? He raised his chin defiantly at Abundio's leaping marlin on the face of the cliff.

"So, is that the name of your team? Good Sport Fishing?"

The Las Ramalitas pangueros broke into their usual chorus of whistles and high-pitched giggles. Abundio nearly gave in to the hot blood he felt rising in his cheeks, but he stuck to his plan. He made a theatrical bow and he pushed his face almost against the nose of the Diagonal Stripe.

"Perhaps you would like to play us... right now."

The jeering stopped. Abundio slammed down his trump card.

"Unless you are... afraid."

The two sides stood facing each other in the middle of the dusty pista.

Quickly and furtively, the men stole glances at each other's feet, counting shoes. Only Abundio kept his eyes level. He had already counted.

Just four of the Las Ramalitas fishermen wore tennis shoes. The other six had been caught barefoot, including the Diagonal Stripe himself, who now spoke up.

"You play too dirty, big man."

Abundio wanted them badly. He poked the Diagonal Stripe hard in the chest and he made the offer that could not be refused.

"You are afraid."

The Diagonal Stripe knew he had been trapped. Even with ten men, a fight with these Amargosa bastards would be costly. Pablo Santos would probably come straight for him and give a good account of himself. Chino Zúñiga was hard and strong and completely fearless. He would do a lot of damage before he could be taken down. And then, there was this big monster. How many would it take to handle *him?* The Diagonal Stripe's knee still ached where they had sewn it closed in Loreto.

"All right... we play."

"Fine! Pablo! Get the men! Chino! We need the wood from the Chevy!"

Pablo trotted off to the village while the others tore apart the wooden platform that had been used to smooth the pista. They used the boards to set up two crooked goals a hundred yards apart in the middle of the runway and they marked each corner of the field with a stack of white rocks.

Within a few minutes, nearly the entire population of Agua Amargosa had seated themselves along the row of stones on the south side of the pista. Ana Rosa Medina and her children came out of their house and occupied the spaces between the first ten stones. Pablo Santos' sons sat next to them. Thirteen more stones held the wives and children of the village pangueros. The americano clients did not appear.

Pablo Santos returned, wearing cleated soccer shoes. He also had his good ball, a hand-sewn Adidas bought in La Paz. Accompanying Pablo were the five remaining pangueros from the village, all wearing tennis shoes.

Las Ramalitas would field ten men. Agua Amargosa could muster only eight, but it would be an even match, considering Pablo's cleats and the presence of El Tecolote Terrible, whose elbows and knees were now spoken of as far north as Santa Rosalía.

Abundio gathered his team in the middle of the field. But before he could speak, María and Socorro came out of the palms. Socorro walked with her arms folded across her chest, making her body look as rigid as a little salt shaker. She came to the edge of the field and stopped. Abundio raised the invisible pebble.

"A moment... "

He jogged over to the women, trying to keep his love handles from jiggling too much. Socorro's expression was grim.

"Husband, is this really necessary?"

"I am going to teach them a lesson, Socorro."

"What lesson?"

Abundio was nonplussed by her complete lack of empathy.

What lesson? How could she ask such a question? Here, in the all-revealing sun, they would battle the chaotic, unpredictable bounce and roll of a ball on rough dirt, and they would pit their wits and bodies against each other, to the absolute limits of their strength. Each side would sacrifice itself without reservation and one of them would emerge victorious, the other defeated.

It was a way of deciding something cleanly, of getting at least the satisfaction of that, of throwing aside for a brief moment the damned curtains that always seemed to be in the way of everything—like gill nets in the night. And if it was only a game of fútbol? If that is all we have, then we must do what we can with it. In the time we are given, we must act, regardless, or we are nothing. *Nada.*

But Abundio had no time for philosophical debate.

"Socorro, I will explain later."

From the first moment, it was apparent Las Ramalitas intended to take Abundio out of the game as early as possible. The tennis shoes converged on him from all sides, whether he had the ball or not, and he stood against their blows until it seemed he must fall from the pain. But he would not fall. He would not fall. He ran and he ran, charging blindly into the glare of the sun, with the sweat foaming between his thighs and running down his bloodied legs, and he would not fall, no matter how many times they kicked him.

Socorro's eyes filled with tears to watch her husband's agony for she could not understand what he was doing or why. She sat stoically on a white stone at the end of the field with María's hands on her shoulders.

One of the Las Ramalitas tennis shoes paid the price for leading the relentless attack against the great Tecolote. Abundio, too exhausted for pretense, swung a blatant elbow at him, catching him square on the temple with a loud crunch, and he fell and lay still.

Another of the tennis shoes limped off voluntarily to the north side of the field and sat down. El Tecolote had evened the numbers, but he could no longer feel his legs, and he could not see his tormentors clearly. He stood powerless in front of his goal, with his chest on fire, raging at them as they closed in on him.

The Diagonal Stripe and two others sandwiched Abundio viciously and all four of them went down. Abundio landed hard on his face. He pushed up on his knees as the ball went past his shoulder and through the wooden goal.

María could watch no longer. She ran to her father and tried to help him up, but he was deadly heavy, and she could not get a grip on the slippery sweat-mud that covered him. Then she saw the black streaks on his foot, and the big toe turned out at an impossible angle, with the bright flap of skin hanging loose.

"Oh God! Papá!"

María whirled around. She spotted Chino bent over in the middle of the field. She streaked to him and pounded her fists on his chest, screaming at him.

"Damn you, Chino! Damn you! Damn you!"

Chino retreated from her fists. She exhausted herself and stood panting and sobbing. Then she looked at his face. His mouth was torn and a middle tooth was pushed inward. His nose was not in its usual place.

María drew back and drove her fists down on her thighs.

"Oh Christ! No! No! No! Chino, just look at you!"

At the far end of the field, Abundio was still on his hands and knees, waiting for his legs to stop shaking. Pablo Santos had recovered the ball. He was taking as much time as possible in returning it for the kickoff. Abundio sucked air deep into his chest. He was feeling almost ready to get up when he heard the whistle blow twice and the voice of Pablo's older son, Rubén, calling halftime.

"*Medio tiempo!*"

They gathered on the south side of the field and drank from the water bottles. Abundio's foot had begun to hurt. His calf would not stop trembling and trying to cramp. He pushed the toe into place and wrapped it tightly in a strip of cloth from the hem of his pants.

"Mijo... "

Chino looked at the foot and shook his head.

"We are defeated, amigo."

"No. Run to the house. Get my boots."

The women were seated again at the end of the field. Socorro seemed calm, but María was still agitated. Chino was glad they weren't present to hear this.

"Amigo, even with boots, you can't play with that toe."

"No, mijo. You wear them."

"Me?"

"Yes. You and Pablo can score on these bastards."

And so, Abundio invoked an unwritten clause in the rules of panguero fútbol, as it was played in the remote fish camps, where pickup teams were of necessity created from whatever raw materials happened to be available. The tradition stated that virtually any shoe, boot, or sandal, cleated or not, could be worn in a soccer match. Further, barefoot players would be given no quarter whatsoever in a sport featuring forceful collisions of the feet. To outsiders, the games resulting from this rule seemed unfair to the lesser shod, and especially so to the barefoot, but to the fishermen themselves the rule seemed natural and inevitable. Otherwise, how could someone able to afford real soccer shoes ever have the opportunity to enjoy them?

Chino ran to the village at a fast trot as Rubén Santos called for them to take the field for the second half. Pablo helped Abundio to his feet. The rag on his foot was soaking through.

"Bundo. Your foot. It will be ruined."

"Accchh!"

"But… is it worth it?"

Abundio felt the anger welling up again. He put his injured foot on a rock and tightened the strip of cloth.

"Listen, you cabrones! Do you want to *be* something or not? For me, the answer is *yes!*"

Rubén's call came again. The Las Ramalitas men were waiting on the field.

"It is a simple thing, amigos."

As they walked out to take their places, each of the Agua Amargosa pangueros shook Abundio's hand.

They were two minutes into the second half, with Abundio playing goal keeper, when Chino came sprinting out in the high-topped combat boots. The tide turned immediately. Chino missed some opportunities but finally crossed the ball to Pablo directly in front of the Las Ramalitas goal, and Pablo dusted it through with a stinging instep volley.

They had tied the score. A thin cheer went up from the white rocks. Abundio looked over to Socorro and María. They had not been part of it.

Las Ramalitas kicked off and Chino quickly won the ball again and began an attack. But now it was his turn to suffer from the tennis shoes. He went down hard at midfield as play swept past him toward Abundio in the goal. Abundio caught a point-blank shot to the chest. Unable to kick, he threw the ball out as far as he could.

María stood and looked down the field. Chino was still on the dirt. His legs were making bicycling motions, but he was obviously not going to get up for a while. María closed her eyes.

"Mamá, they are killing him."

With Chino down and Abundio neutralized, Las Ramalitas had an insurmountable advantage and they pressed their attack straight down the middle of the field.

Abundio crouched low, watching them come. He prepared himself to receive a jolt from his right foot. It looked like the Diagonal Stripe would probably take the shot and El Terrible had decided to charge out from the goal one last time, toe or no toe.

But as the moment of truth began to unfold, three long whistles warbled over the pista, the signal for the game to end. They all looked at Rubén Santos, who stood on his white rock with one hand in the air and the other holding the whistle in his mouth.

Abundio knew the game could not have ended so soon. So did the men from Las Ramalitas, who surrounded poor Rubén and picked him up by the front of his shirt.

"Hey, you little turd!"

"What do you think you're doing!?"

"The game can't be over yet!"

But the Las Ramalitas pangueros knew this was not the time or place. They put Rubén Santos down as Pablo came running up with the others right behind him, and they backed away toward the beach. As they disappeared into the trees near Ana Rosa Medina's house the Diagonal Stripe shouted across the distance.

"You're finished! You sell no more fish at Las Ramalitas!"

It took a moment for them to appreciate the gravity of the Diagonal Stripe's threat. Since the arrival of the tourist anglers two days before, and especially since word of the twenty-dollar bills had spread, they had not thought much about the wholesale price of cabrilla.

Abundio's derisive voice, booming from halfway down the pista, summed up their feelings perfectly.

"You can shove the fish up your asses, amigos! *Backwards!*"

On a hot, late afternoon, in the quiet village of Caleta Agua Amargosa, four dozen people cringed inwardly as they tried to imagine how that might feel.

B<small>Y</small> <small>SUNSET,</small> <small>MOST</small> of the men had arrived on Pablo Santos' front porch and the music had begun. It was monotonous dance music, to the jiggling, staccato beat of grasshoppers and crickets, and the men paid no attention to it as they feasted on pork and beer.

In the Rodríguez house, the women had just finished cleaning up from an afternoon of cooking. Socorro raised the lid of a trunk that was rarely opened. She found the four paper lanterns. They had faded to a light pink, but otherwise they appeared undamaged. She held their wire handles and stretched the brittle paper down carefully.

"We hung these the day Ramón bought his panga. They are Chinese."

María inspected the hand-painted characters.

"I wonder what it says."

"Oh, probably, good luck. Or whatever."

"Are there candles for them?"

"They melted."

Socorro dug deeper into the trunk and found a package sealed with tape. There was a full skirt of green and red satin, appliquéd with sequins, and a white satin blouse with a scooped neck. The blouse had short, puffed sleeves and there were three petticoats for the skirt.

"Oh, mamá! How beautiful!"

"I wore this the night your father and I moved to our house on Isla Coronado. Here, try it."

"But mamá, it is for you."

"Don't be silly."

María stepped into the skirt and pulled the blouse over her shoulders.

"It is a little tight."

"And short. Quite short."

On Socorro, the skirt had come to the ankles and the generous folds of the blouse had concealed the contours of her upper body, revealing just a hint of cleavage above the neckline.

On María, the skirt came to just below the knee. The scooped neck of the blouse strained to hold back its contents.

"Is it… immodest, mamá?"

"Scandalous. It was never intended to have that effect."

"Should I wear it?"

"Of course."

Socorro dug to the bottom of the trunk. She brought out a pair of black high-topped shoes, fastened in front by long rows of closely-spaced buttons. The heels were heavy and square. She gave them to María.

"Here, daughter. Try these."

It was useless. María's feet were an inch and a half longer than her mother's.

"I can wear my sandals from Loreto."

"Fine."

Socorro pulled María's hair back and parted it down the middle. She made two long braids which she wound into loops and pinned to the back of her daughter's head. She began to pin a red hibiscus over María's right ear, then hesitated and removed it.

"Hmmm… "

"What is wrong, mamá?"

"In Salina Cruz. I can't remember what side the flower went on."

"Was it important?"

"Very."

"Why don't we put a flower on both sides?"

"Perfect!"

They powdered María's face and shoulders and put the bright red lipstick on her and they finished with just a little mascara on her long eyelashes. In the warm lantern light of the Rodríguez house, Socorro stood back to appraise her handiwork.

"Chino is very lucky… "

María began brushing her mother's hair.

"Mamá?"

"Mmmm… "

"Is it a mistake?"

"With Chino?"

"Yes. And... well, everything."

Socorro loved to have her hair brushed. She rocked back and forth and hummed softly to herself. And—as she had done so many times during the past four months—she tried to let the image of María and Chino form. But for some reason, she still could not see them clearly. She held María's hands and kissed them and she looked into her daughter's dark eyes.

"I cannot tell, María. But try. You try your very best."

María braided her mother's long gray hair and carefully tied the loops in back with the good red ribbon. She added a hibiscus over each ear. But she knew her mother would not be comfortable with the powder or lipstick, so she did not suggest them.

Socorro dug to a bottom corner of the trunk, where she found a fine silk rebozo woven in geometric patterns of bright blue and green, with tassels of gold at each end. María had never seen it before.

"Mamá, it is so lovely!"

"It was my mother's. She carried my sister in it, from Salina Cruz... "

"Your sister... María?"

"Yes. She would have been your *tía* had she lived."

Socorro found a square-cut white blouse, intricately embroidered across the shoulders. She put it on and went to the small, cloudy mirror that hung over the shelf and she looked at herself in the lantern light.

"María. I would like some lipstick tonight."

"Of course, mamá!"

When everything was ready, they turned off the lantern and stepped out to the darkened porch. The doorway of Pablo Santos' house glowed yellow through the trees, and the music was louder. The dancing had begun.

"Do you have the lanterns, María?"

"Sí, mamá."

"We should be going, then."

In the dark, Socorro brushed a loose strand of hair from her forehead and patted it down.

"Do I look all right?"

"Mamá, you look beautiful!"

Hand-in-hand, they started through the trees toward Pablo Santos' house. When they reached the gully, María stopped.

"Mamá… ?"

"Sí, María."

"I am going to have a baby."

Socorro was silent as they walked slowly through the trees toward Pablo's house. When they reached the edge of the music, she turned and held her daughter's arm.

"They depend on us, María. To make the best of things."

"Sí, mamá."

"Your child will be a fine man, like his father and his grandfather."

María bent down and looked closely into her mother's dark Indian face, burnished amber in the lantern light.

"Mamá, you weren't doing it again, were you?"

"Doing what, my love?"

"You know, mamá! Looking into the future."

"Well… maybe… just a little."

"Mamá, please don't! You know how it frightens me."

"There is nothing wrong with it."

"Mamá, promise you won't do it anymore."

"Well… all right."

As they entered the circle of light, it was María's turn to stop and take her mother's arm.

"Are you sure, mamá?"

"Sure?"

"That it's a boy."

"Sí, María. It was very clear."

THE KITCHEN OF Pablo Santos' house was in a semi-enclosed side porch facing south. Its walls were made of cardón cactus ribs, loosely spaced to allow the escape of heat from a block-shaped adobe cooking stove in one corner.

The roof was made of palm thatch so carefully constructed as to be completely watertight. Mesquite rafters spaced two feet apart ran from the main house to the outer wall of the porch. Crossing the rafters at right angles was a series of stringers made of doubled branches the thickness of a thumb. Finally, hundreds of fan-shaped palm leaves had been trimmed into half-circles two feet wide, and they were lashed to the stringers with their fluted faces sloping downwards. The leaves were tied in an overlapping, staggered pattern that was not only watertight but also created an attractive design suggestive of fish scales.

For the fiesta, Pablo's cooking porch had been largely emptied of its contents. Some cast-iron pots and pans still hung from the ceiling and the box-shaped coffee grinder was still attached to the center post of the room. But, apart from the adobe stove itself, everything else had been moved outside to the space in front of the house.

The long wooden table was covered with platters and bowls. There were chunks of pork, boiled in its own fat, several fried chickens, an iron kettle of simmered beans, plates stacked high with hot tortillas, fresh tomato salsa in Socorro's stone molcajete, and a galvanized steel washtub full of sodas and beer. Floating in the washtub were three small chunks of ice, the last remnant of a full bar, bought that morning in Loreto by Abundio and Chino, and wrapped in newspapers and plastic bags for the ride south.

Music for dancing came from an eight-track tape player, wired directly to the battery from Pablo's pickup.

A wide half-circle of wooden chairs had been set up on the dirt in front of the porch. Within the half-circle, the pangueros were dancing with their wives. The children played tag, running in and out of the light from a row of lanterns hung along the edge of the porch roof.

As they approached the house, Socorro grabbed her daughter's hand and pointed toward the porch.

"María! Look at that!"

Sitting together on the bench at the far end of the porch was Agua Amargosa's most unlikely couple. Fra Nacho, in crisp white shirt and black pants, sat beside Margarita Santos. They were so close together their knees were actually touching, and they smiled and swayed in unison as they watched the dancing.

Fra Nacho had put on his shiny black shoe and he was tapping it in time to the music. His toothless mouth was opened wide in a jolly smile.

Margarita had pulled back her shawl. Her hair, untouched by the decades, was as shiny and impenetrably black as a raven's wing. From a distance, her white skin, straight nose, and high forehead made her look like a Spanish *condesa*. María drew a breath.

"Mamá! Look! She is beautiful!"

Socorro too, saw the classically formed features she had never fully appreciated before. The stories must be true, she thought. Margarita must have been quite attractive in her early years.

Inexplicably, Pablo Santos had brought his sewing machine outside. It sat on the dirt to the left of the porch, and Pablo stood beside it, talking to the americanos in Spanish as they tried to eat their dinners.

Abundio and Chino were nowhere to be seen. The Rodríguez women, mother and daughter, sat with Ana Rosa Medina and several of her children. Ana Rosa had drunk a few beers.

"Socorro! María! Sit down here! María! Don't you look devastating tonight! Socorro, it's such a pity you couldn't have more children!"

Socorro rose to check the food. The pork was almost gone. And the chickens too. The tortillas and beans had hardly been touched. These americanos ate a lot of meat. Well, no matter.

Socorro was returning to the chairs when she caught sight of Abundio coming out of the darkness in the company of a tall stranger. The stranger wore a brand new white dress shirt with the sleeves rolled to the elbows, a striped necktie, and very tight black pants. His socks—showing above a pair of new leather shoes—were patterned in bright yellow and red. His hair was cropped very short and held rigidly upright by a stiff, waxy dressing that gleamed in the lantern light.

"Chino!"

María had risen from her chair. The dancing and music stopped as everyone turned to look at the new arrivals. Abundio pushed his charge to the porch and bowed to Socorro with a wide sweep of his arm. Chino's grin was stopped short by the crack in his upper lip. Apparently, the partners had thought to set aside a generous reserve of beer somewhere. Abundio stood with his feet wide apart. His voice was full of outlandish inflections.

"Well... Se-ño-ra Rod-ri-guez... how do you *like* him?"

Abundio had put on a white shirt and his best pants and he had tied a red handkerchief around his neck. He wore only one shoe. On his right foot, the discolored head of his big toe peeked out of Socorro's bandage. He reeked of the same cloying, waxy hair dressing Chino wore.

They all stood silently, waiting for Socorro's response.

She looked at María, bright against the dark night, transfixed by the sight of this new Chino. Her daughter seemed to glow with an inner light, so slim and nubile, in the same dress she herself had once worn on Isla Coronado.

Socorro tried again to see the images of her María's journey. She tried to see if it was Chino who stood beside the dusty road of life and raised a hand for her in the hot afternoon sun, who stood, as a silent, comforting shadow, beside her bed, late in the closing moments of her final night. And she saw at last, very clearly, that it truly was Chino. It had been Chino Zúñiga all along.

As everyone watched and waited, Socorro crossed the lantern light alone. She extended her hand, as if commanding Abundio to kiss it, and she strained to raise her small, delicate voice loud enough for all to hear.

"You are the bravest, most handsome two men any woman ever dreamed of."

There was a robust cry among the people of Agua Amargosa and the dancing resumed, hand-in-hand, side-by-side, in the old way, as the night deepened over the village and the sky wheeled silently above. They danced like puppets on invisible strings suspended from the stars, their faces waxen and flat in the yellow lantern light, and slowly, the beer and the monotonous beat of the music, the old, compelling rhythms, and the approaching full moon and the tides of the caleta all had their effect, and they left themselves and were drawn up by the invisible strings, up above the dark arroyo, and up, up into the bosom of the night itself.

And in the dust, a while later, the young one, Danny, lay moaning, and María held back the wood-hard arms of Chino, and she pleaded for the promise of the coming day. He's a boy, Chino! Just a drunken boy! He only wanted to dance with me! He meant no harm! And—thank God!—there were apologies and excuses offered and accepted by both sides, and even a toast raised to the luckless partners, *the two greatest fishermen in all of México!* And there were sly winks and sideways glances exchanged by everyone—even between Socorro and Pablo!—when the toast was translated into Spanish.

And, in the smallest hours, in the nadir of the night, after they had emptied themselves completely, they walked back to their houses, one-by-one, and two-by-two, beneath the invisible, slowly moving gegenschein of the midnight sky. And the mantle of darkness settled softly over the caleta, as the tiny village of Agua Amargosa slipped once again into the deep, dreamless sleep of the dead.

BUT NOT EVERYONE rested on this night. For, against the south wall of the arroyo, Chino Zúñiga found himself sitting on the stump of an old olive tree, trying to keep himself awake as he waited for his best friend and fishing partner. Abundio had been mysterious and adamant that they meet at the old well and Chino wondered what could be keeping him.

The crunch of gravel came up the arroyo and stopped.

"Amigo?"

The bushes snapped and cracked and pushed apart, and Chino saw the round shoulders in the moonlight. Abundio had lost the path somehow and had reached the well by cutting across the streambed.

"How is the foot, amigo?"

"Bah!"

Abundio had been thinking of the thing that would have become his son. She had buried it somewhere nearby, perhaps under this old tree where they now sat.

He straightened a leg and reached into his pants pocket. He handed Chino a small object, wrapped in oiled cloth. It was hard and heavy for its size. Chino unwrapped the cloth and held the lustrous, polished gold up to the moonlight.

"It is a Rolex, mijo. Solid gold. Do you know its value?"

Chino stared as though his partner had suddenly grown a second head.

"What... is this?"

"It is yours, mijo."

"But amigo, where did you... I mean, how did you... ?"

"It was given to me many years ago. Now, I give it to you."

"Bundo... I... I will always treasure it."

"No, mijo! Don't let it burden you! You must sell it!"

"But why, Bundo?"

"To use for the sport fishing business. In any manner you think wise. You speak English. You are almost americano, mijo. You will know what to do. You will be able to keep the bad ones from cheating us."

"But Abundio, from the beginning, you have always been... "

"The boss?"

"Yes."

"We both know I am... not capable, mijo. You are the obvious choice."

Chino ran his fingers over the watch's rich leather band and felt the weight of its slightly rounded, rectangular case. He noticed the tiny gold crown inlaid on the face, almost invisible in the moonlight.

The obvious choice? For seven slow revolutions of the great wheel of life he had hidden behind this man. And now, his benefactor was offering to give up his place at the head of his own table. Chino looked down at the bandage on Abundio's big toe. It had come partly unwrapped. He wished he could do something to ease the pain.

He thought of his first encounter with the dark figure of Margarita Santos. She too had wanted to help Abundio. She had come to Chino, with fresh bruises on her face, as he slept on the beach beside the new Evinrude. She had offered him all the best fishing spots. Enough, she said, to build a fine house like her brother's. And all he must do in return was take care of him. Take care of *whom?* Why, Bundo Rodríguez, of course!

So the deal had been struck, and Chino had never asked about the mysterious bond between Abundio and Margarita, and the two men had never once discussed it. In the end, what did it matter? It is all tied together in a big bundle of time, Chino thought. The giving and the taking. The endless rows of El Centro, a satin-lined box of cuff links, a kitchen full of broken dishes, a man's only daughter, an airplane bringing money. It is all tied together and each part is fixed to every other part, as though time were a stone, and not a river. And for my part, Chino thought, I must stop this hiding from myself. I must tell him about María and let the damned wheel of life take me where it wants.

"Bundo... "

Abundio's big fingers folded the gold into Chino's hand. He put his arm around Chino and hugged him tight.

"Is she happy, mijo?"

Chino watched a tear glissade down Abundio's deeply shadowed cheek. The big man had been expecting the pies after all.

"Yes, amigo."

"The Rolex. It is for you both. Go to her now, mijo. They are waiting for you."

ABUNDIO SAT ALONE on the stump of the old olive tree, feeling the sadness settle again upon his shoulders.

In the distant, sultry night, he could hear the blowing sound made by the waves breaking in the outer channel, and he knew the spume was beginning to fly, and the Four Horses were beginning to dance and toss their glowing manes above the wine-dark sea.

The swell outside had been building all through the afternoon and evening. Twice during the party, Abundio had gone down to check it. There had been a visible surge on the beach, much larger than when Pablo had stuck his twig into the sand. And to the north, near the three rocks at the high tide line, Abundio had seen the distant flash, flash, flash of the nighttime luminescence, as a one-foot surf spilled itself onto the sand.

But there was still no wind, and Abundio was certain the chubasco was far to the south, past La Paz, past Cabo San Lucas, perhaps as far as Manzanillo, perhaps even as far as Acapulco. But if it was that far away, it must be the mother and father of them all, to send swells such a distance over the sea, to leap against the Four Horses and break on the shore of the inner caleta.

From July through September, Abundio knew, most of the chubascos born in the blood-warm sea, a thousand miles south, followed the coast a short distance and then veered out over the Pacific before they could reach the Baja peninsula. But toward October the bad ones came. It was at the end of the hurricane season that the chubascos sometimes turned sharply east, leaping over the mountains and blasting the coast between Cabo San Lucas and Loreto with cataclysmic wind and rain.

They needed this one to turn west, away from the coast. Or, at the very least, it must linger another day, it must dally over the blood-warm sea, gathering its strength for just one more day, before it struck them.

Abundio stood and raised his long arms high above his head, and he opened his palms to the starry, late night sky above the arroyo. He called on the ancient, unknown forces that controlled the winds. And he called on Socorro's invisible spirits, on the damned officials in La Paz and México City, on The Virgin of Guadalupe, on the memory of his father, on the blue-red eye of morning, and most of all, on the living candle flame that burned beneath the dark waters.

"Please, give us just this one day."

From out of the dark, a small, black-and-tan shepherd dog whimpered and came groveling, with her tail and head lowered to the sand, and she shivered and lay down between Abundio's feet. He squatted low and cradled her soft, narrow face in his hands.

"Ah, mi perridita. I am sorry. I have no fish for you tonight. But you do not understand, do you? You hope for something. Even though you will not receive it."

"Bundo, do you hear the bird?"
"Sí, Nacho. There are many of them in the bushes."
"And the crabs. Did you see the crabs tonight?"
"Sí, Nacho. Will it be a bad one?"
"Very bad."

On the dark porch, Abundio and Fra Nacho listened closely to the bird calling in the arroyo. It was the black-feathered sea bird, the *pajaro chubasquero*, or "chubasco bird," that came to land only when driven by the fury of a tropical storm. Its plaintive call, like the sound of a rusty barn door swinging in the wind, had not been heard in the caleta for decades. Abundio, in fact, had never seen one before. But tonight, the beaches and the arroyo were alive with the restless, noisy, long-winged birds, who had been arriving all afternoon.

And tonight, the hermit crabs had left the water and marched inland. They had pulled themselves to dry land, dragging their borrowed shells with them, up the beach and into the palm trees. Some of them had gone as far as the houses and Abundio had even seen one near the old well. It was still another sign, as if they needed one, that an unseen chubasco was indeed coming from a thousand miles away.

The two old friends listened to the distant surf. The sighing, crumping sound came, and a few seconds later, there was another one, and another. It was as if the world were panting, as if it were breathing deeply to ready itself for a great exertion.

"Nacho, should we go out in the morning?"

"There will be other days."

Would there? Abundio rolled a hard lump of dirt between his fingers, and he felt the gritty sand come loose and fall away. How long had they waited for these clients? And how long could they afford to wait for the next plane to land? Was there *really* such a thing as a sport fishing business? Or, was this just another trick of the magician's handkerchief?

"Nacho. Do we deceive ourselves?"

"In the end, we are all kings, Abundio, lonely and absolute masters of our own destinies."

"Kings? Of what!? Of this worthless arroyo? It might as well be the moon!"

Fra Nacho carefully peeled the wrapping from a black claret bottle that he had kept hidden beneath his cot. He used a screwdriver to force the cork down into the bottle, and he poured two tall glasses out, full to the brims. The deep red wine was warm, and very rich, and it spoke of leather and smoke on a winter day.

"This is the very finest barolo ever made. It is from Torino. I have always kept it as a reminder, a reminder of my... "

Fra Nacho's voice trailed away to silence. He was sitting in the grass, beside the girl with the almond eyes, halfway up the shoulder of Monte Cavallo on a Sunday in July. There was a picnic of good Austrian black bread, and emmentaler, and two bottles of the finest barolo, bought in Torino and carried on the train to the station in Pordenone. Below them, the angled trapezoid farms of the Adriatic plain stretched out like green patchwork, and there were church bells ringing everywhere in the glowing afternoon haze. They decided to save one of the bottles of barolo for Christmas, but they had never opened it. That was the last day they ever spent together.

Fra Nacho raised his glass high, spilling a little wine on the dirt.

"A toast, then! To the king of the moon!"

He emptied his glass and drew a deep breath and let it out slowly.

"Do you like it, Abundio?"

Abundio knew the wine must be very good and very precious to his old friend. Indeed, it had been his only real possession.

"Yes, thank you, Nacho, although I do not fully understand it."

They finished the bottle as a heavy curtain of clouds came in from the east and covered the rising stars of Orion, the lion hunter of winter. A soft night breeze carried the pungent smell of the sea up the arroyo, as far as Fra Nacho's shack, and then beyond it, up the cliffs, and back, back to the mountains and even farther.

"It is late, Abundio."

"Yes. Good night, old friend."

"You will decide in the morning. At first light."

"Yes. In the morning."

Abundio didn't go straight back to the house. He went down to the beach and walked north alone to the three rocks. The surf was knee high now, and the Four Horses were aflame in the blue-black of the outer channel. A fresh breeze blew off the water. In two hours, there would be light in the east.

ON THE DEEPLY shadowed porch of Ramón Ochoa's house, Peter J. M. Grayson III of Providence, Rhode Island, was pinned under the heavy body of the soldier with no face. Considine and Richardson were there too, next to his pistol, and he could hear the moan of the SBD's climbing out over the atoll. And somewhere far away, the high-pitched screaming voice came, and he stood up and followed it through the smoke and shattered palm trees. He found her there, lying in the snow beside the overturned car, still clutching her handbag and fur coat, and he looked down to see the bright chrome strip of metal protruding from his side. And then they were standing around the hole dug in the frozen ground, and they all came up and put their hands on his shoulders, and she was there too, with her parents, and his, and Considine and Richardson, and the faceless soldier, and they all forgave him and told him not to blame himself. It could happen to anyone, they said. On an icy road, after a New Year's Eve party, it could have happened to any of them.

Socorro woke with a start.

A strong smell of the open sea blew in through the door, and the house was bathed in a strange light, like the glow of embers from a fading fire.

She dressed quickly and went out to the cooking barrel. She closed her eyes and raised her face to the sunrise, giving thanks for the miracle of the new day, as she did each morning of her life.

The entire dawn sky was the deep, dark red of an inverted bowl of blood. Not orange, but pure, pure red.

On the far horizon, columns of clouds slumped northwards like lumpy black soldiers, and there were lighting flashes above them. The half-disk of the rising sun glowed dimly through the haze.

An insistent, tapping sound made Socorro look upwards. In the breeze, her dried botete was banging itself to pieces against the underside of the porch roof, cracking its fins and brittle skin against the palm thatch.

The house was empty.

Abundio had gone down to the boats early. And late last night, María had taken the blanket from her cot in the corner. Chino had probably left her sleeping at their place in the dunes. He had probably already met Abundio at the beach.

Standing at the barrel, Socorro formed a picture deep within herself, of Chino and Abundio, catching the sport fish for their clients, and all of them happy, dancing around the candle at Fra Nacho's house, counting the bills, and laughing, and making plans for the future. But then the picture changed itself, and she saw Abundio, alone, in his panga, on an endless, gently rolling sea. But it was not the sea of Agua Amargosa. It was a different, quiet place that seemed vaguely familiar, as though she had been there in her childhood. Her husband stood and waved to her, and he called her name and shouted something, but he was too far away, and she could not tell what it was.

"No more than ten miles, Chino."

"Right."

"If you hear the lines whistle in the wind, stop fishing and come in fast."

"Right."

"Stay to the south. That way you can come back with the wind."

"Right."

"And, Chino… "

"Yes, Pablo?"

"This panga is all I have."

"Understood."

Pablo Santos sniffed the steady southeast breeze. There must be huge winds down there. In the channel, the outermost of the Four Horses sent a geyser of spray shooting into the gloomy dawn each time a swell slammed into it. And to the north, a low surf rolled to shore, bordering the caleta with white.

Even here at the launch spot they would need extra hands this morning to push the pangas out through knee-high waves.

Chino went over to talk to the clients, who stood waiting on the beach beside their tackle boxes.

"Good morning, Howard. Good morning, Shig… Danny."

A light sprinkling of rain had fallen, and drops of water marked the varnished wood of their boxes. Howard was all smiles.

"*Buenos días, Roberto!* Ready to go get 'em?"

"Yes, Howard. But it may be a little rough today."

"Rough?"

"Yes, there is a swell outside."

"A swell?"

"Yes. We may have to come in early. If the wind starts to blow."

Howard frowned as he looked out toward the Four Horses. The sea seemed flat enough. And there was only a slight breeze, blowing beneath a gray overcast sky.

"Doesn't look too bad to me, Robert."

Inwardly, Chino had to agree. To him, the morning looked no different from a hundred others he had seen during his summers at Agua Amargosa. More than likely, these swells and clouds would fade away over the next few days, and calm weather would settle in again, as always. But Chino was alert to the warnings of Abundio and Pablo, as well as those of the other pangueros who had experienced the full chubasco. And Fra Nacho, it was said, had called the likelihood of a chubasco not a possibility, but a certainty. Chino was in no mood to take chances with his clients.

"There may be a storm."

Now Howard turned his frown on Chino.

"We paid for a full day, Robert... in advance."

They had expected this. Chino's reply was as agreed upon by himself and Abundio. He put on his best smile.

"Of course, Howard! If we need to come in early, we'll return your money. Or, we'll take you fishing tomorrow. Your choice."

AND SO, ON a sultry, breezy morning in the last week of September, two pangas were wrestled into the surging, gray waters of the caleta, each with its load of fishermen.

In the smaller boat, Abundio Rodríguez and Peter Grayson clung tight to the southern shore. Gingerly, they squeezed through a narrow gap in the reefs, and they turned south to fish among the submerged boulders at the base of the cliffs.

In the larger panga, belonging to a fretful Pablo Santos, Chino threaded his way out through the choppy, swelly water of the main channel. He rounded the Four Horses and opened the throttle wide, heading straight east. There would be no time for making mackerel baits or looking for the blue current. He would run out as far as seemed prudent, and they would troll feathers south, and Chino prayed that a marlin would hit before the wind did.

On the far side of the high mountains, the Pacific Ocean had risen five feet higher than its highest tide, and a wall of green surf was booming on the west coast of Baja California.

Along a front two-hundred miles wide, between Cabo San Lucas and Magdalena Bay, a torrential rain had been falling since midnight, and the surf was crashing down on the rocky points and on the sandy beaches between them with a roar that had been heard through the night for a mile inland.

The powerful chubasco had been born in the moist heat of the Gulf of Tehuantepec. It had traveled northwest for two days, cutting across the open sea. For a third day, it had lingered two-hundred miles off the coast of Cabo San Lucas, increasing in strength and sending a long swell far up into the Sea of Cortez.

In the hours just before sunrise, the hurricane had veered momentarily toward Hawaii, like a serpent rearing its head to strike. Then, it had reversed its course and accelerated directly into the glow of the rising sun, crossing the coast a hundred miles north of Todos Santos.

SOCORRO AND MARÍA met at the house, and the mother and daughter chattered happily as they enjoyed a breakfast of rich, roast pork burritos. Having no other chores to do for the moment, they decided to go down to the beach to wash dishes and take a short walk together.

They were just kneeling at the edge of the water, when the center of the chubasco crested the mountains fifty miles south of the old mission of Dolores del Sur. It would enter the Sea of Cortez, somewhere near the southern islands, in about half an hour.

"OOPS!"

Pete was having difficulty keeping his balance in the bow of the panga.

"Señor Pete, you should sit down."

"Just one, Bundo. Then we can get the hell out of here."

"Sí, señor. As you wish."

Peter Grayson hadn't been skunked in over forty years. But it was looking more and more like this was going to be the day. He had cast every fly in his two aluminum pocket-cases and he had jigged every lure in his small tackle box. He had tried surface retrieves, medium-depth retrieves, and retrieves along the bottom; smooth retrieves and jerky retrieves; fast retrieves, and slow retrieves; and no retrieve at all.

He hadn't caught a damned thing.

Abundio worked the tiller constantly back and forth to avoid being blown onto the boulders. A stiff breeze had come up from a bright spot in the clouds where the morning sun should have been and the swells were much larger now. The hissing, green mounds of water rolled in one after another and boomed against the cliff, sending spray twenty feet into the air.

To avoid spilling Pete out of the panga, Abundio was forced to stay at least fifty yards away from the cliff and the chaotic waves reflecting from it. And that was the problem. Pete's casts were falling well short of the rocks. Each time he began false casting, the wind caught his looping line in the air and made it fall in a heap behind him, or in the water, or on Abundio in the stern of the panga.

"Dammit!"

Pete sat down on the middle seat, with the butt of his rod on one knee. His line lay in a tangle, partly in the panga and partly in the water.

Abundio studied the horizon. In the south and east, he could see the tops of the swells beginning to lose their shape in the wind. White foam was beginning to roll backwards off the highest crests as the swells moved under them. Between the whitecaps, the water was dark gray, almost black in patches, where its surface was roughened by gusts of wind.

"Señor. We should go now. The wind is coming."

"Is it a chubasco, Bundo?"

"Maybe… yes."

Pete braced his arms on the gunnel as the panga rolled sideways and heavily back. He let his delicate, polished bamboo rod rattle down on the seats.

"That's it then. Skunked."

Abundio reached into a canvas bag that he kept under his seat. He uncoiled a monofilament leader, already rigged with two small hooks and a medium-sized sinker.

Using the point of his knife, Abundio stabbed a rotten, half-dried old mackerel bait and dragged it up on the seat. He cut a belly strip out of the mackerel and popped out both its eyeballs. He put the eyeballs on one of the hooks and the belly strip on the other, and he tied the rig to Pete's line.

Peter Grayson stared at the cliff with his arms folded.

"It won't count, Bundo. I don't fish with bait."

Abundio dropped the line into the water and pushed the rod into Pete's hands.

"There are times, señor, when a fish is just a fish."

Pete's line was hit before it got halfway to the bottom. He braced himself and grinned as he fought the fish up to the boat. It was a juvenile yellowtail, only a foot and a half long, but it felt much larger and sounded twice before he subdued it.

The yellowtail had hit the eyeballs, one of which was still intact. Abundio removed the hook from the fish's thin, gray lower lip.

"Let me see it, Bundo."

Pete measured the fish using the marks he had painted on the shaft of his rod. He took note of the distinct pinkish stripe running down the fish's side, its yellow fins and tail, and the smooth curve of its forehead. Its coloration was much brighter than normal.

"It is a yellowtail, no? *Jurél?*"

"Sí, Señor Pete. Yellowtail."

Abundio checked the horizon again. The roughed water had come halfway to them. Dark gray clouds covered the sky. There was no visible sign of the sun.

"Señor, we go now."

Pete grinned sheepishly. He pointed at the remains of the mackerel bait. They still had half the belly and one of the eyeballs.

"How about just one more, Bundo?"

Abundio had no time to answer. He had already put the Evinrude into gear and he was pushing the tiller over to get away from the cliffs. As planned, it would be straight downwind to the channel. Abundio picked out a large swell. As it passed under them, he opened the throttle all the way. The old panga clung to the backside of the moving hill of water and traveled with it, wallowing deeply as Abundio worked the tiller to keep it balanced on the prop.

BENEATH A QUICKLY darkening sky, Chino braced one hand on the cowling of the Evinrude and the other on the tiller. Carefully, to avoid losing his balance, he twisted his head left and right, scanning the full three-hundred-sixty degrees of the horizon.

Everywhere he looked, whitecaps covered the restless gray surface of the sea. The long swell was still coming up from the south. But the wind had swung around and strengthened, and it now came straight out of the east. It blew long streaks of foam crosswise to the swells.

They were still fishing.

Howard and Shig clung grimly to their rods. They were soaked with the warm, salt spindrift blowing across their faces. Danny lay curled in the bow. None of them had spoken for the past hour.

Chino had long since given up trying to spot a marlin tail. With the water so dark and rough, he would not see it anyway. He had run out to the edge of Pablo's ten-mile limit and put the feathers in, and they were trolling slowly south, straight into the swells.

It seemed that everything in the sea had disappeared. They had spotted no birds, no turtles, not even bait fish. Their feathers had not been hit by so much as a skipjack in nearly two hours of trolling. They had not seen a single living thing the entire morning.

A low whistling sound came from one of the lines as a gust of wind struck it.

Chino looked back to check the feathers. They swam poorly, skittering on the surface as the crosswind pulled the lines into deep C-shaped curves. Another gust hit, and both lines whistled. The feathers came to the surface and stayed there. Chino reduced throttle to sink them, and the panga wallowed left and right.

He shouted forward into the wind.

"Howard!"

Howard and Shig started to alertness. They had been half asleep.

"Yes, Robert!"

"Reel in a little more."

They saw the lines curving in the wind and understood. They reeled their feathers to within two boat-lengths of the panga and the lines trailed a little straighter.

"Howard!"

"Yeah!"

"How much longer do you want to fish?"

Howard checked his watch.

"It's only nine-thirty."

Chino shook his head.

"It's too windy."

Howard looked ready for an argument. He consulted with Shig and Danny, and then turned back to Chino. He was unhappy.

"Listen, Robert! Do you want to get paid for today, or not?"

Chino did not hear him. He was listening to the steady whistle of the lines. And his eyes were fixed on a sudden change in the appearance of the distant water ahead of the panga. The horizon to the south had disappeared behind a long, gray wall of mist. Above the mist, a line of black overcast crackled with lightning, and below it, the sea was a rolling mass of white.

It was still miles away, but it was coming toward them at a terrifying pace.

Chino cut the throttle and threw the Evinrude into neutral. The lines went slack and tangled as the bow of the panga pushed off the wind. Howard was still talking.

"Hey, Robert! What did I say? I said... "

Chino pointed across the port gunnel.

"Look!"

Chino's knife flashed out twice and the feathers were gone. He threw the motor into gear and spun Pablo's panga around to the northwest. Held at full throttle, Pablo's powerful, eighty-horsepower Evinrude shoved the panga down swell at more than twenty-five miles-per-hour. The boat overtook each wave and leapt over its crest and then slammed down on the back of the next wave with an explosive slap.

Unable to remain on the seats, Howard, Shig and Danny squatted on the floor of the panga. They gripped the gunnels with both hands to avoid being thrown into the air each time it jumped over a wave. And each time it came down, they slipped and fell. For a while, they tried to keep their rods and gold reels from banging together, but they soon let them go. Their heavy tackle boxes split open, spilling hooks and lures that jumped about and caught in their clothing. But they paid no attention and held tight to the gunnels.

Chino squatted in the space just ahead of the Evinrude. Each time the bow came down, he looked for the lowest spot in the swells ahead and he steered toward it. Behind them, the lightning and mist were much closer now, and the black clouds had risen up to cover half the sky. They had only a few more minutes.

Chino shouted forward.

"Howard! The scoop! Do you see a scoop up there?"

Howard searched through the equipment bouncing and sliding all around them. He found a bleach bottle scoop in the bow and held it up. Chino nodded and shouted again.

"Give it to me!"

Danny passed the scoop back and Chino put it down and stuck his foot into it for safekeeping. He was sure they would be taking green water the instant the rollers hit and it would collect in the stern where its weight would swamp them unless he could bail it out.

Chino held the throttle open, paying no attention to the destructive pounding. One last time, his right hand went to his thigh and he felt the small rectangular shape in his pocket, wrapped in plastic and oiled cloth. He knew his duty was to fight with all his strength, but he also knew the end was very close at hand. He did not look back. He concentrated on the sky ahead, squeezing the tiller in a death grip, and he began to clear his mind of everything.

The black wall-cloud rose up behind the racing panga, like the maw of the leviathan, and it swallowed them impassively, and they were inside of it. The green water came in on Chino's shoulders, and they twisted sideways to the swell, powerless to resist, and the clients were bailing with their broken tackle boxes and throwing their heavy gold reels into the sea. The water was around their waists, and the driving spray rose above them, hiding the sky and mountains. Chino heard himself screaming at them to bail, bail for their lives, and they did, but the sea kept coming in, and in, and in, and Chino saw it happening, very clearly, and he discovered that he was not afraid of the end. He was not afraid of it at all.

SOCORRO AND MARÍA sat on the beach with their heads tightly wrapped in scarves. The breakfast dishes had been taken back to the house unwashed.

Out in the channel, the reefs between the Four Horses were carpeted with continuous white surf that ran out from the southern shore and connected the islands together. Inside, the caleta was choppy and dark, and whitecaps showed everywhere.

Pablo Santos paced back and forth at the edge of the water. His sons occupied themselves by throwing rocks down the beach. Pablo shouted toward the Four Horses.

"Why don't they come in!?"

For the past hour, Socorro had kept her eyes fixed on the low, craggy point of rocks that framed the view to the south. Both pangas had disappeared behind the point, and it was there they would first be seen upon their return.

The wind came straight off the sea, driving a low layer of gray clouds before it that skimmed over the village and disappeared up the arroyo. The tops of the cliffs were hidden from view.

Socorro looked at her feet. The gusting wind was driving sand against her ankles. High above, the leaves of the palm trees rubbed against each other with a constant rasping sound.

As Pablo passed by, Socorro stood in his way to stop him.

"Pablo, do they suffer?"

"Yes, yes!"

"Are they safe?"

Pablo shrugged. He was not concerned with the rattling of a few palm leaves or the appearance of a few whitecaps in the caleta. He had been watching the flattened perspective of the horizon, far outside the Four Horses. Out there, the black patches in the water, just visible in the offing, told him of monstrous winds. And the sparkles inside the patches, where a shaft of sunlight penetrated a hole in the clouds, told him the tops of the swells were very steep, and they were breaking over themselves. Far outside, where the wind blew unconstrained by trees and mountains, Pablo knew that rollers had covered the sea with white. And he knew that green walls of water, twice as high as houses, were falling everywhere.

Socorro was tugging insistently at the elbow of his sweatshirt.

"Pablo. Pablo… are they in danger?"

Pablo whirled to face her. He caught himself and lowered a clenched fist. His face was twisted with fury.

"They are in God's hands! And so is my panga! I just hope Chino can handle a boat better than your *stupid husband!*"

Socorro could only stand motionless, with her arms held stiff and her head lowered. But María leapt up from the sand, screaming.

"Pablo! You godless pinche *bastard!*"

She hurled a fistful of sand into Pablo's eyes and spat in his face. Pablo struck out blindly, hitting María's jaw and knocking her to the sand. He staggered away with his hands clawing at his face. But María was not finished with him. She chased him down and—with a natural snapping motion inherited from El Tecolote Terrible—she brought her right foot up between Pablo's outstretched legs with enough force to lift him and knock him backwards into the water.

" *…una panga! …una panga!*"

Rubén Santos extended his arm toward the rocky point to the south.

The panga he had seen stayed down in the troughs for half a minute before they caught sight of it again. But finally, it rose on top of a swell and stood out black against the clouds.

It was Abundio's panga, and there were two men in it.

María wrapped an arm around her mother's shoulders. She walked Socorro back to the trees and helped her sit down on a fallen palm log.

The weltering panga came out from behind the point very slowly, yawing sideways each time a swell lifted it into the sky. It came dangerously close to the Four Horses as it tried to find a gap in the breaking surf. At the last moment, it veered out again and turned straight north, skirting along just outside the reefs.

Abundio and Señor Pete could be seen sitting on the floor of the panga, with just their heads showing above the gunnels. Señor Pete was bailing steadily. They could see the scoops of seawater he was throwing over the leeward side.

Slowly and cautiously, the panga rode out each swell. It passed behind the Four Horses, one-by-one. After rounding the third island, it could not turn immediately into the channel because of the surf. Instead, it continued north for another tenth of a mile, almost out of sight, and then turned sharply back toward the caleta and picked up speed. Finally, it reached the sheltered water inside the reef and settled down for the choppy ride to the beach.

Socorro and María went down to hold the boat against the waves while Pete and Abundio tumbled out.

Pete was shivering uncontrollably in the humid, eighty-degree wind. Saying nothing, he walked up to the trees and sat down with his head on his arms. His long bamboo fly rod lay on the bottom of the panga, broken into pieces.

Abundio nearly fell. The outer wrapping on his foot came off and floated away, revealing the dark-stained inner bandage around his toe. He stood beside Socorro, with his big hands on the seesawing gunnel of the old boat, and he searched the beach again and again, looking for Pablo's green panga. Then he turned toward the Four Horses and whispered into the eye of the wind.

" ...Mijo."

THEY PULLED THE panga all the way into the palms and took Señor Pete back to the warmth of Ramón's house and wrapped him in blankets.

In the village, empty tin cans flew through the spaces between the houses, together with chicken feathers and pieces of paper and palm thatch torn from some of the roofs. Loose trash piled up against the bushes in the arroyo, and empty plastic bags caught on the branches.

The rain began as they were walking back to the beach. It came in light sprinkles at first, driven sideways by the wind. Quickly, it grew to a steady, pelting downpour, falling from a cloud layer so low it seemed they could reach up and stick their arms into it.

By the time they reached the beach, the wind was moaning in the treetops, and the rain had grown heavy enough to sting their eyes if they tried to look into it. The caleta was lost in a driving gray mist, and the wind blew the tops off the whitecaps and shredded the surface of the water into long white streaks.

The Rodríguezes drew back into the trees and huddled together in a sheltered niche to watch for Chino. The rain and spray came in solid, buffeting sheets, with short moments of calm in between, and the wind whistled above their heads, getting stronger each passing minute.

The wind chop inside the caleta began to coalesce into long, parallel swells, and lines of surf began to break on the inner reefs and shoals. It was something none of them had seen before, something they would not have believed possible.

Pablo Santos came scuttling down the beach and found them in the trees. He glared silently at María. He stood over Abundio, who was squatting beside a stump, watching the water, with his hands clasped over his forehead. Pablo shrieked into the rain and wind.

"*Idiot!* I told you it was a chubasco! How are you going to pay for my panga!?"

Abundio stood up, very slowly, expressionless.

"Chino... "

"Use your eyes! Idiot! Chino is *dead!*"

Abundio lowered his gaze into Pablo's hate-filled face.

"Pablo. You are the one who is dead."

A ferocious gust hit them and both men wobbled to catch their balance. Abundio's melon-sized fist reached out and twisted the front of Pablo's sweatshirt into a knot, dragging and lifting him until only his toes touched the ground.

"And, Pablo. If you ever touch María again, I swear... I swear on my father's grave... I will hold your legs apart while she cuts off your balls and feeds them to you on a fork."

Pablo's hand came up over his mouth, and he stumbled away through the swaying trees, looking over his shoulder, like a dog running from a shower of stones.

FOR ANOTHER TEN minutes, Abundio stood watching the caleta from behind the shelter of a tree. Then he went to the old panga and put his shoulder under the bow.

The women came running out when they saw what he was doing. Socorro pushed her weight down on the gunnel.

"Husband!"

Gently, Abundio pulled her hands away. He lowered his shoulder again and groaned as he shifted the bow around toward the water.

"Chino must be out of gas by now."

"Husband! It is useless!"

The panga was pointed at the Four Horses. Abundio grabbed its familiar old gunnel and began to slide it into the breaking surf.

Socorro turned to her daughter, her voice shrill and breaking.

"María! María! Make him stop!"

"Papá!"

Abundio cupped his hands under his little girl's chin and stroked her hair. "Chino needs me. He might be drifting. Under the cliffs."

"Do you really believe that?"

The swells were breaking over the Four Horses now, burying them in masses of surging foam.

"There is the possibility."

"Papá... is it for *me* that you do this?"

Abundio shook his head. He looked out, beyond the Four Horses.

"No, María. Not just for you. I must go now."

Something small, a noise, a shift in the sound of the wind, a feeling they were not alone, made them look toward the trees and the black-shrouded figure hidden within them.

Margarita Santos did not know why she had come down to the Malecón. It was a hot July day. She watched the white sail of the panga disappear into the haze on the north side of the bay. And then she went back to the unfamiliar house, and she felt the new life within her, as she sat working at the sewing machine, and the old woman's voice screeched in her ear. *How can you stab me in the back like this?* And she was alone in the market, among the crowds, searching for toys and bottles and swaddling clothes in the carts of the vendors of used things. *And the toy cow, señora? If I were to buy these three bottles and this black rebozo, how much for the old wooden cow?* And each afternoon, she waited on the Malecón for the white sail to reappear. But it never did and she knew without knowing that she must get away. She must take her new things and get away from this improper place.

Margarita came out of the trees. She saw El Tecolote standing beside his old panga, and she rushed to him and threw her arms around him, mindless of the others.

"Don't go, mi amor! I wanted to die so many times! For the memory of our son, don't leave me again!"

A blast of mist-filled wind pushed Margarita's tattered black rebozo down to her shoulders. She stood facing Abundio, shivering, her face porcelain white in the rain, with the water soaking her clothes, running off the tips of her fingers. She had braided her hair into double loops and she had pinned a red hibiscus over each ear.

Holding her, Abundio turned to his wife.

"Socorro… "

Socorro came to him and raised a finger to his lips. She put her arms around them both, in the pouring rain, shaking her head, with her eyes closed and her dark cheek pressed to Abundio's chest.

"We have all caused her too much suffering, husband."

"Socorro… how did you know?"

"That is of no importance, after all."

Margarita felt the weight of the helpless, growing child. Panting with each step, she climbed the steep, cobblestone street leading up from the waterfront, past the Hotel Perla, to the narrow yard where the Buick was kept parked. She opened the door and looked on the floor of the back seat. The cup was still there. He had left it behind.

Gently, Abundio passed Margarita's hands to his wife.

"Please, Socorro, take her home. I will wait here."

The women held Margarita and led her through the palms to her brother's pink house. When they got back to the beach, wrapped in garbage bags against the rain, they saw the groove in the sand where the old panga had been pushed into the surf. A stained bandage lay half-buried at the edge of the water.

They searched among the whitecaps of the caleta for signs of the panga, and they looked for a long time at the exploding fountains of spray around the Four Horses. But they saw nothing. Somehow, Abundio had made it out through the channel.

Socorro and María rolled a log against a tree. Behind this windbreak, they dug a shallow nest in the sand, just big enough to crouch in, and they pressed themselves into it, with their garbage bags snapping in the wind. They could see very little of the caleta. The air was filled with foam and driving spindrift. Even the beach was obscured by translucent sheets of spray peeling off the booming surf.

They watched the water come well above the high tide line. The beach in front of them was disappearing. Already, the pounding, waist-high waves had removed several feet of sand, exposing the bristly roots of the first row of palm trees and a bank of small, black stones that had been hidden beneath them.

The trunks of the palm trees swayed above them and they could hear the sharp crack of wood as the leaves began to tear off and fly away.

"Oh, daughter!"

"Mamá!"

Socorro bent her head down behind the log and formed the picture. She made the sea light blue and mirror flat again, with Abundio standing at the tiller, laughing, as he brought his panga up to Chino's and threw a rope to him. But against her will, the picture changed itself again, and the green walls rose up all around him. She saw the plug driven from its place in the bow and Abundio struggling to keep his balance as he left the tiller and went forward. He jammed his foot as the panga rolled sideways and dipped its gunnel deep into the green, and then he stood upright, with the water above his knees, waving to her, and his mouth was open, moving. He was singing to her, the song his father had given him, the rowing song they sang each night before dinner, and he was saying good-bye. He waved his long arms at her, as she stood with the coiled lines on the windswept beach of Isla Coronado, and he looked deep into her and waved and said good-bye as a hissing swell folded the panga under and it disappeared in a swirl of color, beneath the dark water.

SOCORRO LOWERED HER forehead to the sand, and she wept and she wept, and María could not comfort her. For an hour they huddled together behind the log, holding each other tightly in the driving rain and salt spray, listening to the roar of the wind and surf, not looking up any more.

Oddly, María found herself thinking of the lean-to in the dunes. She had left her blanket folded on the end of the cot, beside Chino's pillow. She wondered if the lean-to and cot were still there.

She thought of the gold watch and she wondered if it was still in Chino's pocket. And she thought of her father, the great Tecolote of La Paz, on his knees, scraping the sand from beneath the cooking barrel, and the love and pain in his eyes as he kissed her good-bye, and left, to give the watch to Chino. All these years! He had kept it hidden! Like the secret wound in his heart! Saying nothing!

María held tight to her mother's heaving shoulders, and she tried to form the image, as Socorro had tried to teach her many times, but she still could not, and she was glad of it because she feared what her mother had seen.

For another hour, the women knelt behind the log as the wind whipped itself to a mad shriek and the surf grew higher and higher. Then a palm tree fell over beside them with a slow, ripping crash. María was thinking they must give up the beach and retreat to the houses when she heard something like the familiar, growling exhaust note that an Evinrude made when its propeller lifted out of the water.

A few seconds later, she heard it again, louder and more distinct, and she peeked over the log in time to catch the stern of Pablo's big, dark green panga as it turned away and disappeared into the sheets of blowing mist and spindrift. She leapt up and screamed into the storm.

"Chino! Chino! He has done it, mamá! He has come back! It is a miracle!"

They ran down to the strip of newly exposed stones at the edge of the water and squinted out through the spray and the rising, six-foot surf. Less than fifty yards out, Chino squatted at the tiller. He had it pulled all the way toward him, with the Evinrude blustering and churning, and the panga spinning in tight, foamy circles. They could see no one else in the boat with him.

Chino caught sight of them and waved. He waited until a breaking swell passed under the panga, and then he came toward them at full throttle. Halfway in, he changed his mind and turned out again, only to be struck directly on the bow by the following wave. The panga pointed its nose straight up into the air, almost leaving the water, and María bit her hand and screamed.

"Chino! No!"

Now they saw the three americanos on the floor between the middle seats and the seawater come pouring out over the transom. The panga came down, slightly sideways, and Chino caught it with the throttle and held it steady against the waves.

Pablo Santos emerged from his hiding place in the trees. He stood beside Socorro and María, peering out over the caleta with his hands shielding his eyes.

"Careful. Careful, Chino. Take your time."

Chino turned the panga through two more complete circles and then tried for shore again.

This time he did not hesitate. He held the Evinrude at full throttle. It growled and raced in the foamy soup as he rode the back of a swell right onto the beach. For an instant, the wave formed a high wall with the panga suspended on top of it. Then the white water crashed down and shot up the sloping beach, all the way to the palm trees, taking the panga with it.

The boat came to an instant stop as its bottom struck firm sand, and the wave receded, leaving it high and dry for the moment. Chino cut the howling Evinrude.

Socorro and María came running. Two of the clients lay tangled together in the bow of the panga. The impact had thrown them on their faces. Blood and rain streamed down their shirts and onto their swimming trunks. But the third one, the young one, was not there.

Chino, still looking like a stranger in his close-cropped haircut, stood motionless at the tiller, not speaking. He came to life as the next wave exploded against the transom and poured a foot of seawater over his back. He raised his arm and pointed into the trees. There was Danny, on his hands and knees in the sand. He had been thrown out over the bow.

Pablo Santos grabbed the gunnel of his panga and tried to drag it out of the surf. He sank to his calves in the slushy sand, struggling desperately, but the half-flooded boat refused to budge.

"Dammit, Chino! Help me! Help me!"

A heavy, solid wave hammered the transom, sending a geyser of water high above their heads. The swash pushed the panga crosswise and almost rolled it over. Quickly, Chino jumped out. He helped Howard and Shig out of the bow and sat them down beside Danny. The women looked for the rods and tackle boxes, but there were none. The panga was nearly full of seawater. The next wave rolled it on its side and pulled it out deeper.

Pablo Santos was on his knees. There was a loud crack as the mounting bolts of the Evinrude broke and the panga turned upside down and washed away to the north with Pablo staggering after it.

Chino was shivering out of control. His lips were dark purple. His breath came in shallow, rapid gulps.

"Cold."

María pressed herself against his violently shuddering chest. His hands were soaked white with seawater and the skin on his knuckles hung in shreds. She wrapped her arms around him and tried to stop the shaking.

"You are home now. Home."

Chino saw Socorro standing, alone, in the trees. He turned to look toward the Four Horses, his eyes piercing the impossible sea.

"Papá?"

María shook her head.

BACK AT THE houses, the wind was shaking the porch roofs up and down and the hard, blustery rain had begun to collect in wide puddles. The clients filled their duffel bags hurriedly and Chino helped them load their things on the fish cart.

Peter Grayson was still dazed from his ride into the caleta. He was distressed at the thought of leaving without saying good-bye to Abundio, and he grasped Chino's arm.

"Where's Bundo? I haven't said good-bye to him."

Chino willed his mind to concentrate on the task at hand as he put Pete's bag on the cart and began to push it toward the pista at a fast trot.

"I'll tell him good-bye for you, Pete."

"Promise?"

"Yes, yes! Come! We must hurry now!"

Howard used the brakes and prop to hold the plane into the wind while Chino quickly untied the ropes and pulled the stakes out.

Shig, wide-eyed, soaked and pale, looked to the pilot's seat in the shuddering, buffeting cockpit.

"Howard, is this doable?"

"Yeah... just barely."

With its flaps pulled in tight and its engine roaring, the wet-silver bird rolled only a few yards down the pista before it leapt into the air, directly into a gusting, forty-knot headwind. By the time it passed over Ana Rosa Medina's house, it had already disappeared into the clouds and was only a memory, lost in the rising storm.

THE PLANE CLIMBED straight out over the Four Horses on instruments. At five-thousand-five-hundred feet, it broke out of the first layer of clouds and tilted its wings north in a shaft of brilliant afternoon sun.

Behind it, the full force of the chubasco was just reaching the caleta. A low rolling curtain of black air mixed with water, not unlike a tornado laid on its side, came in across the Four Horses. The islands disappeared as the surface of the sea turned pure white and rose up and hurled itself toward the village.

The first line of palm trees fell over immediately and crashed backwards into the grove as the wall of white spray engulfed the houses. The front porches were lifted high and torn off and went whirling and tumbling up the arroyo.

Then the houses began to come apart, and people were running, crawling in the sheltered places. They sought to hide themselves wherever they had been caught, ducking from the spinning boards, the sheets of metal, the chairs and tables and cots and shards of glass that flew everywhere.

The village's two remaining pangas rolled sideways and caught the wind. One of them disappeared into the palm trees. The other flipped over and over and did cartwheels in the air, shedding its Evinrude in mid-flight, and it ended up on the far side of the pista, smashed against the cliffs.

Then, when it seemed the storm could not possibly get any worse, the people hiding in the ditches and in the corners of the remaining houses were enveloped, finally, in the midnight rim of the chubasco's inner core. The deluge came not in sheets, but in choking, blinding waves, and the people laid themselves flat on their stomachs, and gave themselves up to it. It became dark, fully as dark as the darkest night, and the lightning came in blinding bursts, giving them glimpses of each other's chalk-white, ghostly faces.

The water came sheeting off the far mountains and down the arroyo behind the village, where it gathered itself into a river ten feet deep, pushing a dam of sticks and boulders before it. For an hour, the water followed the path it had created during the spring rains. It churned down the old gully and passed harmlessly out into the caleta. But then the flood grew suddenly higher and it overflowed among the houses and widened and deepened.

In the Rodríguez house, Socorro watched the cooking barrel wash away, then the sand beneath it where they had dug up Señor Pete's gold Rolex only a few hours before. Then the front door collapsed and the table and chairs disappeared. The wall to her right burst inwards with a flood of water and stones and dishes, and the house came down around her. Not knowing how to swim, Socorro found herself struggling in the torrent, down, down, toward the beach. She clung to an empty gasoline can and tumbled and bobbed in the current and caught herself, desperately, on the roots of an upturned palm tree at the very edge of the pounding surf.

And in the arroyo, Ignazio Bertogna had watched the roiling black wall-cloud come in, and he lay dreaming in the mud beneath the ruins of his shack. He dreamed of sharks and goats, and fireflies, and a bottle of barolo that had finally been opened, and he felt the universe close upon itself, and he let it close, finally, and allowed himself to drift in the eternal, never-repeating silence of the stars.

TOWARD EVENING, MARGARITA Santos stepped over the broken screen door that lay across the porch of her brother's house.

The sky above the caleta was clear. High up, a layer of red and black clouds scudded rapidly to the south with the yellow beams of the sunset sweeping between them like searchlights. On the horizon, columns of spray rose silently all around the outermost of the Four Horses.

Margarita stepped off the porch.

She pulled her long, black rebozo over her head, and she picked her way around the fallen trees and the colorful, shattered pieces of the other houses. She crossed the wide, rock-strewn gully and she stood on the clean gravel where the Rodríguez house had been.

Then she went up the arroyo, heading for the hole in the shield-like root, for the man and woman who reached toward each other in eternity. She found the old well, overflowing with pure, sweet water, and she found the remains of the trail. She climbed as high as she could, to a place blocked by sticks and mud. She could go no higher, so she sat on a rock and looked down at the village.

Two children were playing in the doorway of a house that no longer existed. Through the trees, she saw Chino and María scurrying about in the lowering dark. They were gathering palm leaves and piling them in front of Ramón Ochoa's roofless house.

With the glowing rays of the sunset wheeling all around her, Margarita pulled her rebozo tight on her shoulders and she looked down at the village, and she wept for the past, and the present, and the futures that would never be, for the light and the dark, and the sun and the moon and the sea. She wept for it all.

And as night fell over the caleta, the people stopped in their work and listened to the strange sound coming from the arroyo. A high, thin wail rose up and echoed against the cliffs, again and again, like the call of some animal that had lost its way.

ALTHOUGH EVERY OPERABLE boat in the area was pressed into the search for Abundio Rodríguez, the only trace of the old panga ever found was a piece of the bow, washed up on shore nearly halfway to Las Ramalitas.

Just two weeks after the storm, the cliffs burst forth in a deep mantle of green, and the first of many American planes landed, bringing tourist anglers seeking the dorado fly-fishing expert, Bumbo, and the great seaman, Robert, who caught five marlin for his clients in one day and brought them safely through the full chubasco.

Chino quickly sold the gold Rolex in La Paz. He used the money to hire a Caterpillar that cleared the cliff road and smoothed the pista in less than eight hours. The watch also paid for a priest and an elaborate wedding celebration that kept the caleta on its knees for six days, and it established "Robert's Sport Fishing," which Chino and María operated successfully for many years.

They built a big dining palapa for the clients, on the beach in front of Ramón's house, with screened windows and painted fish on the walls, and Ana Rosa Medina serving up her famous dinners, and Socorro gruffly taking orders and counting up the receipts. Socorro lived to attend the birth of four grandchildren, and Chino and María cared for her until she was buried under the palms, just as she always said would happen.

The Zúñiga children—two spectacularly beautiful daughters and two strong sons—were all educated in México City and Guadalajara with dollars brought to the caleta by the tourist anglers. The first born, Abundio, grew unusually tall and athletic and was gifted in languages.

He played goal keeper briefly for a semi-pro soccer team in Guadalajara before marrying and taking a position as assistant manager of a new hotel in San José del Cabo.

Fra Nacho survived the mud slide that buried his shack. He moved into the village, and as it grew about him, he became a great favorite of the children. He taught many of them to read and write, but he never found another student as capable as María Rodríguez. In his final years, he also became a favorite of the tourists, who took photographs of him and gave him tips as he sat in the shade of the big palapa.

The fish processing plant was eventually built at Las Ramalitas, but it operated for only six years. The abandoned building may still be seen at the north end of the bay. Its blue and white paint is flaking off now and its windows have been broken out. All its usable metal parts have been carried off by the locals.

In 1983, the cliff road was widened with the aid of explosives, and it was connected to a new paved highway, completed a decade earlier, that ran the entire length of Baja California, more than a thousand miles, from the U.S. border all the way to Cabo San Lucas. A diesel generator was brought into the village and a deep well was drilled that solved the water problem once and for all. Most of the shacks were replaced with proper houses and a school was built for the children. A small rural market was opened. Construction on a church was begun, and the name "Agua Amargosa" began to appear on the better road maps.

As the years passed, though, the nets reduced fishing around the caleta so much that Chino no longer had the heart for it, even though the new road was bringing more tourist anglers than ever. In 1989, he sold a major interest in Robert's Sport Fishing to his best guide, Chuy Medina, who was—on that June morning so long ago—the little dark-faced boy who pulled the hogfish from the yellow rock.

The following year, Chino and María left the village forever to live with their oldest daughter, who owns a small hardware store in Ensenada.

And what of the caleta itself?

Well, the inner reefs are almost devoid of cabrilla and pargo now, and Abundio's leaping marlin, in its circle of rocks, has been lost from three decades of storms and neglect. Nevertheless, half a dozen tourist businesses flourish on the beach, some connected by telephone and fax to their booking agents in the United States. The most successful of these businesses is "Pablo's Pangas," a fleet of seven very fast boats now managed jointly by the two Santos brothers.

Each morning, many skiffs filled with sunburnt anglers try for live bait in the waters around the Four Horses. In winter, the boats lower their baits into the deep water around the points for yellowtail. In the warmer months, they troll outside for dorado, tuna, and sometimes marlin, which they now often release. But compared to the old days, they catch very little.

And high up on the new, paved cliff road, arriving tourist anglers invariably slam on their brakes and jump out to marvel at the view, just as Chino did that first day, when he arrived on the fish buyer's truck.

To these visitors, the caleta appears just as it always has, with its islands and colorful reefs, its rich green carpet of palm trees, its perfect, curving beach, and the gentle sea sleeping beneath the sky.

But the newcomers do not know why the pavement loops so awkwardly around the old rockslide on the cliff, nor do they know the story of the lonely, bottle-cap encrusted cross that still stands in the weeds there, the tarnished metal cup, the old dishes smeared with blackened candle wax; they do not see the shadows that come out to wander beneath the palm trees, crossing, and nodding to one another as evening falls.

And, in the darkest dark, after everyone else has gone to sleep, sometimes an old rooster still calls, and Margarita Santos emerges from the faded pink house, the one with the tile roof only partly completed. Bent with age, she lingers for a while around the salty, bitter well. Then, she picks two daisies, one yellow, one white, and she climbs up past the remains of Fra Nacho's old shack to her secret place in the arroyo.

The End

BY GENE KIRA

with Neil Kelly

THE BAJA CATCH
A Fishing, Travel & Remote Camping Manual for Baja California
240 pages, soft cover, 8.5" x 11", $19.95
Second Edition, Fourth Printing 1996   ISBN 0-929637-01-1

*   *   *

UNDERSTANDING SOCCER
Rules and Procedures for Players, Parents & Coaches
79 pages, soft cover, 8.5" x 11", $9.95
First Printing 1994   ISBN 0-929637-02-X

*   *   *

KING OF THE MOON
A Novel of Baja California
342 pages, hard cover, 6" x 9", $21.95
First Printing 1997   ISBN 0-929637-03-8

Available through bookstores and book distributors, or by mail directly from the publisher: Apples & Oranges, Inc.; Attn: Book Orders; P.O. Box 2296; Valley Center, CA 92082. Please add $3.00 for shipping, and 50 cents per additional book. Check or money order only. California residents please add applicable sales tax. Telephone inquiries, 619-751-8868.